LINES THAT BIND

PART FOUR

AMONG THE SHADOWS

BY ANNA LAZARIDIS

LINES THAT BIND

PART FOUR

AMONG THE SHADOWS

ISBN 978-0692881316

Cover design by George D.K.
Cover Illustration by © Forewer/Shutterstock.com
Interior Illustrations by © Vasiliki Mitakou

www.linesthatbind.com

For my daughter

"It is during our darkest moments that we must focus to see the light."

– Aristotle

ONE

PROM NIGHT

MILY KEPT tugging and tugging on my hair trying to fasten it into something presentable for the prom.

"Ouch! Is this really necessary?" I yelled as the comb hit a knot.

"How else am I supposed to style it if I can't comb through it first?" chided Emily as she watched me in the mirror.

"Don't overdo it, Em. I want something simple; a ponytail maybe."

She pulled on my hair once more; this time deliberately. "Can you please let me do my job? It's your prom, for heaven's sake, Caitlin!"

"I know. I'm sorry. It's just that I don't know what's worse; the theme or having to spend the whole evening with Megan?"

"Just look at that dress," said Emily pointing to the gown spread on the bed. "That alone should make you look forward to tonight."

The Tudor inspired gown, which Emily had picked up in

Tirion, was a breathtaking multifaceted contraption with a hand-threaded silver embroidered overdress, embellished with innumerable silver toned rhinestones and pearls, threaded in one by one. The belled-shaped sleeves that gathered above the elbow, with the trim matching the exquisite lacing added to the flair of the times. It was to be worn over an equally beautiful petticoat. It must've taken full-figured Mavis and the rest of the seamstresses back in Tirion hundreds of hours to put this masterpiece together. Emily had a whole list made up of how many dresses she needed to get for some of my classmates who were also attending this year's prom. The list consisted not only of names and sizes, but personality traits, which helped her match the right dress to the right girl. For Emily, it wasn't just shopping; it was a science.

"You can forget about that hooped undergarment. I'm not wearing it!" I exclaimed.

"Stop complaining," she huffed as she continued to braid my hair. "You have to wear the farthingale. It plays up the overall shape of the gown. Besides, it's not that wide."

"How about I wear the long tunic I wore at Tirion? That would work."

She pulled on my hair again. "You're wearing the gown and that's final! Now, stop fidgeting!"

There was no winning with her so I decided to give in and enjoy the pampering; try to anyway. It took about an hour for her to put the finishing touches on my hair, but once she had finished she whirled me around on the swivel-chair and once I caught site of the result in the mirror I exclaimed happily, "Em, I love it. I really do!"

"I aim to please," she boasted smiling.

"Look at all those little braided strands. How in the world did you connect each one of them to the other with pearl beads?" Emily smiled. "How in the world did you create this net-like design all the way down my hair?" I twisted and turned in the chair to get a better view.

"We might have finished earlier if you didn't keep complaining. Now, come on," she ordered, holding out the undergarment. "You need to put on the chemise first," "Let's go! Now, the corset."

"As if the corset isn't bad enough, now I have to walk around with this bell shaped thing under the long skirt."

"Stop with the faces and get in!"

What I kept to myself was that I was quite tender in my back and chest those last few weeks, and now the soreness was even more intense with the sensual vice wrapping itself around my rib cage. "A man definitely invented this," I said wincing. "No woman in her right mind would come up with such a torturous contraption. How did they breathe in this?"

Emily kept quiet and tied me into the corset. She was a good sport; only pulled my hair and slapped my arm a few times. I was sure she wanted to do much worse than that. I was anxious about going to prom, and the only person I could take my frustration out on was my cousin.

"Come, give us a twirl," said Aunt Leslie, walking in my room with a great big smile.

"I can't believe women actually wore this! It weighs a ton," I muttered while swinging around so Aunt Leslie could see the whole effect. "I can hardly breathe."

"You look beautiful sweetie," she exclaimed as she bent down to straighten the hem.

"Mom, its fine; leave it." Emily helped her up. "She's going to a prom not her coronation. The gown is perfect. Come on now, we should be heading downstairs."

I descended the stairs at a snail's pace, concentrating on one step at a time in fear of tripping over the endless layers of lush material.

Taking my eyes off the step momentarily to distribute the weight of the gown and find my balance, I was happily surprised to meet Justin's soft gaze. Looking unearthly handsome in his tailor-made black Tunic and long black overcoat with golden trim; Justin smiled and winked at me as he bowed his head in a courtly manner. Seeing how handsome he looked in his period black knee britches finished with black leather boots and a striking leather belt around his waist, caused me to stop for an instant as my breath caught in my throat.

Upon finishing my descent down the oak staircase, I walked towards him suddenly, his face brightened up, as though he had seen the pleasantest sight in the world. Justin chivalrously offered his hand; ensuring the lavish and lengthy gown didn't cause a swift and unfortunate fall.

"You're a vision of splendor, my lady," he pronounced, and with a charming bow, he kissed my hand.

Smiling from ear to ear, I curtsied and replied, "A pleasure as always, my gracious lord."

It took Kyle all of two seconds to burst out laughing, but it was uncle Abbot's slap on the arm that made him swallow back whatever nonsense he was about to verbalize. "Look at you," my uncle said turning his attention to me; dismissing Kyle's grimace. "You're all grown up, honey."

Having the need to hug him, I slipped out of Justin's hold and wrapped my arms around my uncle's waist. We stood there in silence for a few minutes, and then, Uncle Abbot kissed the top of my head and said in a soft voice; tightening his hold just a bit more, "Where have all the years gone?"

Aunt Leslie approached, and patted my uncle on the shoulder. "Come now, Abbot; the kids must get going."

"Yes, yes; of course," he replied taking a step back; trying to swallow back the emotion in his voice.

"Your Majesty," Kyle finally said, severing the emotionally charged atmosphere, "your chariot awaits."

It was with trepidation that I followed my cousin outside; there was no way of knowing what he had planned. It was then that my eyes widened in pure delight the second I set eyes on my 'chariot'. I instantly threw myself in Kyle's embrace thanking him for the beautiful remodeling of my once dilapidated 55' Ford T-bird.

"Do you like it?" he asked. Unable to answer from the shock, I simply nodded.

Old Betty was old no more. Kyle had revamped my once decrepit heap of scrap metal into a shiny ruby red goddess.

He beamed with pride and headed to the car; we all followed. As Kyle held the passenger's door open he smiled and started to explain, "V8, automatic Transmission, dual exhaust, stylish steel wheels and tinted rear windows," he boasted in one big breath. "Oh yeah, a working air conditioner and heater. I hope it's to your liking."

"You're unbelievable," I boomed, kissing him on the cheek. "I didn't understand one word you said apart from the air conditioner and the heater bit, but it all sounds great."

Kyle let out a husky laugh. "I'm happy you like it. I enjoyed fixing her up."

"I can't believe you did all this. You're unbelievable," I repeated.

"That's an understatement," he jested.

Emily rolled her eyes, "Stop inflating his already oversized head," she huffed, helping me into the car. "His big, fat head won't fit to get back inside."

It was my turn to laugh.

With care not to crease it, Emily tucked the material around my legs. Apparently, Old Betty wasn't built to accommodate long flowing gowns, but I made do.

"Your car keys my lady," offered Kyle, handing me a keychain with my Initials.

"No, this isn't right," I protested, handing the keys back to him. "Kyle, this car is yours. You deserve it. You did all this work."

"Caitlin, just shut up and close the door."

I smiled. "Okay, I'll shut up."

"Good!"

My hand ran over the leather dash board. "I still can't believe this is Old Betty. I mean, look at her, Justin," I exclaimed as he took the driver's seat. He instantly put the key in the ignition and revved up the engine. The sound was spine chilling. "Now, this is a car!" Justin lauded, indulging his male need to feel the engine. "Listen to her purr."

"Should I leave the two of you alone?" I asked, inciting a chuckle from Kyle who was on the other side of the window.

"We should get going, funny girl," Justin quickly responded with a charming smile. "Your friends will be waiting for us."

"You kids have fun now. Don't do what I would do," Kyle said as he hit the roof of the car with his hand.

"Have fun you guys," called out Aunt Leslie. Uncle Abbot simply waved; visibly touched by the whole incident.

Throughout the whole ride, Justin kept turning; looking at me. "What is it?" I finally asked concerned.

"It's just that you look beautiful. You're like fairy dust."

"Fairy dust?"

"Yes. You look amazing."

"You don't look half bad yourself," I said giggling, playing down how miraculously gorgeous he was in his black attire. The blue in his eyes was deeper than ever; accentuating every inch of his masculine features.

Considering the occasion, the ride was exceptionally quiet. I felt nervous, the way I did on our first date. I kept fiddling with the gown; unable to sit still.

"You should know that we couldn't rein Emily in," Justin finally said. "She had the whole town scrambling to get the estate ready for tonight."

"I don't think it's tonight that's she's worried about. Her nuptials are in about a month or so. That's why she's so high strung."

"Marc is the same way," Justin admitted, taking the last left turn to my parents Villa. "Leslie is also stressed about it. She was torn between missing you all the while you were in Tirion and helping Emily out with all the details."

"Poor Aunt Leslie," I exhaled, cracking the window open to get a breath of fresh air. The corset was digging deep into my ribcage. "How did these women ever breathe?" I complained.

"That gown isn't meant to be sat in; not in these deep seats."

Justin lifted my hand to his mouth and kissed it. "We're almost there."

I stopped twitching the moment we approached the grounds. My mouth fell to the floor. Hundreds of lit torches lined the perimeter of the great protective wall. "She's crazy!" I exclaimed at the sheer extravagance.

"We have to park out here," instructed Justin turning off the engine. He helped me out of the car.

"Why out here? There's plenty of space for everyone to park on the grounds."

He tenderly turned my gaze past the towering cast iron gate, and it was then that I exclaimed in utter disbelief, "Oh, My God! Where does she come up with these ideas?"

Horse drawn carriages were waiting to take the guests to the main entrance of the Villa. Even the horsemen were decked out in Renaissance attire. I had to hand it to my cousin; she didn't let any detail slip.

"There weren't any cars back then," Justin stated, helping me onto the carriage. "It's just Emily's way of making everything perfect for you; for everyone."

I held onto his hand while we slowly made our way up the long driveway. The whole route was outlined with a line of fire; lighting our way up the bend; guiding us to the grand structure up ahead. The flames flickered only inches off the ground without a point of origin. They seemed to be hovering, floating magically in midair.

"Simply beautiful," I whispered looking around the enchanted grounds. "Yes, breathtaking," said Justin gazing right at me. I leaned in and kissed him softly, lingering; wanting more and more with each stroke of my lips against his.

"You're biased," I told him pulling back, but not before I kissed him one more time.

"I'm in love," he exhaled deeply, slipping his hand to the back of my neck and pulled me forward against his hungry mouth.

No drug on earth could have taken me to such heights. I was intoxicated by his scent, his gaze and the mere touch of his skin to mine; everything brought me one step closer to heaven. I truly doubted if heaven could be so sweet.

I shifted in my seat slightly trying to make myself more comfortable. My constrained rib cage was starting to bother me even more. I leaned back against Justin's open arm refusing to complain about the discomfort; refusing to ruin the moment.

I loved that the horse drawn carriage was moving so slowly. It gave us ample time to absorb our mesmerizing surroundings; to enjoy each other's company. I was content to sit there with Justin's cheek against my head, his strong arms around me. I lazily looked up towards the sky only to see large lobes of soft light suspended in mid-air all around the vast grounds.

"How in the world did she accomplish that?" I asked happily surprised, with my head tilted even further back against Justin's shoulder to get a panoramic view of the illuminating spheres.

Each one levitated at a different height and angle. They didn't seem to be permanently fixed in one particular place. On the contrary, they seemed to slide smoothly along the night sky, gliding in a gracefully synchronized motion.

"Look over there," Justin said pointing to the few Willows that adorned the surrounding area.

Unlike their towering counterparts, these swaging giants

glistened like star dust under the evening sky, comparable only to large lustrous jewels strategically placed around the grounds bewitching us all the more; creating an unearthly atmosphere.

"Who's gifted enough to do all this and keep it up for so long? It can't be only one person, can it?" I asked turning my gaze to Justin as we were slowly coming to a full stop in front of the grand entrance.

"The whole senior class had a barbeque a few days ago, with the Ellri to watch over them. Your classmates went all out in using their different gifts. And this –," he said motioning to our magical surroundings, "Is what you get when you put the gifted to use."

"Where was I when all this was going on? I would've loved to see them do all this."

"You were recuperating from our small ordeal a month ago," he answered, giving me a quick kiss, and jumped off the carriage.

"Oh yeah – that," I said trying to conjure up a smile.

The mere thought of what Gabriel had done to me sent cold shivers down my spine. I tried really hard not to think about it, but it was hopeless. Every time I even caught a quick glimpse in the mirror I couldn't help but put my hand up against the right side of my face, making sure that the horrific scars were gone. I was lucky, in a sense, that little Hailie was able to work her magic, but unfortunately there was nothing she could do about my overwhelming fatigue and the rawness in my ribs. Gabriel had worked me over real good. I was quickly made aware that night that even though I was in transcendence my earthly body felt everything my ghostly body did; more even. I had to be more careful in the future.

"Here, give me your hand." Justin's voice responsively snapped me out of my thoughts. This was no time to think about morbid past events. I smiled, and let Justin help me off the carriage. His tight hold around my waist set off an alarming stabbing-like pain that shot up my spinal cord. I bit down hard and kept it to myself. Nothing was going to ruin my night; not when my escort looked so delectable.

The atmosphere around me was truly magical; straight out of a fairytale. Long flowing material, in a rich deep burgundy, draped the whole length of each column emphasizing the massiveness of the entrance. The same rich color was spread over the steps.

We met up with Tyler and Megan as soon as we reached the main hall. "You wouldn't wear the school uniform in Tirion, but here you choose to wear it at your prom?" I commented.

"I couldn't come up with anything better to wear," he said giving me a kiss on the cheek. "You look beautiful," he added softly against my ear.

"You both look great!" I exclaimed, including Megan's wench costume in the equation.

"Thanks Caitlin." She smiled. "You and Justin really look amazing, too."

"We aim to please," boasted Justin, taking my hand.

Small talk aside, Emily went beyond the call of duty. The fresh coat of paint returned my parent's home to the marvel that it once was. The once stripped walls were now adorned with numerous oil paintings and family portraits.

"Come, it's this way," instructed Tyler, taking Megan by the hand. Now that was something that needed getting used to; the sight of Megan and Tyler holding hands was something I wasn't expecting. For some reason I found it funny, but kept a straight face as I followed the group to our destination. The exterior, full arched mahogany trimmed doors with artistic iron grille were left ajar, directing us out to the side courtyard where no expense was evidently spared in the ornamentation of each circular table. Gilded pillar candle holders were used for centerpieces giving off just enough light to accentuate the romantic atmosphere that my cousin was so desperately trying to accomplish, and did so quiet efficiently.

"Everything is so beautiful," I whispered.

About an hour into the evening, and a tummy full of delicious delicacies, which were perfectly served by waiters dressed in the appropriate attire made of fabrics and materials chosen for Tudor costumes, Justin took me by the hand and excused us from the rest of the group. I didn't know where we were heading. He silently led me away from the festivities to the farthest part of the sculptured gardens, but then he stopped abruptly and turned to face me without saying a word.

He seemed to be contemplating something, but instead of verbalizing what his expression was screaming, he cupped my face and said instead, "You're beautiful," and kissed me tenderly.

"Justin, is everything okay?"

"Yes, everything is fine," he answered unconvincingly.

With my hand caressing his cheek I insisted, "Tell me what's going on"

"I just wanted to –," He broke in mid-sentence and gave me a little twirl. I bit down hard, wincing at the pain that seemed to grow deeper and greater as the hours passed.

"Wanted to what?" I asked attempting to giggle in order to

make light of his inability to tell me what he really wanted me to know.

"I just wanted to have you all to myself for a few more minutes," he lied. I could tell that it wasn't what he wanted to tell me, but I didn't make an issue of it. "These past few weeks have been crazy, and with all the hoopla that's going on over there, I just wanted these few minutes with you," he added, holding me tight.

"So you only want me for a few minutes, do you?" I asked smiling.

He traced the outline of my face with his finger and softly kissed me on the lips. I reached up and indulged myself in his nectar, passionately kissing him in return. "I've loved you for so long," he professed softly, leaning his head against my brow, and in one unexpected swift move he lifted me off the ground in his strong embrace and kissed me fervently. I swallowed back the need to scream from the sheer pain that tore right through me. Just as fast, he returned my feet to the ground smiling devilishly.

"Marry me," he blurted out, smiling at my surprised expression.

"Not just yet," I answered caressing his jaw. "Not just yet," I repeated even softer, quenching my need for his lips on mine.

Justin twirled me around amused. "You're going to have to say yes sometime."

I looked into his thoughtful eyes, "You have to promise me one thing, Justin."

"What is it?" he asked seriously.

"That you'll never get tired of asking."

"Tired of asking you?" He smiled, shaking his head. "Never!

You heard what the Nobe Council said. It took us seven life times to finally find each other. What's another couple of years to make it official?" I reached up to steal a kiss. "This prom is growing on me," I admitted, seeing how everything was beyond my expectations.

Justin smiled. "I wouldn't actually call this here your prom. The prom is over there with the rest of your classmates."

"Why did you have to remind me? I prefer being here with you." I pouted.

"Come on. Wouldn't want Tyler to think I'm intentionally keeping you away from this momentous occasion, now would we?"

"And why should we care what Tyler thinks?"

"Because you care about what Tyler thinks," Justin answered conjuring up one of those forced smiles. I had nothing to say to ease his furrowed brow.

"Come, let's get back to the prom," he said, and led me to the dance floor in awkward silence.

T he corset was nauseatingly tight. I tried to be pleasant but now, three hours into our prom, the damn thing was cutting off my circulation.

"I need to be excused," I finally uttered. Justin simply stood up displaying a strained expression.

The downstairs' bathrooms were occupied so that only left the ones upstairs. I slowly made my way up trying desperately to catch my breath, when I suddenly felt a hand on the sleeve of my dress. Surprised, I jumped and turned to find Justin standing beside me. There must have been some reason as to why I didn't feel him approach, but the pain was so acute that I brushed the incident aside, concentration on keeping my balance.

In seconds his left hand was on my back supporting my weight.

"Why didn't you tell me you were in so much pain?"

"I thought you felt what I felt," I murmured through the pain, taking a deep, shaky breath.

"That's not important now," he said, leading me up the stairs. "Where does it hurt?"

"It's this stupid corset. I really need to get it off!"

"In here," he instructed, opening the door to the closest room available. "Now, what can I do to help?"

On other occasions I would've been mortified at the prospect of Justin undressing me, but now; now was different.

"Undo the gown," I urged in short deep breaths.

In a few swift moves he unlaced the whole length of the gown. "I have a new respect for zippers," he said, trying to crack a smile.

I quickly shrugged off the overdress and the looser petticoat and farthingale, but it was the corset that really needed to come off. With one hand across my chest, I held up the tight contraption and leaned against the wall with the other for support, allowing Justin to undo the chords that tied in the back. It hurt – it really hurt.

The looser Justin made it, the more unbearable the stabbing pain became. As soon as he undid the last of the undergarment I attempted to take a much needed deep breath.

"Ahh!" I cried feeling faint.

"God Caitlin," I heard Justin exclaim as he traced his fingers down my back, "What the hell is this?"

"I can't –" I tried to speak but there was no more air left in my lungs, and in seconds everything went dark.

Breathless
Illustrated for Lines that Bind - Among the Shadows

TWO

PARASITE

I WOKE FROM A DREAM, and what a sad dream it was. Yet unlike other times, it left me with no memory of the circumstance, but only the residue of sorrow that wound its way deep in my heart. I drew a shuddering breath. *I must still be dreaming,* I thought, as I looked around the dark and gloomy surroundings which seemed to be encapsulating me.

I listened in sheer silence to distinguish any hint of sound, but nothing; a deathly calm clung in the musty air. In my attempt to stand, the ache in my side brought me back down, pinning me to the ground.

Lying there motionless, I had nothing but a canopy of dead branches to look at which blocked any sort of light from above. My morbid backdrop reflected the underlying feeling that lingered from my dream.

Gnarled and twisted trunks rose to unfathomable heights from the dry coarse earth. Only a few random, rogue streaks of sunlight made their way through the tightly woven canopy, enhancing the eeriness of my decrepit surroundings. I lay there, on barren earth, in a small opening among the towering giants; caged in, and all alone.

What is this place? I wondered in the midst of that dead forest. I tried to sit up once more only to fall back in pure agony. Then, quietly, Justin's voice was back in my mind; my waking mind. "You shouldn't move. Please, sit still," I heard him say.

The moment I blinked back in excitement at the sound of his voice my dismal surroundings disappeared and the cold stone walls of the Chamber of Enlightenment came into clear view.

"What happened?" I asked confused. I clutched the cotton sheet to my breast. I looked down at my bare shoulders and blushed. "Justin? What happened?" I repeated alarmed.

Hurriedly, I lay back on the plush Persian rug and pulled the cotton sheet up to my chin.

"You fainted."

"Fainted?" I asked confused, pulling the white material around my body. Even the slightest move sent tremendous waves of unparalleled stabs even deeper. With two long strides Justin was next to me, helping me wrap the material around my body. "You really ought to stay still. There's no way of knowing the damage."

"What's the matter with me?"

"I really don't know, but please don't move. I summoned Tyler. He should be here in a minute."

I twitched with discomfort. "Where was I? Just now, I mean?"

"Nowhere in particular. The Energy Stone is picking up on the distress you feel, projecting the most suitable surroundings to your deepest thoughts. Now, stay still!" He tucked the cotton material even tighter under me.

"How in the world did you get me down here?" I asked wincing back in pain; ignoring the fact that he obviously saw me naked from the waist up.

"The Villa has a passage as well."

"But there are only five doors. How is that possible?" I was fidgeting; squinting from discomfort and tenderness in my side.

"You don't listen," he chided, adjusting the pillow under my head. "Don't move!" He continued to tuck the sheet under my body making it impossible for me to budge. "These doors represent each family group; not one individual structure. I thought you understood that."

"You mean that no matter where we are in the world, we have access?"

"Yes," Justin exclaimed. "Now, stop moving."

Just then, from the other side of the room I suddenly heard Emily's irate voice. "How dare you yell at me!" The sound of the door locking didn't take long to follow. She came and stood next to Justin, visibly angry, holding a change of clothes in her hand. "How was I supposed to know this was going to happen? I don't have a freaking magic ball!"

Justin stood up towering over her. "You had to go overboard, didn't you? I mean really Em; a corset? Does she look like she needs one? She's perfect!"

That was probably the nicest thing anyone had ever said about me.

Emily turned to me and then back to Justin. "It was part of the outfit. How was I supposed to know?"

He shook his head dismissively.

"Don't blame her," I added, cringing in pain. "I should've spoken up."

"I'm really sorry, Caity. You just looked so beautiful," she beamed as she walked up to one of the doors. "I didn't know it was going to hurt this much. You have to believe me," she added, blindly placing her hand on one of the palm prints.

The instant she touched the imprint on the old wooden door the three distinct clinking sounds were heard. Seconds later, Tyler emerged looking as annoyed with Justin as Emily was.

"Why do you insist on pushing? I said I was going to be right down," he barked at Justin. "There was no one to bring me down here, or did you forget that little detail. I'm not allowed to come down here without a guide!"

Justin was clearly in their heads driving them crazy with worry. "Well, I'm here and so is Em. Don't worry, you won't get in any trouble," promised Justin apologetically. "Now do something about the pain."

"Where does it hurt?" Tyler asked kneeling right next to me.

"Her ribs and her back are all bruised. Look!" Justin instructed as he was about to raise the cotton sheet.

"What do you think you're doing?" I yanked the white fabric even higher up my neck. Horrified, I held onto the cotton material for dear life. It was bad enough that Justin had seen me naked, I wasn't about to let Tyler do the same.

"Both of you turn around," ordered Emily, helping me up into a sitting position.

Grunting and squealing in pain, I finally was upright.

"I know this hurts but here, let me slip this on." She pulled the loose fitting T-shirt that she had brought over my head and folded it up just enough to expose the injured area. It still didn't leave much to the imagination but at least it was something. She caringly helped me back down, and took the time to cover my underwear clad bottom with the sheet. "She's ready," she ordered, causing both Tyler and Justin to circle around.

"Ouch! That looks really bad," exclaimed Tyler, kneeling next to me. He traced his fingers down my ribs, examining the extent of the injury. "Your skin is much softer than I imagined it would be." He winked at me teasingly. "It's pale as ivory, so smooth and warm."

"Falcone!" Justin howled. "Do what you came here to do before I make you one with the floor!"

Tyler smiled devilishly before placing each palm on either side of my ribcage, causing me to jolt at the mere touch. "Sorry Caity," he apologized, and then turned to Justin worriedly and added, "This was not caused by any sort of undergarment. It might have irritated it, but it wasn't the cause. Her injury is way too deep, and there's no way this happened today."

"I did have some soreness in my side and back since Tirion, but nothing like this."

"Why didn't you say something?" asked Justin caringly.

"I know. I'm sorry. I should've paid closer attention to what Hailie had said back in Tirion. She had mentioned further injuries, but I assumed she was talking about something skin deep; about my banged up face, nothing this serious."

"Damn him," I heard Justin yell. "I should've killed him then and there!"

"Gabriel must've kicked me in the ribs at some point after I fell unconscious. Everything that happened that day is a big blur. By the extent of the bruising, he must've kicked me more than just once. It's the only logical explanation, isn't it?"

Nobody answered. It was as though they didn't even hear what I said. Instead, Emily approached Justin and stroked his back in an attempt to calm him. "It's over now," she said. "What's done is done. Thankfully it's nothing serious, right Tyler?"

"Nothing I can't fix," he boasted, gazing at me; smiling. "But you should know it's going to be painful."

"Great," I whispered.

"Are you ready?"

I nodded, not sure of how much more painful this could get.

"I'm going to –," Tyler's explanation was quickly cut short with two of the doors swing open with force. "You're going to do absolutely nothing, Tyler!" Marcellus yelled waving one of the doors closed as he entered the chamber. Tyler's father was furious. "How dare all of you! What do you think this is?"

William and Uncle Abbot strode in from the second door looking as Marcellus did; angry. My uncle instantly came to my side and brushed his hand across my brow. "You should've said something earlier, sweetie. Why do you insist on keeping things to yourself?"

I was about to respond when William's roaring voice interrupted. "Justin, how can you sit by and let this happen?" he asked, clearly livid at his son's involvement.

"She's in great pain, father. What did you expect me to do? Tyler is the only one who can help Caitlin. Just look at her."

Justin's plea visibly fell on deaf ears.

"You don't know what you're saying, son. Have you even considered the consequences? Have you thought about what this might do to Tyler?"

Tyler looked at Justin's father and then to his own dad and

said, "I'll be fine. I've worked on much worse cases in Tirion. This is a walk in the park."

"Oh, really?" asked Marcellus, all the while gnashing his teeth in annoyance. "Go ahead! I'd like to see what my all-knowing son can do." All three Ellri looked at each other and took one step back. "Go ahead son. Work your magic," ordered Marcellus sounding a bit sarcastic.

"Tyler, maybe we shouldn't do this," I advised through clenched teeth. "They wouldn't be here if it's as easy as you say."

"Oh, please! I know what I'm doing! Just hold on tight!"

The second his hands came into contact with my bare skin, a sharp stinging pain caused my whole body to convulse, and without warning the tissue under my skin felt as though it were being shred apart, inciting an onslaught of tears which freely cascaded down the side of my face. Even my jaw ached from clenching my teeth so hard. I feared they'd break from the sheer pressure.

Tyler's healing touch instantly brought my scarred wrist to a rapid and violent throb, where a significant amount of pulsating energy collected into a deathly surge sending unsuspecting Tyler crashing to the floor in a spine-curdling thud. Now, on the brink of collapse, I was inundated with the overwhelming fear of having fatally injured Tyler, but then my ears caught the sound of laughter and I quickly let out a sigh of relief in the knowledge that he was fine.

"I'm sorry," I whispered through clenched teeth. My voice was inaudible; muted. Unable to hear my thoughts, none turned in my direction.

"I guess you don't know what you're doing after all,"

confirmed Tyler's father as he helped him to his feet. "This isn't funny, dad!" Tyler was furious and pushed Marcellus off. "Why didn't you tell me her gift was going to respond? You like seeing me fall on my ass, don't you?"

"You insisted. You were heedless of your Ellri's warning. Thank your lucky stars she didn't kill you!"

My chest tightened.

"She needs help," Tyler's voice cracked. He sounded overwhelmed. "Whatever that bastard did to her it's spreading and its spreading fast."

I lay there feeling cold. I mean really cold.

"Guy's?" called out Emily nervously. "We need to do something fast. Caitlin doesn't look that great."

She was about to wipe my tears away when Justin quickly pulled her hand out of the way. "Don't touch her," he instructed, rather calm. "You'll end up like Tyler. Her gift is still extremely potent." Justin's face was marked with stress and anxiety, but above all, remorse as he leaned in close. "Please, just hold on," he whispered tenderly close to my ear.

My eyes slowly closed in need of sleep when out of nowhere I heard Tyler's angst-ridden voice warning me, "Don't give into it. Stay awake! You have to stay awake!"

"It's cold," I whispered, between short quick breaths.

"Caitlin, please hold on," Justin's voice tattered off in the end. "Don't just stand there," he yelled out to the Ellri.

Like statues they simply stood there; inanimate and lifeless. I closed my eyes momentarily to blink back the insufferable ach, and as soon as I reopened them I was back in the heart of my dreary, dead forest, but this time I had company. Tyler and Emily looked shocked by their new surroundings.

A thunderous clap from the depths of the forest caused my heavy eyelids to snap open; then another deafening sound and another. There, only a few feet from where I lay, a loud rumbling was followed with the roar of trees pulling away, untangling their branches from one another to create a dimly lit path through the decaying forest.

Having no energy left, I closed my eyes, succumbing to the pain. An icy current ran through my veins tightening up my heart; restricting the air flow to my lungs even more. Like a fish out of water I lay there gasping in short, swift breaths. The air caught in my lungs as if some giant hand crushed my chest. The only sensation I had left was that of cold sweat trickling down my bare back and chest.

"You seem to keep me on my toes young lady." The sharp voice penetrated the fog that clouded my mind. I turned my head in the direction of the familiar sound. "Alexander?" I knew no words came out. There was no voice left in me.

He was strolling nonchalant through the woods, up the new formed path; stick in hand. "Save your strength child. Lord knows you'll need it."

Justin stepped back bowing his head as did Emily. Tyler looked around probably wondering why the grounds keeper of the Isle of Indigo was there. He just stood there not knowing what to do. "She needs my help," Tyler finally said, looking at Alexander. "This injury runs really deep. I felt it."

"Yes you did feel it, Healer," Alexander answered.

I suddenly felt weightless as the ground under me was no more and my unyielding torso had been lifted to arms height the instant Alexander stood beside me.

"Now Healer, give this old man some room to work;

wouldn't want your friend to suffer any more than she already has, would you?"

"Be careful, her power is potent," Tyler warned.

"Yes it is, isn't it?" said Alexander, caressing my face.

Tyler was clearly surprised that our visitor was able to touch me when no one else could. "Take it easy, Caitlin. This won't take long," Alexander instructed in a soothing voice as he handed his walking stick to Tyler, motioning for him to step back. "Caitlin, I need you to focus. Concentrate on collecting all your power in your wrist. Can you do that for me?" Alexander asked affectionately.

Struggling to collect what little energy I had in me, soon enough, I felt my arms pulsating from the sheer force that accumulated at the tips of my fingers. "Good girl! Now we need to remove this parasite," Alexander said placing one hand over my head and the other over my abdomen. "This will feel a bit strange."

Even though my confused thoughts fluttered in darkness, I tried to concentrate; tried to banish the fear eating away at me. When in seconds, a thrashing of a whip of sorts snapped my taut torso upwards, causing my stiff spine to convulse violently at his touch. My eyes surprisingly remained open – wide open at that.

Don't scream! I kept telling myself. *Just hold on!*

I wasn't about to give into the pain; wasn't going to give the monster the satisfaction of making me cry; making me scream for help.

Something suddenly changed; shifted somehow. The dangerously charged force in my hands was being drained. The energy I had in my fingers started spreading. Microscopic dim lights spiraled around my levitating body weaving in and out in such a way that it created a transparent cocoon-like casing around me. I could still see everything and everyone, but it was there all the same.

"Hold on child, this unfortunately is going to hurt."

No sooner did Alexander speak the words, when the force field that encapsulated me started altering; vibrating in a way. Then it was as if someone had sadistically cut some invisible strings that suspended me. I fell back in midair; hung there by the mere waist as the cocoon-like capsule dissolved around me into small shimmering droplets of light which ascended higher and higher to some unimaginable height, and the pain intensified. It was as though someone was slowly pulling my insides out with their bare hands, draining me of life.

I screamed from the depths of my soul knowing that no one could hear my cry for mercy.

Make it stop! Please. Make it stop!

Along with the bright, iridescent droplets, a dark hued essence rose out of my battered torso; being forced out of me, and then complete and utter darkness.

Parasite

Illustrated for Lines that Bind - Among the Shadows

THREE

EVEN WORSE

ON THE FLOOR with several pillows propping me up, I shifted uncomfortably trying to make sense of where I was again, but it was in that mental confusion that I heard voices say, "There's no knowing how far they'll go."

"Whatever you're all keeping from her, it's time she knew." I heard Justin's strained voice say. "It's only fair. She needs to know. Hell, I need to know what she's up against. I need to be able to protect her. How can I do that if I don't know what we're up against?"

William patted his son on the shoulder. "It's not your fight son. Leave this one to us!"

"Absolutely not! You weren't the one who had to bring that monster to his knees. Gabriel could've easily killed her."

"Justin might have a point," Uncle Abbot said pacing on the other side of the large chamber. "This is much bigger than Gabriel."

Wait, wait one minute, I thought. My uncle's mouth wasn't moving. *I can finally hear their thoughts. This should be fun!* I smiled at the thought.

"Abbot, you can't honestly be saying what I think you're saying?" Marcellus looked surprised. "Gabriel might not have killed her but the truth most certainly will. She's not ready!"

"Damn it," Justin exclaimed pushing back his hair agitated. "This has gone on long enough. The truth isn't what's going to kill her, but these ridiculous secrets most certainly will. She's been more than understanding. Don't you think it's time you let her decided for once?"

"You can stop eavesdropping now, Caitlin." Alexander's voice startled me. I quickly sat up and looked in his direction. Without a moment's hesitation the cold stone walls of the large chamber altered. Alexander and I were suddenly encircled by a vast sea of wildflowers and sprawling meadows. The warm glow of the sun was invigorating.

Wanting nothing more than to bask in the glorious rays, I lifted my face to the sky and took a much needed deep breath. "Now this is more like it," I smiled, turning to Alexander. "How did you know I was awake? They didn't." I turned momentarily to where the Ellri stood only to see them standing there like inanimate objects. I quickly circled back to Alexander and said smiling, "You really need to show me how you do that."

He picked a handful of vibrantly red poppies and handed them to me. "Maybe someday," he winked, grinning. "You've been a real sport; been through quite a lot these past couple of months."

"Yeah well, I'm glad someone's keeping tabs because by the

looks of it I'm still not worthy of knowing what's going on." I hugged my knees. "Alex, what happened to me? What was that? What did Gabriel do to me?"

He made himself more comfortable as he sat beside me; placing his hand over mine. "In time you'll find out for yourself. Right now you need to grow."

"Alex, not you too! Please, give me some idea of what I'm up against. This is all too weird. Are we even human?"

He chuckled. "As human as they come. We've simply evolved to a higher state, that's all."

"You make everything sound so – so normal. All this is not normal. It's not humanly possible," I said, raising my hands, motioning to our spellbinding surroundings.

"Ah, but it is humanly possible, Caitlin. This –" he said, motioning around, "This is how you feel at this particular moment. This is where your mind wants to be. Just because the average human can't do it doesn't mean it's impossible. The gifted have existed from antiquity and even ions before that. Books have been written; folklore has sung them in verse. You are the purest of them all, millennia in the making. You shouldn't question who you are."

"So, what was that thing that came out of me? What did Gabriel have to gain by wanting to kill me?"

"Even though Gabriel is truly gifted, Caitlin, he is in no way capable of summoning the Animus Habito."

"Soul Dweller?" I looked at him questionably not sure if I was translating it correctly.

"In ancient times they called it the Iuguolo – the Aminus Iuguolo. It took the lives of many gifted."

"The Soul Killer?"

"I'm afraid so. Twisted as this might sound, you should feel proud that the Primoris feels you're a threat. It means your gift is unmatched."

"The Primoris? What's a Primoris?"

"It's a person. Well, used to be. The Primoris Donum."

"What is he? Why? Why does he see me as a threat?" I was suddenly inundated by blood curdling fear. "What does he want from me? Aren't the Korbs bad enough?"

Alex took my scarred wrist in his hand and held it tight. My gift instantly responded to his touch. "This–," he said, tightening his grip, "This is the key. Use it to unlock your secrets. You were the one who dispelled the Iuguolo from your system, not me. I simply guided your raw power. You need to grow to learn all there is to know. What you did today, no other gifted was able to do; with or without my help. You need to find out all there is to know."

"Just tell me already! This search for clues is getting old. This Primoris Donum; what is he? Who is he? Who are you for that matter?"

"I'm glad you're the one," he said laughing, stroking my back tenderly. "You give it such an interestingly innocent flair. You'll do just fine. I'll never leave your side, never did and never will."

"The one what?" I yelled annoyed. "The one what?" I begged. He chuckled again, ignoring my pleas. "Caitlin, now stop playing around and let them know you're okay. They're more worried than they let on, Justin especially."

"I can finally hear their thoughts," I admitted.

"Don't get too excited. It will fade in a few minutes. You're close to ascending, that's all."

I quickly turned my head to the sound of commotion and saw that the Ellri were moving again. I circled to look at Alexander, but he was gone and so were the tranquil surroundings.

"Caitlin?" Justin said approaching me.

"I'm fine; I really am," I pronounced, taking his extended hand, and in one quick swoop he held me in a tight embrace. "Thank god you're alright."

"Of course I'm alright. With you here why wouldn't I be?"

We looked at each other not saying anything further.

"Glad to see you up, child," said Uncle Abbot, severing the silence. I walked into his open arms and he embraced me a bit tighter than usual.

"Where's Tyler and Emily?" I finally asked as I took a step back.

"Tyler, returned to your prom as should you," my uncle said as he caressed my cheek. "You should go and enjoy yourself."

"Enjoy myself?" I enunciated. "Why do you all brush aside the whole ordeal; making everything sound so normal? Are you not aware of what I've just been through?"

"You're fine now. That's what matters."

"You're kidding me, right?" I yelled.

Somewhere deep inside, a spark of rebellion leaped up. "I'm not going to any prom!" I raised my voice even higher. "We're not leaving here until you tell me what all these secrets are all about! And who's this Primoris Donum, and what does he want with me?"

I could tell they were shocked.

"Well?"

The Ellri defiantly turned their backs to me and headed towards the door. "Take her to her Prom, Justin," ordered William, exiting last through the closest door.

"They don't feel you're ready, and who's this Primoris Donum?" Justin asked standing next to me.

"It's someone Alexander mentioned." I wrapped my hands around his waist and buried my head in the curve of his neck. "Apparently, he wants me dead."

I sensed Justin's whole body respond to my words. "What are you saying? What else did Alex tell you? And when did you ever speak to Alex? He disappeared the second you collapsed."

"Exactly what you heard; for some reason this being wants me dead."

"So what is he? What do we do?" Justin seemed to have as many questions as I did.

"I'm not sure. Supposedly my scar is the key to this ridiculous mystery," I gave him a quick little kiss and his whole demeanor suddenly changed. Justin smiled, and hugged me tighter, returning my kiss with even more vigor. It was in that split second that I realized that the only thing standing between Justin and my nakedness was the flimsy T-shirt that Emily slipped over my head. Beet red, I looked around the room searching for something more discreet. Justin chuckled at my discomfort. "You're unbelievable; breathtaking, but unbelievable," he laughed, tightening his hold around me.

"I'm half naked," I yelled, slapping him on the arm to stop him from grinning in satisfaction. "Hope you got an eyeful because you won't be seeing any of that anytime soon if you keep looking at me like that."

He started laughing. "It's your health I was worried about. I didn't even think to look." I raised an eyebrow knowing he was lying. "Okay, okay! Maybe I peeked – just a little," he confessed kissing me on the lips. "How could I not? You're perfect."

"Glad you enjoyed the view," I answered, pushing him away playfully.

From the corner of my eye I saw my gown hanging near the oblong mirror. I tugged on the T-shirt as I walked the length of the chamber hoping it would cover as much as possible. Quickly, I slipped into the rich material without any restraining undergarment this time. The fabric felt soft and smooth, nothing like the inflexible corset.

In no time at all Justin was by my side helping me tie up the dress. "It was much more fun taking it off," he said, kissing me on my exposed shoulder. I didn't comment. His touch sent an onslaught of shivers up my spine; rekindling the hunger I had for him. Before he could even finish tying up the dress I turned around and folded my arms around his neck kissing him softly; tantalizing him mercilessly. His hand caressed my bare back bringing me even closer to unadulterated euphoria.

Justin heaved me off the floor into a tighter hold. His need was all too clear in his urgent kisses and sensual caress. I let out a shriek of excitement and gazed into his hungry eyes as he squeezed me tighter. "You know we don't need to wait. I have complete control of my gift," I offered, kissing him as he put me back down.

"Uhm, really –," he responded smirking. "Is that why you catapulted your little friend across the room earlier?"

"That was different," I said, kissing his sultry lips.

His skin was nectar against my lips. I couldn't seem to get

enough. Having his hand on my bare skin was satanically enticing; any longer and I would have lost any ounce of self-control.

"We have to stop." he said curtly, taking a reluctant step back. I felt wounded. "Here, let me do up the rest of your gown," Justin offered, looking quite distracted by his own thoughts.

"It's been seven months since my return and you're all talking about my ascension. It took my gift eighteen years to surface. Who says I'm going to ascend any time soon?"

Justin smiled warmly. "With or without your gift I want to do this right; proper. Lord knows how much I want you, but we're going to wait until you either ascend or accept my proposal."

I smiled devilishly. "Okay, I'll marry you. I accept!" I blurted out giggling.

He started laughing, putting the finishing touches on my dress. He twirled me around and kissed me hard on the lips. "Let's get you to your Prom, funny girl!"

By the time we returned to the Prom only a handful of couples remained. Thankfully the evening seemed to be coming to an end, and I wanted nothing more than to go home and get out of the gown and into something more – flannel.

Justin was rather quiet and deep in thought. It was only when I started talking that he gave me his undivided attention. "The information that Alexander gave me is aimlessly bouncing inside my head. It just doesn't make any sense, and it's driving me mad."

Prom Night

Illustrated for Lines that Bind - Among the Shadows

He squeezed my hand. "Don't do this to yourself. You've been through enough today."

"Just when I thought it was the Korbs –"

"We'll figure this out," he answered, squeezing my hand tighter. "I promise we will."

"Primoris Donum," I exhaled. The name seeped its chill into my bones. "It means 'the first gift' or 'the first gifted'. I'm not sure. An immortal, right? Maybe even a Nobe. Nobe? Holly Crap! Are they expecting me to go up against a Nobe? They're all out of their freaking minds." I sighed deeply. "Justin, I'm so dead!" Panic swept over me.

"Stop it!" He tugged my hand. "Don't do this to yourself. I said we'll figure this out."

"I'm glad you think so, but forgive me if I don't share your confidence."

Justin was about to say something, but his comment was cut short when we heard, "Where have you two been hiding?" It was Lisa. She approached us smiling. "You missed Tyler's coronation."

"You can't be serious! He's Prom King?" I asked, grinning from ear to ear.

"It would seem so, and Megan of course is queen." I couldn't read Lisa's expression. I wasn't sure if she approved.

"So where is his Royal Majesty?" I asked smiling at the news.

"Right behind you," Tyler exclaimed, tapping me on my shoulder. I hugged him instantly. "Are you okay?" he asked whispering in my ear.

"Perfect!" I assured him.

"Did they tell you what it was?"

I kissed him on the cheek and said softly, "We'll talk later." I took a step back. "You're prom king. That's wonderful."

He shrugged it off by a mere, "Yeah, I guess."

"Congrats man," Justin added smiling. "I always knew you deserved to be royalty. You are, after all, a royal pain in the ass."

Lisa started laughing as did I. Justin's perfectly timed joke smoothed my otherwise dour mood. Tyler, on the other hand, made a wry face at Justin followed by a distasteful gesture with his middle finger, provoking Justin's laughter even more. Within minutes the real royal pain joined our small group, wondering what was so funny. "We're congratulating Tyler on his win," said Justin. "And congrats to you; the crown suits you Megan."

"Thank you. Though it wasn't a unanimous vote as when you and Nicole were elected."

I turned to Justin and stared. "You never told me you were elected king and Nicole queen."

"Who's the ass now?" Tyler muttered.

Justin simply shook his head and rolled his eyes at me and managed a wan smile. "You'd think you have more important things to worry about," he said and stalked off.

"Touchy, isn't he?" Tyler mocked.

I ignored his comment and remained quiet for some time, however, moments later I excused myself, needing to see Justin.

Allowing the pull of our bond to guide me in the right direction, I found him a few minutes later leaning up against the far wall.

"I felt you approach every inch of the way," he admitted, meeting my gaze. He looked away momentarily. "I didn't mean to leave like that. I'm sorry. I – I simply needed to get out of there."

I paused, not knowing what to say. "It's okay. It's my fault."

I saw the muscles in his jaw work. I went to him, and he opened his arms. I stepped inside the shelter he offered, and wrapped my arms around him.

"You need to believe me when I tell you that there was nothing between me and Nicole. I hate that you think I'm keeping something from you; I'm not."

I leaned up and kissed him. "I'm madly in love," I declared, kissing him again, "So you'll have to forgive the teenage jealous fits. Hopefully they'll diminish with age."

"Madly in love?" he asked picking me up.

"To say the least," I squealed with sheer pleasure.

Justin trailed kisses down the outline of my jaw, tormenting me to all new levels, especially now that he nibbled my neck so gently.

"Since I'm not going to be around for much longer, what do you say you fulfill a dying girl's last wish?"

I meant it as a joke; wanting nothing more than to be with Justin in the way a man and woman in love should be, but Justin wasn't at all amused by my grim joke. He pushed me away angrily.

"I was just kidding," I admitted, reaching for his hand.

He motioned it away taking a further step back.

"Justin, I meant it as a joke. Don't be like that. What's the matter? I was a joking!"

"I know," he said, pacing like a caged animal. "It's just that there is nothing I can do." He stopped and looked at me. "Do you know how much that hurts?"

I reached for his hand. "You don't need to do anything."

"All this damn power, Caitlin and there was nothing I could do to keep that monster away from you. How am I supposed to protect you from this?" Frustrated, he kicked the dirt and continued to say, "Gabriel – Gabriel I could handle."

Justin sat down on the stone bench under the towering Oak; his gaze to the ground. I stood there in silence.

"Gabriel was on an even playing field, but this – this is way over our heads. I won't lose you, Caitlin. I just won't."

I kneeled in front of him; my heart a lump of ice within my throat. Justin caressed my cheek. "Anything it takes to keep you safe; I'll do it," exasperated Justin as he sighed heavily.

I leaned my cheek into his hand and said, trying to calm him, "I know that whatever this whole ordeal is, it's big, but for some crazy reason it is something I was born to face. I have to find the courage. I have to face this demon."

"Not alone you don't!" Justin exclaimed. I placed my hand over his. "The Anumus Iuguolo was sent to kill me," I started to say, trying to explain things to Justin; things I, myself didn't understand. "It's killed many gifted before me."

"Is that supposed to make me feel better?" he asked bitterly.

"I'm just trying to say that it wasn't able to kill me. I wasn't supposed to pull through, but I did, and I haven't ascended yet. That should count for something, don't you think?"

"How do you know all this?" he asked quizzically.

"Alexander told me. He even said that my scar is the key and that it will lead me to the truth. He seems to be guiding me somehow, watching over me."

"Alex? But how? He's not part of any family. How is it possible that he knows so much?"

"Whoever he is, he's on our side, and for what it's worth, I trust him. I truly do."

"How is all this connected to the Council's decision?"

"I'm not sure, Justin. It has to be tied together somehow. There's just so much to process. I don't know how I'm supposed to figure all this out. I don't even know where to begin."

He lowered his gaze, again.

"What is it?" I asked taking his hand.

"There's something you need to know about me," Justin started, "About my gift; about what you saw that day in Tirion."

"You know you can tell me anything," I offered, brandishing a weak smile.

"Don't look so worried, Caitlin," he stressed. "I'm fine it's just that I'm not –,"

"Caitlin! There you are," Aunt Leslie exclaimed from a few yards away, startling me. She wasn't alone. Shannon walked right beside her, beaming a radiant smile. I stood up surprised to see them. Justin exhaled hating that he was interrupted.

"Leslie you didn't do her justice," Shannon chirped. "She looks amazing, and this gown is beautiful."

One eyebrow went up as Justin smiled at his mother. "Your timing is impeccable ladies." he said grinning.

"Really? Did we interrupt something?" Aunt Leslie asked, and without waiting for an answer she added, "Well, whatever it was it surely can wait. Isn't that right, Justin?"

"I guess it will have to now, won't it?" he replied, clearly annoyed at having to obey.

"Good! Now why don't we head home, Caitlin. You need to

rest. You might not feel it, but your body's been through enough for one day."

"I'm fine!"

"You only think you are," she insisted.

"I hate being coddled. And you're coddling me – all of you. This really needs to stop!"

Shannon beamed an understanding smile. "Caitlin is right, Leslie. Let's leave them enjoy their evening. Besides, she seems just fine. Justin will see to it that she gets home, won't you son?"

He nodded – smiling for some reason.

I kept my gaze on their back as the two Ellri walked away in silence. Justin folded his strong arms around me and pulled me up against his chest. Eyes closed I let my head fall back against his shoulder. "What was that all about?" I asked, basking in his kisses along the curve of my shoulder.

"I should get you out of here before the Ellri all show up one by one. They're all really worried about you."

I turned in his arms. "Where will you take me?" I asked, lifting myself on tip-toe to kiss his lushes lips.

"You will just have to wait and see," he smiled cunningly.

I stood on the shore, my gown wrapped tightly around me as the wind lashed the waves into a white-foamed frenzy. The silver beading on my gown seemed to dance under the moon lit night; shimmering in its glow. I ignored the long strands of hair that whipped in the wind. Mesmerized by the sound of the waves, I threw my head back and sniffed the salt-filled air, and watched the dark clouds scud across the sky.

"Heavenly!" Justin exclaimed, making me turn in his

direction. "You're absolutely breathtaking," he added, standing a few feet away, looking godly under the soft moon lit night.

I walked happily into his arms, turning in them so that I could look out over the crashing waves once more.

"I'm glad you brought me here," I admitted, taking in a deep breath. "I love the feel of the sand under my bare feet. There is something humbling about it."

"This is where I was supposed to bring you that night," Justin confessed, causing me to turn to look at him. "This is where Marc and Kyle brought Emily and Sandy before we left for the Isle of Indigo. I thought I should at least show you."

"Ah, yes! The night I told you about my dreams," I said, recalling how agitated he was that I kept something so important from him.

"Don't you mean nightmares?"

"I wasn't really afraid. Startled at first, but then I got used to them. Since I knew that they were planted in my head I wasn't scared anymore."

"You don't scare easily, do you?"

"No! I guess I don't. Masochistic, aren't I?"

He chuckled. "I wouldn't go that far."

I took another deep breath enjoying the early morning hours, "It's perfect; just what I needed after today." I turned to face the mesmerizing view again and Justin once again wrapped his arms around me. His hold tightened instantly.

Justin didn't speak. Instead, he leaned his head against mine and exhaled. We stood there motionless. The silence said it all. We were both holding back our fears and concerns about what we would have to face. A warm tear rolled down my windswept face betraying my composed exterior. I didn't motion to wipe it; didn't want Justin to see how scared I really was. Moments later, I turned to face him, and quickly noticed how the soft light accentuated his features. Justin remained motionless, looking into my eyes. My heart fluttered at his mere gaze, and in that split second I made up my mind; decided on something I should've agreed to months ago and said, "I do!"

Justin looked confused. "You do what?"

"I DO!" I repeated pronouncing every word.

"You do – do you? But I haven't proposed yet. You'll have to wait till next time," he said, smiling devilishly, shrugging his shoulders.

"You can't be serious!" I exclaimed, slapping him on the arm. "I just accepted your proposal. You can't refuse me."

"I'm not actually refusing you because there was no proposal to be had today." He looked amused.

"What are you talking about? You proposed only a few hours ago."

He looked at his watch for the first time ever. I never understood why he wore it. It wasn't like anyone in Oaks ever needed a watch to tell time. "It's way past midnight," he announced. "So technically speaking, I proposed to you yesterday."

"What's that supposed to mean?"

He chuckled at my flustered state.

"That simply means that you'll have to wait till I ask you properly. But knowing that you've already accepted takes some weight off my shoulders."

Adoringly, I took his face in my hands and pecked him on the lips. "You never know. I might not say yes next time round."

In one swift move he picked me up and twirled me around dizzily. "Whatever your answer, I'll love you forever," he said stopping in mid stride.

"I surely hope so," I answered, melting in his kisses.

Crushing Waves

Illustrated for Lines that Bind - Among the Shadows

FOUR

HALF-DAY

I T WAS AMAZING how the sound of the first period bell brought things back into prospective. Better yet, the end of year finals that were being held in a week was what really stirred me.

The buzz around school was none other than the Prom. It took all of three days to get the senior class back to normal. Tyler unfortunately, wasn't his vibrant self since my bout with the Animous Iuguolo. I could tell he wanted to bring up the topic; wanted to know what was going on, but he chose to keep quiet.

I was pretty calm considering that there was someone out there that wanted me dead, but what worried me most was the fact that not one person brought up the topic. Not a single one!

Though Uncle Abbot and Aunt Leslie went on their usual daily routine pretending like nothing had happened. I could tell they were worried about me. My aunt exhibited it through her overly affectionate hugs and kisses every time she saw me.

Uncle Abbot, on the other hand, had his own distinct way of dealing with the situation. He simply avoided me. He literally changed direction every time he saw me; pretending to need something from anywhere but my direction.

They both continued to slip out on several occasions to one of those last minute meetings with the other Ellri. I was pretty sure that the main topic of discussion was me and what they were going to do with me.

I quickly banished all those thoughts away as soon as I saw the she-devil approaching. "Will you sign my yearbook?" asked Megan from a couple yards away. Her voice was screechy and rather loud considering the distance. She was making sure I heard her because on many occasions, as soon as I saw her nearing, I made a beeline for my next class; ignoring her annoying little voice.

I took the yearbook form her hand. "Sure thing," I said, accepting the feathery pink pen she offered.

Having missed senior portraits, and the last five years there in Oaks, my face was nowhere to be found in the yearbook. So, I simply drew a stick figure where my picture would've been and signed my name under it.

Senior year, I thought. It was hard to believe that it was almost over. Everyone was looking forward to finishing; looking forward to branching out past the tightly kept borders of Oaks and attending University. Not just any university; the most prestigious ones at that; under close watch of course.

"I can't believe it's almost over," Megan said sounding nostalgic. "Have you thought about what you want to do once we graduate?"

"Survive," I muttered knowing she wouldn't understand.

She grinned. "You shouldn't worry so much about the future. You never know how things might turn out. Take us for instance. Would you have guessed that we'd ever be friends? But here we are."

"I see your point," I said not wanting to hurt her feelings. As hard as I tried I was sure that I would never consider Megan trustworthy. I hung out with her strictly for Tyler's sake. Personally, there was way too much history between us to simply brush it off to the side and pretend things didn't happen. Call it childhood trauma or even deep rooted childhood emotional scars. Whatever it was, I wasn't anywhere near forgiving or forgetting as far as Megan was concerned.

I suddenly beamed a great big smile as soon as I saw Tyler walking towards us. "So, did you girls decide what you want to do today?" he asked happier than I've seen him these couple of days.

Without any hesitation Megan gave him a quick kiss on the mouth and with one hand fixed his tussled hair. Tyler seemed rather awkward with her affectionate exhibition. He simply smiled and took her hand in his. "So –?" he continued to say looking quite embarrassed.

I looked at him confused.

"Caity, its half-day today; Senior Class Day!" He looked at me shaking his head. "You weren't planning on staying for the rest of the school day, were you? We can leave at twelve. Why would you want to stay?"

"I didn't say I wanted to stay. I simply forgot; that's all!"

"Okay then, what do you want to do? We don't need to stay in Oaks. We can go anywhere we want."

"Really, they'll let us do that?"

"It's a perk for graduation," said Megan fumbling through her oversized bag. "We can go to Cambridge. Harvard Square is perfect this time of year. We can have lunch and then coffee. What do you say?"

"Sounds perfect," squealed Lisa from behind, causing me to quickly turn my head. "Caitlin, you can ride with me and Gina."

Tyler grimaced.

"What did you think, Tyler," she said responding to his discontent. "How do you figure on fitting Caitlin and Megan in your two-seater?"

As far as Tyler's expressions were concerned, I was an expert; able to decode each and every face he made. My best friend wasn't planning on escorting Megan anywhere, but now he was stuck with her. He was too much of a gentleman to back out now.

He stared at me, begging to get him out of the whole seating arrangement. I smiled at my best friend and turned to Lisa. "That sounds like fun. I'd love a ride," I answered smiling, hoisting my school bag on my shoulder. "Can I invite Justin?"

"Absolutely not!" she exclaimed. "This trip is strictly for graduating seniors. Justin knows the rules. He'll understand."

"The distance," I muttered shifting my gaze back to Tyler. "If Justin can't come along, I'm not sure if I can make it. The pain will be too great to enjoy anything. I'll ruin your day."

Tyler instantly had a twinkle in his eye.

"You're not going to miss out on this," he said letting go of Megan. "I won't let you back out." He smiled that boyishly cunning smile. "Megan can ride with the girls and you'll come with me. If you see that you can't handle the distance we'll just turn right back and that way you wouldn't have to ruin anyone's day."

My gaze turned to Megan to see how she took Tyler's plan. Honestly, I felt really bad. It was one thing not to like the girl but a whole other to require her boyfriend's tending for the rest of the day.

Surprisingly, she looked fine. No contemptuous stare; no fire in her eyes. "It's okay Caitlin," she said obviously understanding my dilemma. "You go with Tyler. He has a point."

"Are you absolutely sure?" I asked wanting to be certain that she meant what she said.

"Of course silly, Tyler's your best friend. I'd want my best friends looking after me," she said smiling. "Speaking of my best friends, I have to tell Kim and Loraine. You guys don't mind if they tag along, do you?"

"The more the merrier," answered Lisa.

Megan was doing her best to get on my good side. I decided there and then that it was time I got over any ill feelings I reserved for her. This year represented the closing of a big chapter in our lives. It'll do me good to turn over a new leaf as far as Megan Gordon was concerned. Burying the hatchet was long overdue. Okay, maybe not burying it completely but at least keeping it a great distance away. Evidently, I needed to try much harder.

"Okay then when do we leave?" I said smiling.

Tyler was visibly happy that I decided to follow along, especially since he tried, on many occasions, to get me to go out and enjoy myself, but I refused every single time.

"We can go now," Tyler exclaimed smiling from ear to ear.

"I need to make a stop at home first," said Megan looking down at her high heels. "I should change into flats if we're going to be walking around all day."

Lisa nodded. "I'm sure we all have something to do before we leave. Why don't we meet in, let's say, an hour in the school parking lot? That should give everyone more than enough time to get ready."

C ash safely stashed in my front pocket, I was ready to go. I would've liked to see Justin before leaving but there was no time. Tyler was already waiting for me downstairs.

"Did anyone let Justin know about our little trip?" I asked once I entered the kitchen. Tyler was sitting with my aunt enjoying one of her famous multi-layered, Black Forrest Cakes.

"Justin should be made aware before the burning sets in. It wouldn't be fair to have him worry that something has happened to me."

"He knows sweetie. He's in the Chamber practicing with Marc and Kyle, otherwise he'd be here to see you off. Now sit down and have a bite to eat."

I motioned that I didn't want anything.

Tyler got to his feet. "I'll bring her straight back if the pain is too much for her to handle," he began, stuffing the last bite of the morsel in his mouth. "Leslie, your cake is to die for!"

"Thanks," she smiled, handing him a glass of water, but then she turned to me. "You shouldn't have a problem. A slight sting maybe, but no real pain," she added taking me by the shoulder. "Now you kids behave yourselves and stay out of trouble. Using your gifts is strictly forbidden around the non-gifted."

"I'm sure you'll keep a close eye on us while we're there," I accused, knowing full well how true my words were.

"Just go and enjoy yourself. Get a good look around the campus. If you like it, you might want to attend next year?"

"Me? Harvard?"

"Yes! Why not? Your grades are surely Harvard material and since Justin's continuing his studies there; where else would you go?"

"It's not that. It's that I haven't thought much about school; about anything for that matter. There are just so many things I need to figure out first."

"Well, that's your first mistake. The only thing you should be worrying about is your finals and what you want to study next year. Everything else can wait."

"Wait?" I exclaimed. "There's someone out there who wants to kill me. How am I supposed to wait? Wait for what? How am I supposed to make plans for my future? I haven't even considered going to college. It's meaningless to make plans when there is a faceless, deadly threat out there. This is no custody battle. It's a hunt for the kill, and unfortunately I am its prey."

Tyler's mouth dropped open in shock, almost dropping the glass he was holding. Thankfully, his quick reflexes saved the crystal from shattering on the hard wood floor. "Who's out to kill you?" He bellowed, "And why am I now hearing of this?"

"No one wants to kill her," Aunt Leslie said maneuvering us to the door. "Caitlin is simply exaggerating, isn't that right?"

My aunt clearly felt that Tyler had to be kept in the dark about the Primoris Donum. I hated to do this, but I simply nodded my head in agreement.

"I was talking about the Korbs," I said trying to divert the conversation. "Have you forgotten that the decision is still pending?"

"The Nobe Council will need to decide on that. Nobody will dare touch you until a decision is made."

I nodded. I didn't say anything more. It was bad enough I had to lie to him; I didn't want to continue talking about my family across the Atlantic.

A stiff silence hung over us for too many awkward moments. Then, Leslie patted Tyler on the back. "Caitlin, did you know that Tyler is going to Medical school?" She finally asked breaking the unyielding tension.

"That's great Tyler!"

"Yeah, well I thought that the more I know about the human body the better I can serve my gift."

I beamed an overly animated smile. I was sure I looked stupid just staring at him grinning from ear to ear. I was proud; really proud. "I'm sure you'll be the best doctor out there."

"Caity, I'll never be an actual physician. I won't have my own practice if that's what you're thinking. I'm studying it just for the knowledge nothing more. Can you honestly see me in a hospital? The morgue? Won't my gift spark suspicion in the outside world?"

"There're so many people that can gain from your gift; people that can't be saved by medical science. Why in the world would you keep your miraculous gift from saving them?"

He smiled and caressed my cheek. Aunt Leslie just stood and observed.

"Believe me, I know exactly how you feel," he said. "But I'm not here to intervene with the natural order of things. I can't play God. Since I'm limited to saving a few each time how am I supposed to choose who lives or dies?"

"Saving a few is better than not saving any," I said trying to make my point.

"I can't be the one who controls someone's destiny. If they are meant to die; if our creator has decided it's their time to go, who am I to intervene?"

Aunt Leslie took a step forward. "Wounds, injuries the occasional migraine, he can help with, but when the question of life and death is at stake, it's too great for any one of us to decide. Even if Tyler's gift allows him to bring somebody back from near death, it doesn't mean he should. We are merely a shadow of our creator. If we start believing that our gifts give us the right to command the natural order of things we're destined for destruction. The creator will decide who lives and dies; none of us have the right to play God."

"Why were we then granted all this power? Shouldn't we use it to do some good? There's nothing I can do, but Tyler can surely make a difference?"

Aunt Leslie smiled and said, "The world is simply not ready for any of you just yet, sweetie."

"And don't forget the limits of my own gift, Caity," added Tyler. "It's as miraculous as it is deadly and addictive."

I breathed in deep and nodded my head in understanding. "Yeah, I guess you're both right."

"You best get going. The rest of your group is waiting," said Aunt Leslie putting an end to the discussion.

Year Book

Illustrated for Lines that Bind - Among the Shadows

FIVE

DANGEROUSLY CLOSE

HARVARD SQUARE was a hub of activity. Being sunny as it was, the outdoor cafés and restaurants overflowed with young people. As we looked for a table to sit, I noticed that Megan seemed to feel a bit out of place without her two friends. Kim and Loraine had made other plans excluding her. They went with another group of seniors to some mall in Boston without even mentioning it to her. It was quite cold and heartless, but then what did she expect? What goes around comes around, and Megan was getting an overdue taste of her own bitter medicine which was visibly hard for her to swallow. But it was poor Tyler who was paying the price for Kim and Loraine's absence.

Megan clung to him like lint to wool. It was amusing to watch him try to be a gentleman, not wanting to hurt her feelings. He found innovative ways to try and break free of her hold. It was quite entertaining to watch her pull him even closer with each attempt of his failed escape.

Serves him right! I thought utterly amused at how awkward my best friend was feeling.

It took us several minutes to find a seat and even longer to be served. But as the saying goes; all good things come to those who wait, and come they did. The food was scrumptious; just what my growling tummy needed. After gobbling down every last bite of my grilled chicken salad, I sat back content and full, sipping on my soda, relaxing and watching the world go by.

"This place suits you," said Tyler smiling from across the table.

"I think you're right. I can surely get used to this."

"Can you believe this place?" added Lisa looking around spellbound.

The historic red brick walkways helped in capturing a certain urban beauty as did the historic buildings that lined every street. The only thing I could do without; that we all probably could do without was the heavy traffic. After so many weeks in a car free Tirion, the slightest sound of traffic was nerve racking. I preferred something in the middle. The quiet small town feel of Oaks is what I loved most. We had the luxuries of the twenty-first century but the tight knit community of days long gone.

"So where do we head from here?" asked Tyler paying for the bill.

"Like any self-respecting tourist, we should pick up a walking tour map at the visitors information booth in the center of the square," advised Lisa.

"Let's just walk around aimlessly. It's the best way to go about it. Looking at the map makes it so, so educational," said Gina pulling a face.

"I totally agree. I like aimlessness," I said. "It's much more fun than following the tour map. It makes things more adventurous; more unpredictable."

"Getting lost, it is then," said Tyler heading off.

Surprisingly, Gina had an acute sense of direction. She seemed to lead us like a seasoned tour guide pointing out the most beautiful and historic sites. She swore it was her first time out there so I assumed she was making good use of her god given gift. It was subtle, but quite useful.

The area reminded me more and more of a regional shopping center. Small stores lined the walkways enticing the visitors to enter. Everything seemed to be within a fifteen minute walk. We strolled along, stopping in every nook and cranny that drew our attention.

The girls hovered over trinkets and bought a multiplicity of ornate findings for their rooms. Personally, I liked nothing more than the outdoor book racks that some stores boasted.

"Books for a mere dollar? How insane is that?" I squealed talking to Tyler.

"You're such a nerd," was his response.

"I love the sight and smell of the old traditional bookstores."

"As I said, Caitlin. You're a nerd."

I laughed.

We stopped in a few book shops some specializing in poetry others in all genres. The musty smell of used books was intoxicating. If I were alone I was sure to spend hours perusing each and every rack. But unfortunately for me, the rest of my group didn't share my insatiable love for literature apart from Lisa, but even she didn't seem as enamored by these finds.

"Nothing educational today," she exclaimed, smacking the

leather bound book from my hand. "Besides, your uncle probably has all these titles in his library."

"I need to get something for Justin. His birthday is coming up," I huffed, hoping that my little excuse would offer some extra minutes in the shop.

"You can get him something in Oaks, now let's go!"

I halfheartedly followed her outside. Just then, I realized that I did need to get something for Justin. "What can I possibly get a guy that has everything?"

"I'm sure you'll think of something wonderful," she said smiling. "Maybe Kyle can give you some ideas. He probably knows Justin better than anyone."

"That's a great idea, Lisa. I'll do that as soon as we get back to Oaks."

Tyler was paying rather close watch to what I was doing all day.

"I'm fine," I mouthed several times as a response to his concerned gaze.

The stinging in my blood was now more virile. It made listening to what the group was saying, even attempting to make their interests my own, even harder. To some extent the conversations kept my mind off of the agonizing void I felt of Justin's absence.

Since our return from Tirion, our bond seemed more potent. Like Velcro being forcefully pulled apart was how it felt each and every time we had to separate. It was maddening having to leave him, having to see him walk away.

I looked up at the sky and took a deep breath to ease my mind. I simply had too many things bouncing around in there.

The bright morning sun was tardily dimming to a soft

orange glow over the banks of the Charles River. We stood on the Anderson Memorial Bridge and watched the day slowly come to an end with all of us enjoying the sight of geese frolicking near the water's edge. Tyler even suggested a sunset cruise on the river, but exhausted as we were from walking around all day we graciously refused, but offered to treat him to an ice cream before our overdue return to Oaks.

Even though I truly enjoyed my day, I wanted – needed to return to Oaks. The distance was slowly tearing my insides apart.

But when, much later, we were about to reach the cars, something drove all thoughts of returning from my mind. Megan suddenly looked as if she were going to faint.

"Megan!" Tyler gasped. Then louder, "Megan, what is it?"

"It's big. It's really close," she whispered leaning against the parked car in sheer terror.

Megan's lost expression was quite alarming. Her fresh vibrant complexion went from a bright healthy pink glow to a ghostly white in seconds.

"What's she talking about?" I asked turning to Lisa.

From the corner of my eye I saw Tyler wrapping his arms around Megan trying to comfort her. The girl was shaking like a leaf. "Make it go away," she kept whispering in Tyler's shirt.

Lisa leaned into me and whispered, "Megan can sense when something bad is going to happen."

"What do you mean?" I asked surprised.

"She can sense devastation and chaos; things like natural disasters or even something manmade. But she has to be close. I mean in the surrounding area. She picks it up like radar only minutes before it happens."

Megan forcefully pulled herself from Tyler's embrace and looked straight ahead toward the long stretch of road. "Brace yourselves!" Megan screeched in a riveting voice, pointing in the direction of traffic. "It's coming!"

I wasn't sure how long I had been staring at her. For a moment I thought I had fallen asleep and was now dreaming, but surely this strange ominous feeling was something all too real; real and frightening.

No sooner had she spoken the words when the deafening sound of tires trying to come to a screeching halt filled the air followed by several collisions of metal hitting metal at high speeds. The source of the sound was a few blocks away, but the eerie sound of people screaming in horror was all too clear.

Instantly, the smell of burning rubber filled the evening air followed by a dark cloud of smoke and then one explosion after the other shook the very ground we stood on. People were running in all different directions trying to save themselves.

"Death is in the air," said Gina with her eyes closed. "Two people I'm aware of; there are many others. Some are trapped under the cars and others deeply cut by the display windows. There are several weak heart beats. I'm not sure but I think they're small children involved."

"What!" I gasped being too shocked to say anything else. I turned to Tyler instantly. "We need to do something. We can't just stand here!"

He shook his head no. "It's not our place, besides by the time we reach them the police and ambulances will be on the scene. What do you expect to do then?"

"Did you say you want to get there fast?" Lisa asked ignoring Tyler's refusal to co-operate. In no time at all, she used her index finger to trace an imaginary square in the air, encompassing the area of the accident, and quite magically the morbid scene of the accident seemed to enlarge all the more, getting closer and closer as if Lisa was zooming in on nature itself, and in seconds we found ourselves in the dead center of the bloody disaster.

Like Megan, Lisa looked exhausted as she clutched the side of the car, breathing rather heavily.

"I can't believe you're making me do this!" Tyler growled at me.

I didn't respond; wasn't about to get into an argument right at that moment. These people needed our help.

"You girls stay here," he snapped pointing to the pavement. "There's nothing that any of you can do at this point."

Gina remained standing, but Lisa and Megan gladly slumped down on the sidewalk only a few feet away from the disaster, each supporting the other.

It didn't take long for the frightful onlookers to start gathering once again. It always amazed me how we humans swarmed to scenes of blood and gore. Instead of following our natural instincts to run and hide we put it all on the line to get one good look at the blood and gore.

The accident was a mesh of carnage and metal. A large sanitation truck had somehow ended up inside the storefront; plowing across all the tables of the outdoor café. Three other cars were on fire while the smell of dead flesh waft in the air.

I was overwhelmed as was Tyler. "There's just too many," he said looking around at all the bodies. "These vehicles need to be lifted in order for me to pull them out. We can't do this! There're just too many people around."

"Tyler! I don't care! We are helping these people."

Just as I was about to lift the twisted metal off the ground with a simple thought; four Ellri clad in white appeared out of nowhere and stood stock still, like sentries on each end of the accident. The high Ellri Nathan stood to the far corner to my left while William to my right. Marcellus along with his brother Claudius stood across the street on opposite sides.

"Oh, great!" exclaimed Tyler on seeing his father.

They didn't approach us, nor did anybody else seem to notice their presence. Not that they could. As soon as the cloaked Ellri appeared the onlookers closest to the scene of the accident were completely suspended in frozen animation, but the further back I looked the less immobilized they appeared. They moved but in a mysteriously slow motion. Like time had somehow lapsed in various degrees and speeds the further back you looked.

The groans and whimpers of the injured snapped me out of my quandary. Without a second to spare, I summoned my gift and lifted every inanimate object off the ground, and I mean everything. The only things left lying there were the blood soaked bodies of the victims. My heart started beating hard against my chest, my eyes filled in tears.

How can so much happen so fast? I wondered hoping that we weren't too late.

By thought alone, I moved each body carefully to the side, out of harm's way before returning the twisted metal back to its original position. Not wanting anything to be out of place when the police arrived, I was careful in repositioning each object as I had found it.

From the corner of my eye, I saw Tyler standing over the

bodies with one hand out as if examining the victims. He didn't stop to help them all; only the ones who were seriously injured. Gina helped guide him; pointed out who was in more dire need.

Like statues, the Ellri stood doing nothing to help the situation. Annoyed at their indifference, I made my way through the broken glass and into the coffee shop. Apart from the shattered furniture, there was nothing that needed my attention. It would seem that nobody was sitting inside at the time of the accident.

"Thank goodness for great weather," I whispered.

I was about to exit the store when Gina walked in. "Wait," she said closing her eyes. "There!" She pointed to the front of the sanitation truck. "A small boy is wedged against the wall. He's in real bad shape. I think Tyler should be here when you pull him free. He won't make it otherwise."

I circled my head to call out to Tyler when I saw him folded over on the ground; over one of the victims.

"Tyler!" I screamed running over to him. "Tyler, are you alright?"

"There's just too many, Caity. I can't. I have no more energy left."

I instantly grabbed his hand and summoned all my power to the tips of my fingers.

"What are you doing?" he asked starring at my throbbing scar in fear.

"I'm trying to help you regain your strength. Now relax, will you? I need you in there."

At once I felt the flow of energy from my fingers into his arm. Tyler instantly stood upright and smiled. "I can read your thoughts," he said smiling. "You are impressed by Megan, aren't you?" Instantly his face hardened. "Who's Primoris Donum?" he asked clearly aware of my deepest fear.

"Later!" I screamed letting go of his hand. "Come on! I need you!" I barked out the order leading him inside the shop.

"You need to be really quick, Tyler," said Gina. "The kid has excessive internal bleeding."

"On the count of three," I said. "One…two…"

I eased the truck away from the boy. The look in the child's eyes was nondescript. Tyler took him in his arms and laid him gently on the floor. "He's too far gone for me to help. I don't have that kind of energy in me; maybe when I Ascend, but not now." Tyler looked at me completely lost.

"I'm sure I can help. I can boost your energy. It will work! It has to work!"

"Not this time, Caity. I'm really sorry. You might make me feel better but I still won't be able to help. I'm limited to how much of my gift I can use."

I kneeled helplessly over the small boy and wiped the strands of hair from his face. He couldn't have been older than six. He tried to say something but no words were coming out. He turned his gaze from Tyler and stared right at me.

"You'll be just fine," I lied holding his small hand. "You'll be just fine," I repeated wanting to believe it myself.

"Caity, we should go," said Tyler pulling me by the arm. "We have no place here. We did what we could."

"No!" I screamed tugging my arm free. "I'm not going anywhere! I'm not leaving this child alone until help arrives."

"Caitlin!"

I circled my head to the sound of Aunt Leslie's soft voice.

"Do what Tyler says, I'll stay with the little Eric."

Like the other Ellri she too was draped in a long, white cloak. Her features were way too relaxed, even for her. There was no way that she wasn't shaken by this disaster. She had to be; how could she not be?

"I can't just leave him!"

"Child, you must! This is no place for you. Help is on its way. You kids must avoid attracting attention. You did all you could; now go!"

She knelt next to the boy and he closed his eyes.

"Is he –,"

I couldn't finish the question. A wave of sadness overtook me.

"He'll be fine. Eric's little body simply needs to rest. Now go and do what you're told."

The familiarity with which she used the boy's name was eerie. She seemed to be unfazed by the circumstances surrounding the half-dead child, but yet in an overly protective manner, she straightened out his clothes and fixed his hair lovingly, the way she used to do with me when I was young.

"Caitlin, you must go," she urged. "Please! Do as you're told this once."

"I need to know that he won't be left alone."

"Sweetie, I'm here now. Nothing will happen to him. Please, trust me. But you must go!"

I was reluctant at first, but then Tyler pulled me by the arm and led me outside. The girls quickly met up with us and we inconspicuously made our way into the crowd.

Coffee Shop

Illustrated for Lines that Bind - Among the Shadows

SIX

LIAR LIAR

W E STOOD ON the side of the road as the crowd returned to a normal human pace. As soon as the Ellri disappeared, help arrived giving first aid to the injured. The ones that Tyler did help were simply sitting there completely disoriented unable to make any sense of what had transpired. "I was sitting over there –," said one of the injured, "how did I get over here?" He wondered staring at the fireman who was helping him up.

The fire department removed two scorched bodies from the wreckage and carted them off under a veil of white.

"Only if we were closer, I probably could've prevented all of this or a least pulled the two drivers out before the explosion," I said turning to Tyler. "I could've been here in a heartbeat. Why didn't I just use my gift at the first sound of the brakes screeching? I could've reached this place in no time. Why? Why didn't I react any faster?"

"You did all you could. Now stop badgering yourself," Tyler said putting his arm around my shoulder. "We all did what we could."

I hated not being able to save both man. Hated having to stand there and watch the corpses being carried away. These people had families, children.

"I should've acted quicker!"

Tyler tightened his hold.

"Only two dead," said one of the firemen sounding rather surprised. "By the extent of the damage I would've thought there'd be more fatalities."

"I was thinking the exact same thing. There're blood stains all over the place but all the victims are gathered in one area," said another.

"Damn it," I whispered. "I forgot about the blood stains. I didn't want to leave any clues of us ever being here."

Tyler quickly looked at me and said, "Stop doing this to yourself; you did great."

"The onlookers probably helped them out," said the other fireman. Both men shook their heads baffled by the scene of the accident. "Was anyone found in the shop?"

"Fortunately, nobody was inside. The guys checked. Even though there's a large amount of blood against the wall and some on the floor, the shop is completely empty; no victims to account for the blood."

I turned my head to Tyler in utter shock. "Where's the small boy? Where's Aunt Leslie?" I whispered.

"There," said Gina pointing across the street to the crowd that gathered around the accident, and there, among the many faces, Aunt Leslie's stood out. She looked down and smiled. I followed her gaze only to see the little boy holding her hand smiling back. She tussled his hair and took him by the hand and disappeared into the crowd. It was the last time I ever saw that child.

"What in the world –," Tyler exclaimed. "How did she –?"

He was too shocked to finish his sentence.

"We should leave," said Lisa helping Megan stand.

I wanted to look for my aunt, but knew better than to leave the girls drive themselves home. Tired as they were, I wasn't about to allow another accident to happen, so I instructed Tyler to take Megan home and that I'd drive Lisa and Gina myself.

"Some trip," whispered Lisa with her head against the passenger's window. "I wonder how they figure on punishing us for using our gifts outside Oaks."

"I truly don't care. I wasn't going to let innocent people die because of some stupid rules. We did what was right. If they don't see that, then none of us deserve to be gifted."

She nodded in agreement and soon fell asleep.

S eeing that it was Lisa's car that I was driving, I dropped Gina off first, and then took Lisa home. Her father was waiting outside visibly worried. "Are you kids okay?" Mr. Griffin asked as he helped his daughter inside.

"I think we'll be just fine. She needs some rest that's all. I can take her up to her room if you'd like, Mr. Griffin."

Lisa gave me a hug and said, "You did enough already, Caitlin. I'll be okay. Dad, make sure she gets home safe."

"Okay, well you go to your room sweetie and I'll take Caitlin home."

"Mr. Griffin that really won't be necessary. I can walk."

"Nonsense! It's too far to walk and after what you guys have been through, I insist." He led me back outside to the car. "No child should be witness to the horrific events of today," he said a few silent moments later as he drove me home.

I cracked a weak smile. "We'll be okay, Mr. Griffin. It was a good slap across the face, but we'll be just fine."

His lips turned up in an understanding smile. "You all acted bravely; carelessly, but brave."

"Carelessly? In what sense."

"Being gifted is a blessing, but a blessing best kept within the safe limits of Oaks."

"I'm sorry, Mr. Griffin, but I don't agree. We can do so much."

"Yes, of course you can, but people out there are not ready for kids with powers like yours. They may love reading about them, or even watch movies with their favorite superheroes, but when it comes to real world dynamics; nobody is ready for any of you. It's best you all keep a low profile."

"We tried to help today, and I want to believe we did."

He remained quiet for a couple of minutes until we reached outside the massive wrought iron gate leading to Uncle Abbot's house. "You were all wonderful today. You truly were, but not without the protective shield of the Ellri. If you guys were found out, lord knows…" He shook his head, banishing some frightful thought that came to mind.

I reached out to open the door when he placed his hand on my arm. "Caitlin, I'm not trying to diminish what you guys did today. I'm just trying to bring light to the real dangers you all face if you are found out."

"I know," I said with a warm smile.

He wanted to drop me off at the front of the house but I insisted on getting out. "The walk up will do me good," I said, easing his anxious expression.

"Are you sure?"

"I'm sure," I reassured him and headed up the long driveway.

The moon, covered in a wind-tattered veil of clouds, was nevertheless bright enough to make out the single silhouette sitting on the front steps. "Justin!" I exhaled quickening my pace, wanting nothing more than to be in his arms. I stared at him and was filled with sudden fierce love for the man. With every step I felt the pull even stronger. If I stopped walking I was sure I'd simply glide in his direction like metal being pulled by a great magnet.

"What a day; quite the adventure," I said out loud, trying to downplay the events, seeing that he was in a foul mood.

"You seem to have had a full day," Justin said rather gravely.

"It would've been nicer if you were there. I've missed you."

"Good, then you won't have a problem with what I'm going to say next."

"What's wrong?" I asked seeing how sour he was. "Did I do something to make you mad?"

He lifted my chin and looked me dead in the eyes. "You're never leaving my side again; ever! Do you understand? Never again," he roared, and kissed me rather urgently on the lips.

"Justin, I'm truly sorry."

"What's there to be sorry about?"

"Then why are you angry with me?"

"I'm not angry with you. I was just really worried."

The pain was back in my voice. "I shouldn't have gone with them. The distance was too great. Sorry if it hurt. Sorry for making you worry."

He swept my hair to the side and then caressed my cheek. "I'm just being selfish to want you with me. You saved the lives of many people today. There's absolutely nothing to be sorry about."

My eyes widened in surprise. "But – but I thought we weren't supposed to intervene!"

"I wouldn't call what you guys did today intervening. You were at a scene of an accident; a horrific one at that. Only cowards would turn their backs. You did what any of us would've done and more." He beamed one of those amazing smiles that left me wanting so much more. "You guys should be proud of yourselves."

"The Ellri. The Ellri were there and did nothing."

Justin just stared, clearly wanting to say much more, but kept it all bottled up. Instead he kissed me again and smiled between his enticing assaults; enjoying my little groans of satisfaction. "I don't see any bags. Didn't you see anything you liked?" He asked kissing my nose.

"Well, I was looking to get you something for your birthday, but nothing seemed good enough. How about you save me the trouble and tell me what you'd like me to get you?"

One eyebrow lifted devilishly as he cracked a deceitful smile and said, "I have everything I'll ever need right here."

I smiled and gave him a quick kiss. "Justin, you did so much for my birthday. How am I supposed to top that?"

"Honestly, you don't need to get me –,"

Our conversation was abruptly interrupted by the glare of

an oncoming car. "What are you doing here?" I asked Tyler as he slammed the car door with force. "Shouldn't you be home resting; eating a mountain of food. You need to regain your strength!"

"Don't you worry about what I need, Caity," said Tyler angrily. "I'm not the one lying to myself; lying to everybody around me."

"What are you talking about?" I lashed out with a hint of resentment.

He looked at me and instantly turned his gaze to Justin. "Did you know that she's in some sort of mortal danger? I was in her thick skull today when she so graciously boosted my power. She's completely scared out of her freaking mind."

"Tyler!" I protested, "I'm perfectly fine!"

"Like hell you are! Did you know about this?" He insisted turning to Justin. "Why in God's name did you people allow her to come along today? If this thing is after her, shouldn't she stay in Oaks? Locked in the basement or something? Are you all trying to kill her?"

"This has absolutely nothing to do with you," I said breaking from Justin's embrace. "You need to back off!"

Before Tyler could even comment, Justin grabbed me by the hand. "He's right Caitlin. You're safer here! I should've at least been there."

Justin's features were solemn – guilt ridden. I hated Tyler for making him feel as if this was all his doing. I pulled my hand free and stepped away from both of them. "I will not be a prisoner in my own home. Whatever this is; whoever this is will not scare me into submission," I yelled. "He came close to killing me once. He most certainly won't have that privilege ever again. I was born into whatever this is; born to face this demon."

My eyes instantaneously betrayed the composure I was trying to keep. Tears of unbridled fear rolled freely down my face as I fought to catch my breath. "Let him come. I'm right here waiting," I said stretching out my hands welcoming my doom. I cupped my face in sheer terror and fell to my knees shedding tears of uncertainty.

"Look at me," said Justin crouching in front of me. "Why do you insist on keeping all this inside?" He shook his head. "Let's not get ahead of ourselves." His voice was calm and soothing. "First, we need to find out what this thing is and what he has to gain by –,"

"Say it, Justin. What are you afraid of? Say it! Why don't you want to accept this? This thing wants to kill me."

"Caity, that's enough," exploded Tyler "Just stop!"

"Tyler is right. C'mon, let's go inside," Justin reasoned, helping me to my feet. "It's not the appropriate time to discuss such things."

"It's never the appropriate time to discuss anything, is it Justin?"

He looked at me in bitter silence and then raised his voice as he asked, "What do you want me to say, Caitlin? Tell me! What could I possibly say to make you feel better? Because anything I say you will find some fault with it."

To sever the tension, Tyler placed his hand on my shoulder "This isn't Justin's fault. I shouldn't have brought this shit up after the day we had. I didn't mean to upset you."

I instantly turned and gave Tyler a great big hug. I held on for quite some time unwilling to let go. Tyler was visibly surprised by my response. He awkwardly wrapped his arms around me and tightened his hold. "You were truly amazing today," he said, kissing me on the forehead. "Those people wouldn't be alive if it weren't for you."

He pulled me away and stared down at me. "Justin's right. This isn't the appropriate time to discuss all this. We've been through enough today. I'm real sorry. I just didn't think!"

I wiped my stupid tears away and looked up at him and attempted a smile. "You're gift is what's amazing. You handed them their life; their health." I leaned in and kissed him on the cheek. "Let me figure the rest out. I promise I won't keep you in the dark anymore. It's just that everything just keeps on coming at me. Sometimes it's easier that I keep things to myself. I don't mean to keep things from you," I turned to Justin, "from any of you."

Justin didn't' speak. I simply kissed him on the cheek and silently headed inside. He remained standing in the frame of the door talking to Tyler. I didn't need to hear what they were saying to know they were talking about me. Tyler sounded angst, wanting to help anyway he could. Justin being older and mature beyond his years, pushed his own uncertainties and fears aside and comforted my best friend; probably promising to keep me safe and out of harm's way.

It was one of those promises you say to keep the other person from jumping off the cliff; a promise that you would go through hell and back to keep, but know deep down that no matter the sacrifice, it was a lost cause. I was certain that Justin would sacrifice everything to keep me safe; that was my biggest fear after all. Standing up to my uncle Caradon back in Tirion without even batting an eye was a clear indication that Justin sooner forfeit his own life than see me hurt in any way. Gabriel and the Korbs were one thing, the Primoris Donum I had a feeling was quite another.

Moments later, as I was waiting for Justin on the landing, Uncle Abbot came out of the den holding a very old book in hand smiling contently.

"Amazing what you can find in one of these," he gently intoned, waving the leather bound beauty in the air. He caressed my cheek with his free hand and smiled even wider. "You sure had a long day."

"Yeah, it would seem that way. You're not avoiding me anymore; that's good."

He smiled. "You were amazing today; really amazing considering you're so young. You exhibited the greatest virtue of all," marveled my uncle, "The moral excellence of all human beings."

I went down the list in my mind of all seven virtues trying to figure out which he commended me on: Chastity, temperance, charity, diligence, patience, kindness and humility. I wasn't sure which he was talking about. Chastity – sure, and by the looks of it for much longer than I'd like, but I was pretty certain he wasn't talking about that. Okay, maybe patience. I've exhibited an insurmountable amount of that, but again not today.

"And what would that be?" I finally asked turning my head to the sound of the door closing. Justin came in looking deep in thought.

"Compassion," Uncle Abbot said tenderly. "Compassion," he repeated and strolling off to the library.

"Is that even a virtue?" I asked sure that it wasn't on any list I ever read.

He turned and said, "The Buddhist tradition call it Karuna. Compassion, the Buddha says, is that which makes the heart of the good move at the pain of others. It crushes and destroys the pain of others; thus, it is called compassion. It is called compassion because it shelters and embraces the distressed."

I could tell he wasn't finished. Out of all the people to question I would choose the one man I knew who could debate the meaning of God with God himself and probably win at that.

"Another example would be the heritage within Western Christendom of compassion as the principle of charity. Jesus assures his listeners in the Sermon on the Mount that, 'Blessed are the merciful, for they shall obtain mercy.' And let's not leave out the Hindu tradition of DAYA or the Jewish tradition of Rahman or 'Compassionate' as its better known. The Muslim tradition considers mercy and compassion the foremost among God's attributes. In the canonical language of Arabic, Rahman and Rahim."

"Okay, okay I give up. It's a virtue," I exclaimed shaking my head from the outpour of information.

Justin smiled.

Satisfied, my uncle turned to head for the library.

"Oh, that reminds me," he said turning to face us once again. "It's rather late young man," he paused, "Make sure your visit is short. My niece might not have the need for beauty sleep, but she is in much need of rest."

"Of course," Justin said trying to stifle a chuckle.

Within a blink of an eye, my uncle went from a brilliant scholar to a half crazed parent concerned with only one of the many virtues; chastity, and hoping that I'd remain virtuous in that particular sector as long as he lived and breathed.

I knew there was a compliment somewhere in my uncle's words, but I was too agitated to hear it. I rolled my eyes at his inability to understand that Justin and I were inseparable.

His inane house rules were becoming all the more annoying, but I knew my uncle lived under a different code of conduct; a code long forgotten by many.

I respected him too much to make a fuss. Not that he ever had anything to worry about where Justin was concerned. Evidently, Justin was as old fashioned as my uncle; if not more.

I finally had complete control of my gift; could finally give myself to him, body and soul. But instead of taking advantage of my willingness to give into this sweet surrender, Justin stipulated conditions on when we'd be together.

With the mere memory of Justin's touch on my bare back as

he did up my gown sent shivers to the depths of my being.

There was nothing sweeter than the agonizing feeling of missing him; of wanting to see him, needing his touch to revive the lifelessness I felt when he was away.

Everything about Justin made this hormone crazed teenage girl want to ravish him. I felt it was my God given duty to make Justin's plight for sexual morality as difficult as possible.

Unfortunately for me, good old uncle Abbot had absolutely nothing to worry about as far as Justin was concerned. He was the poster boy for abstinence; the epitome of what a real gentleman should be.

SEVEN

FRED AND BARNEY

I TOOK A MUCH needed shower to wash the exhaustion away, and quickly slipped into my super comfortable cotton boxers with matching Tee, and headed for bed. It wasn't something any girl in her right mind would wear when she had a guy like Justin in her bedroom, especially when the oversized Tee had a large decal of Fred Flintstone and Barney Rubble spread across my chest.

Thank goodness Emily was nowhere in sight because if she saw me trotting around Justin in this little number she'd hit the roof. Saying something like, "Are you trying to break up with him or something?"

Justin was sitting in the armchair skimming through my biology book. He cocked his head up the second I entered the room.

"You're probably the only person on the planet that can make Fred and Barney look sexy," he said, pulling me into his lap.

I instantly squealed in delight. "So you don't mind that I don't wear that girly lacy stuff?"

He smiled. "Do you like the lacy stuff?"

"Yeah, I guess, but I prefer cotton and flannel."

"And I love you in anything."

I gave him a long lingering kiss.

"You have all this to read till the end of the week?" he asked, turning my biology book in his hand.

"That's just Bio. I have to go through all that!" I exclaimed pointing to the pile of books on my desk.

"So did you like Harvard?" he asked completely out of the blue. "You know you're not restricted to that one school. You have many choices."

"We didn't actually go on campus if that's what you're asking. The surrounding area is breathtaking though."

"Have you thought about where you want to study next year?"

"Well –," I made myself even more comfy in his lap. His content expression was all I needed to start trailing kisses up his sumptuous neck, "I haven't thought about the future much these couple of days."

He pushed me slightly back and his gaze bore into mine. "Don't do that!"

"Kiss you?"

"No, continue doing that –," he said smiling, "Don't let fear prevent you from making future plans."

"I don't want to talk about school. Besides, I'm sure I've missed the application deadline. I might just take a year off. I think I deserve that much considering all I've been through."

He didn't look too thrilled. "You need a higher education.

You have a whole lifetime to take plenty of years off. You shouldn't miss out on such an opportunity. Besides, we can room together if you decide to go to the same college as me."

I smiled and gave him a quick kiss. "Well, why didn't you say so earlier? Harvard it is!" I giggled.

"You just keep getting funnier and funnier, don't you" he said tickling me. "I'm serious about your education. I don't want you missing out on anything because of who we are."

"And who are we exactly?" I asked knowing that my question would put an end to this discussion.

"Ascend and find out," he answered, pushing me off.

He straightened out rather nervously and looked towards the door. I instantly knew the root of Justin's drastic change in mood.

I walked to the door and pried it open. "Uncle Abbot, what can I do you for?" I asked, smiling at his surprised expression. He didn't even have the chance to knock. Unable to read me, my uncle seemed uncomfortable at my unanticipated response.

"It's late sweetie, you have school tomorrow," he finally said eyeing Justin.

Justin sprang to his feet nervously. "I'm sorry," he said getting ready to leave. "I stayed longer than I intended. I should be in the Chamber practicing; see you in the morning Caitlin. Good night Abbot."

In no time at all, Justin exited my room.

Just as my uncle was about to leave as well, and close the door behind him, Justin reappeared, excusing himself as he pushed open the door and strolled nonchalantly back into my bedroom. Unexpectedly, he pulled me against him with one arm and gave me one of the sweetest good night kisses ever;

right there in front of my uncle. I simply stood there willingly; enjoying any bit of him he had to offer. He let me go just as fast and simply turned once again to the door.

"Sorry Abbot, couldn't just leave without saying goodnight, now could I?"

"No, I suppose not, son." Uncle Abbot said chuckling, following Justin downstairs.

Stunned, I stood there with the taste of Justin's lips on my mouth. *What just happened?* I wondered staring at the closed bedroom door.

S leep, as always, didn't come easy. Not now that I was on somebody's death list. I tossed and turned trying to figure out what Alexander meant when he said my scar was the key.

The images of the days horrific event didn't help much either. The shock of seeing what I saw earlier that day on the street slowly crawled its way up to the surface inciting a deluge of spine-chilling images. Then completely and unquestionably out of place I visualized the distinct picture of uncle Abbot holding the leather bound book.

"Amazing what you can find in one of these," he had said waving it in the air. It didn't register to me at the moment he said it but on re-examining his comment I could've sworn it was meant to trigger some kind of reaction. "Argh," I groaned unable to make sense of anything. I hid my head under my pillow in utter frustration and closed my eyes.

Only minutes later as I was drowning my aggravation into my mattress I heard a surreal voice; an echo of sorts; an undertone carried in the air. "Look," a little boy's voice said as it tattered off. "You need to look." I heard again. This time the voice was much weaker and distant. "This way, Caitlin! We have no time."

I should've been scared, but the mellifluent tone of the boy's voice was soothing; nothing scary about it. It was the same voice I had heard in the Chamber of Enlightenment, a while back when Kyle and I tried reaching Justin when my powers were blocked by the Nobe; right before they forced me to go to Tirion.

"Caitlin!" The dulcet voice urged, "Get up!"

I edged off the side of the bed hoping that this was some sort of dream, but that would entail actual sleep which I had none of. "Come on Caitlin! Please hurry!" With a hint of anxiety, I finally stood and uneasily went to the door; unsure of what was going on. "This way; hurry!" The little boy's voice led me down the hall. "Don't be afraid. Come on." I was being led towards my uncle's private study. "Think Caitlin. Please think!" He implored.

Scared of what was to unfold the second I opened the study's door; I took a deep breath and swung it open. There was absolutely nothing out of place, nothing out of the ordinary. Only the intoxicating smell of my uncle's once lit cigar pervaded the room, filling my lungs with its potent scent.

After inspecting his belongings, I found nothing necessitated such haste. I looked around a few more minutes trying to piece together some sort of mystery I seemed to be a part of, but found no missing piece that would alleviate my curiosity, so I took a seat in my uncle's plush leather chair, mindful of the urgency in the little boy's voice.

With my legs stretched out on the edge of the exquisite antique desk, I allowed my eyes to scan the elegant room knowing that I was surely missing something. And there it was; facing me all these years.

"I should've known," I whispered.

"You did it Caitlin! I told'em you'd remember."

I sprang to my feet and summoned the relic from the top shelf. In seconds, the cloth covered book I once held as a child was back in my hands. The familiarity of it was welcoming. The sheer size of it was what I liked most.

"What's this all about?" I asked, hoping the little boy would answer, but there was no response, only silence. I stood in awkward anticipation hoping that the unknown entity, which had led me to the study, would answer, but my wait was futile.

My attention quickly turned to the massive book and without a second thought, I removed the relic from its protective cloth. The brandished leather cover with all five family crests was as I remembered. It was the book my uncle told me about so many years ago over hot chocolate. Even though he never actually allowed me to open it, I knew it was more than just an expensive book that no eight-year-old should play with. It was that particular day that he told me about the existence of The Nobe and what role they played in our life.

For such an important document he hardly tried to take it from me, instead, he let me fiddle with the cover making sure I'd remember it. It was just like the secret compartment in that drawer in my parent's house, which they went out of their way to make sure Justin, remembered its existence so that I could find the letters and the locket.

I carefully placed the book on the desk and with extra care tried to turn the page, but for some reason opening it was impossible. It looked like a normal book on the surface; apart from its size and strange etchings on the cover, but other than that it seemed to be shut so tight that there was no way of prying it open. I went over the cover with my hand; felt around in the hopes that there would be some sort of secret unlocking mechanism, but there was none. Turning the book over however, led me to find an indentation on the bottom left-hand corner. It was branded with a faint etched design of leaves, surrounded by a heart and dart border. Without hesitation, I put some pressure on the concave spot and to my surprise the branded section quickly slid under the leather binding and a minuscule key hole appeared.

"Just great!" I exhaled, knowing that I would never find the key. I pressed down on the lock and the circular etched cover reemerged.

"Hold on," I said out loud. I pulled the silver chain from around my neck and looked down at the locket my grandmother left me. The design was exactly the same as the branding on the lock. I knew it looked familiar.

I breathed deep in excitement. But still there was no way of unlocking the book. I placed the locket against the etchings on the book, but nothing happened. I pressed open the locked compartment again to display the tiny key hole and stared at my grandmother's locket for what seemed forever. I couldn't make any sense of it.

Just as I was about to give up, I slid the locket off the silver chain and it was then that the link that the chain went through seemed to come loose. I went to screw it on tighter, fearing that it would come off completely, when I quickly realized that by unscrewing that top link I accidently found what I was looking for. Surprisingly enough, as soon as I pulled out the screwed section I saw that the link was connected to the tiny key built to fit the miniscule lock in the book.

"Holy crap!" I exclaimed.

The faint laugh of a child was all too clear in the air.

"You're still here, aren't you?" I said, talking to the invisible visitor.

No response.

I looked around and then turned back to the book. If Casper the friendly ghost wanted to make his appearance, I was sure he would when he was good and ready to do so. With no time to waste, I slid the small key into the lock and before I had the chance to do anything else, the tiny key was sucked into the lock and disappeared. Brushing aside my astonishment, I tried flipping the book open but it still remained shut. "Damn it! Now what?" I yelled as I fell back into the leather chair all flustered and annoyed.

"Put your wrist on your family crest," whispered the child. "It's the true key."

"Why didn't you say it in the first place?"

He laughed again.

"Alex had told me that my scar was the key, but I thought it was a figure of speech."

"He does love riddles," the little boy said sweetly. "Now stop talking and do this already."

With the key in the lock, I turned the book over again and placed my scarred wrist over the triangular mark in the center of the leather-bound book which represented the Korbs bloodline, but again nothing.

"Now what?" I asked into the air. "Some help would be nice."

"Use your gift, mortal," the childlike voice said, sounding a bit agitated that it was taking me so long to figure it out on my own.

"Mortal?" I questioned.

"That's not important now, Caitlin. Please hurry!"

"Okay, just give me a second. I'm only a mere mortal, remember?"

His sweet laugh was uplifting.

I smiled and returned to the task at hand. "Here goes nothing," I whispered as I summoned a surge of energy down my scarred wrist and into the book, but what came next was surely unexpected.

Instantaneously, I was thrown back into the chair with a shooting pain from my scarred wrist all the way up my arm, across my back and then down my other arm to my left hand. The pain was excruciating, throwing me even deeper into the chair as I gripped onto it with both hands, fearing I'd faint from the tearing sensation under my skin on both wrists.

It was like the day when my scar first appeared, but now it was happening again on both wrists this time. I sat back with tears in my eyes, clenching my teeth tightly.

"Caitlin, you must hold on," the little boy urged. "Don't give in. You must remain conscious during the conversion, otherwise you will slip into transcendence and all will be lost."

"Easy for you to say," I spat out through clenched teeth.

"Good! Be mad it seems to work for you."

"Please make it stop!" I screamed in pure agony. "Please!"

"Rein in the pain. You are powerful enough to handle the discomfort."

"Discomfort!" I yelled through the exhaustion. "My wrists

are being torn from my body."

"Concentrate, mortal!"

I opened my eyes momentarily and my gaze fell on the massive book. The image that I witnessed was sobering enough to make me breathe a little deeper and handle the burden bestowed upon me. The insufferable sensation was still there, but it quickly manifested itself into a mentally chilled indifference. The pain was all too real, but now I was simply the vessel it needed to take its course. I somehow became desensitized.

"You see," said the little boy. "You are born to bear a lot, so get used to it."

"How about a little warning next time?"

"Some things are best learned through experience," he said. "Now concentrate because things will get worse before they get better."

"Oh great!"

I didn't once avert my eyes from the leather-bound cover; how could I? The family crests that once decorated the cover were now meshed into one, shifting and forming different symbols.

"Look at your wrists," instructed the sweet voice. "Look at the conversion taking place."

I was too petrified to look at my own hands. The tearing of my skin and flesh as it shifted and changed was all too real. The pain might have been numbed, but the sensation was there all the same. I was too paralyzed with terror to look.

"Caitlin, you have to see what is happening to you. This hasn't happened for thousands of years. This conversion will lead to your ascension. The symbols will tell you who you are."

A small pause at first to collect myself and then I dropped my eyes to my wrists to see what was happening. Both of my wrists were now branded with scars to match the shapes created by the book. With each shape shift on the cover, my wrist would change, accompanied by an underlying pain which was sure to be excruciating were I not immune. New tissue was torn with each and every shift to accommodate the next symbol.

At first, all five family crests came together to form one singular shape, but then they separated again and the book cover as well as my wrist displayed each crest one by one from the youngest to the oldest family to date. With each change I bit back hoping that whatever this was would end quickly. The strangest of all, besides the tearing feeling under my skin, was that I expected it to stop at the Korbs' family crest, knowing that they were the oldest of all five families, but the book continued to shift and create shapes far older than that of the Korbs. It went on and on for a while until it stopped on a shape which looked quite tribal.

"It stopped," I breathed out in utter exhaustion as I fell back in the seat. "Thank god, it's over."

"You did great!" exclaimed my little ghost friend. "Aren't you going to look at you wrists?"

Both wrists now bore identical scars. The skin was too raw to make out the symbols, but it was clear that they formed the exact same one found on the book cover.

Having rested for a couple of minutes, I got up enough strength to walk to the bathroom on the other side of the private office and wrap both wrists with a damp towel to sooth the burn. On returning to the desk, I flipped the book to the first page. To my dismay, there was absolutely nothing written on it. I turned to the next page and the next and still there was nothing written. Discouraged, I flipped through the rest of the feeble book, page after page of absolute zilch.

Irritated at having been put through so much pain and finding myself, yet again, at another dead end; I resorted to slamming the darn thing shut and pushing it to the side.

I fell back on the chair and sighed heavily; exhaling in sheer frustration. At that moment something on the cover caught my eye. There was a twitch. Nothing major, but something did twitch and not only on the cover, but also on both my wrists. I felt something move beneath the skin.

Was I scared?

No, I wasn't scared. I was, without a doubt, petrified.

I didn't know if I wanted to continue with this alone; I was sure I didn't. I needed Justin and needed him quick. He was surely in The Chamber of Enlightenment, but I knew I wasn't allowed down there without a guide, but if Justin was there I wasn't actually breaking any rules. Tyler did it on Prom night and I didn't hear about him getting into any kind of trouble.

Without any time to spare, I wrapped the book with the cloth and pulled the rug to the side. I didn't see any sign of an opening anywhere on the floor. I turned to the desk and opened the top right drawer to see if there was some kind of lever to unlatch the secret opening, but nothing.

"Give me a break already!" I exclaimed downright angry.

My scars started to respond to my anger. Thankfully, I had that part completely under control. It was everything else that seemed to spiral further and further out of reach.

"Open, damn you!" I said, looking at the hard-wood floor.

Honestly, I didn't expect it to work. I mean how did I know my gift could command even this? Surely enough, the trap door withdrew, giving me access to the passageway under the house. I didn't waste any time. I grabbed the enormous book and carried it down the tunnel. Surprisingly, I didn't have to walk but a few yards. I would've thought, seeing how I was feeling, I would most definitely be walking for hours. Thank my lucky stars I was wrong again.

The colossal wooden door separating me and the Chamber stood as a last barrier. Not having ascended, my hand print wasn't engraved on the old wood. There was absolutely no way to gain access. I tried commanding it to open several times but nothing seemed to work.

Without any warning the sound of the door unlocking was music to my ears. What excited me even more was the face I saw the second the door swung open.

"How did you know I was here?" I asked, scanning Justin from head to toe. He was clad only in white linen pants. His well-toned chest was bare and dripping with sweat. What else could I possibly do but stare; and stare I did. He looked down at my wrapped hands and shook his head in annoyance. "I can't leave you anywhere alone, can I?"

He quickly grabbed a towel from one of the chairs and wiped himself down. *Lucky towel!* I thought. "I felt you standing on the other side of the door," he admitted. "You were supposed to be sleeping. You had a very long day."

"A little kid guided me to uncle Abbot's study."

"A little kid?" Justin asked looking confused. "Are you sure you weren't dreaming?"

I stretched out my arms.

"Does this look like I was dreaming?"

"No," he said just staring down at my hands. "What's that?" he asked motioning to the concealed book as he slipped into a white T-shirt.

I pulled the cloth off the book. "I believe this is the key."

Justin seemed stunned. "Where did you get that? You haven't ascended yet. You have no right!" He yelled pulling the book from my hands.

The second he touched the leather binding the book came to life again. The cover shifted over and over again, bringing me to my knees from the pain in my wrists.

"What is it?" yelled Justin sounding concerned.

I removed the damp material that covered my wrists only to see that my left wrist was now brandishing a whole different tribal symbol than the one on my right hand. My gaze fell to the cover of the book and saw a mirror image of the new symbol. "Why is this happening?" I asked, turning to Justin's shocked expression. "What do these symbols represent?"

"This is one of those times that asking questions won't lead you anywhere. There are rules. This book is off limits, Caitlin! Do you understand? You had no right touching it. None of us are allowed to read it."

"There's nothing to read. It's completely blank!"

"You opened it?" His concerned look disappeared and anger took its place.

"I don't know what else to do, and you still haven't told me what these symbols represent."

"Caitlin," He shook his head. "It's not that simple. You're not ready. You must ascend!"

My nerves were reaching their threshold. He was infuriating

me. "I need to know as much as I can about the Primoris Donum and this book might have all my answers!"

He took a step forward and reached out his hand to caress my cheek. I impulsively stepped out of the way causing him to pull back agitated at my response.

"Now you're being childish," he said,, placing the book on one of the soft cushions that was sprawled on the lush Persian rugs. "Why can't you understand?"

"The only thing I do understand is that this thing is out to kill me and came quite close to doing just that. That book obviously has information that will better prepare me. I don't understand why you're fighting me on this? And what the hell do these mean?" I asked stretching out my wrists.

He shook his head again. "I just can't. I'm sorry. You weren't supposed to see the book until you ascended. This wasn't supposed to happen."

I felt an awkward sensation under my skin. The area where the scars were was twitching, throbbing in a way. I looked towards the book and the cover was doing the same exact thing.

"To late for all that now, don't you think?" I asked and casually walked over to where he placed the book. I knelt in front of it and circled my head towards Justin. "I can do this myself. I was just too scared to do it alone!"

"I can't allow you!" He said in a stern voice.

"You know how important this is. Please Justin."

He shook his head again. "Why can't you just do what other ordinary people do when they are warned about something?"

I smiled at him. "You're the one who told me that there's nothing ordinary about me, did you forget?"

He knelt next to me. "I'm definitely going to pay dearly for this," he huffed, looking down at the book, and then shifted his gaze to my scarred wrists. "Do they hurt?" he finally asked.

"Yes, but don't you dare change the subject. You're not getting in any sort of trouble, Justin, because you're not going to do anything; I am."

"What's the difference? I'm your superior. I'm supposed to stop you from doing stupid things, remember?"

"Who reads the fine print?" I asked, giving him a quick kiss on the lips.

"Oh, no you don't! If I'm going to put my life on the line to help you, I surely deserve a better kiss than that," he said with a wonderful smile.

I didn't need to be asked twice. I pulled him by the shirt and kissed him on the lips. I inched my way even closer diminishing any space that separated us. Justin responded just as eager holding me tight around the waist.

"Now isn't this much more fun than reading that stupid book?"

"Good try!" I exclaimed pushing him away. Justin looked at me with one of those irresistible gazes. "This is important!" I pleaded coaxing him to help.

He groaned under his breath visibly unwilling to satisfy my need. "This book contains information that is strictly for the Ascended. We are the only once allowed to read it and only after the Hour of Awakening; no sooner, and that's only for those who are worthy. No one has been able to read it for eons."

"What's the Hour of Awakening?"

"It's a point during our ascension when all we need to know

comes to us from above. We literally are awakened, seeing things from an all new perspective."

"Like what things? And what do you mean it comes from above?" Suddenly I heard a giggle. It was the same sweet childlike voice I heard before.

"Ramiel!" Justin said sternly. "What are you doing in this realm? Go, you have no place here."

"Hurry! Both of you; the book! She must read the book!"

"Ramiel!" Justin yelled.

"Hurry, please! I can't keep them away forever! Bernael is breaking through!"

Justin's face hardened. Evidently Bernael wasn't somebody we wanted around anytime soon. In response to Ramiel's urgency, Justin placed his right hand over the cover and instantly the leather binding flipped open revealing more of the same blank pages.

Justin closed his eyes. "Show me," he whispered and then blew softly over the page. His expression of shock the second different symbols started materializing on the once blank pages was unexpected. "This is a first," he said. "They have never appeared to me before. No matter how many times I've tried."

I simply stared in disbelief over Justin's shoulder at the unintelligible symbols that were burned into the age old paper.

"What sort of language is that?" I finally asked.

"Shh!" Justin ordered.

"Hurry Justin, Caradon can't keep him back for long!" The urgency in the voice was maddening.

"Caradon," I exclaimed clutching my heart. "What does this have to do with him?"

Justin seemed rather calm; considering. The little angelic

voice, however, was anything but calm. "Say his name Caitlin. Only you can unlock the scroll!"

Justin pulled me to his side. "Alexander was right! Only the purest of the bloodline holds the key," he said holding up my scarred wrists, "And these are the way in."

"In where?" I asked scared out of my freaking mind. "What's this all about?"

Justin squeezed my hand. "Just say his name!"

I looked at him confused, and slowly turned my attention to the incoherencies on the page. "Whose name?"

"The one that's out to kill you."

"What! Why?"

Justin looked me straight in the eyes. "Say his name, Caitlin. We have no time."

I looked at the blank pages and said, "Primoris Donum."

I waited but nothing happened. I looked at Justin and shrugged my shoulders in awkwardness. Without warning Justin grabbed my scarred wrists igniting my gift. I pulled away quickly in fear of hurting him. The throbbing was all too intense compensating for Justin's own power.

"Say it again! This time place both hands on the page."

I did just that. Palms down, I put my palms down on the strange book and repeated, "Primoris Donum."

The oversized pages started flailing in the air, and were about to encircle my hand when Justin yanked me by the arm causing me to fall back. He instantly substituted his own hands for mine, placing them in the same exact fashion as mine were. Faster than a heartbeat, the pages wound tightly around his hands, wrapping them like gauze to a wound.

I was too shocked to think. I stood there in awe. Justin didn't seem to be in any pain. He sat there with his eyes closed. By the movement under his eyelids you'd think he was reading.

Only seconds later, one by one the pages seemed to unglue themselves from his arm in layers and return to their normal position, once again blank. But now, it was something on Justin's arm that caught my eye.

His hands and arms were imprinted with the text; symbols of a language long forgotten. This tattoo-like creation seemed to be spreading from his fingertips to his arms, up his neck and down his chest and back. It moved, gliding over his smooth skin like a serpent leaving symbols in its wake.

"Are you okay?" I asked stretching out my hand to smooth the crease in his brow.

"Don't!" He yelled. "Don't touch me just yet!" He continued to keep his eyes closed.

"Justin," the voice said. "You can go safely now. You have all the information you need. Bernael can threaten you no more!"

"You were being threatened?"

Justin didn't answer. For a few minutes longer he remained in complete silence and then opened his eyes.

Shocked at the site of blackness staring back at me, I took an uncalculated quick step back and fell over the cushions. The deep blue color of his eyes was now covered in darkness.

"What happened?" I asked trying to find my footing. "Why didn't you let me finish what I started? You shouldn't have taken my place."

"Don't worry, it's nothing permanent. As soon as the script seeps through, I'll be back to normal."

"What does all this mean?"

"The script can only pass through the Ascended. We are the only ones who can translate these symbols," he said, raising both arms to show the writing. "In order for us to decipher them they have to be transfixed into our being; become one with us. Only then will the scripts decide if we're worthy to know the truth."

"Well –?"

"I know all we need to know," he said smiling. "Now brace yourself," he added, pushing me behind him. "We have visitors, and they are all angry."

Book of Truths
Illustrated for Lions that Bind - Among the Shadows

EIGHT

WAR

I N NO TIME AT ALL, the door leading to the Korbs' world swung open revealing complete darkness. No tunnel; not even a hint of light. The entrance was veiled in occult silence.

I tightened my grip on Justin's hand, fearing the worst.

"Don't worry," he whispered, squeezing me tighter.

It didn't take long for my uncle Caradon to walk through the sheer darkness. Like a ghost he approached with the length of his black robe trailing behind and the worst of all, he wasn't alone.

Caradon, looking rather austere, was accompanied by another man, much younger but just as striking. As they came closer, my uncle tugged on the deep red material that lined the interior of his long flowing sleeves. His action spoke volumes. Caradon was clearly agitated; anxious even. "What's the meaning of this?" He bellowed furiously; folding his sleeves higher up. "Justin you should know better!"

Justin stretched his hand in front of me and pushed me slightly to the back; keeping me at a safe distance.

"Yeah, people seem to keep telling me that. I guess I just don't listen," he said grinning.

Caradon wasn't at all amused by Justin's retort. "So have you deciphered the symbols yet?" He asked staring at Justin's marked hands.

Before he had any time to answer, a strong current of air washed over us and swirled around the room. In no time at all the rest of the massive wooden doors swung open; all but the one leading to Tirion came to a slamming halt. None of the Ellri that walked through those doors looked happy; especially Uncle Abbot and Aunt Leslie.

"You're supposed to be sleeping young lady," My uncle said shaking his head.

I looked around totally intimidated by all the staring. "You know me. I'm a light sleeper," I jested, trying to sly my way out of the already charged atmosphere.

Uncle Abbot walked over to the leather bound book and covered it with the cloth. "You are in a rush to learn too much Caitlin," he said as he wrapped the ancient artifact rather tightly with the light tan material, "Those who rush tend to fall a great deal!"

"Well, I wouldn't need to rush if I knew who was out to kill me, now would I?"

Caradon's companion took a few steps closer. He raised an eyebrow in amusement as soon as Justin took a step forward to block his progress. "Relax young man," he said in smooth tone in response to Justin's instant shift in posture. Justin looked ready to attack, and took another defensive step forward.

"I just want to get a better view of my niece is all." He craned his neck to the side playfully in order to get a better look at me, as if we were playing some kind of child's game. "Eileen, about time we met, don't you think?"

"Caitlin," Justin corrected, acting like a barrier between us.

I slid a glance at the man calling me by my middle name. "Uncle Brett?" I questioned, emerging from behind Justin.

His mouth curved in a wry grin.

He was as tall as Caradon, but ten or more years younger. He couldn't have been a year over forty, I thought. His short raven black hair was in contrast to his brother's long white. Brett had a warmer smile and his amber eyes danced against his pale white skin. I sensed no evil in this man. Unlike his brother, I didn't fear him one bit. I swallowed hard and took a closer look at this six foot two, dark haired, unruly looking character with the most heavy-lidded eyes I'd ever seen.

"Let me get a better look you," he insisted, studying my face. "Yes, well I can honestly say that there is as much of Winston in you as there is Carolyn."

"Thank you," I responded not needing to feign a smile. For me, it was a first where the Korbs were concerned. "Most people tend to lean to one of two sides," I added, continuing to smile.

He raised his eyebrow again. "Well, I'm not most people. I refuse to allow my biases to misguide me. Either way, you are a breath of fresh air."

I smiled again. For some reason I could breathe once again. I didn't know what he did but whatever it was I felt relaxed.

"Fred and Barney, my children's favorite," he said, commenting on my choice of nightwear. "You'll have to meet your cousins someday. It would seem you have much in common."

Mortified, I looked down at what I was wearing. I couldn't believe I was in the presence of all the Ellri, my uncles from the other side of the Atlantic included and I was still in my pajamas.

Caradon didn't seem amused, and turned to the High Ellri and raised his hands in the air. "Nathan, now do you see why she'll be safer with us! This is way too powerful for any of you to protect her. Only the Korbs can."

They were talking in riddles again. Brett turned to face me, visibly aware of my confusion. *"It's best to be kept in the dark about some things."* I suddenly heard in my head.

The piercing feeling of somebody projecting their thoughts in my head was back. Surprised, I stared at my new found uncle.

"You can read my thoughts?" I asked without opening my mouth. I just let the words echo in my head.

"Of course, cool isn't it?"

I half smiled at him. *"That certain aspect of my gift hasn't surfaced yet. I can't communicate with anyone else. Wish I could! I would love to know what was written on Justin's body."*

"Don't fret! Soon you'll be able to do much more than just communicate!"

Justin stared at me with one raised eyebrow. "Just because I can't read you Caitlin, doesn't mean I can't read Brett."

"Caught in the act," said Brett winking at me.

I restrained a chuckle. Didn't think my predicament called for laughter of any kind. But it was hard to care about dying when my uncle made me feel this good.

Justin pulled me back by the arm. "Step back Brett," he barked, "And keep your slithering words out of her head. She might not be aware of your gift, but I sure as hell am!"

My uncle smiled cunningly and retreated. "She's just so innocent. I couldn't help myself. She makes it too easy!"

This was the second time I saw an Ellri backing away from Justin. The first time was in Tirion when Caradon pulled away at Justin's threatening response, and now Brett.

Justin immediately took me by the hand, and the elation I felt around my uncle was instantly gone. Just then I realized that Brett's gift was like a drug, triggering a deep craving for his attention. His warm smile and sweet words were all a ploy to reel me in.

Nathan came over and placed his hand on my shoulder as he said, "This child will not be leaving Oaks. We have all put her through enough."

Caradon just shook his head in disapproval. "Why is this so hard for all of you to accept? Do you know how close she was to facing Bernael? Where were you to keep him away?"

I turned to Nathan questionably. "Who is this Bernael and why was he coming for me? I thought the Primoris Donum is the only one who –,"

My question was cut short by Brett's hardy chuckle. "You should all be proud of yourselves. You have done a fine job of pulling the wool over her eyes. You have led the poor child in the eye of a hurricane with only an umbrella for protection and figured she'd survive on her own. Great guardians you are!"

"Sit the hell down," Justin growled pointing to the chair in the far corner. Lo and behold, in no time at all, my uncle did what he was told. He didn't even protest.

"He's one of the Fallen; Bernael I mean," I heard Marlene say, "Likes to spread darkness and evil. Not a real fun guy to be around."

"Fallen from where?"

"Don't scare her," I heard the tiny voice say.

Marlene looked in one particular direction. "Ramiel, you shouldn't be here!"

I followed her gaze but saw absolutely nothing.

"I helped today, didn't I Caitlin?" The voice asked innocently.

"Yes, you sure did!"

Caradon clearly angry looked at the same blank space Marlene was looking at. "You had no right Ramiel. She hasn't ascended yet!"

"I do my masters bidding and not yours, Varjatus," Ramiel answered raising his voice. "None of you shall ever dictate what I can or cannot do. Remember your place Ellri or I shall remind you of it!"

The sweet voice was now laced with venom. Caradon's cold hard expression made the threat all too real. Whatever this surreal childlike voice was, it was way higher in the hierarchy of the gifted. "It's time she knew," the child added.

"Not yet," yelled Justin. "She needs to Ascend!"

I turned to Justin for justification, but instead, I received a blank stare.

"Time cannot wait for her gift to evolve." Ramiel's voice was back to a loving whisper. "She needs to know at least what she's up against. Caradon was right. Bernael was quite close. And the Animus Iuguolo was only a prelude to what Abaddon has planned for her."

My eyes widened at the sound of yet another name, and one that wished me harm. "Who's Abaddon?" I asked, swallowing back the fear. In an attempt to feel safer, I threaded my arm through Justin's and held on rather tight. He responded by kissing me tenderly on the head.

"Your executioner," answered Brett from across the Chamber. All the Ellri uniformly turned and stared. "What did I do now?" He asked innocently enough. "You all heard Ramiel. My niece has a right to know!"

Justin's posture instantly stiffened.

"Where's the Nobe in all this?" I asked not waiting for Justin to respond to Brett's outburst. "Why aren't they helping?"

No one answered.

"The Primoris Donum is a Nobe, isn't he? Is he responsible for this Bernael and Abaddon?" I finally asked.

Again, no answer.

I slid my arm from Justin and began pacing, arms folded against my chest to hold back the tears. I didn't speak. I couldn't. I kept silent. When I was finally in control of my emotions once more, I waited until I had enough air in my lungs to breathe. I manically tried to arrange all the new names in my head. "Okay," I finally said looking around to all the frozen expressions. Evidently they were all waiting for me, waiting to see how I would react, "Is someone going to actually explain what's going on? Or would you have me do something crazy to get the bastards attention!"

Caradon looked at me with what could easily be described as pride. "You're fearless, like a Korbs should be," he said, smiling for the first time. It suited his features. It made him look warmer and, dare I say, approachable.

ANNA LAZARIDIS

That moment, the sound of the last door drawing open grabbed my attention, causing me to turn my head in the direction of the commotion.

"Don't you dare say that again, Varjatus!" I heard Ava say just before she stepped through to the chamber, "I will cut out your tongue and feed it to Satan's dog if you ever compare my niece to your kind."

Along with Ava came my aunt Rebecca, John and my Uncle Richard. They too didn't seem thrilled to be gathered here.

Caradon simply dismissed her comment, clearly wanting nothing to do with her. "Justin is the only one that really knows what's going on," Caradon started to say looking at me. "The book has only been read once, thousands of years ago by a pure blood bearing the same scar as you, Caitlin. At the time of your birth we tried to get Eileen to open the book and tell us what we needed to know to defeat this thing but she refused. She was the only one who bore the scar after so many ions; none of us had access without her help."

"Justin said only the worthy who have ascended can read it. Is it the same for the Ellri?"

"We can read it freely, but some scriptures within the Book of Truths; the most sacred ones are kept under lock and key. Only the selected few are born with the right of entrance. It's now all imbedded in skin."

I looked down at my new scars. "So how was Justin able to attain the information only now and not before?"

"It would seem your Bond is more than what we originally thought. You are both so intertwined that the scripture couldn't tell where you began and he finished." Uncle Abbot offered, and exhibited the sweetest of smiles towards Justin. "But you somehow knew that, didn't you son? You knew it would work."

"I acted on impulse," Justin answered. "I didn't want anything to happen to Caitlin. She hasn't ascended yet and I couldn't risk the repercussions."

Uncle Abbot didn't seem to be totally convinced by Justin's explanation, but it was Ava who broke the silence when she addressed our little ghost, "Ramiel, summon your master," she ordered. "We need to put an end to this."

"Yes'em, right away," said the sweet little voice.

I looked down to what I was wearing once again. How was any demon going to take me seriously with The Flintstones staring back at them? *I should've worn my Metallica Tee*, I thought smiling at how, amidst all this danger, I was thinking about my attire. Uncle Brett stared and smiled, clearly aware of my juvenile worries.

The Ellri were staring at each other communicating in the only way they felt comfortable; the only way they knew I couldn't possibly listen in.

Justin wrapped his arm around my waist. His eyes now were lighter than before, not the royal blue I learned to love but an ash grey instead. The markings were slowly fading as well. What remained were only traces of the dark symbols. He leaned over and gave me a kiss on the cheek and whispered, "You seem to be taking all this quite well."

"Just stay close to me in case it all surfaces. I tend to have a delayed reaction to bad news," I said, feigning a smile.

"I'll be right here. I'm never leaving your side," he gave me another soft kiss on the top of the head. "They'll have to go through me first," he added in a low whisper. "Let them try!"

Justin's confidence was at an all-time high. It wasn't what he said, but how he said it. He meant every syllable; no false hope as far as I could tell. It was the symbols I was sure. Something in the book gave him the reassurance he needed, the extra boost of confidence. A few minutes later, Justin pointed to the far wall across from us. "Your friend is coming," he said to me as he brushed his lips across mine.

"My friend? What friend would that be?"

There in the middle of all this mayhem I heard a voice I'd cross oceans to hear. "What is it now?" Alexander asked, walking into the Chamber through the thick stone wall, only inches from Brett. "Put your foot in it again, did you son?" he asked Brett as he patted him on the back. He didn't wait for an answer; instead he walked straight towards me.

Brett snapped to his feet and bowed. They all bowed deeply. As deeply, I suspected, as they would for someone much higher in the hierarchy than all of them. I was about to do the same when Alexander started laughing and laughing hard. "Don't do it if you don't mean it, sweetie," he jested, stroking my hair. "I see you figured it out after all."

My smile couldn't get any bigger on seeing him. "I haven't figured anything out," I answered, giving him a much needed hug. "I'm glad you're here."

"Where else would I be?" He squeezed me hard before letting go.

"Alex," Caradon bowed, "She had no right reading the book. Why would Ramiel be so careless?"

Alexander turned and faced my uncle. "If you question Ramiel's actions I don't see why you're addressing me. He's right there. Tell him your grievances."

"Let him try," hissed the young voice.

Alex shook his head and rolled his eyes. "I'm simply too old and too tired to deal with such matters. If you're all going to act like children maybe I should just treat you as such."

I looked to the empty space Alexander was talking to and I still saw nothing. Alex looked at me and probably noticed how confused I looked. "I'm sorry Caitlin. Ramiel is only visible in the Inner Realm. We can all see him clearly, but you haven't ascended yet so you'll have to transcend if you want to get a good look at the Watcher."

"She has more important things than worry about me," said Ramiel in his soothing voice.

After a couple minutes of pure silence, Alexander was preparing to sit but there was no chair to support his weight. I was about to warn him to be careful when as soon as he slumped back, a chair appeared under him in no time at all. He nearly laughed aloud at my look of astonishment.

The rest of the Ellri followed suit, and each took a seat, leaving Justin and me standing in the middle of this massive edifice facing Alexander.

"Where would you like us to begin?" Alexander asked, beaming an all loving smile.

This moment was what I've been waiting for since my return to Oaks. And now that it had finally arrived I didn't know where to start. I nervously racked my brain to formulate a question which would somehow incorporate everything I wanted to know. The questions were way too many; too specific.

"Let's start at the beginning," I finally said not knowing exactly what I meant. Then it came to me. "Why all this fuss over me? Why all this animosity between the families?"

"It's as your Ellri explained. It's a bitter custody battle," he said, fixing the fold in his shirt sleeve.

I shook my head not believing one word. "There must be more to it than that, isn't that right Uncle?" I turned to Caradon hoping that he would shed some truth.

"The Korbs believe; I believe your place is with us. You will be raised in an environment suiting your great gifts and position in the blood line. We are the only ones who can protect you; keep you safe."

I heard Ava hiss in disgust. "Do you plan on protecting her the way you protected her father?" She asked. Each word was dripping in vile.

"We did everything we could to prevent all this. Do you really think we wanted to harm our own kin?" Caradon's tone was harsh and laced with resentment. "If my loving brother stayed with his family; followed our ways we wouldn't be in this predicament now. Eileen had foreseen everything yet he acted selfishly."

I didn't seem to be on the same page. "I don't understand," I said clearly confused, "What do you mean my grandma foresaw everything? She's the one who helped him escape."

Caradon smiled. "She did that only after the wheels were already in motion. None of this would've happened if Winston remained faithful to the family."

"You speak of our brother as if he did something wrong," snapped my aunt Rebecca standing up visibly upset. "I won't sit here and listen to this blasphemy. Winston was and always will be the purest Korbs. Like it or not brother, you will always come in second!"

Caradon took a threatening step forward. "You continue to defend him, continue to support his decision. Isn't this –," he said, raising his hands motioning around to all of us, "Isn't this enough to change your mind about him? He brought all this on. His mulishness has put us all in danger. Winston had no right, Caitlin should have never been –,"

Alexander suddenly cut him off in mid-sentence sounding angrier than I expected. "That's enough you two! I didn't come here to listen to this bickering!" Alexander yelled. "What is done is done, and who was or wasn't supposed to be born is not for you to say Caradon."

My uncle simply bowed in agreement out of respect. I was pretty sure that he didn't see things the way Alexander did.

Justin squeezed my hand aware of how much Caradon's words hurt. I certainly couldn't hate my uncle as I completely agreed with him. I was the root of all the upheaval. I took a much needed deep breath and looked around the room. My gaze stopped the instant I made eye contact with my new found Uncle Brett. His expression seemed to reflect his deeper understanding of how I was feeling. Having access to my thoughts gave him an inside look at how guilty I really felt.

I rubbed profusely at my forehead, trying to make sense of all this. *It wasn't my mother the Korbs wanted dead, It was me, wasn't it?* I formed the question in my head making sure Brett picked up every word.

He simply nodded in agreement.

Alexander turned his head and looked angrily at my Uncle Brett. He instantaneously dropped his gaze to the floor.

I heaved a sigh. In a matter of seconds I felt tears spring to my eyes. I should've been mad at him, but how could I? He was apparently the only one being brutally honest. Agony ripped through me with the realization that in order to find my mother's killer I had to do one thing; simply look in the mirror.

Justin pulled me into his embrace and held me tight. "Ignore him," he said, kissing me on the forehead.

I turned towards my uncle Caradon, but first waited to calm myself. "Is that why my mother suffered? You wanted to stop her from having me?"

"Caitlin," he started to say softly; trying to be as sensitive about this as possible. "I know hearing this hurts, but your birth meant our demise. Our first priority was and still is the continuation of our kind. You –,"

"Just Stop!" Aunt Leslie was on her feet visibly outraged by my uncle's comments. "Caitlin was a blessing. Her birth brought nothing but happiness. How dare you say differently?"

Caradon shook his head. "I didn't mean to imply that we wanted Caitlin dead. I was simply pointing out what it meant to all of us having her come into our world. She's old enough to know; to understand."

"This has to Stop," exclaimed my aunt turning to Alexander. "No child should be exposed to this. Think of what this will do to her!"

Alexander simply looked at me. There was a hint of sadness in his eyes, but he didn't say a word of what he was truly thinking.

"I always knew the truth would hurt, but kill me it won't," I said, turning to my loving aunt. "It's fine; truly it is." The anxiety of what this was doing to me had left its marks on her face. "I need to know. I must know." I finally said, trying to reassure her.

Caradon took a step closer. His long black robe swept along the floor as he glided up to me. "Our intentions have been misconstrued by your Ellri," he started to explain. "After your birth, after your parents went off on their Long Journey, we needed to find you and protect you. Having you in Oaks was dangerous. The Primoris could easily get to you."

He looked at me tenderly. It was the first time that I saw a hint of compassion on this man's face. "We weren't looking to kill you, if that's what you've been told. We tried reaching you in order to protect everyone. Velius is the only safe place. The Korbs were the ones who faced this demon a thousand years ago; the only ones who can face it again and save us all."

I bit my lip thinking about what he said. "Then why, if you were doing all this to help me, why then, did my grandma feel the need to hide my whereabouts? Why didn't she want me anywhere near you?"

"Eileen knew," said Justin drawing everyone's surprised expressions. "Caradon is wrong on one thing. Your grandma did unlock the sacred scriptures a few months before you were born. She knew exactly what was going to happen. The book let her know."

"That's impossible!" Caradon lashed out. "You have absolutely no idea what you're talking about!"

"Wrong again," said Justin grinning – infuriating my uncle even more. "The book keeps track of everything. It is all knowing. Eileen not only was marked with the words of the forbidden language, but later wrote letters to the man we all knew as Winston, telling him everything she knew; everything she saw."

I turned to look at him. "We need to see the letters again. I'm stronger now. We can learn everything she wanted us to know."

He smiled. "It's not necessary. I know what there is to know. The scriptures told me."

"She used the same writing techniques once used between the gifted to get our message across when we didn't want our thoughts to be read, didn't she?" asked Winston. Justin's father looked at me. "It was primarily used to keep the Fallen from knowing our next moves; the same technique that the Book of Truths was written in."

"Who are the Fallen? You've mentioned Bernael was one, but who are they exactly?"

"They are others like us who simply didn't agree with the laws that govern us. Our ancients gave them the name Fallen because they fell from the graces of the Immortal Council thousands of years ago when they refuted the collective body of laws. They thought it was unnecessary to have restrictions on our gifts. It was during the birth of civilization that they spread death and destruction in their wake inciting a war among our kind. Millions of innocent unfortunately had to die. Gifted and non-gifted unlike."

"Which of the five families do they belong to, these Fallen?"

"None!" William smiled at my shocked expression.

"How is that even possible? I thought only the five families were with greater powers."

"Why doesn't she know any of this?" asked Caradon looking around. "Keeping her in the dark sure as hell won't keep her safe. All family members should know our history. It's who we are."

"Don't you mean who we were?" corrected Ava.

"Caradon," Uncle Abbot started to say, "In Oaks we have found that the less the kids know the better they adapt to the world around them. We do after all live among the non-gifted. As soon as they Ascend they learn everything they need to know. It's worked over the centuries and it has kept the children well-grounded and safe."

"I don't care about the rest of the children!" Caradon emphasized. "Caitlin should've been taught our old ways; should've been prepared properly."

They seemed to have gone off on a tangent again.

"Enough!" I yelled. It was my turn to put order to this discussion. "I'm not standing here in my Flintstone pajamas to discuss how I should've been raised. Whichever way you look at it there is absolutely nothing we can do about the past. What I need to know is who these demons are."

Rebecca as well as Brett came and stood next to Caradon. They were only a few feet away looking at me. For some strange reason they each lifted their right sleeve to reveal a strange mark right under the fold of their elbow. It was a round stamp like shape burnt into their skin; much like my scars. It was dark red in color, tribal in appearance.

"What is that?" I asked, placing my fingers over my aunt's mark and then looked at my two knew scars which looked nothing like hers.

"The Korbs family members who are of pure blood, all bare this symbol from birth. It reminds us of our mission," said Aunt Rebecca pulling down her sleeve to cover the mark. "Our mission is to protect and guard our kind."

"Protect our kind from what?"

"Let's just say in a time of war among the gifted we would

be the ones fighting in the front lines; keeping everyone else safe. It's our duty," she explained, caressing my cheek.

Rebecca stepped back and Marcellus, Claudius and Dominick Falcone each came and stood in front of me exposing their arms. "The Falcone family members who are of pure blood bare this symbol from birth," said Marcellus letting me take a closer look.

"Why have I never seen these before?"

Marcellus winked at me, "We know how to keep a secret."

Tyler's dad always knew how to make me smile. His mark, however, was much different from the Korbs' but the inscription was different.

"What does it mean," I asked.

"Our mission," he explained, "is to ensure that everything remains in order. We keep the peace of sorts," Marcellus pronounced shifting his gaze to Caradon. "We prevent wars from happening. We keep the peace so no gifted would need to go to the front lines."

Uncle Abbot along with the high Ellri Nathan and their younger brother Scott also showed me their mark. Again the mark was similar to the others, but yet different.

"The Cathcarts have been designated to educate and maintain the virtues our kind had fought to uphold," said Nathan winking at me. "If we all remain true to who and what we are, no war ever need be prevented."

"How do you go about doing that?" I asked my Uncle.

"We try keeping all of you grounded. Gifts or no gifts you are children with a future. Your priority is education and developing your spiritual world as well as finding your center; controlling the urges that tend to guide each and every one of us to paths better left unknown. It is our duty, as your Ellri, to evoke these virtues; to instill hope for the greater good. No war could ever come from individuals with such morals for only fools rush in where angels fear to tread."

Uncle Abbot stood there staring. "Do you understand?"

"I think I do," I responded giving him a hug. It took me a while to let go.

Later Justin's father along with his brothers Norman and Rick stood in front of me. I let go of my uncle and looked down at their arms. "The Bradfords are the ones who will pass judgment. We see to it that all the rules and laws are just for all. During any war mayhem can easily break out and laws can be easily forgotten. No matter the circumstance, we stand behind the code and see to it that it is upheld."

Aunt Leslie along with Uncle Richard was next. Ava stayed behind. My aunt rolled up her sleeve as did Richard only to reveal a similar mark. It was funny that this was the first time I've ever seen it.

"We the McDevitts are to regulate duties in time of crisis," she said smiling. "We see to it that in a time of war each gifted knows their limits and above all their strengths. We would command the armies on who shall face who on an even match of powers."

A shiver crawled down my spine at the thought of any of these brilliant people having to be put in such positions.

I looked down at my scarred wrists which looked nothing like any of their symbols. "How did you come by these symbols? Who has given all of you these orders or missions as you called them?"

"The Ancient did thousands of years ago after the war took

the lives of so many," explained Nathan. "These marks not only serve as a badge of duty but also as a reminder of those horrific years. If we uphold our duty, if each family works together to do their part; peace remains among us."

"Ava why don't you have one, or do you?"

She smiled. "I forfeited my right to Ascend to become Nobe and with that came the removal of any mark that signifies allegiance to any one family. I'm what you would call a free agent."

"Why would you do that? Why would you forgo your right to immortality?"

Ava looked at Alexander momentarily and returned her gaze back to me just as fast. "Let's just say, it was something I felt compelled to do. One life is more than enough."

I looked at her suspiciously but decided against pushing the subject. I didn't' want to go off on another tangent. "That still doesn't explain why all this is happening. What part does the Primoris Donum play in all this? Is he even the first gifted or is it simply a title he gave himself?"

"Only two people know, and Justin is one of them," said William looking at his son. "None of us have the ability to read that part of the book. It's off limits. We only know bits of history. Millenniums ago; there were many great families with powers. However, after the war only a few survived. And the ones that did survive diminished in power by coupling with the non-gifted. That's why there are so many gifted individuals out there with minimal abilities. Each of them, if they could trace their ancestry back would be surprised to know that they belonged to great families long gone."

"Weren't there any survivors of these older families?"

"You have to understand Caitlin that during the war it was Nobe against Nobe. Powers our minds can't conceive. Immortals don't ever die of natural causes, but there are ways they can be killed," said Brett. "The ones that did survive the bloodshed, the ones who supported a balanced government were given the name Ancients. But even they didn't last for more than a couple centuries after the war. They had somehow disappeared; killed off one by one. Only one remains till this day; the one ancient who knows history better than the book itself; the one who has organized our five families into the stronghold that we are today. He is the one who wrote The Book of Truths; the book Abbot is holding. It was written in his mother tongue; the symbols of the forbidden language."

"How can one individual be responsible for all this? It sounds like a myth of sorts."

Alexander chuckled.

"Caitlin, we are the myth and the legend. The ancient world had no other way of explaining our powers, so they made up stories about different gods, angles, demons. You name it, they wrote about it. We may have evolved as far as gifts are concerned, but unfortunately our human thirst for power was never extinguished. It was imperative that the five families be united. It was the only way to keep the urge of obtaining supreme power under control."

"Well, is someone going to tell me who this living Ancient is? If he knows so much he can help. Where do we find him?"

The room fell in complete silence.

Justin leaned in and whispered. "You're looking at him."

Looking for a Gift

Illustrated for Lines that Bind - Among the Shadows

NINE

HUMANLY IMPOSSIBLE

SHOCKED WOULDN'T begin to describe what I felt. This man was special; knew there was more to him, but still, to hear that he was the only living dinosaur of our kind was pretty surprising. My guardian, my savior was an immortal. Seeing my reaction Justin leaned in again and whispered. "Did you hear what I said?"

"Oh, don't worry I heard you alright. Like I told you before I usually have a delayed reaction when it comes to overwhelming news."

Justin smiled and kissed me on top of the head. "I found out the moment you unlocked the book; amazing isn't it?"

I nodded. Even the word amazing didn't capture the essence of what this man was; no word for that matter was ever going to be good enough to describe Alexander.

Alexander stood up and they all bowed their heads again. "Caitlin, don't look at me like that. I'm but a man."

"Of course you are, just the grounds keeper, right Alex?"

"That's right," he smiled. "Nothing special about a grounds keeper, now is there?"

I was overwhelmed. I took a step closer. Looked at him for a few minutes and then gave him a great big hug. "I'm glad it was you who survived. Wouldn't like to see this world without you in it," I said wailing up in tears.

"The feeling is mutual," he answered, pushing me slightly back to get a better look at me. "In my six thousand years of existence, I must admit that you have left the most lasting impression. Such inner beauty is hard to find, young lady. You make me want to live another six thousand."

"Are you a Nobe?" I asked wanting to know as much about him as possible.

"If you mean have I ascended into the higher order; I have, thousands and thousands of years ago. In my time the third stage of ascension had no name. We weren't even aware that it happened. We simply felt our powers grow stronger. After the war the surviving gifted had gone into hiding for millenniums. We didn't have much of governing bodies. I looked for thousands of years to find any surviving bloodlines, but had absolutely no luck. Two thousand years ago I came across a small clan of truly gifted individuals. Nothing that could be remotely compared to the ancient families, but they had great potential. The Korbs clan was then but a couple of centuries old not gifted enough to ascend into Ellri or Nobe. They seemed quite civil with a working government. It was the only family I had come across through my travels that had figured out the secret of attaining more power with every generation; the purer the bloodline the stronger the gifts."

Alexander started pacing and talking. "Centuries later, I

came across several McDevitts and slowly the other families. It took centuries for the gifted to reach immortality. Personally, I didn't think it was possible. I truly thought at one point that the third stage of ascension was a thing of the past. It took hundreds of years and numerous generations, but the first Korbs Ellri had ascended into an immortal. After that it was only time that more and more would emerge. Before a struggle of power could erupt I figured on implementing the governing body of my day where a council would reign over the Immortals keeping a balance. There was always fear of the Fallen to reemerge as it did a thousand years ago but the families stood their ground. The Fallen had no chance with a united front."

He rubbed his forehead. "Only if my people knew what your families knew a thousand years ago. If the families were united no one would've lost their lives." Alexander shook his head in deep thought and sighed deeply. "Caitlin, this is how your families came to be. Marriages between the families kept the bloodline pure making them stronger and stronger as centuries past."

"But Alexander if you are the only remaining ancient, then who are the Fallen?"

He breathed in deeply. "At the start of my own history the world was in the Mesolithic-Neolithic transition. The clans were organized as are the families today, but at a much smaller scale. Seeing that our gifts as immortals were greater than the average family member we decided to establish some sort of governing class. It wasn't as intricate as yours is today. People might have been gifted back then, but they were raw with hardly any civility or any sort of education. They were truly difficult times. Especially for those of us who saw images of the future. It was frustrating that things took so long to evolve for mankind. The immortals sat down and drew up plans on how to form this governing body and came to a consensus that we would never allow one person to govern us." He looked up to see if I was still paying attention. He smiled at my wide eyed expression. "You always did like listening to stories."

"Who wouldn't I? I mean you're like a living –"

I was looking for the right word, but couldn't find any.

"Fossil, I'm a living fossil," he said chuckling.

"I would hardly call you a fossil. You don't look a day older than my Uncle Abbot."

He was visibly content. "As far as appearances go we're approximately the same age, isn't that right Abbot?"

"Yes, that sounds right," Uncle Abbot said grinning. "Although the body you inhabit doesn't have my rugged good looks." What laughter there was around me was forced and brittle. But there was little of it. I didn't have the heart to joke around. "What happened to your own body?" I asked cutting the laughter short.

"When Ellri are ready to ascend and take the Lo –," For some reason he looked around apologetically. "Once an Ellri ascends there is absolutely no need for a physical vessel to carry our energy force. We are one with nature. We can choose to look however we like."

"So why choose a middle aged man and not something younger?"

He laughed wholeheartedly. "Choose to look young?" He laughed even louder.

"Sure, why not?"

"I'm over six thousand years old; fifty is young!"

"Thank You," snapped Uncle Abbot defending his age.

"Here, here!" said a few of the other Ellri in their fifties.

"Okay, okay I got the point!" I yelled looking around at the people who raised me. "Can an Ellri choose to keep his form? Look the way they did before ascending into Nobe?"

"Of course, The Watcher has kept his form."

I looked confused. "Who's the Watcher again?"

"I am," said the sweet little voice. "I don't belong to any of the five families either. I ascended when I was only eight about three thousand years ago."

I recoiled in shock. "But I thought that Alexander was the only Ancient alive. How is that possible?"

"I'm not considered an Ancient," said Ramiel. "I was born thousands of years after the war. Alexander found me just before I ascended. He said I was special because it was rare for someone so young to become an Immortal; a Nobe as you call us."

"If you don't belong to one of the families then how is it that you're so powerful?"

"I don't belong to one of your five families, but my master tells me that I once belonged to a great clan. One of the older ones, the ones that were killed millennia before you all came to be."

"How is it that you don't know your family or have no memory of one?"

"He was only an infant when the Fallen attacked his village," Alexander said, staring into space. "Lucky for him his powers were latent so when his parents hid him among the non-gifted he was saved. It wasn't that the Fallen didn't know where to find him; they simply didn't think he was worth the effort. "

"I sure showed them," said Ramiel giggling.

I giggled as well at his sweet little laughter.

"The Fallen are descendants of the oldest family," continued Alexander. "We used to congregate together, but the moment we decided that not one person would rule us anymore a rebellion broke out. The oldest family wanted control; started killing off the gifted who didn't agree with their politics, short after the war began. It was a massacre on both sides, lasting only a mere three days and three long horrific nights," Alexander stopped for a minute visibly overtaken by his memories. "The longest three days of my life!"

"If this is too painful for you, we don't need to go on," I offered admiringly taking his hand in mine.

He smiled weakly and lifted my hand to his mouth and bowed slightly before he kissed each of my hands. "For me those days are but indelible memories burned deep in my soul. What we are all here to do is to keep them from becoming your reality. As I was the last of my kind so are the two brothers Abaddon, the angel of death as they called him in ancient times and Bernael, the angel of darkness and evil. Make no mistake about them, the two are no angels. They are two very powerful immortals that have been scouring the planet to do their master's bidding. The Nobe Council has been forcing their hand for too many years, pushing them to comply with the new state of things. They are resilient; even tried to recruit from the five remaining families."

"Gabriel," I whispered.

"Yes, your young admirer was but a tool of their corrupt

ways. Gabriel didn't act on his own; you must've guessed that much. Poor guy was probably promised heaven and earth to reel you in."

Caradon looked frustrated. "Caitlin, don't blame Gabriel for his acts; I am too blame. I was his Ellri. I should've kept him on a shorter leash."

"He's not a dog Uncle. He is old enough to know right from wrong."

"You use the present tense to speak of him. He will not be bothering you anymore, Caitlin. He is but a bad memory."

Suddenly I was sad. "That's really too bad that it had to come to that. You should've exhibited the mercy Justin showed that day and spared his life."

They all looked surprised at my response.

"He almost killed you. How can you feel pity for your executioner?" Caradon said, shaking his head in utter disbelief.

"Can a person be all evil?" I asked scanning their faces. "I'd like to believe that he had other good attributes to offer the world. One mistake in judgment shouldn't condemn you for eternity."

My words enraged my uncle even more. "This is why she needs to come to Velius," he pointed accusingly. "Set her mind straight. Teach her the ways of our kind. Did you hear how easily she forgives? Forgives a person who almost killed her; borders on insanity if you ask me?"

"We're not asking you," Justin responded rather curtly, "It's commendable to be able to forgive; especially your worst enemy."

I wouldn't go that far. I thought. I knew deep down that I could never forgive Megan for how she treated me as a child. It was funny how I had compassion for Gabriel, but none for Megan. I most definitely needed to work through my feelings for her.

Brett started chuckling. "There must be something in the water in Oaks; it's the only explanation," he said looking at his brother momentarily before he shifted his gaze to Justin. "You had the chance to finish Gabriel off and you didn't. How the hell do you expect to stand beside us and fight these demons. Are you going to show the same mercy to Abaddon or Bernael?"

"I will not be governed by my emotions," Justin answered taking a step forward to close the gap between them. "If I allowed that to happen you wouldn't be standing here lecturing me on what I should've done."

This was an Ellri that Justin was talking to. But for some reason, he wasn't remotely scared of any repercussions. There was something different about Justin; I just didn't know what it was.

I pulled Justin by the arm so he could distance himself from my uncle and then asked, "If you all seem to work so great together at a time of crisis than why do you dislike each other so much?"

"Now this explanation I'd love to hear," remarked Alexander delightedly.

Rebecca strolled to my side. She was the only one who had successfully bridged the gap between the families. Once Varjatus herself she now lived harmoniously among the Illumine in Tirion. "It's not dislike we feel," she started to say. "The McDevitts and Korbs being the oldest families have acquired a unique link. An instinct of when one is approaching.

Since we can block out our thoughts we depend on this primal reaction, this nausea we first feel when we come in contact. Its repulsiveness is what keeps the two families apart. Naturally, we prefer staying away from each other rather than feel the urge to vomit."

I stared disbelievingly. "If it's only that, then why are the families split into different groups. Why are the four families called The Illumine and the Korbs The Varjatus?"

Alexander sighed sympathetically. "I should answer that," he said "When I first came to know the Korbs they were cave dwellers. They lived in hiding; mostly dark and mysterious places. Then centuries later, after the first of their young ascended, I noticed that their energy field was a hazy one; grey almost. Unlike mine which was bright and luminous. They looked like bright shadows amidst their dark surroundings, so hence the name. I should point out that they had adopted different ethics and beliefs over the years, but still the name doesn't refer to anything evil. The same goes for the Illumine. First I found the McDevitts and centuries later the rest of the families. They lived in sun washed villages either near the coast or in lush green surroundings. Their aura as some might call it was bright like the sun. That's when I realized that the hue and brightness all depended on where they were raised."

"Don't sugar coat it Alex," Ava sneered contemptuously. "There's much more that separates us than a mere geographical location. We are in no way like Varjatus!"

"Yes, of course!" Alexander smiled apologetically. "The Illumine and Varjatus have numerous differences in their basic makeup, but I don't think you summoned me here to point out the differences. We're here to highlight your similarities; the one thing that binds all of you." Brett snickered under his breath. "Don't you mean the one thing that can destroy us all?"

Alexander turned his gaze away from my uncle visibly bothered by his words. "I prefer to see the glass half full, if you don't mind."

"Where do I fit in? What's my role?" I finally asked.

The moment for questions had suddenly come to an end. In the heavy silence that followed the Ellri all returned to their seats; only Alex remained standing.

"The Primoris is looking," whispered the soft angelic voice.

At once, Justin grabbed my hand and pulled me beside him. "Don't you dare move," he ordered.

I shuddered at the thought of what this all truly meant.

Justin's hold tightened.

Instantly and in perfect synchronization, the Ellri all stood as if responding mechanically to a muted order. They all closed their eyes and held hands.

"The Primoris is close," warned Ramiel.

In response to my ultimate fear of losing them all to that monster, and my instinctual need to protect them all, my power flowed through my veins in a surge of rage and determination to stop it from destroying everything and everyone I loved.

"You are not doing this!" Justin pronounced, getting ready to take hold of my hand. "You need to calm down and let us handle this."

"Like hell I do!" I screamed as I pulled away in my frenzied mindset. Without even a second thought, I closed my eyes, slipped into my solace and quickly stepped out of the physical binds of my earthly body. On entering the Inner Realm the first thing I noticed was what could be described as flood lights.

"Caitlin," the source of the light said. "You shouldn't be here. It's you he wants." In seconds the vibrant light withdrew inward and a young boy stood there facing me. His smile was a pained one.

Seeing how young he was only reinforced my consuming need to protect them all; to face this demon. "If he's coming for me; let him come!" I yelled, angrier than before. "You should tell the others to leave; keep them safe."

I gathered insurmountable power from the energy that flowed freely around me. A raw wave of energy washed over me, bringing my gift to a whole new level. My unearthly body went from a light glow to a bright fiery red in seconds, but I had to find a way to rein it in before I was lost to my own madness and frantic thoughts of annihilating whatever it was that wanted me dead. I breathed in deep trying to harness all the energy that seemed to consume my every cell. I finally homed in on the beat of my own heart and allowed the rhythm to sooth my satanic need to shed blood, and for the first time ever I felt one with my gift.

The Primoris was rather close and quite lethal, I was sure; otherwise my body wouldn't have reacted so volatile.

"Ramiel," I said softly as if talking to an actual eight-year-old, "you have to leave! Please get out of here!"

Without even a goodbye the boy vanished; leaving me stand all alone in complete darkness. The light that emanated from my ghostly presence bounced off the dark mist that slowly made its way towards me.

The sound of nothing but a dull roaring like the wind engulfed the whole of my surroundings. I was alone; in the heart of some putrid scheme; of some sinister intelligence bent on punishing me, but I wasn't going to back down.

Immersed in my own dark and mazy thoughts, I didn't for some time notice the sound of wails and screams. When at last it cut through the fog of my preoccupation, I froze abruptly.

I let the dismal essence of the mist beat upon me. I felt quite boneless and rather stupid for getting myself in yet another life threatening predicament, but that wasn't such a bad way to feel. I was sure I would be nervous, terrified even, but my unremitting need to protect those I loved had burned away my fear.

A s I contemplated what freakish thing the malign mist might disgorge, I took a breath so my voice would be steady, and also to make sure of the words that came out of my mouth. "I don't scare easily," I pronounced, infuriated at the intruder. "What is it that you want?"

Surprised at my own level of confidence, I stood my ground refusing to yield to fear. The blanket of mist rolled in thicker now circling like a wolf its prey. All around me I sensed death and evil.

The sinister darkness was constricting me, pushing against my chest. It reeked of death and despair. I could feel its ice cold touch deep in my bones. This was not the Primoris Donum; This had to be Bernael.

"If you're trying to psych me out you need to do much better than that, I've been conditioned by the best," I said waiting for a response.

For the first time ever I was thankful for Megan's taunting. It would seem her relentless need to bully me had prepared me for the worst. Apparently, I was habituated to deviant beings from a rather young age, thanks to her unremitting emotional and psychological war that was waged against me throughout the whole of my young impressionable life.

A stream of murk quickly encircled my wrist.

Out of nowhere, I heard a snarl like sound. "You bear the mark," it said in a mysteriously hollow voice. The source of the sound was hard to pin point. It wafted in the mist, chilling the air in its wake. "They sent a child!" he exclaimed revoltingly.

"You don't scare me."

"You only think you're not scared of me, mortal," It snarled rather close to my ear.

"You need to come to my high school; I'll show you scary!" I retorted peering through the darkness.

"I can promise you that nothing is as evil as I."

One eyebrow went up as I chuckled at his remark. "You obviously haven't seen the heel toting monster that walks the halls of Oaks High; sporting pink lace and thigh high socks. She is by far the worst I've had to face."

Another snarl; this time even louder. "Mortal," It bellowed, "do not toy with me. Your life hangs only by a thread. You stand breathing before me because I choose to allow you to. I will snuff you out in a blink of an eye."

"And where's the fun in that?" I mocked.

I honestly didn't know what came over me. The fear most people would've felt had somehow altered in my overly stressed mind; transformed itself into a standup comedy routine. I felt somehow euphoric – invincible.

In a blink of an eye the shadow of a human figure stood inches from my face with his fiery red eyes piercing into mine. I didn't flinch. I stood unyielding to his assault. "Do you have anything to add young mortal," he hissed, wrapping a hand around my neck. His long black nails dug deep into my skin as he squeezed tighter. "How much do you value your life now?"

The next few minutes were a blur of strange occurrences. Regardless of my iron clad control over my lethally charged power, I knew deep down I had no more likelihood of stopping this demon than a kitten had of stopping a mountain lion. But this little kitten was mad as hell and ready to beat the lion down.

He tightened his hold around my neck, constricting me of air, but I kept staring deep into his eyes as I forced my throbbing hand through his chest like a knife through butter and held tight to the beating organ that lay beneath the soft tissue, and in the middle of my madness I heard myself say, "How much do you value your immortality demon?"

"How dare you touch me!" he hissed, red eyes narrowing. He bore his teeth as though he might tear out my throat.

Unexpectedly, Bernael slowly let go of his tight hold around my neck and didn't make the slightest move. Not that he had anywhere to go. I was, after all, elbow-deep into his chest cavity.

"How?" He asked.

"I'm but a mere mortal holding onto your evil infested heart. Choose to leave and I'll let go. Choose to fight me, and I'll yank your useless heart out and dance all over it. What will it be?"

The pungent mist suddenly retreated, leaving us in the midst of vast swamplands dripping of stale, musty odor, infested with maggots crawling out of decaying bodies. The dark shadow in front of me instantly materialized into a man.

The only thing scarier than the deep scar running down the

side of his swarthy face was the look he got when he gazed down at my glowing arm imbedded in his chest. "You are still touching me, mortal," he said, brandishing his razor sharp teeth.

"What will it be?" I repeated sternly, waiting for a response.

"What are you?" Bernael asked, visibly indifferent to the situation at hand. "Why do you have two heart beats?" He asked dumbfounded, but intrigued.

I wasn't sure what he was talking about. It was probably the throbbing of my wrist that he was mistaking for a heartbeat.

"Make your choice demon!" I yelled wanting nothing more than to leave behind the hell hole he brought me to, which was lined with unfathomable numbers of decomposing bodies. The smell of rotting flesh was unbearable. The swamp area was some kind of dumping ground for his insatiable lust for blood and carnage.

"Love what you've down with the place," I said returning my irritated gaze back to his blood shot eyes.

"You can't be human!" he exclaimed, ignoring my comment and the fact that I had my hand around his heart.

"I am as human as they come; emotional scars to prove it. Now the question is will you be immortal for much longer?"

He breathed in through his nose, quite deeply. I could literally feel his longs expanding in his chest. "I sense two of you. How can that be?"

I tightened my grip around the warm muscle between my fingers and said with clenched teeth, "The choice is yours."

Bernael didn't respond.

"Do you have a death wish, or something?" I asked seeing that he was somehow amused with the whole set up.

"Don't you have one too, mortal?"

I shook my head. "I don't wish to die."

"Really? Than why are you here?"

I squeezed his heart even tighter.

"I choose to live, young mortal," he said instantly.

It was a bad idea to let him go, but I did. I watched in bewilderment as Bernael retreated. He was instantly wrapped in a cloud of mist again. "You should've killed me when you had the chance, mortal" he said slowly fading away. "I won't be so willing to play along next time."

The mist quickly rolled away draping me in darkness once again. "The bastard was sizing me up," I told myself as I returned to my earthly body. I sat there alone in my solace refusing to rejoin the Ellri. The fear that I was so masterfully drowning deep inside me, quickly crept up as soon as Bernael left. "He was teasing me," I said out loud. "How stupid I must've looked."

"Will you be in here long?" asked the familiar whisper that only visited me in my solace. Its warm glow was welcoming; a total contrast of the blood curdling chill of the swamp.

"I'm afraid to face the Ellri," I admitted, leaning my forehead against my knees.

"I see. Well sitting here won't do you much good."

"I know, but I simply need some more time to figure out why I do these stupid things. How am I supposed to protect everyone if I keep jumping into the fire without thinking about getting burnt?"

"Who said you have to protect everyone?"

"I don't know. It's the way I feel."

It was quite once again. Nobody spoke.

"So many dead," I said shaking the image from my mind.

I instantly felt a warm hand on my cheek. "He was simply trying to scare you."

"Well, he succeeded!"

"He doesn't think so. You didn't flinch once the whole time. Caity, you surprised him and Bernael is not used to being surprised especially by mere humans who haven't even ascended yet. The backdrop was a way to distract you; to see how you'd react in the midst of death and despair."

"He did this once before in Indigo Caverns, but then I didn't know who the monster was that pulled me under the water. What a sick and twisted gift to have," I said, pushing some loose strands of hair out of my face.

"He wasn't always evil; nobody really is. It's just so much easier to follow the wrong path in life because usually there aren't any real rules to abide by or any limits to overcome. After so many thousands of years he feels at home among the dead."

"What a loser!"

"I guess that's one way of describing the infamous angel of darkness. Now, enough hiding from your family, they are all worried. Take a deep breath and open your eyes," ordered the Nobe, and I did just that. The second I emerged from my solace, I found myself sitting in the middle of the Chamber of Enlightenment on a plush Persian rug. Across from me was the most beautiful of God's creations. Justin was holding both my hands and smiling at me.

I honestly didn't expect such a warm response; blazing mad was what I expected to see. I smiled back realizing how close I came to never seeing him again. I eased myself into his open embrace, and held him tight. "I'm sorry, I wasn't thinking," I whispered in his ear.

Justin pushed my hair to the side with both hands. "You were wonderful; crazy, but wonderful. Wasn't she Alex?"

I circled my head to the side and saw that it was only the three of us. The Ellri were all gone.

"I have to admit, she was rather entertaining," he said, trying to smother a laugh. "High heeled toting monster? Where did you come up with that?" he asked shaking his head enjoying the joke.

"Megan!" Justin and I said in unison. We automatically burst out laughing at how in synch we were. The smile quickly disappeared from my face in the realization that I came so close to dying. I closed my eyes and exhaled deeply.

"Why didn't he kill me?" I asked staring at Alexander.

"Don't sound so disappointed. If it makes you feel any better he will surly try again. He spared your life because you intrigued him." Alexander explained. "As I said before; you leave a lasting impression."

I shrank into myself. "He thinks I'm not human."

"I know isn't that great! You guys really confused him."

"Us guys? What are you talking about?"

Alexander pointed to Justin. "Caitlin, you didn't think that your other half would let you face the demon alone, did you? Why do you think Bernael felt two heart beats? He doesn't know about your Bond; doesn't know that anything of the sort exists."

Justin smiled. "It was all Caitlin. She's truly amazing," he boasted caressing my cheek. "But next time," he murmured, and put his hand under my chin to lift my lips to him. "Next time you shouldn't act purely on impulse!" His lips were fierce against mine, spiraling my fears to the farthest corner of my mind.

"You both did great today; showed him that it won't be easy," said Alexander with a proud smile across his face.

"Why was he the one who came for me? Why didn't the Primoris come?"

"The Primoris probably doesn't think you're worth the effort so Bernael was sent to –"

"To take measurements for my coffin?" I asked exhibiting a feigned smile.

"No," said Justin smiling at my black humor. "Bernael is meant to scare you. Abaddon will be sent to kill you if the Primoris Donum feels that you are a threat."

I scratched my head in frustration and bit my lip. "Alex you never told me who this Primoris is and what in the world he wants with me? I mean why does he see me as a threat?"

"Caitlin, haven't you had enough history for one day? Justin knows all there is to know. The sacred scripture has been inscribed deep into his soul. He and I are the only living people who know all there is to know; apart from the Fallen, that is. I trust Justin. He will know when it's the right time for you to know the rest." The second he finished his sentence he disappeared into thin air.

Hours later I awoke gasping from a dream of smothering darkness to find myself half-strangled in a knot of cotton sheets.

I quickly sat up grunting as I unwrapped myself from the tangle of bedclothes.

"Caitlin?" Justin's shadow appeared on the wall near the door. "Are you alright?"

"I had a strange dream." I shrugged, wiping my forehead from the cold sweat.

"Do you remember what you saw?" he asked, perching himself on the edge of my bed.

I thought for a moment. "Not really. It sort of slipped away. Something about a lake." I shook my head. It was gone.

In one swift move Justin pulled me into his embrace and kissed me lightly on the forehead trying to ease my tension. "It's just as well."

"What time is it?" I asked nestling my weary head in the curve of his neck.

"It's about four in the morning, and you have school in a few hours."

"You'd think confronting the angel of darkness would at least get me out of first period Calculus."

His laughter uplifted my spirit. "It's the end of your senior year. I wouldn't call what you have lessons."

"Do you think my uncle will let me sleep in for the day?"

Justin tucked me back in bed and fixed the covers snug around me. "You never sleep in. You hardly ever sleep. Now get some rest." He kissed me again and strolled to the armchair.

I sat up and pushed the covers off. "Do you think you can break the rules just this once and lie down next to me?" I asked pleadingly. "Just this once, or at least until I fall asleep?"

I didn't need to ask twice. He was next to me in no time.

"Now go to sleep," he ordered kissing my shoulder.

I snuggled into his outstretched arms and kissed him quickly on the lips. I looked into his eyes and slowly leaned in and kissed him again; this time I took my time enjoying the flavor of his sultry lips. His arms responded to my touch by bringing me even closer. His lips were hard against mine taking what rightfully belonged to him. In the brief second when his lips were free, he whispered my name. The sound of his voice was intoxicating, causing me to lose myself in the moment. There was nothing as sweet as surrendering myself to him.

"I love you," he whispered as he slightly pulled away putting an end to what I started. He ran his fingers through his tussled hair and looked up to the ceiling.

"If you loved me so much you wouldn't have pulled away," I accused him.

He looked at me from the corner of his eye not amused.

"Your attempts to corrupt me are, to say the least, enjoyable," Justin said as he unexpectedly grabbed me by the arms and pinned me under him trailing kisses down my neck. I squealed in excitement. His little moans of satisfaction were arousing my need for him even more.

I was about to pull my arm free from his grip when he forcefully pinned it back once again.

"Oh no you don't temptress. Your hands are staying where I can see them."

I giggled at his crocked little smile.

"Besides, Fred and Barney had enough excitement for one night. I don't think their little animated hearts can handle what I want to do to you."

"What is it that you want to do to me?" I asked seductively.

He leaned in and kissed me passionately.

"Ascend first and find out later," he mused, swinging himself off the bed.

"You're cruel! You like torturing me, don't you?"

"Trust me love, I'm the one being tortured. As I told you before, I want to do this right. I love you too much to make this any less important."

I wasn't going to question his ethics especially when mine were the ones waning. I've done nothing but think about my first sexual experience. It was rather hard to think of anything else when I had a guy like Justin around. But I never thought about it in terms of losing my virginity; didn't seem such a big deal since the man I'd be losing it to would be Justin.

I suddenly blushed at the mere thought of Justin having all of me. My heart started palpitating as I was fighting to catch my breath.

Justin quickly came to my side again and held me close. "What's wrong?" he asked holding my face in his strong hands. "Don't worry about Bernael? He can't get to you here, Caitlin. You're safe; relax."

I stared at him as I was embarrassed to tell him the real reason behind my anxiety attack. "I won't let anyone hurt you," he said stroking my back.

"I love you," I whispered against his neck.

He inched me away and stared into my eyes. "I love you more!" he said hugging me again.

"That's humanly impossible," I muttered melting into his embrace.

He instantly tightened his hold and kissed me tenderly. "Haven't you heard? Humanly impossible is what I'm real good at."

TEN

FANCY-SCHMANCY

NABLE TO SLEEP in anticipation for my first final, I paused momentarily in front of my window as I wrapped my comfy cotton robe around my waist. The past week was agonizing. Studying was a drag and the images of decomposed bodies kept swirling in my mind making the nights unbearable and any meal less than enjoyable.

Aunt Leslie hated that I went off food. It wasn't that I wasn't hungry. That day in the swamplands with Bernael, had left an indelible taste in my mouth; a taste of rot and stench. It's hard to explain, but nothing tasted right. It's not that I didn't eat; I simply didn't enjoy it. I only forced food down for my aunt's sake because I hated that she worried so much.

As I stood there watching, exhaling deeply, and thinking about how a whole week had passed and Justin had yet to divulge any information pertaining to the Book of Truths, the automatic sprinklers went off in the distance, watering the lawn, and by the looks of it, some of the garden furniture.

I barely saw him in the days following our confrontation with the angel of darkness. He insisted on giving me space to study. I didn't need space; I needed him. But I knew he took advantage of the time he spent away from me in the Chamber, practicing and perfecting his gift with Kyle and Marc. Something had definitely changed as far as Justin was concerned. It was a subtle change; not something I could easily explain, but I knew him well enough to sense the shift that seemed to have taken place in the past few months.

I first felt the difference back in Tirion, when he surprised me that rainy day outside the castle. Back then, I thought it was me, but once things had settled, the inexplicable feeling of change had remained; growing with each day. I wanted to ask him; hoping that nothing serious was going on, and then the whole thing with the Fallen came up.

The water sprinklers changed direction.

"I need to Ascend!" I sighed as I leaned my forehead against the cold window pane.

Moments later, feeling even more defeated, I walked over to my vanity and sat there staring into the mirror. "What in the world does he see in me?" I asked, looking at my disheveled reflection. "He deserves much better," I huffed, and picked up the brush to detangle the mess on top of my head. It took a while to pull through the waist-long strands. I wasn't exactly brushing, because that would entail the brush actually going all the way through. What I was doing would be best described as raking; trying to yank through the knots. Cursedly tired of waiting for someone to tell me what my role in all this drama was, I yanked even harder taking my frustration out on my hair.

Tyler was amazing. Although he made me tell and retell all the things that had happened to me, I was unwilling to mention the existence of the Book of Truths; didn't want to break any more rules. He was as shaken by everything as I was. He hated being left out; hated not being able to help, but I felt it was enough that I was losing sleep over it all, there was absolutely no need for him to worry about the future.

I was over his house most of the week. We studied together, ate together even played video games. I loved hanging out with him, but at the same time felt guilty for keeping him away from Megan.

Having Emily all wrapped up in her wedding plans I needed somebody to take my mind off all the horrid images of death that kept resurfacing, and Tyler was perfect. We never mentioned the accident in Harvard Square; none of us did. I knew that we had all changed somehow after that day.

"Finally," I exclaimed finishing with my hair. I pulled it up in a ponytail and then slipped into my jeans and sneakers. Bag in hand I headed downstairs to eat breakfast before I headed off to school on foot. Yes, on foot. I decided last night that the walk would do me good. It was about a thirty minute walk; exactly enough time to clear my head before tackling Calculus.

Aunt Leslie was downstairs drinking her coffee and reading Home and Garden. Since our return from Tirion she was mostly preoccupied with the upkeep of her breathtaking flower beds; knee deep in natural fertilizer. "Good morning sweetie," she said putting down her magazine. "Couldn't sleep again?"

"No, I slept," I assured her as I walked over to the fridge and pored myself a cup of freshly squeezed orange juice. "I decided to walk to school; that's all."

"What a great idea! The morning air will do you good."

I smiled and took a sip. "That's what I'm counting on," I finally answered after swallowing back the burn in my mouth.

She crossed her hands and simply looked at me.

"What is it?" I asked, placing the glass down and stared back at her. "Did something happen?"

"No! It's nothing serious, sweetie. It's just that you've been neglecting your practice sessions. I would think that with all this hanging over your head you'd at least want to reach your full potential as far as your gift is concerned."

"You don't need to worry about me. I promise I'll get back in there. It's just with finals I can only do so much. I don't know if you can understand, but I want to act normal for a couple of days; keep my mind off –"

She smiled warmly. "Yes, of course I understand," she acknowledged, patting my hand, "Just thought I'd mention it; whenever you feel ready to be yourself."

"I'm sorry. I didn't mean it to sound that we aren't normal. You must know how strongly I feel about that. It's just that I need time; time away from all this."

She patted my hand again. "Sure sweetie. I understand. Now you need to eat something." She got up and brought over a carton of milk and corn flakes, "That glass of orange juice isn't going to be enough to keep you till lunch."

I reached over and grabbed a bowl. "Aunt Leslie, can I ask you something?"

"Of course, sweetie."

"It's about the day of the accident in Harvard Square."

She sat back down across from me. "Sure, what would you like to know?"

I looked at her stunned. I didn't actually expect her to be so willing to discuss the topic.

"What is it Caitlin? What would you like to know?"

"What happened to that little boy? I mean, what did you do to him?"

"I took him home."

"Home?" I asked in a state of uncertainty.

"Yes, home. He wasn't supposed to be there that day. Eric lives only a block away from the coffee shop where you found him. Apparently, he had sneaked out and ended up facing death in the face. The waitresses keep him well supplied with candy, so he goes there with his mother on a daily basis. That particular day she had to take care of things around the house so Eric took it upon himself to go for a walk, and look where it got him."

"Tyler said his wounds were irreversible and that there was nothing he could do to help."

"I'm not Tyler," she said with a sly wink.

I smiled at her response. "How did you know the boy? You seemed to tend to him as if he were your own."

"It's part of my gift. I can tell you anyone's history. Anything they've experienced in their life."

"Really! You've never told me this," I exclaimed. "I'm glad that you were at least there to help. The other Ellri were just standing there doing nothing!"

Her mouth turned up into a crocked smile. "I wouldn't call what they were doing nothing, Caitlin. They were there to keep you all safe. The Nobe were around as well."

"Really! The Nobe and Ellri?" Geez, you guys really don't trust us, do you?"

"It's nothing like that, sweetie. We were there to make sure you guys came out of that ordeal safe. Abaddon was circling, waiting for more dead. He wasn't exactly happy that you and Tyler were there to intervene. There was no way of knowing how he would have responded were we not there."

"Wait! You mean to tell me that Abaddon, the angel of death, was there the day of the accident?"

"Caitlin, he's anywhere there is death and destruction. It's where he derives his energy from. It's why the ancient world called him the angel of death. Being a Nobe he is omnipresent; collecting energy from every realm."

"He must be really powerful," I swallowed hard, "How am I ever supposed to beat him?"

"Who said you're going to have to beat anyone? Why would a child go up against a Nobe; a deadly one at that?" She got up and came to sit next to me. "Caitlin, look at me," she ordered, lifting my chin so that I could look her straight in the eye. "You are not going to be facing anyone. The Nobe will be the only ones going up against the Fallen. You are too young. Bernael and Abaddon are only out to scare you. They wouldn't dare make a move; not with all of us watching so close. Alexander has shown much interest in you, and that's saying much for a man in his position; as is Ramiel. They will never allow anything to happen to you."

"I don't want to see any of you get hurt."

"You shouldn't worry about stuff like that. We can all take care of ourselves, and the Ancient is not someone either demon wants to cross. The only reason Alexander didn't intervene with your confrontation with Bernael is because he was testing Justin; testing to see how far the boy has come," she smiled, and shook her head in wonder, "He's amazing. So young and already –" She stopped abruptly and looked at me. "You have absolutely nothing to worry about, but please don't neglect your practice sessions."

"That was all a test?" I sounded angrier than I actually was.

"It wasn't planned, if that's what you're asking. Don't make any mistake about it; the threat was all too real. It was just with all of us there and Alexander as well as Ramiel no Fallen in their right mind would've overstepped the line. Even though we didn't intervene, Bernael was aware of our presence."

I took a deep breath, and then another. "Why are you so willing, now of all times, to share everything with me. Isn't this information off limits?"

"Some things are," she assured, smiling cunningly, "But seeing that you are so close to ascending; even faced Bernael with great courage. I think you deserve some of your questions answered."

"Then will you tell me what the Primoris Donum wants with me?"

She caressed my cheek. "Now that, even I don't know; I wish I did. It'd surely help me sleep at night. Only Justin and Alexander can help you with that."

"Great!" I exclaimed taking a big gulp of my juice.

"What's great?" asked Kyle waltzing in the room looking sleepy. "Good morning beautiful," he chirped, giving his mom a kiss on the cheek. "You too squirt."

"What are you doing up this early? It's not even noon yet?" I jested, smiling. He grimaced and pored himself a cup of coffee. "I have to go into town and get some things for the party."

"What party?"

"What do you mean 'what party', Caitlin? Great girlfriend you are." He sat across from me.

"You kids have a great day," began Aunt Leslie excusing herself. "And good luck on your finals, sweetie."

As soon as she exited, Kyle lifted the cup of coffee to his mouth and said after taking a sip, "Justin's birthday is coming up; did you forget?"

"I didn't forget, but I wasn't aware you were going to throw him a party?"

He raised an eyebrow. "I decided that your man needs a good old fashioned birthday party; beer and all. None of that fancy-schmancy crap."

"Why didn't anyone tell me?"

"I just decided to throw him one this morning, seeing how exhausted he's been these last few days, a party will do him good."

"You are a great friend, Kyle."

"I know. He is lucky to have me."

I rolled my eyes at him. "So, what are we going to do? Where are we going to have it? What things should we buy?"

"Hey, cool your jets, Caity. I said I'm throwing him a party; not you."

"I haven't even bought him a gift yet," I admitted. "Kyle, you know him better than anyone. What do you think I should get him?"

He shrugged his shoulders. "I'm sure he'll love anything you get."

"That's not much help!" I exclaimed, and forced a spoonful of cornflakes in my mouth.

The taste was vile. I knew there was absolutely nothing

wrong with the cereal; my taste buds were completely out of whack.

"Why do you like torturing yourself?" Kyle asked as he pushed my plate away and handed me his cup of coffee. "It's strong; try it!"

I took a small sip. "Thanks, but it tastes no different than anything else I eat or drink." I handed him his cup. "About the present?"

He shrugged his shoulders. "I don't know what to tell you. He's not into much lately. Always down in the Chamber practicing."

"You sound worried. Is he overdoing it again?"

"I'm not sure. He's training with Alexander and Ramiel. They disappear deep into the inner realm; hours on end. Most times Marc and I are there to drag him out."

"Kyle, what in god's name are they doing to him?"

"Oh, relax! He's a big boy. They obviously wouldn't be pushing him if they didn't think he can handle it. Ramiel has been working with Marc and me. Yesterday he even showed Emily some techniques on sensory manipulation where she could actually guide a person's senses."

"They're preparing you guys for war, aren't they?" I gasped.

Kyle shook his head. "A bit over the top, don't you think? Our gifts are growing. All the Ascended have intense practice sessions."

"You sure that's what it is? Are you being completely honest with me?"

"Gee Caity, stop worrying so much. You have finals to think about." He stood up and put his empty cup in the sink. "I know what will cheer you up!"

"Yeah, what?"

"Why don't you come shopping with me after your exam?"

"Really? Are you sure you want me along."

"It'll be fun. But be warned, I have to get all the shopping for the party done today because I won't have any time this week or next to run around getting all the things I need. I'm planning on inviting everyone we know."

"Yeah, I want to come."

"Great! I'll pick you up from school and we'll drive into Cambridge. I'm sure you can find something for Justin there."

I quickly got to my feet and flung myself at him. Kyle fell back on the counter for support. "Is that a yes?" He asked laughing at my response.

"Of course it's a yes. Why else would I be hugging you this early?" I let go and looked at him. "Have I told you how wonderful you are?"

"Not lately," he teased, wrapping his arm around my shoulder. "Can we take Betty today? I sort of miss her."

"Kyle, I told you a thousand times; she's yours. Take her anytime you want," I answered as he led the way out of the kitchen.

"Will you need a ride to school?"

"Nope! I'm walking!"

He looked at me for a second, but refrained from saying what he initially wanted to say. "Make a list of things you want from Cambridge," he said instead. "And tell Tyler to summon me the second you guys are done."

I looked up at the clock; only twenty more minutes and the first final was over. It was much harder than I anticipated, but thankfully Tyler was a great study partner. Most of the things we went over last night were on the exam.

As I was fiddling with my pencil, Tyler turned and made a face for me to stop. Apparently, I was distracting him. I stuck out my tongue and giggled.

"Caitlin, are you finished?" asked Mr. Travis, approaching my desk.

I nodded yes and handed him my paper. He looked it over once and turned to me again, "Don't you want to recheck it again? You do have another twenty minutes?"

Though I had looked over the darn thing four times already, there was something in his voice that urged me to look over the problems again. "Sure, I'll run through it once more," I said, thanking him.

I scanned the paper over and over again and still, I found absolutely nothing that stood out as being wrong so I doodled little flowers on the corner of my sheet and waited for the twenty minutes to pass. As I was sitting there thinking about different things to get Justin for his birthday, quite unexpectedly I felt a powerful stab-like sensation on the back of my head followed by a deafening droning sound of muffled voices. I flinched back at the sheer force of the intensity.

In seconds, triggered by the sharp piercing in my head, tears flooded my eyes. I held my head with both hands trying to apply pressure at the temples in the hopes of alleviating the pain somehow. Nothing seemed to work, the voices started getting louder and louder, bringing the pounding to an intolerable level. Unable to stand the pain any longer, I quickly got up and stormed out of the room ignoring all the stunned faces that followed my rather urgent exit. I ran to escape the voices, but it didn't matter how far I went; the muddled sounds continued all the more intense.

"It'll be okay," I heard the precious child-like voice say. It was the only clear sound among the jumbled up words of everything else swirling in my head. "Block them out. Make them stop," Ramiel continued to say.

I sat on the front steps of the school and put my head on my knees and closed my eyes. "I can't," I cried as I rubbed the back of my neck.

Within seconds, I felt a cold hand on the nape of my neck. I shifted my head to the side and saw Ramiel in his human form. I tried to smile at his cute dimpled expression, but the strain on my head was making me nauseous.

"It's nothing serious, it will pass soon."

"Easy for you to say," I exclaimed through clenched teeth.

"Your ability to read is trying to surface. That's what all those voices are," he explained, continuing to rub my neck. His cold touch was rather soothing against the burning of my skin. "For some strange reason your own gift is trying to snuff it out. It's reacting instinctively, knowing that if you start reading other peoples thoughts, they in turn will be able to read yours."

He sounded amazed – fascinated even.

"I don't care why it's doing it. How do I stop it?"

"It should fade away any minute now. Give it some time."

I looked at him from the corner of my eye and attempted to smile. He was so young – simply adorable. The smile on his swarthy face was irresistible. His thought provoking, deep chocolate colored eyes were what gave his real age away. There was nothing childlike about them. A three-thousand-year old man trapped in the body of an eight year old boy – how insane.

"Stop staring at me and concentrate on blocking the voices out," he ordered with a smile plastered across his face. "It's almost over. The intensity and voices should phase out in no time." The voices did finally fade away leaving me with a splitting headache. "You don't happen to have Tylenol on you?" I asked, smiling at his amused expression.

"Nope!" he answered, elbowing me playfully. "I'd love to help, but let Tyler tend to you. The poor boy's dying to get out here and help. I can feel his distress. He must really care for you."

"Yeah, I care for him too."

"Not in the same way; I'm afraid. Tyler is undeniably lost in you. No matter how much he's trying to deny it."

"Don't you have better things to do than spy on my personal life? What are you doing here anyway?"

"Watching over you; that's why they call me the Watcher. I Watch," he chuckled at his own words.

"Ha, Ha," I muttered. "For an old man you're kind of funny."

"I'm past old. There's no category for what I am. As you grow you tend to choose to look at the funnier side of life. It makes the centuries pass much faster."

"Is it hard? Being an immortal I mean?"

"Not much different than being 'normal' as you call it."

"You don't think of yourself as normal?"

"Do you see many three-thousand-year olds running around?"

I giggled at his animated expression. "No, I guess not." I looked out towards the parking lot wondering different things about our kind. "Ramiel, who do you think is considered normal; us or the non-gifted?"

"We're all made out of the same cast. But still, what is normal?" he scuffed. "We use that term too loosely. A norm depicts a standard prototype. Nothing under god's creation is standard. We are all individually blessed with such differences that it makes this world an amazing educational habitat. We have so much to learn from each other. Every person has something to offer, something to teach." He looked at me and shook his head. "Why do you have that stupid grin plastered on that beautiful face of yours?"

I smiled. "What you said is so true. It's just strange coming from an eight-year old."

"You see, and Alexander wonders why I remain in the Inner Realm. Nobody takes me serious on this plane."

"Trust me, Ramiel, we all take you serious!"

"Good to know, Caitlin," he beamed, and without any warning disappeared into thin air. It was within seconds of his vanishing act that the double doors to the school swung open, and students flocked out completely absorbed with how they did on their exams.

"Are you okay?" Tyler's voice was strained. "I was looking all over for you!"

"I'm sorry. It's my head. It's killing me."

"Why the hell don't you tell me these things?" he complained, pulling me by the hand. "Come on, let's go to the car; it's way too crowded here." His Porsche was parked next to Megan's BMW. "Cute! You guys even park in the same area."

"Get in!" he ordered, holding the passenger's door open, ignoring my comment and quickly slammed it shut the second I was in the seat.

"It's just a headache. I would've taken something, but I didn't have any pain medicine on me," I explained as soon as he sat in the driver's seat.

"Here, let me see," he instructed clearly annoyed with me. Tyler placed his hands on my temples. He raised an eyebrow questionably. "This was no headache. Why are you lying?"

"Are you going to help or not?" I asked, refusing to explain every little detail to him.

"Of course I'm going to help. I just wish you trusted me enough to share these things."

"I trust you with my life, why would you even say that?"

He applied pressure to my head with both hands as he leaned his forehead against mine and breathed in deep. "It's a lot harder than I thought it would be," he whispered, giving me a quick kiss on the forehead before pulling away.

I instantly felt better. "Shouldn't your gift be getting easier for you? Why is it getting harder?"

He stared at me for a couple of seconds. "I'm not talking about my gift," he admitted, turning to face forward, and his expression quickly froze.

I turned to see what caused him to stare in shock, only to see Megan staring back. It took me a few minutes to realize how Tyler's affectionate tending must've looked. "Crap! Does she think what I think she thinks?" I asked, circling my head to Tyler.

"Who cares what she thinks," he roared, turning on the ignition. "If you don't mind, Caity; I'd like to go home. Kyle is on his way. You won't have to wait long." I sat there staring at him unable to find the right words to say. "Caity, I need to get out of here, please!"

I got out of his car and closed the door behind me. Megan continued to stand there glaring at Tyler as he agitatedly, spun off leaving me to face the high heeled monster all alone. I felt bad; really bad. If I were in her place I wouldn't have been able to contain my anger. She seemed rather calm considering.

"Megan," I started to say, "It was nothing. I had a migraine and he helped. That's all it was."

She feigned a smile. "That's all it was for you, maybe," she responded walking away.

My gaze followed her to her car. "He was just trying to be helpful!" I yelled behind her, defending my buddy.

She threw her designer bag in the back seat and turned to face me. "He can do whatever he damn well likes; it's so over between us."

She was more or less shouting. Everyone turned to look, but quickly returned to what they were doing. Apparently, they were all used to Megan's little outbursts.

"I refuse to be second," she spat out scanning me up and down with such distaste. "Caitlin, look at you. Why in the world would I choose to come second to you?"

Anyone else in my place would've slugged her catty, self-obsessed face. But not me, not when my world had finally fallen back into alignment. It wasn't natural for her to be nice to me. It had thrown me off my game.

Now, I didn't have to be nice to her anymore or pretend to like her for Tyler's sake. This was the Megan I knew and hated. Her ranting didn't surprise me one bit because I knew that it was only a matter of time that she'd return to her spiteful self.

In the distance I saw Kyle approaching with Old Betty. I smiled to myself thinking how funny life was. All these years I felt inadequate around this full-blown spoiled diva and suddenly I felt nothing but pity for her. Kyle drove up and stopped a few feet away. As I opened the door to get into my revamped automobile I turned and looked at Megan who was still staring at me. "Nice to have you back, Meg," I beamed, and slipped into the passenger's seat giggling.

Kyle didn't say one word until we turned onto the main road. He was smiling to himself and shaking his head. "You sure know how to piss that girl off. She's just jealous. She doesn't hate you."

I laughed at his comment. "Oh, she hates me alright, and I wouldn't have it any other way."

"Are you serious?"

"Yeap!" I pronounced and laughed at how fast Megan slithered out of her pretentious skin. "Kyle, it must've been murder for her – pretending to like me all this time. Everybody told me that I should give her a chance; that I might even like her. Well, I guess they were all wrong."

"She's sweet, isn't she?" Kyle asked changing the CD.

"I wouldn't actually call Megan sweet."

"Who's talking about her? I'm talking about Betty. Isn't she great?" he boasted, masterfully changing the subject. "She purrs like a kitten."

"You did a wonderful job with her. Should I even ask how much her makeover set you back?"

"Does it matter? She was worth every penny!"

I loved him for loving my car so much. He liked the simple things in life. Paid attention to the things most people took for granted. He was the best older brother any girl could've asked for; no matter how difficult he made my life sometimes.

"So where's this surprise party going to be held?"

He let out a laugh, almost sounded like a bark. "Who said it's a surprise? How do you expect us to surprise Justin? He reads us all like an open book; especially now."

"I didn't think about that. So where is this shin-ding going to take place?"

"In our back yard – where else would I fit everybody?"

"Nobody knows how to hold small intimate affairs here in Oaks, do they?"

"Why would you want to? We're all family. We all grew up together. Besides, it's not like we can hide the darn event from anybody even if we wanted to."

"I see your point! This will be fun. Everyone loves Justin. They'll want to celebrate his birthday with him."

"Some love him more than others," he accused, tickling me.

"Knock it off you big buffoon!" I squealed, between the laughter. "How can I not love the guy, his perfect by nature."

Kyle purposely turned up the volume on the stereo rolling his eyes at me. I slapped his arm playfully. "You probably love him as much as I do," I accused, sitting back enjoying the rest of the ride.

"I doubt that," he muttered driving at deathly speeds.

ELEVEN

SHOPPING THERAPY

K YLE WAS GOING all out for his best friend. He bought balloons, banners, glow necklaces, light sticks, glow cups in all sizes and shapes and let's not forget the glow straws. You'd think he was throwing a party for a twelve-year-old.

"On my last visit to Cambridge, we didn't get to visit this part of the city. It's less traditional than Harvard square, but as charming." My comment fell on deaf ears as Kyle was preoccupied with his shopping list. "How often do you come here?" I asked Kyle, wondering how he knew the area so well.

"Not much now. In the past I came as often as I could to hang out with Justin. He wasn't doing so well when you were away. His transition into University with you being so far wasn't the best of times for him."

"You're a great friend, Kyle."

He smiled and put on a ridiculously large party hat. "It's easy being Justin's friend," he answered, wearing the oversized glasses to match. "Well, what do you think? Should this be the theme?"

"Clown school? Is that the theme?" I asked, shaking my head disapprovingly. "This party is for Justin, right?"

The girl at the counter was simply smiling at Kyle; checking him out from the moment we walked into the store. "Can you please tell my little sister that parties are meant to be fun," Kyle addressed her, causing her to smile even wider with the sound of the word 'sister'.

"Of course they are," she agreed, keeping her lost gaze on Kyle, "Why else have a party if not for fun."

"You see, Caitlin. It's supposed to be fun," he stated as he handed the love-struck cashier his platinum card. Her smile widened even more. "Just because he's older doesn't mean he can't have fun. Besides, he needs to let go. He's got lots on his mind."

"You're absolutely right. This party's going to be the best Oaks has ever seen!" I exclaimed stroking his back.

"Is that where you guys are from – Oaks?" The cashier asked. "Is that far from here?"

Kyle smiled at the half giddy girl and leaned in as he said, "It's rather far. So far that it practically doesn't even exist."

"That's a shame you live so far," she purred as she handed him the credit card. "We'd love for you to come back and visit."

Kyle beamed a thankful smile again, and grabbed a handful of bags. I thanked the girl and followed him to the car, totting my own share of birthday supplies.

"She was really friendly, wasn't she?" he asked, stuffing everything in the trunk.

"I'll say!"

"What's that supposed to mean?" he asked quite innocently as he took the last of the bags from my hands.

"Like you don't know," I accused him.

"Know what?"

Evidently my free-spirited cousin had absolutely no idea what his gorgeous smile was doing to the female populous. "Nothing, never mind," I said, dropping the subject altogether. He was so used to getting the same kind of response from most girls that he apparently saw nothing wrong with it. "Where do we go from here?" I asked, stepping back onto the curb.

He slammed the trunk shut and twirled the keys on his finger. "It all depends on what you want to get him?"

"You're no help! What do you get a twenty-two year old who has everything?"

He lifted an eyebrow devilishly. "I certainly know what you could give him. It will surely bring a smile to his face."

I slapped him on the arm knowing what he was insinuating. He jumped back in response laughing wholeheartedly at my crimson complexion.

"You are so cute when you blush," he said, pinching my cheek.

I punched him even harder.

"Wait," he said dodging my assault. "Wait! Come on, stop!" he laughed. "I have an idea! Get in!"

K yle pushed against the swollen wooden door that led inside the antique shop on the other side of town. The shop itself was hardly visible from the street; hardly visible from anywhere you stood, really. Wedged between two larger buildings, the store looked to be miniscule and crammed, but what it lacked in size, it more than made up for with its hundreds of years' worth of furniture, collectibles and accessories jammed against its four walls and display cases. Even the narrow wooden spiral staircase that led to the second floor was steeped in precious titbits.

It was the crisp sound of the small bell hanging overhead that made our presence known the second we stepped foot onto the hard-wooden floor. "I think you're going to find something for Justin here," whispered Kyle against my ear.

The small shop was inundated with the scent of antiquities that lined every wall and basically cluttered every available surface area. It made walking around nearly impossible, but it was the outlandishness and mysteriousness of the exhibits that grabbed my attention and sparked my curiosity.

"Ah, young Mr. Cathcart, nice to see you again son," began the old man standing on top of a wooden ladder reaching for something on the top shelf. He stretched and stretched some more; finally he had the box in hand. Without any hesitation he jumped off the last two steps and landed sleek and agile on the floor. Not expecting such nimbleness, considering his age, I smiled at his whimsical expression. "Haven't seen Abbot in quite some time, hope he's well," he continued to say while handing the box to the couple in the corner. "You will love these. They're over two-hundred years old and made of the finest silver." The couple looked excited; especially the young woman who was practically giddy with enthusiasm. "Take your time and have yourselves a good look," the old man advised, and then turned his attention back to us.

"Dad's just fine, Gregory. Emily is keeping them quite busy with her wedding plans."

"Ah yes! Emily and Marc are tying the knot, aren't they? What a beautiful couple? They will surely be a great addition to the family's longevity."

"Don't look so shocked," Kyle said, reaching for a colorful glass perfume bottle. "Gregory knows all about Oaks."

"Of course I know about Oaks. I did use to live there after all," remarked the old man as he handed Kyle a larger, more intricate sample. "She'll love this one, Kyle," he added. "It's older, and more hours went into making it."

The moment the light hit the fragile glass heavenly shadows were cast against the heavily laden shelves on the opposite wall. "Exquisite, isn't it?" he asked in response to Kyle's mesmerized expression.

"How is it possible that you live here?" I asked more interested in the man's history than the perfume bottle Kyle was holding.

Kyle placed the bottle carefully on the counter and shifted his gaze to me. "Gregory is gifted," he whispered. "He prefers the outside world much more than our little town."

The man wagged his index finger at Kyle. "Don't listen to your friend," he told me, pushing his glasses to the bridge of his nose. "Oaks is and will always be, my home. My gift just serves us all better out here, where I can keep an eye out for the others." He winked at me as though we shared some kind of covert secret.

I didn't get it, but didn't make a fuss either; not that I could. The couple was only an earshot away and next to no time approached the counter and placed the wooden box full of silver cutlery on the counter. "We'll buy it," beamed the young lady.

"You made a great choice," added Gregory, wrapping the item with old newspapers before placing it into a gift bag.

Her companion took out his leather wallet and handed Gregory a credit card. "How did you know this is what we were looking for?" he asked.

"Gregory always knows," he responded exhibiting a wide smile, talking about himself in the third person. He swiped the card across the register and returned it to its owner. "Don't use any abrasives to wash them, Silver only needs hot water and mild washing liquid, and don't forget to wipe them dry, otherwise they'll spot."

"How did he come by all these things?" I asked Kyle, seeing that there were no two things alike.

The sound of the small bell on the door drew my attention to the couple who was exiting the store.

"Each piece is quite unique, young lady," boasted Gregory as he approached. "Kyle, here try this," he added, handing my cousin a lighter. "I just came by this a few hours ago. It's got Abbot written all over it."

"Well then," Kyle agreed, "We wouldn't want to disappoint the little sucker, would we now? Dad will surely love it."

Gregory placed the antique lighter on the counter next to the glass perfume bottle that Kyle selected. "Are you looking for something in particular young lady?" he asked, helping me return the felt pen I was looking at back in its box.

"Gregory, this is Caitlin, Winston's daughter."

He looked surprised. "For the love of God, why didn't you say something earlier?" he exclaimed, staring at me. "Winston's daughter," he sighed looking thoughtful. "Why didn't anyone tell me you've returned?"

I shrugged my shoulders not knowing what he expected me to say.

"You were missed child, really missed by all," he went on, exhaling deeply. "Abbot raves about you every time he comes in here. Says you're a genius at school and a book worm at that. When you were young he used to come in here looking for rare books. He always had you in mind when he looked through the piles."

"So this is where he gets them." I looked around smiling; remembering all the times uncle Abbot came home displaying his new purchase. "I always wondered how he was able to come across the rarest editions."

Gregory's round face lit up with satisfaction. His grin stretched from ear to ear as he pushed his glasses back in place. "I carry only the best!" He boasted.

"I can see that. Everything in here is wonderful."

"We're looking for a birthday present," added Kyle, trying to move things along.

"Ah, yes! Yes of course. What would you like to see?" He paused looking at the upper shelves. "Oh, I forgot to ask you Kyle. Did your lady friend like her bracelet?"

"She loves it; doesn't seem to want to take it off."

"That's good to hear. Diamonds have a way of driving young ladies crazy," he finally said as his attention was quickly drawn to my diamond pendant. "I know this piece," he added, "May I?" he asked. I nodded, allowing him to take the pendent in hand. "So it was you all along, was it?" Gregory smiled. "You know Mrs. Bradford would never take this pendant off. It was an heirloom passed down for hundreds of years. Once, many, many years ago when she came in the shop I offered to appraise it for her. Of course she refused saying it belonged to the young lady who would steal her grandson's heart." His smile widened. "And here you are."

Now I was the one smiling.

Kyle picked up a magnifying glass and put it up to his eye. The sheer size of his face caused me to burst into laughter. "It's Bradford's birthday, Gregory. We have another two weeks, but there is no time like the present," said Kyle returning the glass to its rightful place.

"Justin's birthday! Now that's worth celebrating!"

"Well, that's why I brought Caitlin here. She can't seem to think of something to get him." Kyle nudged Gregory playfully in the ribs. "You see Gregory, Justin is special to Caitlin."

"Ah, I see. That surely explains the pendant." He looked around, rubbing his dense beard, clearly trying to remember something. Suddenly he snapped his finger in discovery. "Well you came to the right place young lady. There is something that will make young Bradford extremely happy."

No sooner did he finish his sentence that he disappeared behind a pile of old boxes. "It somewhere around here," he started to say scrambling to find the item.

Gregory carefully worked around the abounding objects, making his way through the pile rather quickly. His voice was fading in and out every time he looked up to see if what he was looking for was further up on the pile. "Ah, here it is! I knew I had it here somewhere." He muttered, blowing on the object to get the dust off. "Justin came in here a few months ago looking for this, but I guess he wasn't meant to find it. The darn thing seemed to have vanished that day, but here it is today."

With care, Gregory removed several layers of tissue paper

that covered the mysterious object that was meant to be Justin's birthday presdent.

"What is it?" asked Kyle.

"It's the eighteen-ninety-seven first edition of Mark Twain's 'Following The Equator, A Journey Around the World'," he beamed with content. Gregory cleared off the counter and laid the book in front of us. "Go ahead, you can touch it," he offered, aware of how hesitant I was to leaf through the pages.

I opened the book and saw that the interior pages were in remarkable shape. It even had the previous owner's name on the second page stating that he had bought it on April of eighteen-ninety-eight and cost three and a half dollars.

"It's the last of Twain's travel books. It's quite rare," he informed us as he turned the pages with the outmost care. "Imagine Justin's surprise if you're the one who hands this to him. It's truly a rare find. You can't go wrong with a book; especially this one."

I circled my head to Kyle. "I think this is it," I commended. "It's in pristine condition, and it's something Justin wants; something he was planning on getting himself. What do you think, Kyle?"

"Is it nerdy?"

I looked at him. "It's a book, Kyle!"

"Yeap, it's nerdy alright. He'll love it!"

Ignoring his comment, I turned to Gregory and asked, "What's something like this worth?"

His furrowed face darkened by my worrying smile. "Do you not like it?" he asked.

"No, I love it! It's just that I don't know if I can afford it."

"Sweet child; why would you be worried about the cost?"

"I do have to pay for it somehow, don't I?"

Kyle put his arm around my shoulder and squeezed me hard. "Gregory, she'll take the book. Wrap the sucker up, will you?"

"Yes, of course," he agreed with an animated smile.

I was about to take my wallet out of my bag when unexpectedly Kyle pushed it right back in. "Unless you have a couple of thousand stashed away in that little thing; that's not going to be of any help."

"Thousands?" My eyes widened. "Kyle, I can't afford this!"

"Don't be silly, of course you can. Now close your mouth. You look stupid."

"Thousands?" I asked again staring at my cousin.

Kyle simply ignored my surprised response and picked up another tidbit off the counter, all the while Gregory was somewhere in the back room packing up Justin's birthday present, and in no time returned holding a tastefully decorated box. The nice thing was that it totally suited Justin's personality down to the elaborate bow.

"I promise that Justin will be more than thrilled," reassured Gregory.

My smile couldn't be wider with gratification. "I hope you're right, Gregory, and thank you."

"Ah, trust me. Gregory is always right," he pronounced causing me to giggle. "Oh, and tell your Uncle Abbot that his visit is long overdue." He pointed to the darkest side of the store. "The chess pieces have gathered dust awaiting his next move."

"I'll be sure to tell him, Gregory," I promised following his gaze to the far dark corner of the little shop were two worn leather armchairs sat around a small hand-carved wooden table displaying a chess game long left unplayed.

"Thanks for everything, Gregory," ended Kyle as he led me outside with gifts in tow.

Sometime later as Kyle was maneuvering through traffic he asked, "You want to get some coffee before we head back?"

"Yeah, sure! Nothing exciting back in Oaks but a pile of text books I have to tackle. I can get to them later."

After several failed attempts at finding somewhere to park, Kyle finally spotted an opening rather close to where we were intending to go. The streets were bustling with activity; mostly young people making their way in and out of the shops carrying several bags in hand.

Once out of the car, I froze the instant I realized where Kyle had parked. There, right across the street was where the accident had taken place. I wouldn't have recognized the area if it weren't for the scaffolding in front of the store.

"What is it?" Kyle asked, placing his hand on the swell of my back. "Are you okay?"

"This is where it all happened, the place where those two people burned alive inside their cars."

He took me by the shoulder and led me down the street. "We can't always help everyone. You all did the best you could."

I stopped in mid-stride and turned to look at him. "I didn't," I admitted, feeling my tears overspill my eyes.

"Caitlin, what do you mean? What is it?"

"I could've stopped it from happening."

"Look at me," he pronounced. "You did what you could."

I shook my head. "I could've been there the second I heard

the wheels screeching to a stop. I had ample time to act." I turned my gaze to the ground. "I didn't react fast enough. It's my fault those people are dead."

Kyle smiled weakly and wiped my tears away. "What are you talking about? You did great! Did what you were meant to do. You chose to help instead of walk away."

Refusing to accept his reasoning, I kept shaking my head.

He held my face in both hands. "Caitlin, I want you to listen and listen good! That day you saved all those people. Yes, two died, but that doesn't give you the right to beat yourself up. If you guys weren't there –" He stopped and kissed wiped my tears. "You were all amazing, we're all proud of you." I leaned into his embrace and let him hold me for a few minutes. "Caitlin, I wish you didn't keep all this bottled up." Kyle stroked my hair as he continued to say, "Not being able to read you is really annoying. It's driving poor Justin crazy. You just keep too many things from us."

I sniffed back the tears. "I'm sorry. I'm just used to dealing with things on my own. You all have your own problems to worry about."

"That's just stupid," he admitted. "You need to let people in, especially Justin. Do you really think that he doesn't know how you feel? Hell, he's going crazy with worry. The Korbs are after you and you say nothing. Gabriel almost kills you and you say nothing. Bernael is up in your face and you still say nothing. How do you think that makes him feel?"

Tears just kept flowing down my face. "I feel numb inside," I blurted out. "Something inside me broke five years ago and then any hint of emotion that I did have simply died the moment they sent me to Tirion." I wiped my eyes looking at his strained expression. "It's not that I don't want to feel things like fear. It just takes me much longer to register the emotion. Anger seems to be the only feeling I genuinely feel. It's the only thing I know won't betray me."

"We're all to blame for what you went through," he began as he held me tighter. "We did this. We did this to you."

I took a small step back. "I need to work through this. I don't know how, but I know I'll get through it. I must!"

Kyle displayed a weak smile. "You will get through it."

"I love Justin. I know I do. I feel it to the depths of my soul, but I need time to be able to open up completely. It's not his fault. It's nobody's fault."

"I understand," Kyle said, with a strained smile. "I'm sorry for pressuring you. I didn't know. I never considered what all this was doing to you. But Caitlin, you must find someone to confide in. Keeping all this bottled up is sooner or later going to explode in your face."

"You're telling me! If it's not one thing it's another. I can't seem to catch a break."

He caressed my cheek again without saying another word.

"Now, where's my coffee?" I asked feigning a smile.

"I'm always here for you. I need you to know that, Caitlin. Don't ever hesitate to come to me. I'll be there. I promise!"

"I know you will," I accepted. "But, enough of this talk. Let's get something to drink!"

Kyle was genuinely concerned, but I didn't want to put a damper on the rest of our day. I was having way too much fun before the whole discussion came up. As always, I put on my ridiculously happy face and made damn sure that my cousin was enjoying himself. I wasn't accustomed to seeing him sad and I refused to cause him to look like that again. I simply adored him too much to burden him with my juvenile inability to work through my emotions. Fun is what we came to Cambridge to have, and fun was what we had.

As far as bedrooms were concerned, mine looked like a bomb went off. My Text books were randomly scattered all over the place, sheets of notebook paper crumbled up and thrown in a pile near the corner. The scrap paper was meant to go in the bin, but my inability to make the basket was what kept them sprawled on floor.

Shopping with Kyle was without a doubt the most fun I had in the last few weeks, but that evening was hardly bearable. I had wanted to see Justin, but Uncle Abbot insisted I keep my mind on my studies. A prisoner in my own room; I did the only thing I could to keep my mind off of Justin; I read and reread everything there was to know for the exam on Biology. I could practically recite the whole book if the need arose.

Frustrated at my uncle's inability to understand my need, I decided to put those feelings to good use; work through them as I'd promised Kyle I would. I stood there, in the middle of my room, and concentrated on sorting out the mess I've made, using my powers to quicken the pace. All at once, everything was up in the air moving around me faster and faster as the minutes passed. The nondescript speed that the objects sliced through the air caused my hair to flail in the draft. The books were neatly being stacked on the desk while the crumbled paper was dispensing itself properly. The swooshing sound that resonated in my ears was triggering my need for speed even more. My bed was being made while my clothes were being folded up neatly and arranged in my drawers. My room looked possessed. Thankfully, nobody was there to witness how I took cleaning to a whole new twisted level. It was an exercise of sorts; a way to keep my mind busy.

Coordinating all the different objects and tasks demanded orchestrated intricate thinking. It was more or less like solving a mathematical equation on the spot. It called for great concentration and a considerable amount of my excess energy. It was either that or bounce off the walls. Cleaning seemed more productive, though the bouncing might've been more fun.

The sudden knock on my door caused me to return everything back to where gravity would have them. "Come in," I announced excitedly, knowing who it was. I tried to quickly comb back my hair with my fingers, but who was I kidding? I was a walking disaster. My hair was all over the place. My nightshirt wasn't even ironed. Of all the times for him to come over it would be on the night I looked like crap.

The second I saw Justin's head poking in the door I beamed with happiness. "Hey, stranger," I began, wanting to sound all cool and mature.

"Is this a good time?" he asked as he approached. "I'm not bothering you, am I?" he added as he leaned in and gave me a quick kiss on the lips. He didn't take a step back, but he didn't make another attempt to kiss me either.

"Come here," I whispered and pulled him towards me by his black T-shirt. His mouth was glorious against mine, taking what I offered with equal want and longing. "I missed you," I admitted between kisses.

He pulled back momentarily and said in a raspy voice, "I missed you too," and smiled devilishly.

"That's nice to know," I responded kissing him again.

Justin pulled away slightly. "Did you have fun today with Kyle? I know he did."

"Yes! It was so much fun. He's hysterical!"

"I love it when you smile," Justin boomed and lifted me off the floor as he hugged me tight. "I love you," he whispered against my lips as he kissed me again.

"I love you too," I answered, and was about to take a step back when Justin quickly pulled me back into his embrace. "Don't –," he muttered, "I need to feel you close."

I nestled in his arms in silence for a few minutes and then asked, knowing that something was wrong, "What's going on?"

"Nothing! I just missed you; that's all." I didn't speak; instead, I remained in his embrace as long as he wanted me there. "Kyle tells me you had lots of fun shopping today."

"Yeah, as I said before, it was fun." I leaned in and kissed him once more. "Are you sure you're okay?" I asked folding my arms around him. "You're acting kind of weird."

"Am I?"

"You seem distracted."

"Do I?" He asked composed as he let me go and walked to the window.

"Justin, what's wrong?"

His gaze remained fixed on the view outside my window as he asked, "Did you mean what you said to Kyle?" He didn't turn around to look at me.

I took a few steps closer and made him turn to look at me. "What are you talking about?"

"Do you really feel numb inside; broken somehow?"

I raised my head to the ceiling and sighed. "Is this what this is all about?"

"Caitlin, you didn't answer my question," Justin exclaimed. "Did you mean what you said to Kyle?"

"Yes, but it has nothing to do with us," I said, trying to explain as I took a seat on the edge of my bed.

"How is feeling numb inside not have to do with us?"

"It's not that I don't feel anything. It's just that I don't have that initial fear or need to run that most people have when in a dangerous situation. I used too, but for some reason those feelings all froze; vanished somehow."

More thoughtful than before he continued to stare. "Is that how you feel about us; dead?"

I smiled at his sad expression and took his hand and put it against my chest. "Can you feel how fast my heart is beating? This is what happens when I'm around you. There's absolutely nothing dead about me when you're here. What I told Kyle has nothing to do with what I feel about you. It's all those other things you all want me to share. I prefer to keep those feelings deep down; drown them if I could."

"You can't carry all this inside, Caitlin. No one should have to feel the way you do." He sat next to me and held me in his arms and said nothing more on the subject, but it was my tears that proved the impact his words had on me.

"I didn't mean to make you cry. I'm such an ass," he sighed, and wiped away my tears.

Emotional as I was I kept quiet, but minutes later, Justin broke the silence by saying whimsically, "So, tell me, what crazy things did Kyle buy for my party?"

I sniffed back the tears and answered while attempting to

smile, "He handpicked everything, and I mean each and every last detail. You'll have to see it to believe it."

"He's gone overboard, hasn't he?" He took my hand and kissed it.

"This is Kyle we're talking about. Overboard is his norm."

"He's going to make me regret agreeing to this, isn't he?"

"The only thing I can say is that Kyle has outdone himself," I laughed. "You're going to have fun. Your birthday is going to be one of a kind."

"Is that supposed to reassure me?"

"Kyle arranged every little detail because he wants everybody to have a great time. So, relax. You'll see; you're going to have fun"

"I surely hope so," he responded as he artfully used his weight to make me slide back onto the bed.

"Is there something you want?" I asked playfully as his hand slid to my back, bringing me completely under his weight.

"There is one thing," Justin muttered, bringing his lips down on mine. His touch was maddening. "You're all mine," he mumbled between breaths. "All mine."

The feel of his hand on my bare thigh was agonizing. Justin slowly pushed my nightshirt higher up until his hand was stroking the swell of my back. I arched my body upward wanting him; needing him more and more with every touch.

"Damn it!" He snapped, and bolted off of me. "Abbot is on his way."

"For the love of –," I cursed different profanities under my breath at my uncle's questionable timing. I scrambled up; barely able to stand. Justin grabbed me just as I was about to fall and chuckled at the effect he had on me. "You don't know what you do to my ego," he admitted as he helped me sit on the edge of the bed. He quickly gave me another kiss and sat on the armchair.

I put my face in my hands and breathed in deep to collect myself.

"Are you alright?" Justin asked concerned.

I circled my head to look at him. "You expect me to be fine after all that? How am I supposed to be fine? You're killing me here."

He started laughing; I mean laughing hard.

"Glad you find my torture amusing," I accused and started laughing myself.

"Don't you mean sweet torture?"

The knock on my door came soon after his comment. Sure enough it was my uncle. "Justin, you said it will be a quick visit. Caitlin has finals first thing in the morning."

Justin jumped to his feet and kissed me on the cheek. "Good luck on Bio."

"That's it!" Seeing him walk away was infuriating. "This is ridiculous," I exclaimed, turning to my uncle. "You all know we belong together. There's absolutely no one that can question our Bond. So, why do you insist on keeping us apart?"

"House rules, young lady," Uncle Abbot said preparing to close the bedroom door. "Justin knows my mind. He knows what needs be done if things are to change around here."

"What's that supposed to mean?"

Uncle Abbot simply winked at me and smiled. "Have a nice night, sweetie," he said, and closed the door behind him.

I fell back on my bed and screamed into my pillow.

Time at the Shore

Illustrated for Lines that Bind - Among the Shadows

TWELVE

THE WALK

S I SAT UP IN bed waiting for day break to finally appear, I couldn't help but wonder why Tyler had broken up with Megan. They had seemed to be getting along pretty well, and surely had to have come even closer after our little incident at Harvard Square.

"What the heck was that?" I snapped, jumping to my feet; startled at the sound of something hitting my window. I quickly swung my window open and saw Tyler looking for another something to throw. He was about to pelt the object at my window without even looking.

"Hey, watch it!" I screamed, visibly scaring him.

Without any hesitation he dropped whatever it was he was holding and wiped his hands across his leg. "I need to talk to you," he began in a hushed voiced.

"Why in the world are you whispering? Everybody probably already knows you're down there."

"Fine," he whined, raising his hands in the air. "I still need to talk to you, now! Will you come down or shall I climb up?"

I stared at him for a couple of minutes and then looked down, estimating the distance of his impending fall. "Unless you can fly, I think I'd better come down there. I wouldn't want anything to happen to that pretty face of yours."

He was about to protest when I quickly turned and closed my window. I slipped into my thin, cotton robe and made my way to the back yard as quietly as possible. Not that I had any chance of sneaking around, but the occasion did call for stealth mode. The two Ellri that slept under that roof knew exactly what was going on. I might've been able to fly under the radar, but Tyler surely wasn't. It was only a matter of time that either my aunt or uncle would intervene.

"What is it that it couldn't wait for another couple of hours?" I asked as I slowly closed the door behind me to reduce the annoying screeching.

"Can we walk?"

I nodded. "Are you okay? Is everything okay at home?"

Tyler was preoccupied with his thoughts and kept quiet as we headed towards the stream. The soft light from the early morning sun fought for its rightful place in the sky casting serene shadows on the dewy ground as we traversed the length of the back yard. I felt at peace and thought it would be best to allow Tyler to speak first, seeing that he was the one who dragged me down there at those wee hours.

"I can't do this anymore," he finally protested as he quickly picked up a small rock and flung it into the stream in utter annoyance.

"Tyler, what's going on? You can't do what anymore?" I asked, but seeing that he refused to look at me, I placed my hand on his arm and repeated, "You can't do what anymore?"

He looked down at my hand and shrugged it off. "This," he pronounced and looked away, "I can't keep pretending around you. It's harder than I thought."

"Tyler, look at me. This is ridiculous. You are my best friend. That means more to me than anything in the world."

He conjured up a smile and said, "I'm leaving right after finals."

"Wait! What! What do you mean you're leaving? Leaving where?"

"Anywhere, but Oaks; I need to get away from here."

I closed my eyes and took a deep breath. "Don't you mean you need to get away from me?"

He took a few steps away. "I just can't! It's tearing me up. There's absolutely nothing I can do, Caity." He turned and looked at me again. "How do I heal this? Please tell me! How do I make these feelings go away?"

I felt like somebody had torn out my heart. His face was pain stricken and I was the cause of it all. "You can't leave," I said, taking a step closer. "I'll stay away. I'll even treat you like dirt. I'll make you hate me. You'll see; I can be a real bitch if I want to."

His mouth turned up to a half smile. "You can never do any of those things and you know it. Besides, it'll probably make me love you even more."

I rolled my eyes at him and smacked him hard on the arm. "You're such a stubborn jackass! Why are you doing this? Why would you ever walk away from our friendship?"

"Caity, what am I supposed to do? Tell me? Do you expect me to play the role of the best friend who hangs around until the boyfriend swoops in and takes you away? Am I supposed to pretend that seeing you with Justin isn't painful? That every day I hate myself for hoping something bad might happen to him; that somehow he disappears from your life?" Tyler was now pacing. "Did you hear what I just said? What kind of selfish bastard hopes that for a guy like Justin?"

"You're not selfish," I stated, trying to calm him. "You don't mean any of it."

"But I do!" he insisted as he stopped and faced me.

I shook my head. "I don't believe you. You can't mean it."

"You don't get it, do you?" he asked pushing his disheveled hair back. "I mean it with all my heart, Caity. That's what's killing me."

"You're just confused; that's all."

"Did you know that Justin was the one who stood by me when you disappeared five years ago? Nobody ever explained why you had left and I was so confused. Justin was the one who hung out with me almost every day to make sure I was doing fine. He was the older brother I never had; still is." Tyler took a deep shaky breath. "I'm sick to want something bad to happen to him, but I do."

"Tyler," I snapped, cupping his face with both hands. "You love him. You'd give your life for him, in a heartbeat; as he would for you. What you feel is guilt; guilt for having these ridiculous feelings for me."

"Even so, I can't stay."

"Megan was right," I admitted rather loudly. "What the hell do you people see in me? I mean really! I'm a freaking mess."

"What are you talking about?"

"Look at you, Tyler! You're gorgeous. All the girls at school are crazy about you. What in the world do you want with me?"

"Knock it off, Caity."

"No! I'm serious! Why? Why me?"

"Really? You really want to do this now?"

"Yeah! I want to know, Tyler. What is it that you are drawn to exactly? Because from where I stand, I'm a freaking mess."

"No you're not. You're perfect!"

"You and I both know that I am anything but perfect. I'm a walking disaster."

"No, you are beautiful, sweet and kind and considerate."

"Great! Just Great, Tyler! Why don't you keep all that crap for my epitaph?"

"Caitlin!"

"Oh, don't Caitlin me!" I snapped. "You know exactly what I'm going through right now. How dare you do this to me now? I was wrong! You are selfish." Now I was the one pacing. "God Tyler, we've been through this already."

He grabbed my arm and pulled me closer.

I stared at him, clenching my hands into a fist. "I swear Tyler, if you try kissing me again I'll – I'll snap you in two!"

"Relax, will you?" He started laughing. "I wasn't going to kiss you; not that the thought hadn't crossed my mind. You simply have something in your hair."

"So why the heck are you just standing there? Get it out!"

Tyler continued to laugh softly. "It's just a small white feather. Look!" He handed it to me. "What the heck were you doing, rolling around in bed?"

I blew away the feather refusing to look at him for fear of being found out. Tyler didn't need to know what Justin and I had been up to.

"You're not leaving and that's final," I began, "Where would you go anyway?"

"To my cousins in Europe for a year or two."

"You're serious, aren't you? You've got everything planned out, haven't you? You're seriously going to leave."

"Can you think of any other way? You have Justin. What do I have?"

I stood only inches away. "If this demon gets me, you might not have to leave after all. Did you ever think of that?"

"Is that supposed to be funny?" he answered, pushing me away. "Why do you make jokes about these things? You don't fool me, Caity. I know how frightened you are."

"Why do you care? You're leaving right? So, whatever happens to me from that moment on is none of your damn business. But don't worry. I'll make sure you're invited to the funeral."

He grabbed my arms with force. "Stop it! Just stop saying things like that. Nothing is going to happen to you!"

"Says you."

"No, says me!" Tyler and I jumped out of our skin at the sound of a third voice. We both turned our heads to see Uncle Abbot standing a few yards away. "Is there a good reason why the two of you are standing out here instead of resting up for your finals?" he asked with both hands on his waist.

"Thought the fresh air would do us good," I sassed breaking free of Tyler's grip.

Uncle Abbot did not look at all amused. "You, young man need to get home and get home now!" he bellowed.

"Yes sir, I'm really sorry. I just needed to talk to Caity. I'll be on my way."

Tyler said goodbye and bounced into action.

"One more thing," began Uncle Abbot, stretching out his hand in a motion to stop Tyler, and it worked. My best friend froze in his tracks, and with one slight twitch of my Uncle's wrist Tyler turned and faced him like one of those wind-up robots that turned on command. "Don't go packing just yet young man. You're not going anywhere anytime soon. So you can get that inane idea out of your head. You'll be ascending soon and you have to perfect your gift," My uncle informed him. "Why can't you kids be responsible?" He asked sounding disappointed. "Why do you insist on putting your emotions before your duty? You are in Oaks to learn and grow. Do you both understand?"

"Yes sir," Tyler assured, shifting his gaze to me. "I should be getting home now."

I waved goodbye and watched him walk away.

"I'm a monster," I said softly.

"You are no such thing," responded my uncle as he put his arm around my shoulder. "You can't help how the boy feels. You're fortunate to have so many people care for you."

"I'm unintentionally hurting my best friend. What am I supposed to do?"

"Give him some space. It'll be easier with graduation. You wouldn't need to hang around each other all the time."

"But it's Tyler."

"I know sweetie. Don't you worry we'll keep him busy; keep his mind on more constructive things."

I looked at my uncle. He had this content smile on his face. "I see that you all have your own agenda with Tyler."

"It's for his own good. His gift is as dangerous to him as it can be towards others. He needs to be able to overcome the urge to do harm; to want to hurt others."

"Tyler wouldn't hurt a fly."

"Not yet," my uncle added, stroking my back.

I was quiet for a few minutes. "Okay, I'll try keeping my distance, but it's going to be hard to be without my best friend. Tyler and I are inseparable – joined at the hip."

"Maybe that's the root of all your problems, sweetie. You have grown into a beautiful young lady. The poor boy has been fighting a losing battle."

I let out a sigh.

"It will take Tyler some time, but now that school is over he won't be forced to see you every single day. It will do him good."

"Is that supposed to make me feel better?"

He didn't comment – simply gave me a little squeeze on the arm. We slowly reached the house without another word on the topic of Tyler. It was better this way. I didn't exactly feel at ease discussing this with my uncle.

"I can't believe high school is over. What now? Where do I go from here?" I said walking up the steps.

"College in the Fall."

This was my opportunity to open up the topic about wanting to take a year off. Even though Justin insisted I go straight to college I still felt that I needed a break.

"About college," I started to say entering the house, "I was thinking about postponing it for a year." His face was expressionless. "With all the stuff that's been going on, I think I need a break, wouldn't you agree?"

"True, you've been through much in the past five years,

especially since your return. I understand why you feel you need some time off," he said as he led me into his study.

I was in for a lecture that I was sure of.

"Here, take a seat," he offered, kicking back in his comfortable leather chair. He took a cigar out of the case and trimmed the tip, but didn't light it – just held it between his fingers and pointed to the bookshelves. "Do you see all these? These works of art wouldn't have been possible if these people took some time off." He looked at me for a minute. "What does that even mean? How can somebody take time off from their life? Life has a tendency to follow you wherever you go. How do you take time off? I'd really like to know."

"I didn't mean –"

He waved his hand dismissively. "I know what you meant, Caitlin. It's just that I don't want you to miss out on your future because you need a break from your past. Things happen. Okay, maybe in our world they're a bit extreme, but that's who we are. Going to college will keep you grounded. It will keep you 'normal' as you say. I won't force you, but you should know that Justin will not be following you. What you chose to do, you chose to do alone."

"Why can't he come with me?"

Uncle Abbot stood up and pulled back on the heavy material that covered the large windows and looked outside. "Let's just say he has other responsibilities. There are things that need his immediate attention. You on the other hand are free to do what you want. None of us will stand in your way."

He just gave me his permission to do whatever I wanted, but for some reason it sounded more like a goodbye than anything else.

His voice had a trace of disappointment – a sound I never thought I'd hear from his mouth.

"I haven't made up my mind just yet," I said, attempting to crack a smile. "I've got the whole summer ahead of me to decide."

Uncle Abbot drew the curtain completely to the side letting in the morning light, and then came round the desk and stood in front of me. "Well then, no use fussing about it now, is there?"

"No, I guess there's not," I agreed, "Besides, who knows what might happen until then."

His eyebrow arched exquisitely as it always did when he needed some time to process some important information. "Nothing's going to happen, sweetie," he finally added, "You need to start thinking positively about your future."

"Easier said than done," I huffed.

"Come, come, these discussions are best left after a good night's rest. Now, go. You need a clear head for biology."

"I need a miracle, not a clear head."

"I'm sure you are well prepared. Now, go on. Get some rest."

A dvanced Placement Biology was hard enough, but this final was annoyingly intense. Mr. Maxwell, as always, found questions that not even god himself knew the answers to. The easiest were the first few which centred on meiosis. Cautiously, I continued down the page to the more difficult ones; the ones that seemed to require a medical degree to answer.

Agonizing over whether I should circle answer A or B, I

unintentionally started tapping my pencil to my head as I returned my gaze back to my paper. Before I could even focus on the next impossible question I noticed that Tyler was looking at me from the corner of his eye. He was clearly upset with me. I knew he would be. I purposely arrived late that morning knowing all the seats around him would be taken since all my classmates would have scrambled to get a seat next to the biggest nerd in class. Once in class, I ignored him and took a seat all the way in the back.

I could feel him staring, trying to get my attention, but all that ended the second Mr. Maxwell handed out the murderous exam. My plan was to make Tyler so mad that he hated me. Deep down I knew I was merely ruffling his feathers, but I had to try something.

As soon as I had finished with the final, I handed it in and exited the door; leaving before the rest of my classmates, and by classmates I meant Tyler. I was sure he was staring at me, but I refused to turn around, refused to look at his questionable expression. I simply thanked Mr. Maxwell and headed out to the parking lot and instead of taking the main road back home I walked the long way, cutting through the large estates. It was the only way to avoid him.

Fifteen minutes into my walk, I decided to cut through Nathan and Marlene's grounds which required a bit of a hike through a small, but dense forest that separated their home from the Falcone's. The landscape was quiet and perfectly serene.

Needing some time alone, I slumped down on one of the protruding roots and made myself comfortable by leaning my head back against the towering tree. The view in that light was mesmerizing. Not more than a few feet away, a deer appeared munching on some leaves. I tried to stay perfectly still not wanting to scare the beautiful creature away. I yanked some weeds from the ground and held them out hoping that the deer would come in closer. To my surprise it did. The creature didn't

Sounds of Nature
Illustrated for Lines that Bind - Among the Shadows

look remotely scared; not at all hesitant as I would've thought. Instead, it moved down to my sneakers and nibbled on them a bit, but figured that the grass was much tastier. Then it took a few steps to the side and continued to graze without a worry in the world.

"Beautiful, isn't it?" I heard Ramiel's sweet voice say.

The deer didn't even budge from the sound of his voice.

I looked around excitedly. "Where are you? Show yourself."

His laughter was therapeutic. "Here I am," he announced, drawing my attention. In those seconds a blinding beam of light suffused the entire area as he slowly took human form. The three-thousand-year old child stood a few yards away stroking the wild animal.

"Why isn't it running away?" I asked.

"Why would it run? This beauty has nothing to fear. We mean it no harm." Ramiel plopped down next to me and leaned his head against the tree. "It's quiet here, isn't it?"

"Yes, it's what I needed today."

"For an eighteen-year old, you sure have a lot going on up there," he said and pointed to my head.

I levitated the pine cone off the ground thinking about the first time Kyle showed me what I could do with my powers. I smiled at the memory of that night.

"Nice little trick," Ramiel admitted, letting out a cute chuckle.

"You're not impressed."

"It's a pine cone; should I be?"

"No, I guess not. I have a tendency to levitate things when I'm frustrated. It's a way to keep my mind busy."

"Oh, I see! Then I am impressed."

"Ha, very funny!" I kicked some dirt to the side.

"No, I'm serious. You found a way to deal with your stress. That's a good thing."

I turned my gaze to him. "Everyone thinks I need to talk about things; open up and share my feelings, but the only thing I want to do is break something. I want to scream! I want –," I huffed and kicked some more dirt. "Ramiel, I really don't know what I want."

"Oh," he exclaimed, looking concerned. "What's on your mind?"

"Everything and nothing."

"That's how I feel on most days," he began as he stood up. He held out his small hand to help me up. "You should find an outlet."

I dusted myself off and grabbed my bag. "Levitating things is my outlet."

He giggled. "You're quite gifted. I'm sure you can come up with a better way of working out your problems."

"What would you suggest I do?"

He didn't answer right away. He seemed preoccupied and kept looking down at his feet.

"Ramiel, is everything okay?"

"Yes, everything is fine. I'm just not used to being in human form. It's awkward. I haven't walked around like this in lord knows how long." He smiled.

"I think you need a break as much as I do."

"Take a break from what, Caitlin?"

"I don't know. From all this! Don't you wish that you were like everyone else out there? Living your life with the rest of the world without worrying about watching over people, or angels of death and destruction?"

He chuckled. "We really don't have a choice of who we are. I was born to be what I am as are you. It's natural to feel overwhelmed at times. It's okay to feel like running away. You're but an infant. You must grow into your comfort zone."

"So you think I'll survive all this?"

"First you need to find an outlet for your frustration like any other gifted individual. Juggling things in the air is good exercise if you want to join a circus, but with powers like yours why stop there?"

"What would you have me do?"

Ramiel's brow creased as he was contemplating something. "How are you with heights?" he asked, and smiled wickedly.

"Not a real fan, but I'm not scared of them, if that's what you're asking."

"Good," he pronounced, "Now give me your hand and brace yourself."

"Brace myself for whaaaaaaaa!" I was suddenly free falling at a toxic speed, screaming for dear life. "Ramiel! Ramiel!" I kept yelling between the screaming fits, as I sliced fiercely through the air, unable to do anything to save myself. "Ramiel!"

"Isn't this therapeutic?" I heard him say in my head. "You did say you wanted to scream, didn't you? So, scream!"

"I'm going to die!"

He chuckle. "No you're not."

"I'm going to hit the ground and die!"

"What ground?" he asked filling my mind with his laughter.

It took me a while to realize, but I finally saw what he meant. I was falling and falling with no end in sight. "There you go," I heard him say. "No ground to crash into, so just let go of it all and get control of your body. You're all over the place."

"Are you kidding me?"

"Caitlin!" he snapped, "Stop analyzing every little thing, and enjoy the feeling of being completely free."

My mind wasn't equipped to process the situation, so I closed my eyes instead and allowed the wind to whip by me as

I continued to descend at a frightful pace.

"How do you feel?" Ramiel asked.

"Scared out of my freaking mind!" I yelled.

"Closing your eyes defeats the purpose of this exercise," he advised. "Open your eyes, Caitlin and enjoy the drop. Scream till your voice dies out."

With hesitation I slowly opened my eyes, and started screaming again at the sheer speed at which I was plummeting. I suddenly felt faint and drained of energy.

"I thought you said you're not scared of heights." I heard Ramiel say.

"I don't want to do this anymore," I yelled, "Please make it stop."

"If you want to stop falling, you'll have to stop it yourself."

"What! How am I supposed to do that?"

"Well, you best think of something fast because I think I see land down there." He started laughing again.

"Ramiel!" I yelled again. "This isn't funny! Get me the hell out of this."

"No! Get yourself out," he scolded.

"Ramiel!"

"Look, is that Oaks down there," I heard him say as he let out a boyish chuckle.

My fear of death quickly vanished only to be replaced by anger. With my eyes closed I summoned my gift to return me to where I was; safe and sound on the forest floor.

"You can open your eyes now, Caitlin." Ramiel's sweet voice was lined with pride. "You did it, young lady. Good for you."

I looked around and noticed that we were in the exact spot

where we started. "Did I even move from here? Was it some kind of trick?"

"I'm many things, but a magician I am not."

"So you're saying that I was really falling to my death."

"Don't be so dramatic. Yes, you were falling, but to your death you were not. It was invigorating, wasn't it?"

"Was it? I couldn't tell. All the screaming got in the way."

He started laughing. "I'm sorry, I thought it'd help you let loose."

I grabbed my schoolbag off the ground and headed up the path through the woods. "Next time a little warning would be nice."

"Next time, you can do that without my help."

I turned to him and pulled a face. "There won't be a next time."

"Oh, come on Caitlin, you know deep down you want to try that again. I know you are a perfectionist and getting control of that fall will haunt you unless you perfect it."

"And why would I need to get control? Wasn't the whole thing meant for me to let go?"

"Well it was in a way, but it can also help you home in on your emotions. Just then, you stopped falling because anger kicked in and you wanted it to stop. Can you imagine what you can do if you had absolute control of what you felt? You can be anywhere you wish and do anything you set your mind on, and I mean that in the most literal sense. Next time –,"

"Next time!" I exclaimed cutting him off.

"Yes, how do you feel about deep sea diving?"

"Will that be with or without an oxygen tank?"

Ramiel shrugged his shoulders and smiled wickedly, "I'm

having fun, Caitlin. Thank you for that."

"I'm happy that my near death experience has brought you so much joy."

He leaned in and pushed me playfully as we headed along the stream cutting across the Falcone property and then over to Justin's estate.

"That's sweet," Ramiel said out of nowhere.

"What is?" I asked, looking at his quirky little smirk.

"Your heart is beating faster. Should I ask why?"

I blushed. "I guess I can't hide much from you, can I?"

He shook his head no.

"I can feel how close Justin is. That's what's causing my heart to beat like it is."

"Oh, I see. It's amazing how you both can sense each other. I felt the potency of your bond in Tirion." I stopped and stared at him. "You were there, weren't you?" I didn't wait for an answer. "Of course you were. All the Nobe were. Are you part of the Council? Alexander was there as well, wasn't he?"

"Yes we were there, but it really doesn't matter what seat we hold."

"Why Tirion? Why do you all chose to meet there?" I asked.

"You still don't get it, do you? Once you step into the Inner Realm you can be anywhere. It was you who was in Tirion, not us. The Energy Stone gave you entrance. Much like the doors to the Chamber of Enlightenment; much like your solace, if you ever learn to access the good bits."

"You see how annoyingly frustrating everything is? Ramiel, there should be a manual."

"I'll take it under advisement." He laughed as we continued down the path

"I transcended without leaving my physical body in Tirion, but then so did Gabriel."

"He has ascended. Once you ascend your gift will be one with your earthly body. You will slip in and out in a blink of an eye, more so than any other. That's what you just did on your free-fall."

"I figured as much."

"Once you ascend you will harness the power of your ability to transcend with your earthly body, but you need control. I pulled you into the Inner Realm without you even realizing it."

"I'm doomed to die, aren't I?"

"No! You are simply learning our ways. There's much to take in for someone so young."

"Can Justin do the same?"

"Ah, Justin," he said in admiration. "That boy can do so much more. Truly gifted he is. Your bond has accelerated his evolution. He is a wonder by any means."

"What does that mean? Why are you all so enamored by him?"

"Aren't you enamored?"

"Yes, but I can assure you for different reasons."

He started laughing again. The sweet sound was like a melody in the wind. "Do you know you blush every time you talk about him? I don't even have to mention his name and you're brighter than the sun."

I didn't comment.

We were nearing the crumbling wall that divided the two properties. "This was truly invigorating," he admitted, "No wonder Alexander takes those long walks,"

"Yeah, it's supposed to clear the mind."

"We're going to have to do this again, Caitlin."

"Of course, but I should get you one of these,"

I pulled out my MP3. "You can listen to music while you walk."

"I already listen to music. It's all around us."

"I can't hear anything."

"That's because your mind is preoccupied with nonsense."

I took a minute to register what he said.

"I should be going," he voiced, slowly fading away.

Not ready to let him leave, I quickly asked, "Ramiel, would you like something to eat? You eat don't you?"

"Thank you for your gracious offer, but I must decline. Maybe some other time."

I looked at him surprised.

"What's that look for," he asked.

"I don't know. I was expecting you to say that you don't eat; that immortals don't need food."

"We are living organisms, Caitlin. We just serve a different realm. We are not dead."

"I just can't imagine the Nobe eating, that's all?"

"You probably ate with a Nobe and didn't even know it."

"How can that be?"

Suddenly, Ramiel started shape shifting; changing into different people that lived in town. He transformed from one person to another effortlessly. "You see, it's that easy."

"That's so cool! You can be anybody you chose."

"Only in appearance; we don't actually take the body of another human. Not unless he's soul has left the vessel. But even then we would never morph into somebody that has died. Can you imagine the tribulation if their loved ones suddenly saw the dead walking around ordering French fries? It's spooky."

"So how does one know that they are talking to the real person and not the Nobe?"

"They don't! That's the whole point of taking human form. We are meant to blend in, make sure everything flows as it should."

"Apart from you and Alexander, no other Nobe ever appeared to me in human form."

"The only reason my master chose to appear to you is because somebody wasn't playing fair. There are rules that we follow, and when those rules are not upheld he steps in to remedy the situation. You didn't know who he was until recently."

"I suspected he was special," I admitted, scrambling to find another question. "Why do you call him master? You're both Nobe! Why would you feel inferior to him?"

He smiled. "By no means do I feel inferior. I do it out of respect. There is nothing about Alexander that evokes superiority. He says he's six-thousand years old, but I suspect he's much older. He is one of the dinosaurs. I'm pretty sure he's older than either of the brothers – Bernael and Abaddon. The power that Alexander has comes from way back. He's the one who put that scar on Bernael's face. You should see what he did to Abaddon when he tried to take the life of a non-gifted. The Ancient is the reason why the Fallen keep away."

My eyes couldn't get any wider. "The war – why did all those gifted have to die if he's so powerful?"

"I can only speculate, but I believe that the Ancient saw our doom. Saw our future. He would never intervene with the natural order of things. If the gifted were dead set on killing each other the best he could do is try talking them out of it. Try to bring peace. It's the reason he's so bent on bringing balance to the Nobe. He wants peace – a utopia for our kind."

"Does Alex really think that something like that is even possible?"

"Caitlin, Justin now knows everything. He can tell you exactly who Alexander is and the other one which I'd rather not mention. It was all in the Book of Truths." Ramiel looked away into the distance once again, and fell in deep silence. "I've said too much as is."

"Please don't stop now."

For some reason Ramiel started laughing.

"What is it?" I asked. "What's so funny?"

"Alexander just informed me that I'm a Watcher not a Talker." He laughed again. "The walk was wonderful, Caitlin. Thank you for allowing me to tag along."

"Ramiel," I quickly said, stopping him from disappearing. "Am I pathetic for wanting a break from it all?"

"No, you are in no way pathetic."

"What then?"

"You are but a child thrown into situations beyond your grasp and asked to solve problems; problems that you yourself did not create."

"So what now? What am I supposed to do?"

"Sink or swim, Caitlin; it's your choice. But keep in mind that these waters are full of creepy critters that are out for your blood," he warned before disappearing.

I stood in serene surroundings until I turned to head home.

THIRTEEN

THE BIG BAD WOLF

THERE WAS ABSOLUTELY no way of avoiding anyone in Oaks. A few yards up ahead, I spotted Tyler sitting on the bench under the Willow tree. He knew I always sat there when I needed to disappear.

"You're impossible," I yelled as I approached him. "What are you doing here? Wasn't the cold treatment hint enough to stay away?"

"You're being ridiculous," he roared, "So what now? You're going to pretend I don't exist?"

"You know what they say; out of sight out of mind."

Tyler shook his head. "How about distance makes the heart grow fonder; did you think of that?"

We both started laughing at our stupid conversation and I took a seat on the bench. "I'm sorry. I thought I'd give it a try and see how things go."

Tyler sat down as well. "Well, thanks to you I might not do well in Bio. I couldn't concentrate."

"I didn't mean for you to do bad on the exam."

"Don't apologize to me. I can afford one bad mark. You need to apologize to the whole second row who was copying off my sheet."

"Oh no! I didn't even think of that."

"You're wicked," he accused, chuckling at my inability to keep a straight face.

"Was Megan at least one of those who copied? Please say yes!"

"You're really enjoying this, aren't you?"

"Shouldn't I be? It's tiring to always be nice."

He was quite again and wrung his hands in front of him. "Don't blame Megan. I told her how I felt about you. I didn't think she'd take it so hard."

I shoved him lightly. "Why did you go and do something so stupid?"

He squirmed away. "What did you expect me to do? It's the truth. I simply told the truth. What else was I supposed to say? Sorry Meg, we have to end this because you're annoyingly obnoxious and getting on my damn nerves. Is that what I should've said?"

I started laughing and kissed him on the cheek.

"What was that for?" he asked beaming.

"All this time I thought you had completely lost your mind for dating her. I mean the girl is beautiful, but still; how could you?"

"She wasn't always like that. When you left she was real cool to be with. You seem to bring out the worst in her."

"Well she can go back to her cool self if she wants. School is over. She won't have to set eyes on me ever again."

"You realize we live in a small town, right? I mean you'll run into each other eventually."

"Not if I can help it," I pronounced, getting to my feet. "So, what are you doing here, anyway?"

"We have to study for History, did you forget?"

I pulled him to his feet. "No, I didn't forge. I just thought I'd study alone." I started giggling, "Wouldn't want to cause you any more emotional scars. How will you be able to concentrate with all the love you have for me?"

"In a good mood, are we?" Tyler asked, playfully pushing me to the side. "Now you're being silly."

"I'm silly? You're the one who's declaring your love for me and I'm the silly one?"

"I meant all that and you know it!"

"I know you meant it. It's just twisted. Of course we love each other. We've been best friends since birth. It's not romantic love you feel. It's the love you feel for a sister."

"I have a sister, Caity and trust me; I don't feel this way about her. You are constantly in here," he admitted, pointing to his head. "I can't get you out of my freaking mind. It's maddening. It really is and the things I want to –"

I couldn't help myself. I acted on impulse. I slapped poor Tyler so hard across the face that my palm stung on impact.

"What the hell was that for?" he barked, holding his reddened cheek.

"I forbid you to think of me in that way ever again. It's sick and twisted!"

"That hurt, Caity!" he complained rubbing his cheek.

"You big buffoon; it serves you right!"

"You know, you've made a habit of slapping me," he

laughed, "I like it! You're so feisty and hot when you're angry."

"You're sick!" I exclaimed stumping away. "Sick!"

I stopped before I entered the house and turned to him again. "Next time I'll put a little extra something in my slap to remember me by." He started laughing that annoying laugh of his. "Are you coming inside or are you going to continue laughing like an idiot?" I fumed, holding the door open.

He laughed even louder as he followed me to the kitchen. Uncle Abbot was there with Aunt Leslie trying real hard to stifle their laughter.

"Oh, go ahead laugh," began Tyler taking a seat. "Is nothing sacred in this town?"

Kyle came in along with Emily and sat at the table. "Is that your palm print on his face?" Kyle asked me.

"I didn't mean it to be that hard."

"Sure you didn't," said Emily getting an icepack from the fridge. "Here Tyler, keep this on for a few minutes."

"You're kidding me right?" Tyler said. "I can bring people back from the dead, but you don't think I can fix a slap across the face?"

"Then why the heck do you still have that mark across your cheek?" Emily asked and sat down across form him.

He chuckled and winked at me. "It simply feels good."

I was about to attack Tyler again when Kyle held me back.

"Let me go! The boy is demented. I need to set him free," I screamed lashing out at Tyler.

My uncle simply got up and walked out of the kitchen.

Kyle held me tighter. "You don't want to hurt your friend, now do you?"

"Yes I do! Someone needs to slap some sense into him."

"Allow me," said Justin as he walked into the kitchen.

The overly hushed atmosphere was quite tense with Justin still standing there staring at my best friend. Nobody had said a word. Tyler's head instantly lowered.

Aware of how bad my best friend must've felt I went and stood behind him and folded my arms around his shoulders.

"The only one that's allowed to touch him is me!" I took the seat next to Tyler, after giving him a soft smack on the arm. In seconds the mark I left on his face disappeared.

Tyler was about to get up to leave when Justin stopped him by saying, "Tyler, you came here to study, right? I think Caitlin needs your help."

I nudged Tyler in the ribs. "That's right, I do. So what are we having for lunch? I'm starving," I announced, trying to break the icy atmosphere.

"What, you're actually going to eat?" asked Kyle responding to my feigned enthusiasm over the aspect of actually eating.

Justin turned and stared at me. "Haven't you been eating?"

Aunt Leslie motioned everyone to sit at the table while she served lunch. "Caitlin's been off food for a while now," she informed him, serving me a heap full of mashed potatoes.

Both Tyler and Justin turned and stared at me.

"What? What are you both looking at?" I yelled, pushing the dish aside. Kyle instantly chuckled under his breath. I kicked him hard under the table and the smile was instantly wiped from his face.

"You need to stop hitting people," he complained. "It's not lady like."

Emily shook her head. "I knew you looked a bit different, but I didn't expect you to be starving yourself."

"I'm not starving myself," I barked. "I just have this real bad taste left over from my visit with Bernael."

"Bernael!" Justin began as he stood up. "Why haven't you said anything? Why the hell do you keep this stuff from me?"

He was mad. I mean real mad, and nobody looked up. Instead, they all chose to stare down at their plates except for my aunt.

"What do you want me to tell you?" I began, "So, I haven't eaten a square meal in the last week, so what? It's not worth getting bent out of shape over."

"You never think anything is worth getting bent out of shape over, do you?"

I stood up infuriated that he wanted to start this argument in front of everybody. "What is that supposed to mean?" I yelled angrily. I shifted my gaze to Kyle knowing we had the same conversation in Cambridge. "This is your doing, isn't it?" I accused my cousin. "Stupid me, and here I thought I could confide in you!"

Kyle was about to speak when Justin motioned him to stop. "This has nothing to do with Kyle. This is all your doing and your incessant need to keep everything bottled up."

"So you all side with Justin; is that it?" None spoke. "Fine," I exclaimed and was about to leave when Justin grabbed my arm and pulled me to a full stop. "Where are you off to again?" he asked annoyed.

I instantly pulled away. "Is this some kind of intervention?" I asked, seeing that my uncle came to stand opposite me, looking rather concerned. "Why are you all doing this? Why now of all times? You don't think I have enough on my plate; is that it?"

Aunt Leslie took a step forward. "It's because you have so much on your mind that we worry. You're locked away somewhere in there," she began and pointed to my heart. "We can't just sit back and watch you beat yourself up and now you're even off your food. I'm worried that this is the start of something bigger."

I could feel my anger percolating. "I'm perfectly fine," I repeated through clenched teeth trying to restrain my temper. "I've already explained why I haven't been eating. I'm sure it'll fade away soon." I took a deep breath and circled to face my uncle. "I'm fine!"

Tyler pushed back his seat and stood. "You're such a bad liar," he accused, shifting his gaze to my aunt. "She's been distant in school too. She can't seem to concentrate on anything."

"Why would you say that? Everything is fine at school. I've kept my grades up and we have fun, don't we?"

"Sure, you laugh on the surface, but we all know you do it for our sake. You always do things to make others happy."

"Since when is that a bad thing?" I yelled.

Justin ran his fingers through his hair. "Why are you so unwilling to break out of this shell? Do you really think I can't feel how depressed you've become? With your Ascension being so close I'm afraid that you'll be consumed with all these suppressed emotions. You will be an easy target for Bernael. He feeds on this negative energy."

"Bernael!" I snorted contemptuously. "Do you think he matters to me? None of them matter. Don't you get it? There is nothing left for them to take. I feel absolutely empty!" I glared at Justin, hating him for forcing me to say these things. "I'm dead inside, remember? Is that what you want to hear? Are you all satisfied to know that I feel nothing?" Tears started to sting my eyes. "I died the minute you sent me away five years ago. Something broke inside of me and I haven't been able to mend it. There's nothing that these demons can do, that you all didn't do yourselves."

Emily looked away visibly upset.

"Don't turn away," I told her. "You all want to know what I carry inside me, don't you? Why turn away now?"

She looked at me with tears in her eyes. "Caitlin I'm so –"

"I don't want your pity," I yelled cutting her apology short. "I hit bottom at thirteen. Do you really think that Bernael can ever top that? Do you really think I didn't pray for death? I prayed for it every painful night. Prayed that it will all stop, but as you all know it didn't."

Justin took a step closer.

"No!" I yelled, pushing him away, ignoring his strained expression. "You started this. You're going to stand there and listen."

"Caitlin –," Uncle Abbot said coming closer.

I lifted my hand and motioned for him to stop. "I don't need your gift to calm me down Uncle. You all want me to feel all this; express my deepest emotions, my suppressed feelings. Well, there you have it. I don't fear death because I stared at it in the face night after night at Stone Hurst. I fought the urge. knowing how much easier it would've been to end it all." I took a deep breath and scanned their tense expressions one more time. "The reason I don't fear anything is because I'm my worst enemy." I scuffed. "I realized that at Tirion when I was so willing to dive off that damn cliff; so willing to end it all."

I laughed and cried together as I stood there feeling naked.

"There's nothing that anyone can do to me that I haven't thought of doing to myself. So you'll all have to forgive me if I don't flinch in the face of evil. Sorry, if I don't scare easily. Your lives are the only things that matter to me and if that means forfeiting my own lifeless soul to save yours; then be it."

I felt exposed and refused to be the object of their pity. Justin called out my name as I pushed past my uncle and exited the house from the back entrance.

I stood there, on the steps to the back yard with clenched fists and said under my breath, "Take me to the woods." Within seconds everything was a blur, as the sound of the wind swooshed past my ear and minutes later I came to a complete stop. Once again, I found myself in the serene environment of the dense forest where I knew nobody could track me nor read my thoughts.

I walked around aimlessly wondering why they all pushed so hard. I was dealing with things just fine on my own. *I was, wasn't I?* I thought taking a much needed deep breath. I shook my head irritated at how easily I got mad. They all meant well and I simply snapped.

Just then, as I stood looking up at the canopy of trees the feeling of evil trailed up my spine. My wrists instantly started to thud against my skin and a dark grey mist started crawling its way around my ankles as it did the last time I came into contact with it. This time Ramiel wasn't there to warn me. Nobody was there to save me.

"Bernael!" I yelled agitated beyond belief. "I've already seen your unforgettable face. Why toy with me now?"

A husky laugh bounced off the trees causing the birds to flutter away from the sinister sound. "You're going to be fun to torture," he taunted as he materialized in front of me.

I didn't move; didn't even flinch at the sight of him. A well balanced individual would've most likely have fainted or at least tried to run away. But there I was; cold and unaffected as the very dirt I stood on.

Bernael took a step closer and trailed his long dark finger down the side of my face. "I don't know if I should start by ripping out your heart or snapping your neck," he slithered as he stared at me with his blood-red eyes.

"I'd go with the neck. I doubt if you can find a heart anywhere in there," I mused, pointing to my chest. "There were others who beat you to it." He smiled. "A genuine smile coming from the angel of darkness; I couldn't ask for anything more out of life."

"You are a rare one; I'll give you that," he slithered as he folded back his long flowing sleeves.

"What you call rare, others might call stupid," I began, staring at his exposed arm, and there in the fold of his elbow was a mark much like the ones the Ellri bore. Distinct in that it was more prominent against his dark skin.

"I wouldn't call you stupid young mortal," he hissed, kicking back his long rob as he effortlessly glided across the moist earth, moving in a circular motion as he looked up to the sky with his eyes partially closed. He was clearly checking for something; a possible intruder, maybe. Whatever the reason for his actions, he looked like a predator laying claim to his prey.

"If you have any kindness in you, don't call me mortal. Caitlin will do." I said drawing his attention.

Instantly he was only inches away, staring at me. He smiled again. His razor sharp teeth were a frightful sight, but my eyes focused only on his disfigurement. "It must've been an unusually deep wound to leave such a defined scar," I began softly, unintentionally speaking my thoughts. The scar ran from the hairline of his brow all the way down the side if his face just missing his eye.

"Does the sight of my scar scare you mortal?" he asked purposely ignoring my plea as he took a step away.

"No more than your teeth," I said smiling. "To be honest the whole appearance is really working for you."

He came even closer to my face; his breath was surprisingly warm against my stone cold complexion. Bernael closed his eyes and inhaled deeply through his nose. "I smell no fear in you," he snarled in a deep raspy voice and took a step back; swiftly circling the perimeter again. Seconds later he was up in my face again. "Are you always this transparent with your emotions?" he asked taking another whiff.

"Apparently not," I huffed, thinking that it was those emotions that brought me to the forest in the first place. "It would seem you bring out the best in me. Strange isn't it? I feel more comfortable around you than I do with the people I love. How distorted is that?"

Expressionless, he stared at me as he said, "I sense tremendous anger, hatred even, and much self-inflicted pain." Bernael stroked my cheek with his hand. "You seem to wear your scars on the inside young mortal." He inhaled again. "Ah yes, there it is; young, untamed love; deep seeded for someone so young, but yet you are entirely devoid of fear; I sense none."

He kicked the opening of his robe to the side visibly

annoyed with the material that draped over his earthly body. Bernael seemed ridiculously uncomfortable in his human form as was Ramiel earlier. Again he fell silent as he seemed to be distracted by something. He stared up at the sky and took a sniff of the air.

"Don't let my cool exterior fool you," I began, trying to explain my lack of the basic human trait. "I do fear you."

"To fear is to cherish your own life. You cherish not. You fear not. I sense what you feel way deeper than you yourself are aware of. I know what is in that soul of yours mortal; know how bleak you see everything. You question your own reason for living. It is endearing to see someone so young who does not value their own life."

Bernael turned his head up again, sniffing the air for something.

"You can sense all that, can you?" I asked as I swallowed back the pain that truth alone could incite. "How did you find me anyway? Nobody can sense me or read my thoughts to locate me."

He circled to face me. "I can feel pain. I am drawn to it, and you have been this way for many, many years mortal. From the time you lost your parents. I don't even have to search for you anymore. I sense it as intense as you do."

"So, you always knew where I was?"

"Yes, your pain was my pain," he said indulgingly.

"Sorry to hear that," I muttered as I dropped my gaze to the ground. "That's an awful gift to be stuck with."

Without warning, he grabbed me by the neck and dangled me in the air. "I wouldn't say awful. I thrive on it. It quenches my thirst."

I didn't fight him. It made no sense to pretend. He could kill me faster than I could blink.

"You give up too easily," he offered, releasing his hold.

I dropped to the hard uneven earth like a ragdoll, and slowly sat up with my back against the tree. "So, will this execution take long?" I asked, rubbing my throat. Unlike the last time it burnt where he touched me. "Is this how painful your scar was when you first got it?"

He didn't answer. Bernael again sniffed the air with his eyes closed.

"Why don't you get a healer to fix your scar?" I asked, getting to my feet as I dusted myself off.

He looked at me and smiled. "Why would I want to ruin this masterpiece? It's a reminder."

I placed my hand on my neck trying to extinguish the burn from his touch. "A reminder of what?" I finally asked.

"To return the favor to the person who put it there."

The second he finished his sentence my gift soared out of control. Bernael was talking about Alexander. There was no way I was ever going to allow that to happen; no matter how powerful this demon was.

"Ah, anger," he snarled, "Most powerful of all emotions; leaves a good taste in my gut."

I was literally glowing. I hadn't even transcended but my body was pulsating to the beat of my heart. The glow got brighter and brighter.

"Impressive for someone so young, but what now young mortal?"

"You stay the hell away from Alexander or –"

"Or what, infant?"

"I'll send you to hell myself." I yelled.

His laugh was more like a bark. Bernael took a step closer. "Hell is but a place where evil presides. Trust me child, I am much worse than any hell you can fathom. Do not presume to know me. I can cause you great damage."

"Why don't you come closer and test your theory, demon," I yelled completely beside myself. My need to protect Alex was overwhelming. My gift was escalating even more as I spoke.

Bernael took a step closer but stopped abruptly.

"Let me save you the trouble old man," I yelled, lessening the distance between us. "Does this make you uncomfortable?"

He smiled knowingly. "I'm impressed by your bravery, insignificant mortal child. It's stupid, but impressive."

"Touch me if you dare," I challenged.

He hesitated, "I don't wish to kill you just yet, child." His voice slithered deep into my subconscious. It was like an echo in the wind.

"Kill me? You can't even touch me!" I bellowed hating everything about this grotesque being.

A deep menacing growl came out of his mouth taking me by surprise. With blazing speed, his fierce grip was once again clasped around my throat, this time burning every inch he touched. I felt inconceivably frail and drained of all source of energy. I felt faint.

Bernael pinned me against the tree with a back-breaking slam and inched closer to my face. With his free hand he traced his finger down my jaw line and his black nail felt like a serrated knife slicing through my skin.

"So frail," he began in a soft sensual voice. "Piece by piece you fall apart, rotting slowly from the inside. One wrong move and you'll end up like me young mortal." He looked deep into my eyes and then leaned in to whisper in my ear. "Take it from one who knows; sometimes even to live is an act of courage. I have also forgotten the taste of fear long ago. Continue on this path and you will soon become as I am."

Deep in the Woods
Illustrated for Lines that Bind - Among the Shadows

He let go of his grip and took a step back to look upon me in distaste. I could hardly stand or able to lift my head to look at him. The taste of my own blood slowly made its way down my face and to my mouth.

"You're a coward!" I screamed with tears rolling down my

eyes. "Why don't you just finish this here and now? He wants me doesn't he? Well, what are you all waiting for?"

His expression was strained. "I will not fulfill your wish today no matter how much you push. I will not be your executioner just yet."

Bernael suddenly turned his head to the side taking another deep sniff of the air. With a low moan he simply vaporized into a light grey mist and disappeared amongst the trees.

Curious to see what might've triggered his sudden departure, I turned in the direction he was looking to, and to my unbounded astonishment and relief, the figure that appeared out of nowhere was Justin himself, who stood there looking furious.

"Oh great!" I exhaled. "If it's not one thing it's another!"

He walked over to me in deafening silence. Drops of blood trickled onto my shirt as I attempted to lift myself into an upright position, but it was hopeless as I had no energy to keep my balance. Justin was about to lend a hand, but I pushed it away. "I don't need any of you!" I spat out. "I was just about to deal with all these pent up emotions as you were all so gracious to point out. Why did you interrupt?" I asked glaring at him.

His expression was unyielding, but still, not a word.

"What? No lecture? No yelling at how I keep my feelings to myself." He extended his hand for me to take. "Please Caitlin." His voice was shaky, his teeth clenched. "I'm this close to going after him for doing this to you. Let me help you."

Justin pulled me into his arms. I leaned my head against his chest and cried into his shirt. "What's wrong with me?" I sobbed, feeling faint. "I don't feel –,"

Before I could finish my sentence, everything went dark.

FOURTEEN

PROPHECY

I SLIPPED IN AND out of sleep for a couple of hours, but Justin was nowhere in sight. The inflamed mark around my neck was what kept me from thinking that it was but a bad dream. I put my hand up to my face only to feel the bandage that covered the cut Bernael had so graciously left me. Surprisingly, it didn't hurt as much as the burn around my neck.

"Stupid!" I muttered as I pushed myself in a sitting position. "What the heck was I thinking? Real stupid Caitlin; real stupid," I whispered, leaning my head back up against the headboard. "Why do I do these things?" I mumbled, burying my head in my knees.

"Glad to have you among the living," Justin jested as he entered his room through the open French doors, which led to a balcony overlooking the lush green fields that made up the Bradford property.

"I went and outdid myself again, didn't I?"

He cracked a weak smile and sat on the edge of his bed. "As long as you're okay, that's all that matters."

Tears started to roll down my face as soon as I met his gaze. "Justin, that's just it, I'm not okay. All of you were right. I'm a basket case."

"It's my fault," he admitted, and softly wiped my tears with his hand. "I shouldn't have pushed you. Not now; not with all this hanging over your head. You just seem so in control sometimes, but I can feel how you really are underneath. I was wrong. You should deal with these issues your own way."

"Yeah, okay!" I huffed as I pushed myself off the bed and headed out to the balcony. "You saw how I deal with things. I'm a complete and utter mess." I crossed the marble tiles and leaned against the cast iron hand rail. Within seconds, Justin came and stood behind me. "He's not going to kill me," I noted, turning to his concerned expression. "He'd rather torture me first."

"He's just playing with your weaknesses. He doesn't like that you've made it so easy for him."

"Made it easy? That's an understatement. I'm not remotely in the same league as he is."

"I wouldn't go that far." Justin leaned with his back against the dark patina rail. Caringly, he pushed my hair behind my ear with one hand. "He's just more experienced in using his gift. He knows you're special. He saw it in the way your gift responded." Justin almost smiled again. "Trust me, you had his full attention."

Shaken by the thought, I looked out at the beclouded horizon. "It wasn't his attention that I wanted," I confessed, feeling even more ashamed for wanting to end it all.

"I know," he muttered sounding sad.

The tension between us was palpable as we both stood there in utter silence. Justin finally took a deep breath and turned his gaze to me and asked, "Where does that leave us?"

"Us?" I pronounced, looking at him questionably.

"Yes damn it; us! Where do I fit in – in this suicidal path you've chosen to take? Apparently, what we have isn't enough for you."

"You are everything to me," I cried.

"Am I?" Justin yelled. "Is that why you're so willing to end it all? You love me so much that you want to tear out my soul?"

"You know it's not like that," I pronounced looking away momentarily, unable to handle his disappointed gaze.

"Then what the hell is it?"

I circled my tear stained face to look at him again. "I'm drowning! Don't you understand?" My voice was shaky with every syllable I uttered. "I'm suffocating from it all, but it's you that keeps me sane. You are the only reason why I'm still standing here. Don't ever doubt that. I can't allow any of them to hurt you!"

Justin held me by the arms and leaned his head against my forehead. "How do you think that makes me feel? I don't need saving Caitlin. What I need is you! I need you to fight for what we have; fight to live to enjoy it." He kissed me lightly on the top of my head. "This destructive path you're on is submerging you into darkness. Sooner or later, it will consume your every thought.

Feeling stupid, I lowered my head and said as I wiped my tears with the cuff of my sleeve, "Bernael warned me of the same thing."

Justin coaxed my head up so that I could face him. "He of all people should know how these feelings can drown a person."

I sniffed back the tears. "How do you mean?"

He slowly ran his hand down the length of my cheek. "Bernael wasn't born into darkness; nobody is."

"So why is he the way he is?"

"Pain – lots and lots of pain," Justin began as he took a step back. "He's not the monster that you see. His real human form is that of a sixteen-year-old. That's how old he was when he became immortal. He had ascended days before the war broke out. His family was one of the many who wanted power over the Council; power to control all life."

"Sixteen!" I exclaimed stunned.

"Yes. It is written that the Fallen are of the first pure blood lines. They ascended much younger than we do. Bernael was angelic in appearance. Alexander describes him as the 'Kiss of God' in the book."

"So how does he go from being angelic to being the demon that he is now?"

"More or less the way you're slipping," he explained, turning sideways to look at me. "Bernael's gift was rather unique growing up. He was able to absorb all of humanities pain and anguish. He senses things in people that no one else can explain. He brought hope to the people that he touched. His gift, of course, had the darker side to it, but he never delved into the darkness; not until his family was all killed in the war. He drowned in sorrow; suffocated as you put it. Alexander tried for many, many millennia to bring him out of it, but nothing seemed to help. Bernael blamed Alexander for not putting an end to the war. Even tried to attack him once, but once was all he got. Alexander brought him to his knees and branded him once with the mark of servitude to the darkness on his arm and a second time for trying to lash out on him."

"I saw the branded mark he has on the inside of his arm, and I can guess the deep scar down the side of his face was the other?"

Justin nodded. "Yeah, that would be it."

"Alexander must've been really hurt to want to do that to him. It doesn't sound like something he would do, unless he had no other choice, but still, where was Bernael's brother in all this? Why didn't Abaddon help him?"

"They're not actual brothers. They belong to different bloodlines. Abaddon is much older and chose the darkness way before his first ascension. He was a healer like Tyler, but loved the feel of taking life much, much more. It's easier for them to kill than save. When they save a life their energy is drained leaving them tired and miserable, but when they take a life they feel euphoric, like being high on drugs. The two demons met up many years later."

My neck suddenly started to burn. I fanned it with my hand, but nothing seemed to help.

"You didn't even blink when he held you by the neck," Justin said as he pulled my hand away. "Let it heal itself."

"You were there?"

"You didn't think I'd leave you in the middle of the forest with the big bad wolf, did you?"

"So it was you that he sensed."

"He wasn't sure what he sensed."

"So why did you let him do this to me?"

"You're the one intent on dying. Consider it therapy."

"Why doesn't anyone understand what I'm going through? I don't want to die!"

Justin raised an eyebrow.

"Okay, well now I don't. I never actually do. I think I'm going through menopause or something."

Justin started laughing. "Menopause?"

"Oh sure, laugh! How else would you explain these drastic mood swings?"

"You've blown a fuse. You need time. You were right, you do need a break!"

I started pacing back and forth from one side of the balcony all the way across to the other. "I challenged Bernael; called him a coward," I muttered, turning to Justin who was leaning with his back against the rail. I inhaled deeply the second his gaze caught mine. His white linen shirt caught what little beams of light escaped from the cloud covered sky. It created an ethereal outline against his toned body, accentuating every curve and perfectly sculptured muscles.

"I should be on medication," I continued to say smiling at the way he made me feel. "I do fear him, now. But when I'm there in the middle of everything, something takes over; something snaps. The fear vanishes completely. I don't know how else to explain it."

"It's your gift," I heard a third voice say. The simplicity in the tone stopped us cold as we turned to find Alexander's airy apparition slowly taking form through the flowing curtains that waved in the soft breeze. "Your gift responds instinctively and allows the adrenaline to take over, but take Bernael's warning to heart."

Alexander took a step forward materializing into his usual

human form. "If you don't find a constructive way to express all this anger you will lose yourself to it."

"Why would a demon like Bernael feel the need to warn me? Doesn't he want me to be like him?"

"He wouldn't wish that on his worst enemy," Alexander began, "and his enemy you most certainly are not."

"Wait, I'm confused. He doesn't see me as his enemy, but yet he wants me dead? How is that possible?"

"Bernael doesn't kill. He has never actually killed anyone. He can most certainly drive you to the brink of insanity, but death will be of your own doing. He's that dark voice inside your head that impels you to do wrong; to taste the other side of life. He makes everything dark and sinister seem tempting and appealing."

Alexander's voice had a hint of admiration.

"You like him, don't you?" I accused.

"I loved him once," he admitted, taking a seat on the soft cushioned chair. His voice was low and lined with a tinge of sadness. Alexander was meditative; preoccupied by his own memories. The ancient slowly turned his sullen face to me. "Bernael sees his former self in you, Caitlin. You astound him with your inner strength. In you, he sees his alter ego."

"Am I supposed to be flattered?"

"Flattered no, but alarmed yes. He hates that you are so willing to do the one thing that he never could."

"What? Kill myself?"

I put my hand to my neck as it stung all the more.

"No!" he chuckled. "Even a fool can do that."

I should've been offended, but I knew I acted stupidly.

"Bernael would never sacrifice himself for another human.

Your selfless need to give it all up to keep everyone safe has shaken him."

"It's not selflessness that guides me. It's pure insanity." I took a seat on the floor in front of Alexander as would a child being told a story. "I reacted in response to my own anger," I continued to explain. "Everyone was right and I refused to see it. When I think of death I think of it as a way out. There's nothing courageous in the way I acted."

"A man I once met said that courage is knowing what not to fear," Alexander began as he softly caressed my wounded cheek. "You Caitlin fear and fear greatly. The mere thought of losing the ones you love triggers this need to protect them. The reason you don't fear evil is because you don't see it. Even with Bernael you felt sorrow. The greatest gift you have Caitlin is not all this power that courses through your veins, but your ability to forgive and to feel compassion."

"You've met Plato?" I shrieked, finally remembering the quote from one of my readings.

"Is that who that was?" he asked as he beamed a bright smile.

Justin chuckled quietly at my stunned expression.

"Enjoying yourself, are you?" I asked.

"I love that out of everything you've been told today, Plato is the one that has had the greatest impact," Justin jested.

"Do you blame me?"

He simply shook his head and smiled.

"Caitlin," Alexander began, turning my face towards him. "The reason behind your self-destructive tendencies is because you are still in shock. Even though you don't feel it, your mind has been trying to deal with so much information. The gifted slowly come into all this knowledge; you were forced to face it all at once. You've been bombarded with quite a lot in these few months."

"It's why I need a break!" I insisted, looking over my shoulder to Justin for some understanding. "One minute I'm fine; the next, I'm challenging an almighty immortal to a dual."

"And then?" Justin prompted.

"And then the feeling vanishes, and I feel like a fool for acting so impulsively. Each time it's as if everything is closing in on me. I really need to get away from all this; some kind of break."

"Not so fast young lady," said Alexander grinning. "There are people out there who face more dire circumstances on a daily basis and they unfortunately do not live a privileged life as you do. The only thing you need to do is to sort through your feelings. You are part of a family so act like it. Think of the impact your death would have on the people who love you. You need to control the rage that guides you."

"Easier said than done," I mumbled. "The second Bernael mentioned that he was planning to get back at you for giving him that scar, my gift reacted on its own."

Alexander placed his palm over my bandage. "Bernael brews in his own self-loathing. There is no one he hates more than himself. He's not mad at me for scaring him. He's mad because it reminds him of who he once was." He took a deep breath. "The boy was glorious."

The warmth from his hand seeped right through the bandage. It was a strange sensation, but his touch was soothing.

"He can be that again, Alex. I'm sure of it. I saw it in his eyes; heard it in his voice. There's still some good in him."

Alexander cupped my face with both hands. "This is why you don't fear him. Instead of seeing the demon everyone else sees, you see the angel fighting to get out. Make no mistake about it; he is evil to the core. Any hint of goodness vanished thousands of years ago. He revels in darkness." Alexander turned and stared at Justin. "I'm dying to see how she reacts to his brother Abaddon."

"What's the matter?" Justin quickly asked, sensing the tightening in my heart.

"Any time somebody mentions his name my insides turn. I don't know why?"

"It's because you know he's out to kill you," said Alexander.

"Why? Neither of you have told me why. Why is he so hell bent on killing me? What did I ever do to him? Who is this person?"

Justin took my hand. "It's not what you did to him that he worries about, but what you'll be able to do in the future."

"Why do you insist on talking in riddles? Why would I want to do anything to him?"

"The Primoris is considered by many to be the oldest of our kind and is thought to be our maker of sorts," Justin started to say.

"Rubbish!" Alexander looked annoyed.

Justin ignored Alex's outburst and continued. "Nobody knows how old this person – thing is, and you know with age comes power. It probably is the most powerful of all the gifted."

Alexander grimaced. "Don't believe the hype Caitlin."

I giggled. "Is he or isn't he the most powerful?" I asked, wanting to finally know what I was up against.

Alexander showed a tight smile. "The Primoris is quite powerful, but choses to send his two errand boys to do the dirty work."

He could not hide his look of discontent.

"Why do you hate him so much?"

"Hate?" Alexander swiftly got up once he uttered the word and stood at the rail in silence.

"Caitlin –," Justin made me turn to look at him. "The Primoris killed Alex's family." I gasped in shock. "He decapitated his youngest daughter."

"Alex is this true?" My question met a wall of silence.

Justin reached for my bandaged face. "You don't need this anymore," he said as he peeled off the gauze.

My hand flung to my cheek and around my neck. "It's healed," I whispered softly, and then turned to Alexander to thank him, but realized it wasn't the time. I then turned back to Justin and asked, "When did all this happen to his daughter?"

Alexander turned momentarily and explained, "It was before the war; way before anything really."

Averting any eye contact was the only way to hide my own discomfort.

"Caitlin, don't be like that," Alexander offered halfheartedly, feigning a smile.

"Why would anyone do something so horrendous?" I finally asked outraged.

He circled and looked over the railing. His face was calm; calmer than I've ever seen him. "They weren't actually my biological children," he muttered, gripping the railing tight. "I only have one true child, but I loved them all the same." He inhaled deeply. "I raised them like they were my own; found most of them abandoned by their families. Some of them were orphans and left to die, but they were all gifted in different ways." He hit the wrought iron with his palm and turned to face us.

Justin laid his hand upon the Ancient's shoulder. "I can tell the story another time. You shouldn't have to relive the whole thing again."

Alexander patted Justin with a fatherly hand. There was a strange aura of fragility about the Ancient.

"No son, this is my story to tell," he began, and turned his gaze to me. "Aisilin was my youngest. She was but a baby when I found her and only eight when he took her life. She had a scar much like yours, but hers was present at birth. Her gift wasn't as evolved as yours is Caitlin, but for her age she was miraculously powerful," he sighed.

I reached out and took his hand. "Please Alex. You don't need to do this. It's way too painful. I can't stand seeing you like this."

He smiled weakly. "I'm in no pain, child. Thousands of years have passed since that horrific day. My old eyes have seen much worse."

"I know how it feels to lose the people you love," I started to say, taking his arm in my hand. "The pain never goes away. We fool ourselves by trying not to think about them, but the second we picture their faces it returns in torrents; suffocating us, submerging us into a deeper grief. Please, for your own sake let's drop this topic."

"I'm fine," Alexander admitted and stroked my cheek tenderly. "Oh Caitlin, many mistakes have been made in the past few years. You should have never been put in the position you are in now, no matter the circumstances. It was wrong."

"What are you saying?" I asked, saddened by the whole topic.

"Nothing, sweetie," he masterfully stated. "It's just that the pain of losing someone will always be there. It's a simple reminder of the love we have for them."

Tears started pricking my eyes again. "I'm fine too," I said, trying to banish the sadness that instantaneously crept its way to the surface. "I came to terms with their loss a long time ago as well."

A worried frown creased his brow as he looked at me. "Have you really?" he asked questionably.

"Yeah, I'm fine. Now, about the Primoris," I coughed back my true feelings, suppressing the need to scream.

He lifted an eyebrow and looked to Justin.

Justin simply shook his head and rolled his eyes.

"I'll be fine. I'm more interested in the story. What does he want with me?"

"There is this legend," Alexander started to say. "It's said that one person alone would unite all the bloodlines, but in order for this amazingly gifted person to take reign a Guardian would be born to pave the way; to squash anyone who stands in the way of the Chosen One from taking their rightful place at the head of the Nobe Council. The Guardian would be the General of all Generals, who will lead all armies to a brilliant victory where light will triumph darkness."

"Sounds like a nice story," I admitted.

"It's not a story, Caitlin. The Primoris believed itself to be the Chosen One; the rightful leader. When my sweet Aisilin was born with heightened abilities he became restless. The monster believed that the reason she was marked was because she was destined to become either the Chosen One or the Guardian. The Primoris wasn't going to risk its place in the hierarchy." Alexander exhaled deeply. "It took her precious life on a beautiful Sunday morning while she was playing outside with her older brothers."

My wrists started to throb with exuberant energy, reacting to my deep rooted need to rip out the demon's heart and serve it to Alexander on silver platter. "I will tear his head off," I growled, taking a step back. "I will destroy him!"

Surprisingly, Alexander chuckled at my threat. "What did I say about getting control of this rage?"

"Control!" I yelled. "I can't control this!" I admitted. "I have to find this monster."

"This is what you need to work on. Don't let your anger control your actions. Don't feed its insatiable appetite."

I closed my eyes and started taking slow deep breaths. It was then that I noticed Justin holding onto my scared wrist. I yanked my hand away instantly.

"How do you do that?" I asked at his ability to touch my throbbing wrist without being the least bit hurt.

"Our powers are somehow interwoven. Your gift can't tell me from you."

"What's that supposed to mean?"

"Most gifted would need to take the Oath of Unity to reach this stage in their relationship," Alexander started to explain. "You two seem to have gone way beyond that stage. You're gifts are evolving at an alarming rate."

"Isn't the Oath of Unity supposed to be taken during the marital ceremony?"

"I guess?" said Alexander shrugging his shoulders. "It wasn't so complicated when I was young. In the last hundred years it's been made into a ceremony. The Oath isn't something to be taken lightly or is it something you need witnesses for, but you both still need to take it for the unity of powers to be complete." His face suddenly beamed.

"What's that smile for?" I asked.

Alexander patted Justin on the back. "Can you even imagine the possibilities?"

Justin simply smiled and shook his head.

I exhaled deeply. "Would either of you care to fill me in?"

"The Oath will take your bond to a whole new level," Alexander began, "I personally haven't witnessed anything like it in all my years. Nobody knows what to expect. We're all waiting on tooth and nail. All five families are excited about this upcoming event."

I turned to Justin. "Is he talking about what I think he's talking about?"

He nodded and wickedly winked at me as he said, "You, me; a walk down a certain aisle."

I rolled my eyes at his smug expression. "I'm a basket case, remember? What happened to working out my feelings? Expressing my emotions? Why in the world would you want to be tied down to a freak like me?"

"Don't even go there. Stop looking for excuses. If Alexander says you'll be fine; you will be."

Alexander was visibly amused by our conversation. "I'm dying to see how you'll be after the joyous event."

"Me too!" beamed Justin.

"I haven't accepted your proposal," I reminded him.

"No, you're mistaken. You did accept."

"No I haven't!"

Justin smiled. "You did accept, but I simply didn't propose that day."

I shook my head in annoyance. "Anyway, where were we?" I asked, dropping the subject. "Why did the Primoris allow you to live, Alex?"

"Caitlin that's not important," Justin intervened shifting his gaze from Alex to me. "The thing is that the legend is believed to be just that; a legend. Since Aisilin there have only been two others who had a scar like yours. The last person was your grandmother."

"Was she in any danger?"

"The Primoris has grown skeptical of the legend. Who's to blame the monster? Your grandmother was never in any danger. Bernael did have her under close scrutiny, but nothing came of it. But when your scar appeared only a generation after the previous holder it raised flags of concern."

I scanned both their faces. "But you said it's only a legend. Nobody knows if it even means anything, and who was the other person? You said since Aisilin there have only been two others who had a scar like mine. My grandma was one, but who was the other?"

The two stared momentarily at each other.

"What? What aren't you telling me?"

Justin scratched his head anxiously.

"What!" I exclaimed annoyed.

"A thousand years ago, on the brink of a second war Abaddon was sent to kill the second known person to bare the same scar." Justin didn't seem to be too thrilled telling that part of the story. I could tell by the way his voice trailed in hesitation. "The child was but a fifteen-year-old girl of pure blood. She belonged to the Korbs clan, one of the first of her kind to ascend. Deondra, had an uncanny ability to foresee the future, possessing the most sought after gift; the gift of prophecy. The second she would place her palm over her scarred wrist, she saw visions of the future as clear as day. When Abaddon finally broke through the different barriers the Nobe put up to keep him away from the child he was shocked to find her waiting for him in the middle of a vast field of poppies. He was taken aback by her serene manner. It bothered him that she wasn't afraid to face him."

"Hah!" I exclaimed spooking Justin. I giggled at the way he jumped at my outburst. "So I'm not the only one who isn't scared of the boggy monster."

They both chuckled.

"You're absolutely adorable!" Justin said, smiling adoringly.

"You think I'm adorable?" I asked blushing.

Justin laughed softly. "Should I continue with the history lesson or do you have anything else to add?"

"Continue," I said eagerly, still flushed at the way he looked at me.

"Abaddon was dead set on knowing why she didn't fear him. Deondra told him that she knew that her time had come; even saw what dress they'd bury her in. You can imagine how aggravated Abaddon was with her willingness to go without a fight. He questioned the validity of the legend believing that the Chosen One or even the Guardian would be fighters. He believed that they would never yield to any threat. She told him that she was not the one the Primoris should be afraid of. She was but a messenger to warn him of the day of reckoning. The day when darkness would turn to light, when evil would turn to good. Abaddon, like some person I know –," he hinted raising an eyebrow, "Didn't like riddles. Just as the demon was about to snuff out the young girl's life she stared him in the eyes and stretched out her hand to caress his face. 'You will bow your head in reverence to the light', she had told him smiling at death himself. 'Wail in lament for the mercy that will be shown you. I die in peace knowing that I did what I came into this world to do. Follow the signs and you will find your redemption. The second of the two is who you seek.' Abaddon, being the loathsome person that he is, tore out the child's heart and left her blood soaked body to drench the soil that it fell on."

I gasped in horror. "Poor girl!"

Justin looked at me and half smiled. "Deondra's blood was said to have made the poppies a shade darker in color."

My eyes narrowed in speculation.

"What?" Justin protested grinning. "I'm just telling you what I read in the Book of Truths."

I looked at Alexander confused. "Where were you when all this was happening? Why didn't you save her?"

"Deondra saw what I saw. Her future was but a shadow of her life. I cannot intervene; cannot shift life's plan. If I altered her future, you would not be here today."

"You could've put an end to all this, couldn't you?" I was accusing him of a horrid crime. "Why do I suspect you to be even older than you let on; older than the Primoris? How would you know all there is to know unless you were there from the beginning? He fears you, doesn't he? It would explain why he would be in hiding. Why else would the most powerful gifted need to hide? Hide from what, but another more gifted."

He was about to look away when I took hold of his arm and turned him to face me. "Alexander, why in the world would you allow any of this to happen?"

He frowned as considered his next words. "I am a mere cog in the wheel of life; an old one, but still an insignificant cog. Who I am is of no importance to any of you. Why I chose to do what I did is again of no importance. I answer only to a much greater power; a power we all should pay homage for breathing life into our unworthy souls. I live to guide not to intervene."

"So what's my role then?" I asked. "I still don't see how Deondra's warning involves me?"

Alexander sat down again. "She had pointed out that the second of the two is who he sought. The second of the two is presumably you, as far as Primoris is concerned. First your grandmother bore the scar and then you. It has never happened before. My daughter was the first, but that was thousands of years ago, then came Deondra at the turn of the previous millennium and then in this century came two; back to back; first Eileen and then you. And then this –," He lifted both my scared wrists. "You bare the symbols of our kind on your skin; the original symbols."

"You know the future. Am I or am I not the person who Primoris seeks."

He shook his head reluctant to speak.

"Oh, come on!" I huffed.

"Caitlin, that's just it. I don't know. I've tried to see, but something blocks me; there's a window there, but it's as if someone has hung a blanket over it. I have only a vague sense," Alexander frowned again. "There's definitely a great journey before you, but where it leads, I cannot tell. I should be able to see, but I cannot. I sense great change of some sort ahead of you. Your future is a blank canvass. I can't see anything. Everything about you is a mystery. From the moment your scar appeared it was like you were erased from my radar. I can sense you; have since you were in your mother's womb, but for some reason your gift is keeping you well hidden; hidden from us all."

"Not well enough!" I sighed.

"For the past month or so I can't see Justin's either."

"As it should be," said Justin.

"I agree young man. Seeing the future is more a curse than a gift."

"Alexander, I'm branded on both wrists now," I began looking down at my hands. "Doesn't that change the legend?"

"Actually it validates it. You have been branded with the one sign that makes all the difference to the Primoris."

"What's that?"

"It marks your rightful place among us."

"I still don't understand what that means."

"Your scars represent not one, but all families. They represent your true calling. They state your position among the gifted and that alone is the Primoris' downfall no matter how much the monster wants to deny who you really are. It represents your ability to transcend, to reach a level of power that only the purest of the bloodlines can do."

Alexander stood up and added, "You don't seem too satisfied with my explanation."

FIFTEEN

SNEAK

I GRIPPED THE RAIL RATHER tight and looked past the sprawling property concentrating my gaze on the woods in the distance. Even though it was still early, the overcast sky gave the impression of late evening.

"What do we do now?" I asked looking hopeless up at the sky. "What if I used my gift like Deondra did?" I asked. "If I hold my scarred wrist I can see images of the future too. I haven't tried it from that day in Uncle Abbot's office, but if it would help, I see no point in waiting."

"No!" snapped Justin. "You will do no such thing. Have you forgotten what happened the last time you accidentally accessed that part of your gift?"

"I'm stronger now. I have control and it might show me what Alex can't see in our future."

"Caitlin, neither the past nor the future is important," Alexander explained. "You need to learn control. Learn how to curb your anger and work through the rest of your emotions."

"Okay, but what do I do in the meantime with all these demons who are out to get me? Do you expect me to just sit around and wait?"

"They're out to get us all, make no mistake of that. They hate that they are not the ones holding the reigns over us all."

The anger was back. "They won't touch a hair on any of you, not if it's the last thing I do!"

"We all know how much you want to protect us, but it's you who needs protecting right now or at least until you get complete control and Ascend. There's no point in putting yourself in unnecessary danger. Think of the people who love you, and now that you know what you are up against, you realize how important it is to perfect your gift. You have more than just the two of us looking out for you," Alexander said heading indoors. "Just don't make it any more difficult than it has to be."

As soon as he reached the fluttering sheer curtains he seemed to become one with the material; transparent and ghost like. "Perfect your gift," he pronounced, as he vanished into the white fabric.

Justin stood behind me and messaged my shoulders. "Take one day at a time," he whispered in my ear.

I melted into his embrace and leaned my head back against his chest indulging in his warmth. His soft lips against the curve of my neck sent shivers of delight down my spine. "I'm sorry for earlier," I muttered, basking in his attention.

Justin wrapped his hands around my waist and pulled me closer. "Just don't do it again," he whispered between kisses.

I couldn't help but close my eyes – lost in his touch. "You know –," I said turning in his arms.

His eyebrow went up in anticipation of what I was about to say. "I know what?" he asked smiling.

"You heard what Alex said. We are already bound to one another, more than any other couple."

"Yeah, so?" he said, fiddling with my hair.

I kissed him on the lips as I circled my arms around his neck. "So, I see no reason to prolong this."

He smiled magnificently. "Caitlin, you're not implying that I take full advantage of having you in my bedroom, are you?"

I leaned in and kissed him ardently and his response was immediate, lifting me closer against his hard body. Wanting nothing more than to respond to his playful comment I eased slightly back and looked into his eyes. "I don't care where you take advantage; just take it," I said shamelessly,

His husky laugh was uplifting. Justin twirled us around in a circle triggering squeals of happiness. "Don't think I don't want to," he muttered as he kissed me on the lips, loosening his hold. "Taking advantage of you is all I think about."

His hand stroked the side of my face as he gazed into my eyes. My face instantly turned three shades of red. "Sweet," he whispered brushing his lips against mine. I leaned in and relished in his every kiss as Justin's mood banished any morbid thoughts that lingered from the day's events.

"I need to get you home," he said kissing me one last time.

"Why in the world would you want to do that?"

"You have to study for tomorrow and your buddy is waiting for you there."

"Tyler," I sighed. "What am I going to do with him? I feel awful."

"What's there to feel awful about?"

Frustrated, I fell back on Justin's bed. "He just makes things much harder than they have to be."

"Reminds me of someone else I know," Justin laughed.

I threw a pillow at him, but he masterfully caught it in the air and placed it back on the bed.

I reached out and caught Justin's hand as he was about to reach for the top drawer. "Does he actually mean what he says? I mean does he really think he loves me?"

It was a strange question to ask ones boyfriend, but Justin was the only one who would know Tyler's mind better than Tyler himself.

Justin took a moment, and then came and sat next to me focusing his gaze on our intertwined fingers. "He's a great guy, Caitlin." As he said it he lifted his face to look at me and his features were much softer. "It was real hard for Tyler when you left. It was as if someone pulled the rug from right under him." He looked away, towards the balcony deep in thought. "You guys were more or less glued to the hip since birth. When you were sent away, he literally had his best friend ripped out of his life without any warning," Justin explained as he finally turned to face me. "Tyler does love you, but I think it's more the fear of losing you again that scares him most. The need he feels of wanting to be with you is, as far as I can tell, a way of keeping you close; keeping you from ever leaving again."

"I knew he didn't actually love me. He's such an idiot," I muttered making a mental note to explain things to him.

"Caitlin, he does love you! He loves everything about you."

"But you just said –,"

"What I said was that he fears losing you. That alone has manifested itself in a –," Justin took my other hand as well. "In a way Tyler is obsessed with you. Not in a dark creepy way. He just feels the strong urge to be around you. He needs to see you and make sure that you're perfectly safe. Trust me Caitlin, the poor guy is suffering."

"Damn it," I whispered, putting my head in my hands. "Why would he feel that about me? We're best friends for heaven's sake. I feel the need to protect him all the time too. I care for him, but that doesn't mean I'm in love with him. Why can't he see the difference?"

Justin sat back against the headboard and made himself comfortable. I slid up and leaned my head against his chest. It felt perfect being in his room. Everything about it was an extension of the man I loved.

"Just don't alienate him. Tyler is doing his best to work through this. He knows that his feelings will do more harm than good. You need to be patient, but feel free to slap him as often as possible." Justin chuckled at his own words.

"Very funny," I said looking up at him.

"What? It'll save me the trouble of doing it myself."

I pushed myself up and looked at him seriously. "You will do no such thing. Tyler is off limits. Do you hear me? Promise me that you'll never hurt him. Promise that you will protect him no matter what."

Justin swiftly grabbed me by the waist and spread me next to him on the bed. I looked up into his breathtaking smile.

"I love that you want to protect everybody," he admitted as he lowered his head into the curve of my neck. "God you smell good," he muttered, kissing me down the length of my neck.

I didn't make a sound. I hardly could breathe from the intoxicating affect he had on me. "Caitlin, you're making staying away nearly impossible," he moaned into my neck.

I didn't answer.

It was one thing to joke with him about taking full advantage, but a whole different thing to actually doing it.

He quickly slid back to his side of the bed and stared at the ceiling. I stretched my arm across his chest and nestled my head under his chin.

"I can stay like this forever," I finally confessed, cozying up even closer.

Justin kissed me on top of the head. "Forever? Are you sure you wouldn't tire of me?"

I lifted my head and gave him a quick kiss on the lips. "Tire of you? Not in a million years!"

"A million years?"

I nodded. "I was going to say more, but I hate to exaggerate."

He squeezed me tight and smiled. "So –," he finally said raising an eyebrow. "What did you get me for my birthday?"

I instantly sat up and smacked his arm lightly. "I'm not telling! Wait, how do you not know?"

"Kyle is blocking me out and he's doing a rather good job at it. I guess he feels that the surprise is worth the wait to go to all that trouble."

"Oh, it is! It truly is.

"Just a hint," he said tickling me.

"Not unless your life depends on it," I giggled, trying to break free from his hold.

"Fine!" Justin said, feigning being mad. "Then I guess I won't tell you what I got for you."

"Why in the world would you get me anything?" I pushed

him away. "Justin it's your birthday not mine. Why would you buy me something?"

"I don't need a reason to get my girlfriend something," he stated, standing up.

He went to his dresser and pulled out a change of clothes from the top drawer and headed for the bathroom. "As soon as I take a quick shower I'll take you home. Tyler is getting restless."

"Why don't you just beam me over there, superman," I smiled making him stop dead in his tracks. "It's much faster."

His expression wasn't at all what I expected. Justin looked as if he wanted to say something, but instead tried to smile. "I prefer to drive," he said instead, and disappeared into the bathroom.

There was something in the way he looked – something he wasn't saying. While he dallied in the bathroom, I strode outside onto the balcony and took in the light breeze.

"What a day," I exhaled emptying my lungs of all the rancid feelings smoldering beneath.

Somebody should warn students about Advanced Placement History. Better yet, they should be warned about AP Exams altogether.

Apart from quizzing each other on the systematic overview of world history and analyzing the economic, political and social transformation of the United States since the time of the first European encounters; there was really not much left to say to Tyler. He intentionally kept his distance by sitting at my desk instead of on the floor as we always did when studying for exams.

I had to do something, had to break the ice somehow. I brought my hand up to my neck considering if I should tell my best friend about my earlier run-in with Bernael. I was never sure how much everybody in Oaks actually knew.

There were so many secrets going around that it was hard to keep track of who knew what. They read each other's thoughts, blocked each other's thoughts; it was impossible to know how informed they each were. It explained why nobody talked about anything that involved our gifts.

"I acted really stupid today," I began as I pushed my text book to the side. "I honestly have had enough of history these past few days. I'm up to here in details of past events."

Tyler circled his head momentarily and looked at me, but returned to his notes only seconds later. He wasn't going to make this easy on me.

I climbed onto my bed wanting to give my back side a break from the hard-wood floor. Sitting on the soft mattress Indian style, I simply let my gaze fall on my friend's back, hoping he'd say something.

It took him all of two seconds to slam his book shut and turn to face me. "You should come with a warning label," he finally blurted out as he got to his feet.

I didn't respond; thought it'd be best to let him get things off his chest.

Tyler started fiddling with one of my dolls on the top shelf. "I got you this one, didn't I?" he asked holding up the porcelain ballerina.

I nodded.

He then returned the doll to the shelf and leaned back against my desk. "You're unbelievably hard to hate," he said trying to smile. "God knows I've tried." Tyler looked down contemplating what to say next. "I'm an awful friend. I realized that today."

"No you're not, Tyler. You're a great friend."

"No, no I'm not." He looked up and faced me for the first time since morning. "I'm the last person you need to push you. I'm really sorry for dumping all this on you. You have so much to deal with right now, and I shouldn't have said anything. I should've dealt with all this without mentioning anything. What I feel is not important." He stood completely upright, but didn't take a step closer. "I was a complete jerk to bring all this up."

"What you feel Tyler is more important to me than any of the things that are going on," I admitted as I got up and stood in front of him. "I need you to know that I'm always going to be here for you. Like it or not, I'm never going to leave you no matter how many times you make me want to kill you."

He showed a tight smile as I took his hand and held it tight. "I need you in my life. I won't survive any of this without you. I wouldn't have made it in Tirion without you."

Unexpectedly tears filled my eyes in the realization that he had saved me from so much misery while I was causing him this much pain. "I do love you," I confessed, swallowing back the tears. "I love you because you are the only one who sees me; who knows me. I do love you Tyler, but unfortunately not in the way you want me to love you."

"Damn it, Caity," he groaned pulling me into his arms. "This is entirely my fault. I swear I'll get through this even if it means banging my head against the wall till I lose consciousness."

I sniffed back my runny nose and looked at him. "Can I be there to watch?" I said, attempting to smile.

He chuckled and squeezed me tighter. "I knew you'd like that. You'll see we'll be fine Caity. I promise."

"Not if we don't pass History," I scuffed.

I instantly felt much lighter. I hadn't realized how much all that was weighing me down. Tyler and I slowly returned to studying. It was never going to be the same with Tyler, that I was sure of, but still, I wasn't going to allow our slight discomfort ruin eighteen years of friendship. I refused to live without him in my life.

Between our little study breaks I told him about my confrontation with Bernael. His reaction was more or less as I expected. He wouldn't have been Tyler if he didn't lecture me on how stupid I was or how little I valued my life. What I did, however, was keep my conversation with Alexander a secret. Tyler didn't need to know about the legend or anything pertaining to the Book of Truths. I even omitted telling him about my injury knowing it'd upset him even more.

"So do we just wait and see when he'll try attacking you again?" he asked with a raised eyebrow.

"I guess so. It's not like I have any other choice."

"That's absurd! We should be able to do something!"

"Don't worry," I reassured him, "The Ellri will guide us and The Nobe will protect us. There's really nothing you and I can do. We are insignificant in comparison to all their powers. We haven't even ascended yet."

"Guess you're right," he accepted, turning back to his notes.

The evening wore on with Aunt Leslie bringing us snacks to munch on.

M r. Myers walked around the classroom. "Pens and pencils down," he said, "And make sure your full names are on the answer sheets and pass them up."

I looked over to Tyler to see how he did, but he was talking to Lisa. As I was about to collect my bag up off the floor and put my things away, Megan stretched out her perfectly shaped leg and kicked my bag completely out of reach.

Enraged at her audacity, I turned and glared at her. In turn she made a face and turned to talk to her two best friends, but Kim and Loraine didn't seem to share in Megan's immature ploy to make me angry.

"Get a grip," I whispered, and calmly reached for my bag. Megan wasn't able to use her gift under the Shield of Knowledge, but I was. "Breathe," I told myself.

"What the hell was that all about?" Tyler protested as soon as he caught up with me down the hall.

"Oh, it's nothing. Megan is just being Megan. I wouldn't want her any other way."

Tyler stopped and looked at me. "Okay, what have you done with Caitlin?" he asked smiling.

"I'm right here. It's just that we're graduating in a few days and I refuse to get into a confrontation with her. I have more important demons to worry about."

"I see your point. If you want I can talk to her," he offered, opening his locker.

"Thanks, but that won't be necessary. I can handle Megan on my own." Tyler pulled out a bar of chocolate and tore it open and took a great big bite.

"You need to lay off those things. You'll ruin your teeth," I told him.

He chuckled and opened his chocolate-filled mouth. "You want some," he said laughing.

"You're gross!" I exclaimed hitting him again.

He devoured what was left of the bar and collected his books. "I need my energy for later."

"What for?"

"I'm going for a practice session in the Chamber later on today. They told me to be well stocked."

"We have finals. Why in the world are they making you do this now?"

"As a distraction," he said, taping his finger on my nose.

"Am I the one their distracting you from?" I asked abased. "You should all just take me out and shoot me. I seem to be more trouble than I'm worth."

Tyler chuckled and closed his locker. "You are so worth the trouble," he mumbled thinking I didn't hear him.

I didn't comment. Just as we were about to exit the main building my eye caught Megan leaning up against Old Betty.

"This isn't going to end well," I muttered.

Tyler shook his head in discontent. "What in the world does she think she's doing?" he asked aggravated. "You know what? Just ignore her. She's trying to rouse you."

"She's doing a hell of a good job."

Tyler quickly took me by the arm and led me back into the main hall and through to the back lot. "I'll drive you home and we'll come back for your car later," he said, smiling contently. "It'll be fun to see how long she waits for you to show up."

"But, she'll see us drive off."

Tyler's eyes were brighter than ever. "Not if you duck down into the seat. She won't be able to see you."

"I love how your twisted mind works," I giggled, letting myself in his car. I slid down the passenger's seat as far down as I could possibly go.

"You're actually enjoying this, aren't you?" he asked putting the car in motion.

"Are you kidding me? Consider this therapy. It's either doing this or letting my anger take over."

"Good," he noted, pushing my head down. "Now keep quiet!"

Tyler stopped the car for some reason and slightly opened the window. "Hi girls, you're looking beautiful as ever."

I rolled my eyes at how annoyingly sincere he made his compliment sound.

"What are you ladies waiting for? Don't tell me you're having car troubles."

Thanks to Pete Lazzo's Harley, I wasn't able to hear an answer.

"She should be right out," answered Tyler. "She was called down to the office earlier."

"Thanks," Megan said obnoxiously.

"My pleasure," he beamed and rolled up his window. I remained hidden. "Get your ass back in the seat," he ordered driving at excessive speeds.

"How long do you think she'll wait?"

"Hopefully till hell freezes over," he laughed, keeping his eyes on the road.

Within minutes we were already halfway home.

"Why do you all feel the need to go so fast?" I asked in response to the sheer speed he banked the curve.

A wide grin spread slowly across his face as he geared up

and stepped on the gas pedal. "We're in Oaks, what can possibly go wrong?"

I shook my head and turned my gaze to the side window. Everything was going by at an alarming speed when out of nowhere Tyler yelled. "Hold on!"

He slammed so hard on the break that the Porsche swerved to a complete stop throwing me violently forward – missing the dashboard by a mere inch. Thankfully, I was wearing my seatbelt otherwise I'd have flown right through the windshield.

I squinted, trying to make sense of the reason behind his immediate stop. "What are you doing?" I screamed glaring at him. "What was that for?"

He continued to stare straight ahead as if bewildered, but now something else was working behind his eyes – tightness came to his features. "We have to get out of here now!" he barked putting the car in reverse.

I followed his gaze and saw what Tyler had sensed long before the object ever came into view. An eddy of black smoke rolled towards us, approaching at great speeds, slicing through the air like a bullet. Only a few feet away the cloud-covered monster coalesced out of the darkness and stood before us.

"Bernael," I muttered exhaling anxiously. Something cold clutched at my innards.

Tyler turned to me, his face fearful. "We need to go," he said slamming his foot on the gas pedal.

In that moment of horror, Tyler accelerated zero to sixty in seconds as he spun his Porsche round and headed in the opposite direction. Through the side mirror I saw Bernael fade into a coiling shadow, a wide rope of blackness that drifted quickly behind us. In no time at all, the gloomy stream encapsulated the sports car draping us in complete darkness.

I felt my knees weaken. What monstrous thing was happening before us, as relentless and inescapable as the clutch of a nightmare? Tyler automatically slammed on the brake not being able to see where we were going. There was a hum of eerie sounds – voices of the damned. Sounds that only hell itself would favor.

Bernael once again stood in front of us with his real form restored.

Tyler being the boy that he was, instead of freaking out he chose to stick his middle finger out at the demon – provoking Bernael even more.

I was about to pull on the door handle to get out when Tyler pulled me by the arm. "Where do you think you're going?" he asked angrily.

I wrenched my arm free keeping my eye on the angel of darkness. "You have to go. He's after me!"

"Like hell I do," Tyler yelled, getting out of his car before I could even object.

I felt my own terror surge out. "Tyler, don't!" I screamed in fear of his life. "Get back in! Tyler, Please." I was begging. "You have to go!"

Bernael shifted his gaze at me and smiled cunningly. He was going to use Tyler to get to me; that I was sure of. My gift responded immediately charging to unthinkable levels. I quickly ran and stood between Tyler and the demon – taking a step closer wanting nothing to happen to my best friend.

Bernael was visibly amused. When I stopped, he stopped. When I tried to move more swiftly to shield Tyler, he headed me off, forcing me to shrink back to avoid contact with him.

A voice as ragged and deadly as the thrush of freezing wind scraped through the air. "This is undeniably amusing mortal, but I'm not here to play."

To my horror Tyler came and stood next to me. Now, I had no way of keeping him out of harm's way without hurting him.

"There is no hell deep enough for you monster," Tyler said taking a step forward. "You stay away from her."

Like a hungry lion spotting his prey, Bernael spread his wide-sleeved arms and collapsed back into shadow and without any warning; shadowy coils sprang around Tyler, tightened as they looped around him.

I was in utter shock – my eyes remained open, that much I was sure of, but my mind simply stopped, refusing to believe what was unfolding in front of me. With unfathomable speed a stream of clotted dark ran through Tyler's chest rendering him limp, suspending him inches off the ground.

"Tyler!" I screamed utterly useless.

After a long moment Tyler fell to the ground, twitching. The jerking movements slowed, and then stopped.

I began to cry. Shoulders quivery, unable to hold up a moment longer; I fell to my knees next to my childhood friend.

"You fear me now, don't you mortal?" Bernael said in a voice more powerful than cannons blasting in battle.

I looked down at Tyler's motionless body and circled my head to the Fallen and that's when I mentally snapped and an overwhelming urge to see the fallen angel's blood draining from his lifeless body came over me. Raw hatred surfaced with waves of unadulterated rage. My gift was spiraling completely out of control as was the fury. My arms glowed a fiery red preparing to deliver this monster to his maker.

"How does it feel to hate?" He hissed smiling. "Multiply what you feel right now mortal by a billion and you will have an idea of what I'm capable of."

For some strange reason his words hit me like a freight train going one hundred miles an hour. I was nothing like this demon and I never hoped to be. He was using Tyler to push me off the edge, to cause me to lose every ounce of humanity.

Without a second thought, I breathed in deep and closed my eyes. It took several attempts, but the ill feelings I had were gone; my gift extinguished as fast as it ignited.

Bernael looked on in utter shuck.

"You obviously have enough malice for the both of us," I began, kneeling back down next to Tyler. "There's no need for both of us to hate, is there?"

I turned my back to him and concentrated on Tyler.

Tyler's lips pulled taut, his eyes emptied. I gave a little squeak of alarm and turned to glare at the fiend who was standing there smiling.

There was something going on that I did not understand. I could only stare terrified. Tyler looked like a man trapped beneath crushing weight.

"It's me you want," I screamed standing up. "What did you do to him?"

Bernael grinned as he took a step closer. "He'll be begging for death by the end of the day."

"You're a monster."

"I am a monster, mortal. Make no mistake about it."

"Tyler did nothing to you. Why would you do this?"

"Do I need a reason?" he sneered contemptuously.

Honesty

Illustrated for Lines that Bind - Among the Shadows

SIXTEEN

FORGIVENESS

J UST AS I WAS ABOUT to take an offensive step forward, I felt a light touch on my shoulder. Instantly, Bernael retreated several yards away.

"Justin, let me at him," I quivered with anger trying to break from Justin's hold.

"Caitlin!" he pronounced sternly. "Check on Tyler."

I looked over to Bernael and caught his provokingly alluring grin which automatically triggered the monstrous feelings I tried so hard to smother.

"Caitlin!" Justin pronounced, shaking me by the arms. "This isn't the time or the place for heroics; Tyler needs you."

"Bernael needs to be stopped," I yelled. "He needs to be put down."

"Caitlin!" Justin barked out. "Go to Tyler, now. We'll handle this!"

"We? Who's we? What do you mean?"

Just as I turned to glare at the bastard who hurt my friend, the Ellri appeared, forming a ring around the monste.

Bernael seemed to be trapped within the human circle, morphing in and out of human form gliding in circles like a caged animal trying to find a way out. Whatever the Ellri were doing, kept Bernael limited to the confines of the circle.

"Where are Tyler's parents?" I asked kneeling next to my friend, seeing that the two Ellri were not part of the circle.

Justin's full attention was on Bernael. "Stay here with Tyler," he ordered and walked away.

I reached out to touch Tyler's brow. "You'll be okay," I whispered hoping against hope.

Huddled over Tyler, I was trying to think of ways to help, but there were none. Hiding behind a mask of a composed exterior, my eyes filled with frightened tears. I looked towards the ring of Ellri only to see the unsteady black shape that had been Bernael attempt to break through the confines. Apparently, he was trapped against his will and had no means of breaking free of the human barrier the Ellri created around him.

My fear beat higher, rising like storm-tossed waves in fear of losing my best friend. I leaned down and grabbed Tyler's arm in my hand and tugged. He was unmovable as stone. "Get up, damn you!" I shouted, and yanked as hard as I could.

My head snapped up in response to the menacing roar coming from the depths of Bernael himself. The sound was a hollow wail, like the droning on engines. He wasn't backing off, wasn't going to let any of them restrain him. Bernael kept circling the entire inner perimeter in his ghostly self, trying to find a way out. His attempts to attack the Ellri were in vain.

The sheer force of their combined gifts catapulted the demon back to the center of the circle as if hit by a charge of electricity. Bernael crouched in the middle clothed only in darkness, and hissed contemptuously at his wardens' refusal to set him free.

It was amazed to see the Ellri able to contain a powerful Nobe like Bernael. Some higher power was surely working overtime in keeping everyone safe. I quickly turned my gaze to Tyler's pale complexion.

"There must be something I can do," I whispered rubbing my brow in utter frustration. Without a second though, I placed both hands on his chest allowing my gift to pass to him in the hopes of giving him the energy he needed to pull through. My hands instantly glowed as did Tyler's limp body. His eyes were dangerously dull and there was no sign of life apart from the very faint heart beat against my palm.

Again the angry growls of the beast trying to break though the circle caught my attention. The sound of Bernael struggling stung my heart as if a cold icicle had sheathed itself within me.

"Damn it Tyler!" I screamed seeing that nothing was happening. The only thing I did accomplish was to burn a hole through his shirt where my hands lay. My hand prints were brandished on his chest. "Tyler please," I begged "Please get up."

Long moments later, he inhaled and clutched onto his chest with his right hand. "Tyler," I gasped praying that he was all right.

"I can't breathe," he whispered in short deep breaths.

Evidently, Tyler's gift was working overtime. My hand prints were slowly vanishing from his chest with every breath he took.

"I can't heal this," he muttered, closing his eyes again.

"Tyler?" I asked seeing that he took way too long to reopen them. "Tyler," I screamed seeing that he didn't respond. I shook him vehemently to wake him, but nothing seemed to work. I stretched out right there next to him and placed my head up against his chest. The rather soft beating of his heart was the only thing that kept me from throwing myself on Bernael and ripping his evil heart right out of his chest.

As I held onto Tyler I wrapped him in a beam of light. I wanted him to absorb as much of my energy as he possibly could. "Please Tyler, wake up," I pleaded tightening my hold around him.

Another venomous rasp from the demon drew my attention.

Without letting go I circled my head to the Ellri and saw Justin standing in the middle of the circle opposite Bernael.

"What is he doing?" I muttered frantically. Justin was putting himself in unnecessary danger. The Ellri were there. He had no place playing the hero. I immediately got to a kneeling position keeping one hand around Tyler's arm.

"Let Tyler go," I heard Alexander's familiar voice say.

I shifted my gaze to the bright being only inches away. The light faded around him as the sun fades behind the moon during an eclipse. "You've done all you could. Your friend needs to pull through on his own."

Seeing Alexander suddenly made me realize how the Ellri were capable of such an impossible feat. Only another Nobe would have enough power to contain another Nobe.

I looked at Tyler before standing up. There on his shirt I noticed wet patches soaked through to his skin. I instantly raised my hand to my face and found the source of the tears.

Strange really, I was so intent on helping him I hadn't noticed that I was crying. Reluctantly, I let go of his hand and kissed him on the cheek. "I need you," I whispered in his ear before letting go.

"Come Caitlin," said Alexander offering his arm. "Let's see what Bernael really wants."

Wiping my tears I followed Alexander to the circle. In perfect synchronization the Ellri automatically broke formation allowing for us to enter into the circle.

Bernael instantly recoiled. "Father," he hissed, bowing his head. His gaze instantly fell to where my hand wrapped around Alexander's arm.

Alexander lifted my hand to his mouth and gave it a quick peck before lowering it to my side. He strode to where Bernael stood and stared at the angel of darkness.

For a second there, I could've sworn that a wave of sadness washed over Bernael at the sight of Alexander showing me so much affection; like a child who was jealous of his parent's devotion to his younger sibling. That's when I knew that no matter how evil he was, there was still good somewhere deep down.

Instead of looking towards Alexander, Bernael kept his gaze on me. "Don't think for one minute that the Ancient is capable of love, young mortal," he seethed in a raspy echo. His voice was dripping in virulent gall. "This is what he does to those he holds dear." Bernael pointed to his scarred face and turned to face Alex. "Father, will you show her the same love you showed me?"

The two immortals stood there in deathly quiet.

"Kneel!" roared Alexander causing the ground to tremble.

"I will do no such thing," answered Bernael.

"You dare defy our rules!"

"I'm not sixteen father," Bernael hissed, "you have absolutely no power over me."

The second Bernael spoke a ring of fire appeared over the heads of the Ellri.

Stunned, I edged closer to Justin needing to feel safe. "You'll be fine," he whispered. The flames instantly took human–like form. The Nobe council materialized creating the outer circle; levitating several feet in the air behind the Ellri.

Just as my mind fought to accept the miraculous spectacle, streaks of fire streamed down from the sky only to morph into the bright unearthly Sentinels. They stood in a third circle a few feet behind the Nobe. They too were suspended even higher than their masters before them.

"Kneel to hear your sentence," said Alexander with pain stricken voice.

This was hard to watch. I knew how much Alex loved Bernael, knew how much he had hoped that this demon would return to his former glory.

Impulsively, I backed up even closer to Justin as I looked up and around unable to believe what my eyes were seeing. Like an upside down three-tiered cake they all stood awaiting some sort of sentence. Bernael looked around and smiled. He seemed relieved somehow, happy to be put through this trial. His gaze stopped the second his eyes met mine.

A great curtain of sorrow swept over me.

"Kneel!" Alexander barked drawing Bernael's attention.

Bernael spat at Alexander's feet and grinned sadistically. "I will never kneel to you. You are not my master."

Unexpectedly, there, only a few feet away, Alexander morphed into a majestic radiant being that he truly was. "You will kneel in front of the court," he bellowed pointing to the ground with his hand.

Bernael tried to turn into shadow, but for some reason he couldn't.

"Kneel or be witness to your own demise," roared Alexander causing my skin to crawl.

Bernael took a step back. "Do as you wish," he said and pulled his hood over his head.

Two of the Nobe Sentinels appeared before Bernael and forced him to kneel. "You will obey," the one Sentinel said in a volatile voice. "Kneel Fallen!"

Bernael didn't speak. He fell to the ground in sheer silence awaiting his sentence.

"No!" I screamed at the top of my lungs taking a few steps forward. Justin instantly grabbed my hand and pulled me to his side. "I can't allow them to do this," I said, pulling my arm free from his vice.

"Caitlin," Justin yelled, trying to reason with me. "You have no place in the circle. You have no say in this matter."

I didn't really care where I stood in any circle or what my place was in this hierarchy. I couldn't allow them to do this to him – do this to anyone. Even though Bernael was who he was, I couldn't be part of this. This isn't who I was.

I momentarily circled my head and to my even greater relief saw Tyler pushing himself up against the car into a sitting position. I took a deep breath happy to see that he was going to be alright.

Uniformly, the two Sentinels turned and stared. "Step back," they ordered stretching out their hands in a motion to stop me.

"No! You step back," I yelled, seeing that they were still holding Bernael down by the shoulders. To my surprise, the gargantuan Sentinels backed away from Bernael responding to my command. Bernael lifted his head slightly and looked at me visibly shocked at my inability to cooperate, but even that slight movement caused the Sentinels to hold him down again. That instant, two other Sentinels descended and stood rather close causing me to look away from their radiance. They were about to place their hands on me when out of nowhere I heard Justin's threatening voice. "I dare you to touch her."

The Sentinels looked back and forth to Justin and then to Alexander. They seemed at a loss – confused about what to do.

"Leave her," Alexander said waving them away. The two brilliant beings returned to their place among the rest of their kind.

I mouthed 'thank you' to Justin and went and stood in front of Bernael. "If this is what we are, I want no part in it," I declared, looking into the brightness that was once Alex.

In seconds he returned to his human form looking rather stern. "Caitlin, there are rules," he said in a softer tone.

"Yes I know. I won't pretend to understand them, but all this is just a bit too extreme, don't you think?" I pointed to the suspended beings. "I'm sure that these rules exist to keep us human. Is this humane?" I asked motioning to the way the Sentinels kept Bernael pinned to the ground. "Is this, what being gifted is all about?"

"What you protect is human no more," said Alexander. "His intention concerning Tyler overstepped every rule."

"Alexander, he is human, don't you see? Bernael is more

human than most. He feels things that we can't even imagine. Please don't do this."

The Sentinels released their hold on Bernael as if responding to a muted order. He in turn removed his hood and got to his feet. "Mortal, I don't need your pity," he slithered.

"I don't pity you," I pronounced rather curtly turning to him. "The taste of your evil still lingers in my mouth as a reminder of how loathsome you are. I truly hope you rot in hell for all you've done."

He looked baffled by what I was saying. "If so, then why would you do this?"

"For my own humanity, my own peace of mind, you sick, twisted animal. For my personal belief of doing onto others as I wish them do onto me. Make no mistake of it, Bernael; I do hate you."

"Compassion is a weakness mortal. Maybe you should keep it for somebody more worthy."

I smiled. "Everyone is worthy of compassion even beautiful beings who wrongly chose the darker path in life. They, more than anyone, need to be shown mercy. The ability to forgive monsters like you is a great way to measure our humanity."

"You know not what you speak," he shouted. "I will get to you mortal and revel in seeing your torturous soul beg for mercy."

Justin took a menacing step forward, but I quickly motioned for him to stop. Thankfully he did as I wished.

I smiled at Bernael's threat and turned to Alexander. "He has paid dearly," I began, "Losing his family was hard enough. We both know how that is."

I purposely brought up his past in the hopes that those

forgotten moments would bring some light into this demon's sad existence.

"Don't you dare speak of things your little mind cannot comprehend," he roared acidic.

I purposefully ignored him by keeping my back to him. I looked up as if addressing the court. "I'm his intended victim, am I not? I want no harm to come to him. Won't allowing him to live be punishment enough?"

In no time at all the Sentinels as well as the Nobe vanished into thin air leaving only the Ellri to keep Bernael in check.

Alexander smiled warmly and caressed my cheek. "Your words are sincere Caitlin, but I just can't leave him be. His crime must be punished,"

I looked to Bernael and noticed yet again that he cringed the moment Alexander showed an inkling of affection.

"Forgive him," I said smiling.

Both man looked at me as if I were crazy. "What kind of punishment would that be?" wondered Alexander stunned that I would even mention such an inane idea.

"There is no revenge so complete as forgiveness," I pronounced, quoting the 19th-century American humorist Josh Billings.

"I'm not out for revenge, Caitlin," Alexander responded.

"What then is all this?" I asked. "Alex, you said it yourself, Bernael feeds on all this chaos. Thrives on knowing that he still has a hold on you," I explained. "Bernael still loves you. You know this. He's dying for your attention. Forgive him and cut the lines that bind you for all these thousands of years. Remove his reminder of the hate he so much loves to hold onto."

"NO!" screamed Bernael from the depths of his decrepit

soul. The very ground we stood on shook. "Father, don't listen to this child. She knows not what she speaks."

Alexander took a step closer to Bernael. "It's time son. We both need to put an end to this," he accepted, reaching out to touch him.

Bernael instantly fell to his knees. "No father, please don't!" He begged taking hold of Alexander's ankles, pressing his forehead against them in total submissive humbleness. "This is who I am. Don't listen to the girl she knows not."

"No child," Alexander said softly as he placed his hand on top of Bernael's head. The demon lifted his face and gazed at the ancient. "This is not who you are, but what you've become," said Alexander stroking Bernael's cheek. "Oh, I do miss you." He sighed deeply. "If I did this – if I led you down this path I'm truly sorry. Forgive me." Alexander stroked the deep scar on Bernael's face and made it vanish from the monster's face the same way he made mine disappear the day before.

"NO Father, DON'T!" he gasped bringing his evil hand to his cheek. "Damn you!" he growled backing away. "Damn you all." Bernael was furious. He turned and bore his eyes into mine. "I will be the one that rips out your heart mortal, make no mistake about it. It will not be my brother, but I who will savor in the taste of your blood."

In milliseconds, before I could even understand what was happening, Justin had his hand around Bernael's neck. "If you as even breathe around her, the only blood you'll be tasting is your own!" he roared angrily as he let go of the monster and took a step back.

Bernael grinned devilishly. "Alexander will not always be

there to protect you," he said inches away from Justin's face. "Don't think for a minute that I'll hesitate to kill you next time."

"Enough," yelled Alexander waving his hand in the air.

In seconds Bernael bowed his head and disappeared.

I had opened my mouth to say something else when a slight sensation of movement passed through the air around me. At first I thought it was the light wind that brushed across my face, but then a faint blue glow sprang up in the emptiness. It was not like any light I had seen, for it illuminated nothing else; it was only a pulsing sky-blue streak hanging in the air.

"He's gone," said the sweet child's voice. "Bernael is nowhere in sight master." Ramiel was apparently watching everything, informing Alexander of the demon's actions.

"Good, good," answered Alexander in a low sullen voice. "Keep your wits about you; he'll be on the prowl."

"Of course," Ramiel said fading away.

J ustin's embrace was exactly what I needed. He held me tight – as tight as I held onto him. After a few minutes he led me to where Tyler sat. Aunt Leslie and Uncle Abbot were already there looking after him. He seemed to be in some pain and unable to stand on his own.

"Finals week is a killer," Tyler said as soon as our eyes met. Even after what he'd been through he was still trying to make me feel better. Teary-eyed, I kneeled down and gave him a tight hug.

"Don't be like that. I'm fine, Caity. Are you okay?" he asked taking my hand.

"Yeah, I guess." The tears didn't seem to stop. "You scared me," I admitted, giving him another hug.

"You both need your rest," said Aunt Leslie as she helped me up off the road. "Justin will drive both of you home."

We both nodded in agreement and looked on as one by one the Ellri crossed the road and slowly disappeared into the woods, fading like ghosts into the lush greenery.

"That's just so cool," exclaimed Tyler while Justin was helping him in the Porsche. "Come on Caitlin," he smiled patting his knees, "you're going to have to sit on my lap."

Tyler's smirk was enough to cause Justin to smack him on the back of the head. "Don't make me leave you on the side of the road like road kill."

Tyler shut his mouth and sat quietly in the passenger's seat.

From the corner of my eye I saw a figure traversing the fields on foot. I knew it was Alexander. *He's walking it off.* I thought. It was all too much, even for him. He loved Bernael more than he wanted to admit; admitting it would've meant loving the monster he'd become.

"Justin, can you take Tyler home? I need to do something first. I'll walk home,"

Justin followed my gaze across the field and instantly understood what I had in mind. "Just don't be late. I'll be waiting."

I gave him a quick kiss on the lips and watched them drive off. Using my gift, it merely took seconds to reach Alexander. The whole landscape flew by me at the speed of light. I couldn't even tell I was moving.

"Took you long enough," Alexander jested, attempting to smile.

"You know old man," I jested as I took his arm in mine. "You shouldn't keep all these feelings bottled up."

He stopped and turned to me. "You're sure you're only eighteen, right?"

I laughed. "An infant by any measure."

He shook his head in disbelief. "You did today what I tried to do for thousands of years. You touched his soul, touched his heart. How? How did you know?"

I smiled. "I saw it in the way he looked at me. The reason Bernael finds me interesting is not because of who I am or what I might become, but what I am to you."

He looked baffled. "What do you mean?"

"For a person who knows everything you sure don't know the basics."

He chuckled.

"Bernael wasn't curious about me on terms of my gifts, but he wanted to see what it was about me that kept you interested. He loves you, Alex. He really does. I saw it in his eyes today. He was jealous of how comfortable you felt around me. He lusts for your attention; for your caress. He might be thousands of years old, but he is still that sixteen-year old that lost his family. In his eyes he seeks your approval."

He shook his head in wonder. "Sorry if I sound repetitive, but are you sure that you are only eighteen? Your insight is remarkable."

"Blame it on the years of purely observing life rather than living it," I said saddened.

He patted me softly on the back. "You did great controlling your anger today. I was real proud of you."

"I have to admit it's much harder doing the right thing. It takes more energy to stay in control."

Alexander nodded.

"Alex, how did it feel saying what you said to Bernael?"

"Let's just say that I've experienced every emotion over the course of my long life, but today I must admit was like no other." He turned and looked at me. "I don't have the words to describe what it is I feel."

"That's a good sign, right? It means you did the right thing; I'm glad." I nudged him knowingly. "What will happen to him now?"

He half smiled at my attempt to bring him out of his current melancholy state. "Caitlin, you really didn't think that you could change him, did you?"

"I think we made a difference in his life, brought a ray of light into his deep dark existence."

Alexander smiled. "The damned hate the light."

"I don't believe that. They just forgot how the evanescent warmth feels against their skin. Trust me Alex, Bernael felt the warmth today. I know it in my gut."

He stroked my back fatherly like. "I surely hope so; for his own sake."

"And me? Where does this leave me, Alex?"

"You are left to fend through finals and pass with flying colors." He smiled and slowly faded into nothingness.

"Alone in the middle of nowhere once again; this was turning into a nasty habit," I told myself.

I followed the road back home because I simply didn't feel adventurous enough to go through the woods. Not that the road had less evils to overcome. Unfortunately, the one true demon I was trying to outrun since morning was now only a few yards away getting out of her BMW.

"This day just doesn't let up," I whispered, approaching

Megan with every step. She looked as if she was about to speak.

"Choose your words wisely," I warned, walking past her.

"Who do you think you are?" she screeched as I continued down the road. Kim and Loraine stood on the side avoiding eye contact.

"Hi girls," I said, as I continued on my way.

I suddenly felt Megan's hand on my arm. "You're not going anywhere, till I say you are," she shrieked holding me tight.

I looked at her hand on my arm and then turned my gaze to her. "You don't want to do that," I began, shrugging her off. "This really isn't a good time; trust me."

"Why couldn't you just stay away," she fumed. "Everything was perfectly fine until you got here. Why the hell did you have to come back?"

"Like it or not Megan, Oaks is my home, so get used to it."

She instantly grabbed my scarred wrist looking down at the triangular mark burnt into my skin. "What the hell is that?" she asked disgusted, dropping my hand with force. "Look at you Caitlin, You are a freak!" she said and shoved me with one hand.

The deep breath I took was the only thing saving her from my wrath. I had anger issues – I knew this, but what person wouldn't have reacted in this situation? I took another deep breath before I simply pointed to her car.

"What?" she asked obnoxiously grabbing my arm again; this time even tighter than before.

I took yet another deep breath.

"What are you pointing at, freak?"

I smiled. "Don't you live in the opposite direction?" I asked. "Here allow me." I focused my gaze on her precious little car.

In seconds, the automobile was in the air awaiting my next command. "It's up to you Megan. Where would you have me put it?" Her hand instantly unclasped from my arm. "I thought so," I muttered returning the vehicle back on the road. This time it was facing in the direction of her house. "I told you Megan, any day but today. I had enough."

She stared helplessly. "You are a freak!" she screamed in distaste.

"Yes, I know. I'm freaking awesome," I smiled, swallowing back the need to strike her.

That second, Justin pulled up to the side of the road in his Audi. He slid out and stood there waiting. In no time at all, his smile soothed this agonizing need to pulverize her.

I turned to Megan and smiled again. "See you tomorrow," I spat out and dashed across the street and into Justin's embrace.

"You should've thrown her car in the ditch," he laughed once we were back in the car.

"Have you learned nothing today?" I smiled, and kissed him on the mouth.

"I learned that you are the most amazing person I have ever met." He took my hand and lifted it to his lips. "What you did today was beyond anything any of us could hope to do."

"I refuse to believe that there's nothing good in Bernael. There's a spark in his eyes and there's nothing evil about it. Now Megan, she's a whole different story."

Justin shook his head laughing. "Take it from me, there is not one kind thought in that mind of his. Bernael's all evil."

"It might not be a thought, but there is something."

Long quiet moments later, Justin pulled up to the house and turned off the engine. With his arm around my waist, he led me to the door. "Apart from school, you won't be leaving my sight from now on."

I instantly stopped and turned to face him. "You promise."

Justin smiled.

"What? I miss you all day. I need to see you more. You spend way too much time in the Chamber of Enlightenment and not enough time with me."

"I promise," he said, taking me into his arms.

I looked into his glorious deep blue eyes. "Is Tyler going to be okay?"

"Unfortunately, yes," he admitted, smiling mischievously.

I smacked him laughingly on the arm. "Be nice!"

There was no final to study for that night. Let me rephrase that; I had a final first thing in the morning, but I simply didn't have to study for English Lit. I felt quite ready.

In a fleeting moment I came to a decision I wasn't sure I was ready to make. "I know what I want to study at University," I declared while Aunt Leslie served an early dinner.

Kyle and Emily both turned to me.

Justin simply smiled.

Aunt Leslie looked over to uncle Abbot beaming excitedly. "That's great Caitlin. What's your major going to be in?"

"Literature, but I haven't decided on what kind yet," I declared as I picked up my glass of ice tea.

"That is most certainly a great idea child," said uncle Abbot grinning from ear to ear. "It's nice to see you making plans for your future."

"Yes, there is only one condition to my studying at university come September."

"What's that?" asked uncle Abbot, ready to agree to almost anything.

Justin raised his brow in apprehension.

"I apply to university like everybody else. No phone calls, no ridiculous donations. I want to get in the old fashion way."

Kyle chuckled deeply. "As if that's ever going to happen," he said, rolling his eyes.

"As you wish," promised uncle Abbot, glaring at Kyle. "There's no question of you not being accepted. They'll be lucky to have you."

Aunt Leslie was simply glowing. "We should celebrate. Lord knows we've been through enough today." She came round the table and gave me a great big kiss on the cheek.

"That's a wonderful idea," agreed my uncle as he got up. "A celebration is what we need." He headed to the wine cellar and in no time at all was back in the kitchen waving two bottles of wine. "Mission Haut-Brion nineteen-eighty-two," he boasted, placing the bottles on the table.

"Great job dad," Kyle beamed as he got up to fetch the bottle opener.

Emily brought out the expensive crystal.

"Why would you bring these out? There's wine glasses in there," I said, pointing to the kitchen cabinet.

Emily shook her head. "Didn't you hear what dad said? He brought up an eighty-two Mission Haut-Brion. You don't pour a one thousand dollar bottle of wine into any ordinary glass cup."

I almost choked on my ice tea.

"Château la Mission Haut-Brion is located in the Graves region near the city of Bordeaux," explained my uncle. "The vineyard has been operated since the 16th century and their selection is wonderful."

"To a bright future," said Uncle Abbot, holding up his fine crystal, "To all of you, and to your upcoming nuptials darling," he added winking at Emily.

We drank up and celebrated my decision to enter the world of the living and Emily's future with Marc.

"I can help with your applications," offered Justin visibly happy with my decision.

"I'd like that."

"We'll get to it tomorrow," he said, lifting the wine glass to his lips.

Reaching for some cheese, Emily looked at Justin. "It'll have to wait for later on in the evening."

"Why?" I asked wondering what she had planned.

"We're going to look for a dress, silly; a dress for you to wear to my wedding. Did you forget?"

"Is that tomorrow? I completely forgot."

"Gee Caitlin, show some enthusiasm for my upcoming nuptials."

Kyle glared at her. "You self-centered snob," he blurted out. "Don't you think Caitlin has had enough on her mind? Cut her some slack already."

Emily was about to apologize, but I motioned for her to stop. "No Kyle," I began, "Em's right. Her wedding is important. I'm stupid to have allowed it to slip my mind. I'm truly sorry Em."

"Don't apologize to her, Caitlin. She's gone overboard."

Annoyed at her brother, Emily stormed out of the kitchen and headed up to her room.

SEVENTEEN

GONE MISSING

IRST WEEK OF finals had finally come to an end, and by the end of the following week the only thing left to do was attend the graduation ceremony. The official end of my childhood; the end of having school as an excuse to get out of doing things I hated.

Not being forced to see Megan the she-devil on a daily basis was one of the many perks of graduation. The hateful looks aimed at me the previous week were enough to last me a lifetime. She didn't even try to conceal her true distaste towards me anymore. Megan was now quite crude and acidic on each and every encounter. When she was with Tyler she was, at least, marginally civil towards me, now however, she chose to be downright cruel, and I loved her for it. Every time I passed her in the hallway she'd either pull a face of sheer loathsomeness or deliberately push past me.

I didn't react, nor did I bring down the whole building on her head as she deserved; instead, I sort of enjoyed being bullied, and the more I seemed to enjoy it, the more frazzled she became. It was the one thing in my life that was as it should be. Over the months, however, I realized that I wasn't the only one on her hate list. Fostering such hatred towards others was definitely a warning sign of rather deep rooted issues; the type only medication could cure, but who was I to judge.

Tyler, on the other hand, was a no-show. Not only did he not return to school after the incident with Bernael, but our teachers never once inquired into his absence as they usually would. Even my aunt and uncle's response to Tyler's absence was strangely delivered. They mentioned that he needed to rest up; that his body was in much need of recuperation, but it was the tone in their voice that hinted to something deeper.

Straight after my last final I had decided to drive over to his house to see for myself. His car was there, but when I knocked on the door nobody answered. I even walked around the grounds hoping to find him in the back yard, but as everywhere else, Tyler was nowhere to be seen.

Even Emily side-stepped the issue of where Tyler was. I must've asked her a dozen times while we were on our little shopping trip in town looking for a dress for me to wear at her wedding. She kept changing the subject by handing me another dress to try on. For some reason she believed that pink would suit me. "This is my wedding," she kept saying trying to talk me into wearing yet another ridiculously pink poufy dress.

I shoved the article of clothing back into her hand. "This is my body," I responded. "Have I done something to make you mad?"

"Caitlin," she begged, holding out another dress.

"You can't be serious!" I exclaimed, looking at the

preposterously short cocktail dress she was displaying, hoping I'd wear it.

"Come on Caitlin, this isn't actually pink. It's almost white," she pronounced, pushing me back into the changing room.

"I give up!" I yelled, refusing to wear anything else. The sales girl stood there agitated with my aversion to clothes. "You're right, Em. This is your wedding, so why don't you just pick whichever one you like and surprise me on the day of the event? I promise I won't complain. I'll wear anything you pick out, but please don't torture me like this. You know I hate trying on clothes."

She smiled wickedly. "You promise you won't make a fuss."

"I promise," I huffed as I slipped back into my comfortable Levi's.

She rolled her eyes as soon as I walked out of the dressing area. "You and jeans," she noted, shaking her head. "Is that what you'll wear at Justin's birthday party?"

"Not exactly this, but something comfy; it's a barbeque for god's sake. What do you expect me to wear, a gown?"

"Since we're here, why don't you pick out something pretty to wear?"

"It's a barbeque!" I insisted, lifting my hands in the air in utter frustration. "Kyle said nothing fancy-schmancy."

"Kyle's an idiot," she pronounced and started going through the racks. "You need to look nice, trust me."

"I'm not trying anything on. I had enough!" I snapped, and fell back into the velvety cushioned armchair that adorned the changing room.

The sales assistant walked away looking as if she wanted to slap me. I couldn't really blame the poor girl. She did stand there for more than an hour waiting to see which dress I'd finally pick out.

"Melanie, I'll be back without this pain in the neck," Emily offered as we finally headed for the exit. "Could you put those dresses to the side, I'll come back and pick one."

Melanie, the over-dolled up sales assistant, smiled and wished Emily good luck. I suspected that the good-luck was aimed at me, and the tremendous patience my cousin was exhibiting. To my defense, I never wanted to go shopping in the first place.

Once in her car, Emily simply stared out the window. "Fine," she finally crowed, putting the car in gear. "I'll just get you something later."

The ride home that day was exceptionally quiet. I had a million questions to ask her about her plans and preparations, but I simply didn't feel it was appropriate to bring up the topic just yet. Clearly not over how childish I acted in the store – she continued to drive in silence. A little while later and only minutes from the house she finally turned to look at me. "You really need to grow up," she stated in a condescending tone.

I kept my mouth shout, knowing that she already had a lot on her plate. She looked at me once again with a side glance and smiled, visibly aware at how much effort I was putting into being calm and rational.

"I know I'm being a pain about this whole wedding thing," she finally started to say. "But some help on your part would be nice."

"You're just trying to do too many things at once, Em," I admitted, trying to defuse the situation. "And I'm sorry too. You know how I hate shopping for clothes, but that still doesn't give me the right to rain on your parade. Whatever you need, I promise I'll be there. You name it I'll do it, but please no more shopping."

She parked the car in the garage and slid out gracefully. Only a few steps behind her, I collected the rest of her bags and entered the house.

"I didn't mean to pressure you about the dress," she answered, once we were in her room. Emily fell back on her bed and put her hands up to her face as I discarded the bags right next to the place where she left the ones she was holding.

"Why don't you get a professional to do everything?" I asked, sitting next to her.

"It's my wedding. I want to do it on my own. It will take me longer to explain exactly what I want to a wedding planner. Marc is being really great, but even he is getting on my nerves lately."

"Marc is wonderful," I acknowledged, patting her leg. "You're just overdoing it. What can I do to take some of the pressure off?"

"Well," she started to say sitting up. "If you really want to help –,"

"Of course I do silly. Now what is it?"

"I need your awesome powers the day before the event. I need you to set up everything outside. Do you think you can do that?"

"Is that all?" I asked. "You want me to set up the chairs and stuff."

"Well, it's more than just the chairs. I don't want the professionals doing it because they'll just piss me off. If you do it, I can make changes in an instant."

"Yeah sure. That won't be a problem. I simply need to have an idea of what you want and everything else will fall into place in minutes."

"I know! That's why I want you to do it."

"Anything else?"

"Well there is one more thing." She was hesitant – looking like she got caught with her hand in the cookie jar.

"What is it?"

"You promise you won't tell anyone?"

I raised an eyebrow. "How is it that no one else knows?"

"They don't, trust me, but you have to promise not to tell anyone, not even Marc."

"Yes. Okay. I promise. Now, what is it already?"

"How would you like to be a godmother?" she asked staring at me, waiting for a response.

It took me a few seconds, but it all finally sunk in. "No Way!"

"What? Why? I thought you'd love to be my baby's godmother."

"Your baby's godmother?" I just couldn't wrap my mind around the whole meaning of the word. "We're going to have a baby?"

Emily smiled. "Well, technically speaking, me and Marc are, but I'm glad you see it that way."

"Em," Silence filled the air between us. After a time, I stopped staring and hugged her. "This is so wonderful. I mean how." I shook my head. "I know how. What I meant to say is when. When did you find out?"

"I didn't – I mean, I'm not really sure yet, but all the signs are there. It does explain my mood swings, right?"

"Yeah, I guess. I'm sure there's a test you can take. How does it work for our kind? I don't know how things like this are done, Em." I was babbling on and on, and then I asked, "Who else knows?"

"No one, I want to be sure that I am first. I don't dare tell mom. You know how traditional she is about these things. She'll kill me. She's looking forward to a 'white' wedding."

"Oh please, Em. Leslie is many things, but naïve she is not. She knows exactly what you and Marc have been up to."

Emily pulled a face. "I know, but still she will be disappointed."

"Don't be ridiculous! She won't have a problem with it. She'll be wonderful. You guys are getting married in a few weeks anyway."

"It's not that she'll have a problem, but she'll surely give me one of those looks that I'll carry with me for the rest of my life."

Remembering my aunts all too familiar expression of disappointment, I realized that Emily had a point. "How do you expect to keep it from everyone?"

"Leave that to me, but we're getting ahead of ourselves. I'm not sure that I am yet," she pondered as she stood. "Nobody can read your thoughts so the only thing you need to do is keep your mouth shut. Do you think you can do that?"

"Yeah, of course! But won't they know?"

"I told you, don't worry about that," she exclaimed, turning to face me.

Emily started to wring her hands, and the only time she would do that was right before she had something major to ask; something she felt guilty about asking. "Out with it," I smiled warmly. "What else would you have me do?"

Her smile was even brighter. "I need your help with the Nobe."

"The Nobe?" I looked at her questionably. "What does the Nobe have to do with this?"

"Caitlin, I don't know how the Oath of Unity will affect the baby – if there is a baby."

She was pacing.

"We're talking about the unity of our powers. I don't want to put the baby in any harm."

"Oh, I haven't thought of that." I also got up off the bed and walked over to where she stood. "Why don't you simply ask them?"

"Don't you think I've tried summoning them? They won't respond to me, but maybe if you intervene, they might show up."

"It doesn't work that way. I don't call on them. They simply appear. But I guess I can ask Alexander for a favor. What would you have me say?"

"Find out if it's going to be a problem."

"But I thought you didn't want me to tell anyone."

"Are you even remotely aware of who the Nobe is?" she asked raising her hands. "Do you really think they don't already know?"

"How am I supposed to know who knows what around here? Nobody tells me anything, and when they do I'm supposed to keep it from everybody else, but then I find out that everybody else already knows."

Emily giggled. "You're so right. I'm sorry."

"It's just really frustrating trying to figure out how you all can be in tune with each other and yet keep so many secrets."

"That's easy. I'm surprised Justin didn't explain all this."

"He told me you can block each other out. He didn't go into much detail. Not that he had any time, what with all these things going on."

"He's right. If we want to keep something personal we just block everyone out. It's not rocket science. It's a simple thought process, it works automatically. You're lucky because your gift does it for you."

"I always considered it a handicap."

"Are you kidding me? I'd love to have all my thoughts to myself."

"Can you block out the Ellri?"

"No, not really, but they wouldn't probe unless they thought it was necessary. The voices we hear on a daily basis are frustrating enough. None of us like to intentionally listen in on other's thoughts because it takes too much concentration and it makes the other voices all the more loud. It's like trying to listen to a radio program through interference. It's not fun. However, for people like Justin there is no interference. He can easily concentrate on an individual and hear his mind as clear as day."

"I guess I'm lucky then," I admitted. "I might never possess this ability."

"It would be wonderful to block people out permanently," she huffed, patting her flat belly.

I placed my hand on top of hers. "I can't believe you're going to be a mommy." I gazed at her smiling. "You're going to be so great. If you're half as good at being a mommy as you are being an older sister, you'll be fantastic."

Emily instantly hugged me. "I really, really hope I am. Marc would be an amazing father," she sighed worriedly. "I have to make sure everything will be okay."

"Don't worry, Em," I assured. "Everything will be, and after Wednesday when finals are over, I'll be all yours to boss around. I really want to help as much as I can."

Emily gave me another quick hug and took to her purchases.

Standing there watching my cousin go through all the items she had bought was an awakening; nothing would be as it once was. We were all growing up. Emily was going to be a married woman and a mother at that. In no time at all, my eyes brewed over with tears at the mere thought of my own parents.

Was my mother as happy to find out she was pregnant with me? I quickly wondered.

Knowing nothing about the way they met or even the slightest true memory of how it was to have her around was painful, but over the years it had become bearable enough to brush off quite easily.

I shook my head trying to banish the sadness from my system. This was a happy occasion. There was no need to ruin it with memories of the past.

Apart for the shopping bit, the day was fun. It had been a long time since my cousin and I spent time together. Her joyous news left a permanent smile on my face for days. Even Justin noticed my change in mood. He was visibly uplifted by my happiness.

Nobody knew why I was happy, but they didn't seem to care. They concentrated on the moment rather than asking the reasons behind the change.

Tyler however was still nowhere to be seen and no one clued me in on why he was missing.

A s every other night at about seven I waltzed down to the kitchen to sit with the family for dinner. The only difference about that night was that I was the only one standing in the spacious room. The table wasn't even set, and that's when I realized how quiet the whole house had been all day.

I hadn't noticed it before because I was engrossed in John Milton's Paradise Lost, but now the house was abnormally quite. Even the gentle whir of the refrigerator was muted, and then I heard the tap on the rooftop, followed by another. Rain began to dance on the shingles, and the trees seemed to whisper as a breeze careened through their branches.

"Where is everyone," I whispered, getting a soda from the refrigerator. The fizzy drink helped in soothing the distaste in my mouth. Though the feeling wasn't as astute as it was the first few days, there was still a hint of bile in everything I ate or drank.

Drink in hand; I headed back to the study to continue my reading. I deliberately poked my head in each room as I walked by; making sure that everyone was truly gone.

"They're all in the inner realm," said the sweet angelic voice.

"Ramiel, what are you doing here? And why aren't you appearing in person?"

"I'm not actually here," he said chuckling. "I'm supposed to be watching over the sacred event."

I stood in the middle of the foyer looking around in all different directions not sure where the voice was going to come from next. "What event?"

"Over here," he said. In seconds a dull light appeared on the second step. "Everyone is at Tyler's ascension."

"Really!" I squealed. "So, he's fine then?"

"He's better than fine, he's Ascending, and he has gained his full gift. Now it's up to him how he uses it."

"Tyler will do wonders, I'm sure of it. But why hasn't anyone said anything? I was worried about him."

The dull outline suddenly faded.

"Ramiel?" I called, wondering why he disappeared without a sound.

"I'm right here," he finally said. "You're not the only one I have to keep an eye on, you know."

"You mean there are others causing you as much problems as me?" I asked grinning.

Didn't know if Ramiel was going to follow me or not, but I made my way to the study nonetheless, and for an instant held the door open for him to pass.

"Just about seven billion others are as messed up as you," he said smiling.

I felt stupid standing there knowing full well that he really didn't need the door to be held open. He laughed and glided right in.

"I thought you watch over the gifted, why would you need to keep an eye out for the non-gifted as well?"

As soon as he approached the comfortable sofa, Ramiel slowly materialized into the sweet little boy I grew so fond of. "What's the difference?" he asked, plopping down on the furniture seemingly in much need of rest. "Everybody needs watching over."

I took the seat next to him. "So what exactly do you watch for?"

"I see through their eyes, through their thoughts. It's my job to observe human kind, to relay what I see back to my master."

"And then what?"

"Then, the Nobe Council decide what the best way to intervene is."

"So the gifted do help out. We actually do use our powers for the greater good."

"Of course," he boasted as he rested his head back on the cushion. "Thousands of years ago we, the Nobe as you call us, have come to regard ourselves as the keepers of balance. We are each powerful enough to bring turmoil and destruction to this planet, but where's the challenge in that? Alexander saw to it that we placed ordinary people above any of us. He taught us to consider the non-gifted and the gifted as equals. But the Fallen didn't agree with the whole idea of being equals to the weaker, less gifted individuals. The Varjatus as well consider themselves superior on the evolutionary chart than any ordinary human."

"Well, that certainly explains the Korbs' superiority complex," I muttered.

Ramiel grinned at my comment. "You can't blame them for believing they're better. I hate to admit it, but taking their gifts into consideration they are quite powerful."

"Just because you have greater power doesn't exactly make you any better."

"True," he agreed, and stood up. "I really need to get out of here. I'm getting way too comfortable being in my human form. I'm afraid I'm going to lose my edge."

"Do you ever get a day off?"

"Why would I ever want one?" He strode around the room momentarily and turned to look at me. "I really like hanging out with you, Caitlin. I'm happy that I can finally be myself around a mortal. You make me feel young again."

I giggled looking at his eight-year-old façade. "Thanks for doing what you do."

He started fading away as he spoke. "People like you make it all worthwhile."

Moments later, I realized that I missed my opportunity to ask him about Emily's dilemma. Ramiel of all people would know what to do.

Book in hand, I slumped back into the armchair and was once again lost in its writing. I didn't know how many hours had passed, but I was nearly done the whole book. In that instant, I heard the door to the study open.

"I can't believe he's ascended." I heard Kyle say.

He was talking to somebody without being aware of my presence. I poked my head around the large armchair and noticed that he was talking to Marc.

"We really need to keep him under close watch. There's no telling how he'll turn out. I really feel bad for the guy. Bernael really did a number on him."

I quickly closed my book and stood up surprising both of them.

"Really Caitlin, you need to do something about your gift," said Marc visibly shocked to see me. "Not knowing where you are is spooky."

"What's going on with Tyler?" I asked worriedly.

They both looked at each other unwilling to share their knowledge.

"Don't do this to me," I begged, placing my book on the antique desk with a thud. "Tell me! What's happening with Tyler?"

In seconds Justin walked in and without saying a word, both Marc and Kyle walked out of the study without a hint about Tyler.

"Why do they do that?" I began, "A simple answer is all I ask for. How hard is it to answer a damn question around here?"

"Don't blame them," Justin said, as he took my hand in his, "They're simply following directions. Tyler is one of the Ascended now. Whatever happens to him is none of your business."

I pulled my hand away and walked to the window. The heavy material was pulled slightly to the side giving way to the soft evening light. "Just tell me one thing, Justin." I started to say turning to face him. "Is Tyler going to be okay?"

Justin didn't answer. He just stood there and stared.

"If anything happens to him it's going to be my fault. Bernael was using him to get to me. Do you have any idea how that makes me feel?"

"How many times do I have to say this? None of this is your fault. Tyler needs to work some things out on his own. His gift will guide him. The Ellri and all the Ascended will be there to help him," Justin offered, taking a few steps closer. "Caitlin, you had nothing to do with what is happening to Tyler."

"Is he going to be okay?" Anxiety set free the tears that fear could not. "If anything happens to him I won't be able to live with myself. He means everything to me."

The instant the words came out of my mouth I wished I hadn't said them because Justin's expression suddenly changed. He didn't much like the way I talked about Tyler. It was one thing to tolerate our friendship, but a whole different thing to hear me talk about my friend with such emotion.

"I'll see to it that he's fine," he stated coldly, and headed out the door.

I didn't have much time to respond. He slammed the door shut behind him and left me all alone to pull my foot out of my mouth. "Good going," I whispered.

"You have a knack of clearing a room," Ramiel joked, appearing in the far corner.

"Now you're just snooping!" I accused him.

He laughed. "I told you from the beginning, you intrigue me."

I sat back in the armchair sulking. "I keep making a mess out of everything. If it's not one thing, it's another. Emily was right; I do need to grow up."

"Don't rush to grow up. Take it from me; it's not all it's cracked up to be. Screwing things up is what eighteen-year-olds do. Enjoy it."

I shook my head. "I would if I didn't keep hurting people on the way."

"Justin's not hurt. He wants to make you happy." Ramiel closed his eyes, and looked up at the ceiling. "He's with Tyler as we speak."

"You told me Tyler will be okay. What's this I hear about Bernael?"

"He will be okay. Now stop worrying!"

He looked up again.

"What is it?"

"Nothing that we need to worry about just yet."

This was my chance to ask him about the Oath of Unity. "Ramiel what can you tell me about the Oath a couple takes?"

He smiled. "So you're finally getting hitched to Justin?"

I made a face that caused him to laugh.

"No, I'm not! I just wanted to know what happens if the woman is pregnant. Can something happen to the baby?"

His little brow tightened. "You're still a virgin, why would you care about things like that."

Beet red, I looked down at my hands in utter shock. An eight-year-old was bringing up my virginity.

"Why do you look like you're going to be sick?" he asked. "You are a virgin, aren't you?"

I flinched my head up. "Can you please stop saying that word? It's strange hearing it from a small boy."

Suddenly, and without any warning he shifted forms. Now, instead of the adorable eight-year-old I had the town's practitioner standing in front of me – robe and all.

"Does this look make you feel more comfortable?" he asked smiling.

Though the exterior was different, the facial expressions were all the same. Ramiel's expressive eyes shone through.

"I prefer your original look. Dr. Pier always scared the crap out of me." I said smiling.

Back in his adorable self, Ramiel came and sat next to me. "Why in the world would you need to know about being pregnant?"

"Just humor me."

"It's a serious problem. The instant the Oath is taken an immense surge of energy is distributed between the couple. There's no telling what it can do to the unborn fetus."

"So, what can be done to secure the safety of the child?"

"Well, that's easy. Don't take the Oath."

I sprang up. "No, that's not an option," I cried. "They are meant to take the Oath."

"Emily and Marc will be just fine."

Shocked I turned to him. "How did you know?"

"I'm The Watcher, remember? I'm an all mighty immortal." He chuckled.

"But you said that the baby will be in danger."

"Yes of course, if there ever were a baby." He got up and traced his fingers over the book shelves. "I'm sorry to say, but our Emily will find out she's not pregnant after all, her mood swings are all her doing."

"Oh, no!" I fell back down in the seat. "She was looking so forward to starting a family."

"Don't look so glum. There are many children in her future."

I finally smiled. "Are you sure of that?"

He raised an eyebrow. "She'll need you tonight. She's on her way back from the doctors as we speak."

"I don't know if I should be happy or sad."

"Marc and Emily new the risk they were taking. The gifted should not dally in the art of love prior to Ascending in fear of a pregnancy, and the Oath is quiet the same."

Before I had a chance to ask anything, Ramiel looked up towards the ceiling and his features instantly froze. He disappeared in seconds.

"What is it?" I asked looking around.

"Be quiet!" he ordered. His voice was tight, but I thought there was a hint of rage there. "Caitlin –," His whisper was sharp and ominous; "You must do what I tell you and do it to the letter. Do you understand?"

"What's going on?" I asked with my heart in my mouth.

"Abaddon is lurking and he knows you're alone. The Ellri have been summoned, but they can't come just yet. The Ascension is not entirely finished.

"Where's the Nobe?" I asked turning my head in the direction of the voice.

"I'm right here," he said half laughing.

"Oh yeah, sorry." I smiled. "So what am I supposed to do?"

"Shhh!" he ordered once again.

I froze on the spot. The angel of death was coming for me and I was sitting there talking to an invisible eight-year-old.

"Caitlin, he's approaching. Don't say a word. Don't make a sound. No matter how much he provokes you. Do not talk to death, or you will be welcoming him into your realm. Stand still no matter what he does. He won't harm you while I'm here; might try to scare you, but that's all. I can try to stop him, but I will set off a war that none of us want. So do as I say and don't flinch."

I stood there motionless. It wasn't every day that I had death come to my door, literally. In seconds my head started to thud right at the temples. With each second the incredulous pain increased all the more. *Of all the times to have a headache,* I thought. I rubbed the back of my neck trying to remedy the situation, but nothing seemed to work.

"I said don't move," whispered Ramiel.

I grimaced from pain closing my eyes and let my hands drop to my side.

Moments later, only a few feet away, Abaddon made his appearance; slowly taking human form right there in front of my eyes. It started out as a faint apparition, but slowly solidified into the most breathtaking being my eyes had ever fallen upon. I was in awe of his beauty. Spellbound, I stood there staring. I was surely not expecting something as angelic. His brother, Bernael was traumatically more in tune with his evil ways; he even looked his part as the angel of darkness, but Abaddon – Abaddon was nothing like Bernael. The marvel bestowed upon me was stunning in every way.

He smiled gloriously and took a step closer. Sweeping the floor was the flowing white material that draped his tall figure, which only added to the allure, along with his long blond hair that cascaded down the front of his chest and the length of his back.

"You take pleasure in death, do you?" he asked in a honeyed voice. "Am I to your liking mortal?"

His grey eyes bore into mine. He had one of those faces you couldn't help but stare at. Every aspect of his features was divinely symmetrical.

"Is this how appealing you view death?" He was studying my face. "It's been quite a while that I looked so enticing. Most people conjure up frightful creatures, but here you are making me look pretty; more angelic than the angels themselves. You must love the taste of death to have manifested such a beautiful creation."

I took Ramiel's advice to heart and kept my mouth shut. I wasn't sure how I was responsible for his appearance, but I knew better than to open my mouth and say something stupid.

Abaddon turned his head up and looked up towards the ceiling closing his eyes momentarily. "Ah, Ramiel old friend, what are you doing here?"

"You are testing my patience demon," hissed Ramiel in a menacing tone. There was nothing childlike in the sound of his voice. It vibrated off the walls causing me to take an involuntary step back. "Abaddon, think your next steps wisely or I shall not think twice before returning you to your master without a tongue."

The demon's eyebrows pulled together. "Knowing that she means so much to you will only make this much more entertaining," answered Abaddon as he shifted his gaze back to me.

"You will bow your head in reverence to the light," Ramiel stated, repeating the words of Deondra's prophecy.

Abaddon took a step back and stared at me. His deep set eyes fell directly to my scarred wrists. "The second of the two is who I seek," he muttered to himself. "So it is you," he spoke, turning his gaze to my eyes. "You are the next I am meant to take. I hope you make it more fun than the last two. Aisilin was way too young to enjoy and Deondra made it too simple." He circled me again. "From what my brother says, you'll be worth the wait."

He stepped away, and walked around the room staring down at his feet. He seemed amazed at his own human form. It must've been quite some time since he appeared in an earthly body. He looked bothered, but amused at the same time.

For some unexplained reason my mind kept repeating lines from Paradise Lost:

> *For those rebellious, here their Prison ordained*
> *In utter darkness, and their portion set*
> *As far removed from God and light of Heaven*
> *As from the Center thrice to the utmost Pole.*
> *O how unlike the place from whence they fell!*
> *There the companions of his fall, overwhelmed*

With Floods and Whirlwinds of tempestuous fire,
He soon discerns, and weltering by his side
One next himself in power, and next in crime

Over and over again I kept repeating the verse, and unintentionally, without considering the dire consequences of going against what Ramiel said about keeping absolute quiet, I spoke the lines as a whisper, drawing Abaddon's full attention.

"What did you just say?"

As quiet as the first time, barely an echo of my own voice, I stared at him and continued to recite lines from my reading:

A Dungeon horrible, on all sides round
As one great Furnace flamed, yet from those flames
No light, but rather darkness visible
Served only to discover sights of woe,
Regions of sorrow, doleful shades, where peace
And rest can never dwell, hope never comes
That comes to all; but torture without end….

Abaddon came even closer and I raised my gaze to his expressionless grey eyes.

"What you see before you is the real thing, young mortal. No writing can surmise the extent of what we are." He came round to the other side, leaning in closer. "I am the demon that you read about; the Fallen that so many books describe."

I practically stopped breathing, but not due to fear, but to the ridiculously intoxicating sensation that gripped my chest as his cold breath feathered across my cheek. There was something about him so appealing, so heavenly addictive that I was sure to follow to the end of the world had he asked it of me. Against my better judgment I smiled.

He stood behind me and whispered in my ear. "You seem to enjoy my presence, mortal."

"Why wouldn't I?" I asked, turning to face him in a mesmerized state, which visibly surprised him.

He laughed harshly. "You are intrigued by me, are you not? But know that yours will not be a peaceful death; I can assure you that."

"I've been ready to meet my Maker for the longest time," I finally admitted, staring at his flawless features. "Whether my Maker is prepared for the ordeal of meeting me is a whole different matter."

Ramiel chuckled.

"You're a vulgar young thing, aren't you? You jest as you know not what I'm capable of," he uttered in annoyance.

"I don't care to know what you're capable of. Whatever it is the end is all too clear."

He looked furious. "You mock me!"

"I do not. I'm just pointing out the obvious. You take my life and then what? You won't be able to hurt me anymore. So, in a way you'll be doing me a favor."

"You send me this child!" he yelled staring at the ceiling. "I'm supposed to fear this infant? The child is suicidal," he screeched, talking to someone other than me.

"I am no such thing!"

"Ahh, but you are."

"You know nothing about me!" I protested loudly.

"But I do young mortal. I know more than you think. Just look at how you see me. Am I not appealing to you? Did you not seek me out on several occasions? Back in your dorm room where desperation brought you to your knees or even in Tirion when you so willingly jumped off the cliff – were you not suicidal then?"

I dropped my gaze to the floor.

"Don't look away from the truth, young, insignificant thing. You bask in my attention because you hunger for what I have to give. You hunger for the darkness as much if not more than any of the Fallen. You are like us more than you want to admit."

"You're wrong!" I yelled. "I'm nothing like you."

"Why then, would you not fear us? Why is it that your natural instincts don't lead you away from me, but instead towards me? I am the fear, and the darkness; the nightmares that keep sane people awake."

"I don't fear you!"

"Ah, but you should."

"Why don't you do what you came here to do? Toying with me won't get us anywhere."

"Again, you challenge me. But you fear not, because you know not my wrath. There is a scary monster under your bed, young mortal, each and every night; make no mistake about it, and he is blood thirsty and hell-bent on taking your last breath painfully as you scream for mercy."

My breath caught in my chest as Abaddon quickly stretched out his hand to touch my shoulder.

"Keep your eyes closed!" bellowed Ramiel in my ear.

"No mortal, keep them open," Abaddon ordered. "This will be a great lesson for you."

EIGHTEEN

PURGATORY

S ILENCE ABRUPTLY dissolved into shocked cries and eerie screams. I was standing in the study no more. The smell of sulfur was overwhelming, burning my lungs with each breath I took.

The cavernous edifice was anything but welcoming. The stench of rot inundated the air. Strangled screams caught in my throat, threatening to choke me. I held them back and retreated into the place in my mind where nothing touched me. It was a place I found during those five years that were stripped from my life so ruthlessly.

Looking around my hellish surroundings, I suddenly felt a familiarity to the place. I knew I've never visited that God forsaken area before, but there was something about it. Then like a cold slap across the face it all came to me.

"This isn't real," I muttered, turning to my escort. "This is all in my mind, isn't it? It's from a book I love, 'The Devine Comedy'."

I recognized it by the morbid scenes my own mind had conjured up while reading Dante's Inferno. The scene that materialized in front of me was that of the bridge that crossed the tenth gulf of hell, from where Dante heard the cries of the alchemists and forgers, who were tormented, but not being able to discern anything on account of the darkness, he descended the rock, that took him to the last of the compartments in which the eighth circle of hell was divided, and then saw the spirits who were afflicted by divers plagues and diseases.

"This isn't real," I repeated, "It can't be."

"Quite sordid thoughts for one so young," Abaddon hissed. "What part do you think I play in all this?"

"I don't want to be here anymore," I stated softly, fearing what it all meant. "None of it is real."

"That's where you're wrong. All your senses can't be mistaken. You feel the desperation and the pain. How can all this be anything but real?"

"It can't be," I turned and looked at death in the face. "It's in my head. It's all in my head."

In that instant a stream of dark mist crawled its way to our feet. The surrounding area spun into a gray swirl of confusion as the image of a man burst with startling clarity, and in a raspy voice Bernael spoke, "You have to do much better than that dear brother." The monster appeared only a few feet away, bringing with him souls tormented by venomous and pestilent serpents. "This child doesn't scare that easily."

He was in black, his features shadowed, silhouetted against the night, prowling around me with long, tireless strides and without any warning he grabbed my arm and pulled me up against him with his back to his brother. He leaned in and spoke softly against my ear, "You seem to attract evil young mortal," he slithered, tightening his hold on my upper arm. "It's in your blood; born into it as many of the Fallen were. It calls to you, yet you willfully defy it."

I futilely struggled again and again, but only felt more pain as Bernael sank his claws deep into my skin to restrain me. The minute he let go I took a defensive step forward, but with a mere stretch of his hand he stopped me in my tracks as if I were but a ragdoll to do with as he pleased.

He took a step closer and stroked my cheek with his razor sharp nails. "You took everything from me," he sneered, as he took yet another step forward, causing me to take one back. "He will disappoint you, I promise." His voice lowered. "Father knows no love. He will be your downfall; make no mistake about it. Nothing is above the law in his eyes, nobody more important." With every step Bernael took forward he distanced me from his brother. "Be warned about your Alexander. He loves not."

My eyes brimmed with tears as the sense of pain emanated from his every pore. Without restrain I dropped my arms, refusing to fight his tight grip. Bernael instantly let go and his gaze remained transfixed to mine. With one hand I reached up and placed my palm up against his chest. Instantly, he took a big step back. "You dare touch me!" he roared.

"Are you finished playing with your toy, brother?" asked Abaddon from a distance. "I grow weary of these games. She is of no true threat. Taking her will be easier than the other two."

Bernael's gaze was locked onto mine. He didn't budge.

"Come brother, let me finish this."

Again Bernael didn't move. He was the only thing standing

between me and Death himself. "She's not worthy of your gift, brother," Bernael finally said. "Allow me the joy of playing a bit more with the child."

Both immortals quite suddenly pulled away from me and without any warning I felt a hard tug on my arm as just as fast I was pulled back into a vacuum, and forced out of the dark, dismal pits of hell only to reenter the comfortable surroundings of the study.

"What the hell are you doing?" Justin yelled, grabbing my other arm – shaking me lightly.

Disoriented and with a pounding headache, I just looked at him trying to make sense of what had happened. The horrible sensations faded, leaving me nauseated and shaking, clutching onto his strong arms as the room spun around me.

"Why are you yelling at me?" I finally asked, trying to gain my balance. My knees were about to buckle under me when Justin instantly tightened his grip and held me upright. He helped me to the armchair.

"It's not like I asked for any of this to happen," I whispered, resting my head on the pillow. After a long silence, I added. "My head is heavy."

"Lie down for a minute," Justin bade me in a gentle voice. "The feeling will fade soon enough.

"Why do they insist on bothering me?"

"Ramiel warned you!"

My eyes felt too heavy to keep open.

"Rest for now," Justin said, pulling the soft knit throw over my shoulders.

Several quiet minutes later, I took a deep breath and turned to Justin who was sitting across from me. "I just can't seem to follow the damn rules," I acknowledge, trying to erase the look of disappointment from his face.

"How is it that nobody has seen the Fallen in over a thousand years and you –?"

"That's not fair!" I muttered standing up. He offered his hand for support, but I motioned that I was fine. I walked over and leaning against the desk. "They keep coming to me!" I complained.

"Of course they do! You keep making it so easy." He started pacing. "Why did you have to speak to Abaddon?"

"He was pushing my buttons! What was I supposed to do?"

"Keep quiet and be afraid like any normal individual in the same circumstance."

"Justin, we have already established how freakishly abnormal I am when it comes to fear. Why lecture me now?" I asked, mustering a ghost of a smile.

He strode over to where I was leaning and placed his hands on either side of me; blocking me in. I leaned back dazed by his breathtaking smile. Justin stared for a while without a sound. My heart accelerated with every hint of his breath upon my brow. Slowly he leaned in and brushed his lips against mine – soft at first, hovering over my mouth between each kiss. One hand moved to the nape of my neck, combing his fingers around the roots of my hair.

"You need to pay closer attention," he muttered, drawing my head closer; kissing me even harder.

"Oh trust me," I chimed, responding instantly to his merciless sweet torture; finding it rather hard to concentrate on anything else apart from the longing buried inside of me, "You have my full attention."

My heart was racing. Our bond was getting stronger and it took much more energy to restrain my natural urges. Justin pulled back and looked at me with one eyebrow raised. "I'm serious!"

"So am I," I beamed, catching my breath.

Slowly, I pulled Justin by the shirt bringing him even closer. Sliding myself further back on the desk, I unintentionally caused things to fall to the floor. Ignoring everything, but the affect his lips were having. I wrapped my legs around his waist and pulled him up against my body and he instantly gave out a little moan of satisfaction.

"Caitlin –," he whispered in a low groan between the passionate kisses he was trailing down the side of my neck.

My name on his lips was maddening. There was nothing in the world that I wanted more than Justin. Sinfully aware of my need for him, Justin bowed my body against his leaving absolutely no room for misinterpretation. He wanted me as much as I him.

"Get a room you two!"

Justin instantly backed away at the sound of Kyle's voice. For the first time ever, he seemed disoriented and stunned, almost tripped over one of the smaller tables.

I looked at Kyle menacingly as I pushed myself upright. "What do you want now?" I asked hating that he interrupted something so great.

"The Ellri want to talk to you in the Chamber."

"And this really couldn't wait?" I asked, pulling my hair back into a loose bun. I reached over the desk looking for something to secure the makeshift hairdo. "Ah, here you are," I whispered as I picked up the pencil and used it to tighten the loose strands. Then, I turned to face my ill-timed cousin. "This better be important."

Kyle shrugged his shoulders. "What can I say? I'm just the messenger."

I went around to the other side of the desk and picked up all the tidbits that fell to the floor in my moment of weakness.

"Why did they send you? Why didn't they summon me?" Justin asked in wonder.

Kyle grinned sadistically from ear to ear. "It would seem dear friend that it wasn't the head on your neck that was doing the thinking just now."

"Kyle!" I yelled, crossing the room to punch him.

What stopped me from clobbering my cousin was Justin's sinful smile. He was enjoying Kyle's stupid comment. The mere thought of having such a strong effect on Justin made me giddy – for him to lose his concentration only meant one thing – he enjoyed it as much as I did.

Kyle rolled his eyes. "Come on you two. You can ravage each other later. The Ellri are waiting."

This time Justin didn't spare him the punch on the arm.

"Damn it Bradford, can't you take a joke!"

"You only get one each time Cathcart. Now let's go; they're growing impatient."

The scene in the Chamber was all too familiar – I was standing in the middle and everybody else stood around me. I was going to get an earful, I was sure.

"Do you purposely defy our warnings?" asked Nathan the High Ellri. "Or is it that you think you know better?"

"Neither, everything just happens. Honestly, I don't mean to get myself into these predicaments. How was I supposed to know that Abaddon was going to pay me a visit?"

William put his arm around my shoulder. "You're putting us all in danger by talking to him. He seeks a way in and today you nearly gave it to him."

"But he appeared on his own. He let himself in."

"Caitlin, what you saw today wasn't the demon himself, it was Abaddon testing you. The man is monstrous."

"Are you sure, because what I saw was far from a monster. The guy was angelic."

"What you saw," continued Justin's father, "was how you perceive death or better yet, how you perceive the idea of death. You don't fear it like most people. You actually welcome it with open arms. That's why he appeared so appealing. He picked up on your deepest feelings and emerged as this godly creature. It was all in your mind."

I looked towards Justin. He was sitting on one of the far chairs simply listening.

"How is that possible? How is it possible that the whole scene was in my head? I saw him! I spoke to him." Then I simply stopped talking and looked around. "Okay, maybe the cave was a bit farfetched, but other than that he and Bernael were all too real."

"Caitlin darling –," said Aurelia with her deep Italian accent. "If Abaddon actually did appear, you wouldn't be standing here now. He is a very powerful immortal who appears only to take life. What he was doing to you today was toying. It was all a mind game. He took you to the depths of your own subconscious without you even knowing it."

"But Ramiel said that Abaddon was there. Why else would

he warn me? It couldn't all be in my head, could it?"

Aurelia took my hand. "You're too young to understand all the details. The Watcher wasn't lying to you. Abaddon was in a way there with you, but up here; in your head not physically. The reason you weren't supposed to talk to him was because the more you talk to the monster the more infatuated you become, and the deeper into your mind you permit him to probe. By talking to him you allowed him access into your thoughts. That's one of his gifts."

"Well, this is why you need to stop with these secrets. If I knew all this beforehand I wouldn't have allowed him to take me on a tour through hell at nine o'clock at night, now would I?"

"Don't worry your pretty little head," Aurelia said, smiling. "Justin pulled you out in the nick of time."

"That's another thing –," I snapped as I turned to look at Justin. "How are you able to do all this, and why in the world does everybody back away from you?"

Justin stood up so fast that he looked animated. He clearly wanted to say something, but William cut him off. "Justin simply surprised them. The brothers can't read him as they can read the rest of us, so to them he came out of nowhere."

"No, there's a lot more to it than that," I accused, taking a few steps closer to Justin. "What aren't they telling me? What are you keeping from me? What were you going to tell me at the prom that Leslie and your mom interrupted so masterfully?"

"Caitlin," Aunt Leslie said standing next to me. "This isn't the time for this discussion. Justin will explain everything when the time is right."

"And when will that be?"

He took a step forward ready to say something only to be stopped again by his father. "Justin will tell you as soon as you Ascend; no sooner!"

"Justin, don't listen to them. Tell me, what is it?" I asked stepping away from my aunt. I went over to him and took his hands in mine. My voice almost broke. "What is it?"

He looked around towards the Ellri momentarily and then circled his brilliant gaze at me. "I can't go against their wishes," he said lowering his head once again. "I just can't."

"Fine," I snapped, letting go of his hands.

"Caitlin," he muttered barely audible. "I'm sorry, I really am."

"Don't be," my voice faltered at the end. "I'm sure there's a good reason behind this secret as well." I walked away disappointed and stood at the other end of the chamber. "Is there anything else you all wanted me for?"

Marlene approached. "There is one more thing, sweetie," she said, smiling warmly. "You are forbidden from seeing Tyler."

"What are you talking about? You can't forbid me from seeing my best friend!"

Tyler's father moved in closer. "I'm afraid we can Caitlin. It's for my son's own good. You must stay away."

"This is absurd! Why would I need to stay away?"

Marcellus attempted a smile. "It's either you keep your distance or he would have to move away from Oaks."

Tears in my eyes, I scanned their faces. "Why are you all doing this? What's staying away from Tyler going to accomplish?"

From the corner of my eye I noticed the distaste in Justin's expression. "I'll see him in school eventually," I continued to say. "He has to finish his finals."

"He'll take them later, when he's feeling up to it. We don't want to put more pressure on him than necessary."

"What's the matter with him?" I asked, raising my voice. "Why won't anyone tell me?"

Marcellus, visibly distraught, turned away from me, and in a motion of understanding, Aurelia, took his hand in hers. In that small gesture of affection, I realized something was seriously wrong with Tyler.

"What's going on?" I yelled, causing the whole room to vibrate. They instantly turned to face me. "Tell me now!" I ordered, triggering a vicious tremor from the depths of the earth. "Tell me!" I repeated even louder.

"Curb your anger, young lady," snapped Nathan. "This is not the time for childish tantrums. You must learn your place – must learn to control your thoughts and actions. This ridiculous display of power is what's going to lead you straight to the Fallen."

"That's enough, Nathan," Justin said surprisingly calm. "You can surely understand her frustration."

"What I say is for the child's own good," Nathan added as he looked about the room addressing the other Ellri. "She needs to remember her place! She needs to realize that her every action brings about an onslaught of repercussions for us all. Curbing her little bursts of rebellion is what she needs to concentrate on. Today's events must not be repeated. "

"I can assure you that Caitlin knows her place and respects all of you," Justin clarified.

Nathan turned and looked at me, and displayed a warm smile. "My words are meant as a warning, child. There is no disrespect intended or do I pretend to understand how difficult this whole situation must be for you, but even so, sweetie, you need to realize that horrible as these events might be, you cannot allow things to control your power. What we say is to be obeyed to the letter, and if staying away from your friend is difficult, then too bad. Tyler is to be left alone. Do you understand?"

I dropped my gaze to the ground and nodded in subdued acceptance to the rules of our kind.

In an attempt to lighten the mood, Uncle Abbot patted Nathan on the back and said, "Justin's right. Caitlin has been through so much, and yet continues to excel in school and in all her other responsibilities. I see no reason why we need to punish her. She has had no prior knowledge of our rules. No need of penalizing her for things she knows nothing of. "

"I wasn't aware that there was a question of punishment," I uttered softly as I turned to Justin.

"I second that notion," said Shannon winking at me. "She needs a break. Caitlin needs to go somewhere for the summer."

"Ah, yes," agreed Marlene. "Somewhere beautiful where she can relax".

"Wait a second," I started, "My punishment is going away on holiday?"

"Italy!" boomed Aurelia, ignoring my statement. "Caitlin should visit Italy."

Justin's features quickly darkened, and that's when it dawned on me. "This isn't a vacation you're sending me on, but a family reunion. Hell no," I protested releasing my hand from

Justin's hold. "You can all forget about that. I'm staying in Oaks and that's final. You're little diabolical plan is not going to work. I'm not going to stay with the Korbs; not even for a second."

"It will keep you safe from the Fallen," said Shannon. "Your uncle, as much as I'd hate to admit it, was right. The Korbs are the only ones who can keep the Fallen away. Being of the same blood they have more power over them."

"The same blood?" I asked dumbfounded. "How is that even possible?"

"We have only recently figured it out ourselves. It explains why they keep everyone outside the family blocked out all these years," added Nathan as he took a seat. "Your uncle Brett exhibits many gifts similar to Abaddon; gifts that are clearly inherited from past generations."

"Can this be?" I asked, looking at Justin.

"Alexander, shall I tell them?" Justin asked, directing the question to the empty space beside him.

Covered in an intricately woven white tunic, Alexander's ghostly apparition filled the void next to Justin. Quickly enough, he solidified into human form and said, "You might as well tell them. I'm starting to feel as Caitlin does. I don't know who knows what anymore."

"I really doubt that," I began. "Why aren't they letting me see Tyler?"

He smiled and shook his head. "Oh, no you don't. The Ellri make the rules and you must follow; don't come to me thinking you can break them."

"Will someone tell us if our assumptions are correct?" asked Nathan. "Are the Korbs direct descendants of the Fallen?"

"Yes they are," Alexander informed. "It's why the Korbs are so susceptible to evil. It's the reason behind their great gifts. When I found them they knew nothing about their ancestors, but soon I realized that their gifts were remarkably similar to Abaddon's family eons before the war. It was much later that I figured out that the only reason the Korbs' clan was still alive and intact was because someone was keeping them safe."

"I knew those Korbs were monsters," seethed Lucille.

"And what would that make me?" I asked teary eyed.

"I didn't mean it in that context, Caitlin. I'm sorry sweetie."

Nathan came closer. "That would explain why they're not out to kill her." The High Ellri wasn't talking to anyone in particular, but simply thinking out loud. "She's their direct descendent – the purest of his blood line, but also the purest of the Illumine blood line." He suddenly froze and turned to stare at me. "That would make Caitlin the balance in Light and Shadow."

"Don't get ahead of yourself," Justin advised. "There's one more thing that Alexander hasn't mentioned."

Impatient with the lack of urgency on Justin's part, Nathan spat out, "Well, what is it?"

"The Korbs are direct descendants of the Fallen, but Abaddon is not the purest living member of his blood line."

A hushed silence fell among the Ellri. I've never seen them look that stunned before.

My mind was shrieking, screaming with the need to know what was going on. "Oh come on!" I yelled knowing that they all were reading each other's thoughts wanting to keep the secret from me. "Don't do this to me."

Justin smiled. "I didn't do it intentionally. I simply forgot to verbalize what I was thinking. It's much easier to communicate through thought."

"So tell me then. Who is the purest in their blood line?"

"Well as far as the Book of Truths is concerned you, Caitlin, are the purest blood descendent of the Primoris Donum."

"You mean to tell me that the person who wants me killed is, in a way, my kin?"

Alexander nodded. "I'm afraid so."

"We shouldn't have been kept in the dark about this," said Nathan angrily.

I kept quiet, trying to figure out what it all meant. How was it that I was the purest in a long line of immortals? There was a huge puzzle piece missing and nobody seemed to comment on the fact.

"Caitlin will not go to the Korbs just yet," Alexander announced. His voice barely penetrated the tangle of my thoughts. "She is safe among you. The child has been bounced back and forth long enough. Give her time to work out her emotions and let her Ascend first. The Fallen will come for her, but only to sway her to their way of thinking. We are all aware of how strong minded she is. I don't fear losing her to them."

"I agree," blurted Marlene. "Caitlin has proven herself a formidable opponent. There is no way they will get their claws in her. She's solid."

"Yeah right!" I exclaimed. "Bernael nearly tore my head off and his lovely brother was in my head screwing around with my thoughts. Great opponent I am."

"You're still alive, aren't you?" she asked winking. "That's more than I can say about many Gifted that were killed in their wake."

The shudder ran so deep it made me flinch. "Oh, God, I'm in trouble, serious trouble," I moaned, dragging my eyes away from her. "What am I supposed to do until then?"

Marlene studied me with a worried eye – pushing my loose hair behind my ear. "Do what you always do."

"And what would that be exactly?"

"Annoy the hell out of them. That seems to be working for you just fine," she chuckled as she turned to Justin. "Don't look so miffed young man. Caitlin is the only one who has brought the angel of darkness as well as death himself out of hiding. You can't deny that there's something about her that draws them to her."

"I'm nobody really. Whatever is happening; it's happening without intention, I can assure you," I tried explaining. "I truly don't want to see the Fallen ever again. I might not fear them, in the way you'd like me to, but it still affects me. It sort of pulls me deeper into this hole I keep fighting to escape."

"It's part of the ascension process," offered Uncle Abbot. "That's why you need to work through what you feel before it eats you up alive."

"I know. I'm really trying hard. I didn't even get mad at Abaddon today, or his despicable brother."

"You need to listen," I heard Ramiel say as he appeared slowly in front of me. "You came really close to falling victim. Another minute in that false hell, and you would've really believed that what you saw was real. It would've turned into your little own world – captive in your own mind."

"I'm really sorry Ramiel, but he made it impossible."

"You need to exhibit more control in times of pressure. Don't let them have the upper hand. You might feel on top of things, but that's because they want you to feel comfortable around them. It's easier to manipulate you once you feel in false-control. Caitlin, you need to remember that they are the ones in control, no matter how strong you think you are."

I slumped down on the Persian rug. "There's just too much," I huffed, putting my head in my hands. "I can't take any more."

Nobody spoke nor attempted to come closer. They gave me the space I needed to collect myself.

"Is my being here putting all of you in mortal danger?" I asked finally looking up. "Please, an honest answer if you may?"

"Absolutely not," answered Aunt Leslie. "Why would you even think that?"

Everybody seemed to be agreeing with what she was saying.

I got to my feet ones again "I love all of you for being such bad liars, and –,"

"What is it?" urged Alexander. "There's something you are holding back. Go ahead, tell them."

"I won't lie and say I understand why all this is happening. The only thing I do know is that my only duty – my only reason for living is to keep all of you safe. I'm not sure why I feel this or how I'm supposed to accomplish it, but I know that the intense need to protect all of you is much stronger than any of the gifts I have. It drives me to do what I do. It's what spirals my gift out of control."

Alexander quickly turned his gaze to Justin. The Ellri all stared at the two men in sheer silence. I stood there stupidly – feeling exposed and idiotic. Actually, I felt ignored. After a time, they all smiled and turned to me.

"Is everything alright?" I asked, aware that everyone was

still looking at me with a plastered smile on their face.

"Everything is as it should be," Justin said as he wrapped his arm around my waist. I closed my eyes momentarily, leaning into the arm that supported me. "If you're all finished, I'd like to take Caitlin home," he said.

"Go," said Nathan waving us away. "Enjoy the rest of the evening."

What evening? I thought.

It was past midnight and I still wanted to talk to Emily.

T he house was still quiet as Justin and I made our way up the stairs. "Is Emily here?" I asked in a whisper.

"Yes, in her room. She's still awake and going through her clothes."

I stopped at the landing and turned to face him. "Would you mind if I go talk to her?"

"Why would I mind. She needs you right now," he said and simply leaned in and gave me a quick kiss goodnight before heading back downstairs.

I hated to see him go, but I really needed to see if she was okay.

The knock on her door was meant to be soft.

"Come in," she said with a low melancholy voice.

Her back was turned the moment I entered her room. She fumbled through the clothes spread on her bed attempting to feign comfort.

"So how was your evening?" she asked suppressing a dry cough. "Did you and Justin do anything interesting?"

I didn't answer – I simply put my hand on her shoulder and turned her around to face me.

Emily's beautiful eyes were red and swollen from the tears – her skin was pasty and damp.

"Oh, Emily –" was all I could muster up to say before giving her a hug.

She held on tight releasing the emotions she was so desperately trying to hide. "I'm not –"

"Don't worry; everything will be okay, you'll see. Ramiel has seen many children in your future. So, save your tears for when you'll be begging for some peace and quiet from all the crying and screaming."

She giggled as she sniffed back the tears. "He really said that? He said that I'll have many kids in the future."

"Yeap! Scouts honor!"

"You've never been a scout," she jested as she brushed away her tears with her sleeve and slumped on the bed. "It would've been great, right?"

"Yeah, but it's a good thing it turned out the way it did."

Her brow furrowed. "That's a cruel thing to say."

"I just meant that the baby wouldn't have survived the Oath of Unity."

"What are you talking about?"

"Ramiel said that it's dangerous. You would've had to cancel the ceremony until you gave birth."

Her eyes grew black with sorrow for a moment. "Really?"

"Yeah, Em. It has something to do with the transference of power. You know more about this than I do."

"I really never thought about it. Mom was right about me waiting – about me not rushing things with Marc. She tried to warn me, but I kept calling her old fashioned."

"It was a simple false alarm, that's all. You and Marc will be married in less than a month and then you will have your family."

"I really thought that I was. The signs were all there. I was going out of my mind."

"Well, enjoy your independence while you still have it, because a husband and kids sounds like a whole lot of work."

She smiled and leaned into me. "You're the only one I could talk to about this."

"You can come to me with anything," I said feeling that our roles were suddenly reversed.

"So –," she said standing up. "What have you been up to today? Anything interesting?"

I grinned knowing that she wouldn't be expecting to hear anything of what I was about to tell her.

After twenty minutes of relaying the day's events I could tell Emily had completely gotten over the false pregnancy scare. Her mouth had fallen to the floor the first five minutes of my rendition – now she simply stared lost for words.

Her eyes popped wide open the second I mentioned my visit to the depths of hell. By the time I got to the part where Bernael entered purgatory she was completely frozen.

"And I thought I had it bad today," she teased, taking my hand. "Lord Caitlin, how are you feeling?"

"Insanely calm!" I answered smiling. "I'm sure the shock of it all will surface sooner or later."

"Consider me warned!" she laughed.

We continued to talk till the wee hours, covering every topic under the sun.

NINETEEN

GRADUATION

THERE WAS A void without Tyler, and with each pacing day it was getting that much harder to come to terms with the fact that I was forbidden to see my best friend. Not knowing what was happening to him was what frustrated me the most. "Tyler, where the hell are you?" I whispered, looking out the window.

"Caitlin –," I turned at the sound of my name. Emily walked in carrying my cap and gown. "Don't forget that after the ceremony we're all going to Mr. O'Malley's to celebrate. He's reserved the pub for you guys."

"Yeah, okay," I sighed.

"For heaven's sake, why are you so down? You're finally graduating."

I turned to look at her. "Tyler won't be there today, will he?"

She shook her head no.

"Guessed as much," I huffed as I dropped into the armchair.

"Don't be like that. Today we have graduation and this

weekend we have Justin's birthday party. You really need to pull it together."

"He's okay right?" I asked for the quadrillionth time.

"Tyler will be fine. Now get dressed! You don't want to be late for your own graduation."

"Okay, fine. What should I wear?" I muttered going through my closet.

"Have I taught you nothing?" Emily said, pushing me playfully to the side. "Here wear this," she ordered, and handed me an updated version to the classic little black dress with a flattering scooped neckline which swooped down my back, creating a deep back slit. "Ah, here they are," she added handing me a black pair of heels. "These match perfectly."

I stepped into the dress and with Emily's help I zipped it up, pulled my hair back into a rather tight knot and waited for Emily's approval. She seemed satisfied with the overall look. Just some last touches on my hair and minimal makeup, and she beamed one of her signature smiles. "You're ready!" she exclaimed as she grabbed the cap and gown from my bed. "You might as well wear these once we get to school. You wouldn't want to wrinkle the gown in the car."

"Yes mom," I teased.

With a hard smack on my backside, Emily shoved me playfully out the door. "Smarty," she said giggling. "If it weren't for me you'd probably have gone to your graduation wearing your absurd flannel pajamas."

"It's too hot for flannel; the cotton ones, maybe."

We headed down the stairs laughing.

"Come on you two! We're cutting it a bit close," complained my Uncle.

"I can't believe you're graduating," Aunt Leslie sighed as she hugged me rather tight.

"Come now dear," urged Uncle Abbot, taking my aunt by the arm. "We don't have time to stand around crying. We'll have time enough later."

"That reminds me –," started Aunt Leslie, "Emily, could you grab some tissues?"

"Sure mom," she yelled and quickly disappeared down the hall.

"Come on," repeated uncle Abbot as he headed for the silver Lexis parked in front of the house. "We're going to miss the ceremony!"

"Calm down Abbot! You know they won't start without us."

"Yes dear," he answered in a mechanical manner, and waited for us quietly in the car.

A s far as graduation ceremonies went – mine was more or less like any other. Lisa being the valedictorian of our graduating class gave her speech, inciting several rounds of applause and cheers. The atmosphere was pleasantly charged with teachers and students visibly enjoying themselves.

Megan, however, sat a mere row in front of me and a few seats to the right. I purposely waved to her discretely and smiled, annoying her all the more. Her snotty glances attracted the attention of some of my fellow students.

"What's her problem?" asked Greg Murphy as he sat next to me. Greg was a male version of Megan. Thankfully, he reserved his stupidity for the male members of our class. "Just ignore her," he advised, fixing his cap, "She'll never grow up," said Greg – the one boy who got sent to the nurse's office for sticking a pencil so far up his nose that he had to be sent to the emergency room.

Suppressing a laugh, I simply nodded in agreement and looked up towards the podium where Lisa continued her award-winning speech. My mind quickly slipped back to the days I spent at Stone Hurst.

No sooner had I taken a deep breath to smother any ill memories from surfacing, than my attention was suddenly drawn back to the podium. Mr. Patterson took the microphone calling us one by one to receive our diplomas. I hadn't noticed Kyle being there until I stepped onto the stage at the sound of my name being called. Apparently, somebody was stupid enough to designate him the family photographer.

I looked up to where my family sat and was surprised to see Justin sitting next to my uncle. I smiled at the unexpected surprise. He hadn't mentioned anything about coming, and I never once brought up the event even though he spent night after night testing me, asking me a million questions to prepare me for finals. As soon as our eyes met, Justin winked at me, causing me to smile even wider.

"That's more like it," yelled Kyle, snapping a million frames a second. "Smile Caitlin!"

"You don't need to scream," I said through clenched teeth.

"Come on, a few more shots. You look so cute in your little cap and gown."

I was about to say something, but lucky for Kyle, Mr. Patterson, stretched out his hand to hand me my diploma. "Congrats Caitlin, it was truly an honor," he said proudly.

I shook his hand and thanked him for everything, and then I was made to stand there for a minute or two, to allow Kyle to have his way. "That's my girl!" he coaxed, snapping a thousand more unnecessary pictures. As soon as he stopped, I slowly descended the few steps, hoping that my gown wouldn't snag on my heel and land me face down on the grass, but it was the raucous commotion to the far side of the field that drew my attention.

Students and teachers all seemed to be backing away from something, and by the look on their faces, they were terrified of whatever they witnessed. In no time, I discarded my cap and gown and headed towards whatever they were trying to avoid. Out of nowhere my Aunt grabbed my arm, and pulled me to a full stop. "Get yourself inside the school, now!" she ordered, and quickly let go. "I have to help the others, but you get yourself indoors; do you hear?"

There was just too much happening for her to wait for my

response; instead, she guided people to the back entrance, trying to calm everyone. On the other side of the field, my Uncle, Kyle, Justin and Emily were doing the same thing; leading people to safety.

The stimulus was simply too intensely arousing, to back away, so instead of following orders my curiosity led me across the length of the stage and to the other side of the field. It was there that I saw what everyone was running from.

A thick grey blanket of mist slowly made its way towards the stage, imbuing the entire area with a low eerie hum of muted voices squalling with pain, and as the mist rolled forward the dire sounds resonated all around me in a great crescendo of shrilling cries. The closer the mist got, the clearer the source of the devilish cries became.

To my horror, the greyish volatile mass of vapor morphed into hundreds upon hundreds of smoke-like demons swiftly crawling along the ground in a wave-like motion, drawing nearer as they pushed forward in unison, like a stormy tide ready to crash upon the shore.

It was surely not a sight for the faint-hearted, but I refused to be fazed by the hellish scene unfolding before my eyes, because I knew they were all there for me and I was blazing and ready to face the monsters head on.

"Don't you dare do anything," I heard Ramiel's soft voice in my mind. "Keep your composure and this should be over soon."

"What's going on?" I asked out loud. "What are they?"

"Just keep your wits about you, and don't fall prey to their trap."

A surge of energy quickly made its way up my spine and to

my fingers, preparing me for what was to come. I breathed deep ready to stand my ground.

"Caity!" I heard from across the field. "Caity, come here!"

I turned my head to look. "Tyler!" I yelled. "What are you doing here?"

"I came to see you graduate. Come on, let's get out of here!"

"You shouldn't be here," I warned. "Go inside with the others."

"You shouldn't worry about anything," he cajoled, displaying a soft smile. "Everything is as it should be. You shouldn't fear them."

It was then that an entity appeared right beside Tyler, holding him by the shoulder.

"Who the hell is that?" I yelled, falling into rage, and that's when maddening fury took control of my senses the second I realized that it was Abaddon.

"You forget way too easily, young mortal," he slithered, wrapping his arm around Tyler.

"Abaddon, you stay the hell away from him," I yelled with menacing intent.

"Or what," I heard him say, inches from my face.

He was nowhere near me physically, but sure enough I felt his breath against my skin. The trickery was meant to unhinge me; meant to scare me, but I stood taller. This was a direct and violent assault on the people I cared for, and hell itself could not contain me. As the thought of Abaddon holding Tyler lingered, a tumultuous storm smoldered deep inside me as I looked beyond the field to where Tyler and Abaddon stood.

I looked behind me, and thankfully everyone quickly moved to the far end of the field near the school entrance. Seeing their strained faces ignited my need to protect them all. It was an inner calling, a deep seeded urge to destroy whoever might cause them harm.

The smoke-like demons collectively stopped, and stood at unfathomable heights equal only to the Nobe Sentinels. The field was now filled with rows upon rows of mysteriously airy, supernatural beings, and as if summoned by some higher power, the rows of demons parted in one synchronized move, and Bernael stepped forward smiling wickedly. "You seem to attract evil," he slithered as he took a step closer. "You must feel the pull. Why fight it?"

"I feel nothing," I lied.

"Ah, but you do," he insisted.

"Why here? Why now, Bernael?"

Instead of an answer, he took a step closer and simply stared.

"What do you want?" I asked impetuously.

"Why won't you admit that you feel their power," he started to say, "Tell me how strong the pull is."

"I don't know what you're talking about." I lied again.

"It must be tearing you inside; making it impossible to distinguish right from wrong."

"You know nothing about me. Now, what is this all about?"

He didn't answer at first; instead, he circled around and looked past the field to where Tyler was. "How far would you go to save your friend," he asked softly against my ear. "Join us, and you'll never have to lose anyone."

Fiercely annoyed at how he was toying with me, I turned around and looked him straight in the eyes. "Is that what Abaddon promised you before you sold your soul to him?"

Angrily, he took a step closer, only inches from my face. "Don't speak of things you know nothing of."

"I know that you do his bidding, even though you know it's wrong. You say you can feel every emotion, which means you can still feel love and compassion."

He laughed. "Is that what you occupy your thoughts with? Are you trying to save my soul, mortal?"

"Does it need saving?"

He was furious, but then he said in a more composed manner, "Your friend seems to be enjoying our company. Isn't saving him worth your sacrifice?"

Closing my eyes momentarily was the only way to keep my sanity. My mind and gift had one objective and it was a murderous one.

"You needn't try so hard," Bernael began, "We can teach you the ways of our kind. You can master your power and quench that fire you have inside. You will have the Shadow Guard by your side to fend off anyone who opposes you. Why fight it? Let it reign over you. Become what you were born to be."

My eyes snapped open, and I looked directly at him. "Let Tyler go!" I enunciated. "Let him go, now!"

Bernael started laughing that sinister laugh of his. "You are persistent, aren't you? But unfortunately, you are on the losing side. There is no way of saving them all. At some point you will have to choose among them, and in the end you will sacrifice it all for nothing. They tell you fairy tales to keep you in control. They deny you the truth in order to command you. How do you trust people like that?"

"Am I supposed to trust you then?"

Bernael didn't answer.

"Stop playing with your toy brother," barked Abaddon only a few feet away, "I'm fed up with this child. I got what I came here to get."

"You leave Tyler alone!" I snapped.

"Curb your tongue, mortal," Abaddon roared, unleashing a wave of shrills from the Shadow Guard. He inched closer and said, "The only reason you still have a breath in you is because my brother seems to like playing this game of cat and mouse, but make no mistake about it, I will come for you, so bite your tongue when you address me or I will be glad to bite it off for you."

I took an impetuous step forward. "You will leave Tyler alone," I ordered as the ground beneath my feet trembled and the sky above darkened in response to the rage that spewed from my every cell.

Abaddon looked around him and then back to me. "Your little display of power is noteworthy for someone so young, but let us see how far you will go to save your little friends."

In a blink of an eye, Abaddon was by the school entrance and grabbed one the graduates. The second he turned my classmate around, the irony of it all made me smile. Abaddon, however, didn't know what to make of my reaction, but poor Megan looked distraught and frightened at the hands of the monster.

"How do you plan on saving this beauty," Abaddon hissed as he stroked Megan's blond tresses.

The air around me pulsed to the beat of my heart as my body surged from the collective energy of nature itself.

"Will you not fight to save this child?" Abaddon asked.

I was silent for a moment.

"Caitlin, please help," Megan cried. "Please help me."

"You don't want to die so young, do you pretty little thing."

Megan shook her head. "Please don't kill me."

Abaddon lifted her face to meet his gaze. "That's up to your friend over there."

"Abaddon!" I roared, and my voice seemed to emanate from the bellows of the earth. "You will release her or you will meet your maker!"

Abaddon disposed of Megan to the side like a rag doll. "You dare order me about!"

In response to the magnitude of Abaddon's own power, along with having Bernael present, and the army of hell itself all around me, my gift triggered an anger-induced power binge, which took control of my mind and body; submerging me into an abysmal thirst for blood and destruction.

"Is it death, you wish?" Abaddon asked, coming closer.

I did not back away; instead, I took a few steps forward and with each step I felt the earth crumble beneath my feet. "You will do my bidding," I heard myself bellow only a mere foot away from the angel of death.

Low resonating murmurs made me turn in the direction of the Shadow Guard. In a surging wave of grey mist, the Guard came and stood behind me. I was not fearful of them, but instead, I turned to them, and at once they simultaneously fell back to their crawling position. It was a gesture of servitude, which I did not expect, but gladly accepted. Their murmurs of despair turned into a pulsating hum, like that of the constant beat of a drum, but Abaddon did not let this stand. He let out a earsplitting shrill, and in an instant the Shadow Guard let out wails of pain which droned on and on as they retreated further and further away from me. Abaddon then raised his hand in the air, and the lamenting sounds of hell ceased, and the Guard stood deathly still.

"They are not yours to command," I bellowed, seeing how the Guard stood motionless.

Abaddon's face darkened, and in sheer silence he distanced himself.

"Join us and save the ones you care about," Bernael warned, coming all the more closer the further Abaddon went. "He will make you pay for your defiance, and it will not be pretty, I can assure you."

The minute Bernael finished talking; out of nowhere, two colossal creatures, composed of a greyish liquid-light, broke formation and grabbed both my arms behind my back, and in order to restrain me, they clutched even tighter each and every time I tried to break free. The Shadow Guard seemed to have a death-grip on me and the harder I fought; the more I was being pulled back towards the monstrous legions that awaited Abaddon's order.

One by one, the demons firmly clung to each other, creating two parallel lines behind me, each pulling on one of my arms with unyielding might. As I pushed forward to resist the powerful tug, they pulled and pulled back with no restrain. I was in a tug of war for my life against powerful immortals, yet my power did not concede, nor did I yield from fear; instead my mind was racing with vile and torturous thoughts; all aimed at the Shadow Guard.

"Enough!" I roared, and snapped my arms back, the way one would crack a whip. It was instant; without any hesitance on my part. The moment I pulled free from my keepers vicious clutch, they violently imploded into a mass of vapor and lifted high into the air and dispersed.

"Abaddon," I screamed as I took an aggressive step forward; giving rise to earth tremors and furious winds which stirred around me violently, "It's your turn!"

His deep, sinister laugh filled the stormy atmosphere. "It's time you feel my wrath, insignificant mortal," Abaddon threatened, and like a speeding bullet reached to the far end of the field where the students stood frightened.

"No! Don't!" I yelled, at the sight of Abaddon among my classmates. They were all terrified with tears streaming down their face.

"Is this a friend of yours," Abaddon asked me as he placed his hand on poor Greg Murphy's shoulder, causing Greg to fall to his knees. "No, please," Greg begged in tears.

"It's not my fault," Abaddon explained in a sorrowful tone. "Your friend Caitlin is to blame."

And without giving Greg a chance, Abaddon snuffed him out with flick on his wrist.

"No!" I yelled as I prepared to attack. "He hasn't done anything to you. Stop this!"

Abaddon raised his hand in the air, in a motion to stop my advancement, and said while holding Lisa by the arm, "If you want to save at least one, you will remain rooted to that spot."

Unable to make any move without putting Lisa in harm's way, I remained a simple spectator to Abaddon's sadistic display of power.

"What's your name, lovely," Abaddon continued to ask.

"Lisa," she answered teary eyed.

"Sweet, innocent young girl, I hate to do this, but your friend left me no other choice." With one touch of his hand, Lisa and many others fell to the ground, cold and motionless; victims to my inability to protect them.

"Why are you doing this?" I cried. "Why?"

"How many will it take for you to come with us?" Abaddon petitioned. "Will you accept the Fallen as your own? Will you side with us on matters of balance?" He had his hand on Gina. "Will you accept Shadow law?"

"Enough!" I yelled, from the bottom of my soul. "I had enough! Stop this! Stop this now!" I screamed with tears rolling down my face.

"Okay, fine," I heard Kyle say. "No more pictures; I get it. You don't need to make a scene."

Disoriented, I looked around and saw the graduating class all looking at me from their seats.

"Caitlin, you look like you've seen a ghost? Are you okay?" asked Kyle coming to my side.

I scanned the grounds again and realized that everything and everyone was as they should be. "It was all in my head," I whispered.

"What's that?" asked Kyle stroking my back. "Are you sure you're going to be okay?"

"Yeah, I'm fine," I lied, and headed back to my assigned seat.

I looked around the grounds just to make sure there were no demons lurking about, but there was one left. To my dismay, Megan turned and looked at me. "Freak," she mouthed, and turned around again.

It didn't bother me one bit; I had other things on my mind. I fiddled with my diploma and dropped my gaze to the ground hoping that Tyler was safe. Over and over again, I played each dismal scene in my head hoping to understand the meaning of it all. It all felt so real.

As soon as the ceremony finished, Kyle insisted we all pose for pictures, so we did. I looked in the distance trying to banish the bleak memories from my mind. "Over here, Caitlin," Kyle directed, seeing that my head was turned away from the camera. This was supposed to be a joyous occasion and I was, yet again, slipping into darkness.

"Caitlin –," Justin's voice instantly snapped me out of my haze. No sooner had Aunt Leslie and uncle Abbot turned their backs to congratulate friends of the family, Justin grabbed me by the waist and pulled me in for a great big kiss.

"Congrats," he beamed and kissed me again.

"Thanks," I said faintly.

"Aren't you excited? You're officially finished with high school."

"Yeah, it's great." I tried to sound enthusiastic, but who was I kidding. The e vision of all my classmates dead against the ground jolted me.

"What's the matter?"

I shook my head and forced a smile. "Everything is great." I leaned in and kissed him lightly on the lips. "I'm really glad you came," I added, taking his hand, "wasn't sure if you were going to show up."

He took a step back. "Where else would I be, and why in the world would I not be here?"

I shrugged my shoulders and leaned in and gave him a kiss. "I'm just happy you're here."

"Abbot –," Justin began as soon as he saw my uncle approach.

"Yes, Justin," my uncle answered wrapping his arms around my shoulder – squeezing me lightly.

"Would you mind if I drove Caitlin to the party?"

"She's all yours," he beamed, and patted him on the back. "We're going home anyway."

Kyle continued to take pictures the whole time we were standing there; annoying the hell out of everybody.

"You will all thank me later," he boasted, as he tried taking a close-up of Justin. "Come on man! Give me one of those million dollar smiles that drive my little sis crazy."

Justin pulled the Camera from Kyle's hands. "I think you've taken enough for one day."

"Hey! You're infringing on my freedom of artistic expression," Kyle complained, pulling the camera back. Justin chuckled and punched his best friend on the arm. "Damn it Bradford! That hurts!"

"Will you two act your age?" Uncle Abbot implored shaking his head in disapproval. "Caitlin –," he began turning to me. "We are so very proud of you, sweetheart."

"You are both the best parents any kid could've ever asked for. Thanks for putting up with me all these years," I confessed giving both my Aunt and Uncle a hug.

Emily was desperately trying to dry her eyes while Kyle was taking pictures of the heart-warming affair. "Can you all turn this way," he instructed, inciting an angry look from my uncle. "What now?" Kyle asked, putting the camera back down. "I was trying to capture the moment."

"Come on love," my uncle offered, taking my aunt by the

shoulders, "Let's leave the kids enjoy the rest of their day."

We all stood there in silence watching the adoring couple walk away hand in hand.

"We should be heading to the Raven," announced Emily, taking Marc's hand. "We won't find a seat if we don't leave now."

Justin looked over to my beautiful cousin and her fiancé. "You guys go on ahead and save us a seat," he instructed. "I want to show Caitlin something before we head to the pub."

"Fine, just don't be too late. It's not my graduation."

"We'll be right behind you," Justin reassured her.

Emily and Marc headed off, hugging each other tenderly.

"Caitlin –," Justin began, "I need to talk to Kyle before we leave; is that okay?"

"Of course, I'll wait by the car," I answered, desperately needing to step away from all the festivities.

I walked to the parking lot, all the while trying to make sense of what happened in the field with Abaddon. The second I reached Justin's car, I slipped out of my heels, leaned up against the car door, and exhaled deeply trying to sooth my intolerable migraine. My thoughts ran wild with morbid scenes of dead bodies scattered throughout the area.

I leaned further back against Justin's sleek black Audi, trying to find some balance and clarity with what had happened on the field. Keeping the incident private was a way to keep the Ellri from lecturing me again. In all likelihood, they already knew about what had transpired, whether real or not, I was sure they were aware of it, and the only reason my Uncle and Aunt didn't bring it up was to keep from ruining my graduation with such talk.

For some reason Justin was taking much longer than I had anticipated, and I was left standing there alone. Several parents were kind enough to stop and congratulate me, and then Lisa and Kim walked up to me and gave me a hug. I held on a bit longer than the occasion required, but both girls were huggers so they didn't make a fuss. They were ecstatic to be finishing, and laid out plans on how to conquer the world.

"You're coming to the Raven, aren't you?" asked Lisa.

"Of course, wouldn't miss it."

Lisa turned to Kim. "Told you she'd come."

Kim pulled a wry face as she shoved Lisa playfully. "Kyle took our picture," she squealed changing the subject. "He was like, 'You pretty ladies don't mind if I take your picture, do you?'" she giggled, sounding like a very bad version of Kyle.

"He doesn't sound like that," dissented Lisa. "When in the world did you ever hear him talk like that?"

"Anyway –,' Kim added abruptly, ignoring Lisa's protest. "We should head off before everyone gets there first. I wouldn't want to stand all day. I'm sure the whole town is going to be there and the seats are limited."

"Okay, well, I'll see you guys there then," I announced, holding back the need to hug them again.

As they walked off, Lisa turned and said, "Don't be late."

"I won't. I promise," I called behind them, as I watched them distance away.

Absorbed in their quirkiness, I jumped out of my skin when out of nowhere I felt a hand grab me around the waist. "Come with me," Tyler murmured, pulling me by the hand until we stood behind Greg Murphy's ridiculously oversized SUV. The car was apparently as big as his ego.

Surprised to see him, I simply stared, and then reached up and touched his cheek to make sure he was real. "What are you doing here?" I asked in a confused state of mind. "You should be somewhere safe."

Tyler looked at me in bewilderment. "Are you okay? he finally asked, taking my outstretched hand.

I didn't answer.

"I can't stay long," he started to say; "They'll kill me if they knew I was here."

I caressed his cheek again, and then gave him a long overdue hug. "How can they not know you're here?"

"That's not important," he noted as he cupped my face in both hands. "Can you slip out tonight, and meet me by the stream?"

The lucid image of Abaddon holding him jarred in the back of my mind as I continued to stare at Tyler.

"Well, can you?" he repeated

"Sure, but why all the secrecy?"

"I'll explain later on tonight; be there at about midnight after everyone's asleep, okay?"

I didn't want to let him go. "Stay, please," I begged. "They're keeping me from seeing you." I added, wanting to clear the air. "I don't want you to think I'm staying away on purpose; I'd never do that".

"I know," he offered. "Midnight tonight," he repeated, giving me a quick kiss on the cheek. He didn't take a step back; instead he leaned his forehead against mine momentarily. "I've missed you," he whispered, and without another word, he quickly walked away.

Graduation Ceremony

Illustrated for Lines that Bind - Among the Shadows

TWENTY

TRUTH BE TOLD

J USTIN'S VOICE startled me. "Why are you hiding back here?" he asked, poking his head around the SUV.

"It was getting rather crowded out here, and this seemed the quietest place." I lied as we headed back to his car.

"You know, you look exceptionally gorgeous today," he beamed, holding the car door open.

"Graduating does that to a person." I inched up to him and lessened the distance between us.

His smile caused my heart skip a bit.

With heels, I was much closer to his mouth than usual. It was actually quite nice to stand at this height next to him. I didn't feel so microscopic. Justin eased in and kissed me softly on the lips. He was about to pull away when I took him by the collar and pulled him back towards me. "Not so fast," I muttered taking advantage of our closeness.

"I love you," he whispered as he slipped one hand to my back and held me close.

"I love you more," I answered, sealing my proclamation with a kiss.

"Humanly impossible," he jested softly against my lips, and then backed away to hold the door open for me to get in. He gave me one last kiss and headed for the driver's side. I contemplated telling him about Tyler, but I wasn't really sure how it was possible that Justin didn't know; how the Ellri didn't know.

Justin threw my cap and gown in the back seat, and drove off to the after graduation party at the Raven in sheer silence. The ride was too quiet for my liking. There was definitely something up with Justin

"You know don't you?" I accused. "You know about Tyler."

He didn't talk for a few minutes. Once he parked the car in the over-crowded parking lot, he turned in his seat and started to say, "I'm not going to tell you what to do. You never do it anyway." He tried to smile.

I looked down wringing my hands. "What would you do?"

"If I were you, I'd do what the Ellri told you and stay away. He shouldn't have come to see you today."

"What I'm going to say is going to come out all wrong, so just bear with me," I requested. "I miss him, Justin; I really do. He should've been there today for the ceremony. I love him to death and what the Ellri are asking of me is cruel and painful. I have to see what he wants. My best friend wants to talk to me. How am I supposed to stay away?"

Justin didn't respond; instead, he reached for the door handle in silence and slipped out of the car. Without hesitation, I got out myself and walked over to where he stood.

"What's wrong?" I asked reaching for his hand.

"It's really nothing," he replied, displaying a faint smile.

"Don't say it's nothing when you look like you want to tear someone's head off. Now tell me what's really bothering you?"

Justin reached out and took both of my hands in his. "I want you to be honest with me," he began hesitantly.

"What is it?"

He looked down at our hands instead of looking me in the eyes and started to say, "Did you ever stop to think who you'd be with if you weren't born with this bond. If you didn't feel the pull we share."

"No!" I quickly answered. "Why in the world would I think of something like that?"

Justin raised his gaze to meet mine. "I'm just saying that if we weren't born with this bond we share, you would've had a choice of who you wanted to be with."

"What are you getting at?" I asked annoyed. "The same goes for you, Justin. If we weren't tied by this bond you and Nicole could have made a go at it, right? Is that what you want?" I was about to storm off when Justin quickly pulled me into a tight hold. "Not so fast," he ordered as he held me tighter. "You're being ridiculous; you know that, don't you?"

"Not much different than what you're saying."

He shook his head. "What I meant is that what you and Tyler have is so natural; it's not forced. There has never been any power that binds you to him, but yet you love him freely."

"It's not the same," I tried to explain.

"Let me finish," Justin quickly added. "What you feel for me was forced upon you from birth. You had no choice in how you felt about me, but with Tyler you built what you have from scratch. I just can't help but wonder if what you share with him is the real thing. Would you have felt that strongly about me if there was no bond?"

I stared in amazement. "You're kidding me, right?" I asked. "Of course I love Tyler. He's been my friend since birth, but that doesn't mean that I'm in love with him." I interweaved my fingers with his and looked him straight in the eyes. "Bond or no bond, it has always been you that I love. I don't know how my life would've been without this connection we share and I simply don't care. This is who we are, who we were born to be. I love you, and this ridiculous Life Bond we share does not define the depth of my love for you; it doesn't dictate what I feel in my heart."

"I just –"

I cut him off with a kiss. He smiled and kissed me back. "Get it through your thick skull. I love you," I pronounced, looking into his dark blue eyes.

"Just making sure," he laughed, and wrapped his strong arms around me.

"I'm still going to see him, I hope you know."

"Just be careful."

"Why would I need to be careful with Tyler?"

He pushed back a loose strand of my hair behind my ear. "You know what?" he began to say, "I changed my mind. I don't want you to go. He's not stable yet. There's no telling what he'll do."

"Tyler would never do anything to harm me."

"He's not –," Justin stopped. "I can't believe I can't tell you."

"You can't tell me what?"

He looked frustrated. "Just drop it, and do whatever the Ellri advised, please!"

"I'll take it under advisement," I said giggling. "Now, come on, you don't expect me to miss my graduation party, do you?"

He smiled as he pulled me closer by the waist. "Do you really want to go inside?"

"Beats standing out here arguing, doesn't it?"

"We're not arguing now," he said sheepishly as he nuzzled my throat playfully.

I took a step back and smiled. We are going inside no matter how much I want to stay out here with you, okay?"

"Yes ma'am," he teased and took my hand, escorting me into the pub.

The morbid image of my classmates sprawled dead on the field lingered in my mind long after my return home from the Raven. It was rather difficult to look them in the eyes during the graduation party without shuddering at the thought of what-if; what-if it were true; what-if I'm useless in protecting everybody; what-if my being in Oaks put them all in imminent danger?

All those what-ifs played in my head as I stood on the landing for lord knows how long contemplating what to do about Tyler. First, the Ellri had warned me to stay away, and then Justin insisted I stay in that night, but even so, I headed for the back door knowing that my friend needed me. Friendship aside, something deep down told me that I was going to regret going down to the stream where Tyler planned for us to meet. Every fiber of my being urged me to head back inside, but my need to see what Tyler wanted was what impelled me forward.

Moments later, I was able to make out Tyler's silhouette standing near the stream; leaning up against the old Oak tree.

"Hey, there," I gushed happy to see him; causing him to turn around.

"You startled me," he gasped, and displayed a wide smile.

"So, what's with all this secrecy?" I asked, getting straight to the point. "Are you really okay?"

"Yeah, I'm fine," he answered as he threw a shiny pebble in the stream causing it skip on the surface of the water.

His voice was hoarse with disuse, and weak. I wondered how I didn't notice that earlier.

"Justin knows you're here, doesn't he?"

"Maybe, I'm not sure," I began, standing next to him as I faced the stream. "It's not like you can hide much from him these days."

"No, you surely can't." He spoke in a condescending tone.

I picked up a small rock and threw it, trying to mimic Tyler's awesome ability to make the object bounce on the surface of the water. Unlike Tyler's, mine sank to the bottom the second it hit the water.

"You need to use your wrist," he advised, throwing one himself.

I wiped my hands on my jeans and turned to face him. "You didn't bring me out here to throw rocks, did you?"

He shifted his gaze and stared at me.

"Why don't they want me to see you?" I asked trying to squeeze some kind of answer from him.

"With our ascension comes all this knowledge, things you're not supposed to find out until you ascend yourself."

"Tyler, I know all this already. What does that have to do with staying away from you?"

"Caity, everyone knows I can't keep things from you. The

second I learned all this information, you were the first person I wanted to see, to tell you everything I've learned."

"Are you serious?" I exclaimed. "Is that really the reason, because if it is, it's pathetic? We can't hang out because of more secrets?"

"You just don't get it, do you," he began.

"What don't I get?"

"It's about Justin, about you, about all of us," he finally spat out and kicked the dirt.

"About Justin?" I asked horrified. "What does any of this have to do with Justin?"

Tyler simply stared at me for a minute before he said, "Gabriel had absolutely no chance going up against him in Tirion. The poor bastard didn't know what he had got himself into until that day. And then your parents –,"

"My parents? What about my parents?" I gasped.

"Whatever anyone said about their death is a lie, they're –,"

"Tyler," came Marcellus' forbidding voice, "What do you think you're doing?"

Tyler's expression was stern. "She needs to know the truth. Why have you kept all this from her? She has every right to know."

"You – home – Now," his father barked angrily pointing at Tyler. "You've been warned of the repercussions. It would seem that you only learn the hard way."

I took a step closer to Marcellus. "Please," I implored, "he didn't tell me anything."

"Caitlin, you need to get home," he ordered unbending. "Now!" he yelled.

I looked at Tyler and then back to his father. There was

nothing I could do to calm Marcellus, his concern was beyond reproach. The second I turned to head back towards the house I noticed uncle Abbot standing there like a statue waiting for me.

"I don't want Tyler to get in trouble," I stated the second I reached my Uncle. "He did all of this for me."

"Tyler has made his bed," my Uncle warned taking me by the arm. "Now, let's get you inside."

"Tyler is right. I need to know the truth if it involves Justin or even my parents."

"You need to go inside," he commanded. "It's rather late."

I felt my face harden as I looked at him. "I need to know!" I demanded unwavering.

"It's time for sleep child. Your answers will come in time."

In that split second as I was about to enter the house I heard Marcellus' menacing voice echoing throughout the grounds. "Abaddon," he screamed in utter vengeance. My heart constricted at the mere sound of Abaddon's name.

"What the hell is going on?" I swore, looking in the distance. "We need to help them."

"Go inside," ordered Uncle Abbot. "There's nothing you can do just yet, not when Abaddon is involved."

"I'm not leaving Tyler with that monster," I croaked. "Don't you guys get it; he wants Tyler!"

The commotion in the distance drew my attention, but it was my Uncle's soft caress against my cheek that made me turn away. "Caitlin, you are in no position to help just yet, no matter how strong you might feel. There are many things that you still need to learn before going one on one with an immortal like Abaddon."

"Wait just a second," I quickly said, realizing the obvious.

"You know all about my vision at the graduation ceremony, don't you?" I accused.

He simply nodded.

"Why in the world didn't you say anything; explain it all to me? I have been going out of my mind all day thinking about all those deaths and how there was nothing I could do. Why in hell, did no one say anything?"

"Look," he started to say impatiently, "There are tests that we all have to endure to see how we would react in dire circumstances. The Nobe simply needed to see how much your gift has evolved and how far you were willing to go to save people."

"I failed them all. I let them die."

"You didn't fail anyone. It was a stupid test and you did far better than anyone expected. Your gift draws the darkness as much as it summons the light, but for some reason you fear your own power."

My attention was once again drawn to the commotion.

My Uncle shook his head. "It's not your fight, sweetie. Not today and hopefully never."

I looked at him angrily and then turned again to where I left my friend and his father. To my surprise, right there only a few feet away, Justin suddenly appeared out of nowhere; pointing to the house. "Inside Now!" he yelled.

"I'm not going anywhere until I know Tyler is okay," I answered defiantly.

"Caitlin," he fumed, "This is not the time. You must go inside." Justin's gaze turned to my uncle and said, "Abbot, get her inside right now!" The moment his order was verbalized, Justin vanished into the darkness.

My blood instantly rushed to my head and arms in response to Justin's own anger.

"No Caitlin," exclaimed my Uncle the second he noticed my throbbing wrists. "You need to relax and do as you are told. Your presence right now would only add fuel to the fire."

I looked past my uncle. "You know I can't just leave them," I said, shifting my gaze back to my uncle's concerned expression.

"I know sweetie; don't you think I know? But just this once; this one time do as I say, and trust me to know better."

I smiled, and kissed him on the cheek. "I'm afraid not uncle. Whatever is going on is drawing me like a magnet. There's no fighting the urge to protect them. I'm truly sorry." And with that said, I closed my eyes effortlessly and sliced through the grounds faster than the wind itself, but once I reached the place I thought was the source of the commotion, I found no one there. Would this have been a dream, it most definitely would've been one of the most powerful, but confusing. Tyler, Marcellus even Justin were all gone, and I was left there feeling like a fool.

Turning to head back home, a painful image caught my eye from the opposite bank of the stream. No one was around but only a young man about my age, maybe even younger; robed in a rich dark fabric. He was sprawled on the ground quenching an apparently unquenchable thirst; splashing water on his miraculously soft features.

Being in plain view, I quickly slipped behind the large Oak to hide from the trespasser. Unaware of my presence, he continued to look into the water, visibly shocked by his own reflection. That instant, he lifted one of his hands and ran it down the side of his face as if feeling for something that wasn't there. "Father," he roared looking up to the sky. "Why? Why?" he continued to wail returning his gaze to his reflection.

"Bernael?" I whispered to myself as I emerged from my hiding place and edged closer to the stream causing the young man to lift his beautiful face towards me. Instantly, he pulled his oversized hood over his head as if ashamed to show his brilliance. He drew away from the water clutching the earth as he withdrew further and further back; surprised, scared, I wasn't sure how to describe his reaction on seeing me.

"Where did you come from?" he sneered from across the stream. "Why didn't I sense you?"

The voice was that of Bernael, but the face; that face was nothing like the monster that haunted my existence. Without hesitation, I summoned my gift to take me to his side of the stream, and I quickly stood only a few feet away from the angelic figure. His skin was surprisingly as pale as mine if not paler; nothing like the dark, monstrous creature he once was.

"Bernael?" I asked again, wanting to make sure it was him.

He didn't speak at first; instead, he kept his head lowered, hidden under his oversized hood.

"You're beautiful," I began, staring at him, "Alexander was right; you are magnificent."

He remained silent, crouched on the ground.

As long moments passed, I continued to stare with keen caution and watchful prudence, waiting for him to say or do something.

Bernael finally looked up, raising his brow in amusement. "And you mortal, are but a water nymph sent here to torture my conscious."

His face lit up – gloriously smiling.

"Water Nymph?" I flinched back, unsure of what he meant.

His gaze dropped to my feet and at that split second I realized that I wasn't quite on land yet. I was suspended millimeters off the surface of the gurgling water beneath my levitating body. Surprised that I hadn't noticed, I smiled and took a step forward, reaching sturdy ground.

"That was weird," I laughed, looking back at the stream.

Bernael shook his head. "You think that's weird? There's nothing weird about your gift. You are a splendid creature."

Something in what he said tugged at my mind. "What's with the compliments?" I asked.

Bernael reached up with his model perfect fingers, and pulled back his hood revealing long flowing, light chestnut hair, slightly pulled to the side into a long braid reaching mid-back accentuating his flawless features.

Ignoring my question, he slowly stood and walked to the water's edge kneeling over the stream. His straight locks fell to the side, skimming the top of the running water. "I haven't seen myself in thousands of years." He heaved a sigh as he smoothed his hand over his cheek; studying his own reflection. "Funny, how we never really look at ourselves."

He slowly circled his head and gazed at me with his dark almond shaped eyes.

Feeling a twinge of sympathy I, shifting uncomfortably in the spotlight of those long eyes, darker than any brown I've ever seen and piercing, shrugged not knowing what to say.

"This is not who I am anymore!" he bellowed at his mirrored image. With one swift and agitated move, he ran his elegant hand over the water dispersing his reflection.

I remained silent; not really sure what I was supposed to

say. Bernael's voice echoed through my mind, mournful yet angry, powerful and cold as ice.

My gaze remained on him as my mind took note of how angelic he was. Unlike Justin's chiseled features, Bernael's were delicate and soft; the type of boyish good looks a sixteen-year-old would display, but this was no ordinary sixteen-year-old, and neither were his unearthly good looks. Beneath the mass of cascading tresses were elegant cheekbones and a nose of Botticelli straightness. He was assuredly beautiful by any measure.

"This is not me," he growled again menacingly.

His handsome face was no longer pleasant.

In that instant, I knew what was to follow, but my acceptance of the fact did not make it less of a blow as I stood there witnessing how a dark grey mist rolled in and hang over the water. Serpent like, it moved towards Bernael and wrapped itself around him, engulfing every inch of him. Instinctively, I stepped back, gasping in shock as the shadowy figure I knew all too well suddenly appeared where the angelic creature once stood; a shape exaggerated by the dark fog.

"Much better," he slithered, stretching his hands in the air. He turned and stared. "You don't look happy to see me in this form."

I cracked a weak smile. "I'm still shocked at how beautiful you really are," I admitted. "Why would you ever choose to look like this?"

"This skin suits me," he stated, straightening out his long black robe.

Looking around, I slowly came to the frightful realization that I was standing alone opposite one of the most powerful

Immortals. Bernael swore to get back at me for having Alexander remove his scar. Was this the time and place where he'd do it? I wondered glimpsing over my shoulder at the tree lined surroundings. Nobody knew where I was. Uncle Abbot was the only one aware of where I was heading, but even now; I was way past that point. Would anybody be able to reach me in time if I needed help?

"What's on your mind young mortal?" Bernael asked, looking rather perplexed. His eyes showed the mind inside the overweight, overworked camouflage. I realized with a start that I was facing great danger.

"What now?" I asked, trying desperately to sound confident. "What will you do with me? And where in the world is everyone else? I expected to find your brother not you."

He looked at me now, and his look was no longer in the least friendly. "Abaddon has his own agenda when it comes to the Ascended. Your little friend is a Healer much like my brother."

"So? What does Tyler's gift have to do with Abaddon?"

"Thousands of years are quite long to go without a friend; a partner is what my brother seeks. Tyler will be perfect; Abaddon's personal little pupil."

"No, you can't be serious. Tyler will never side with the likes of him!"

Bernael smiled. "Healers are the easiest to recruit. Their gift is easily manipulated. Abaddon will only need to offer him the taste of death, and your little friend will be hooked for eternity, addicted to the sheer ecstasy that taking a life offers them."

My wrists started to throb with the mere thought of Tyler being exposed to such evil. "I need to find him. Take me to him!" I ordered.

He let his gaze fall to my hands. "You want me to help you save your friend?" he scuffed, pulling his robe to the side and walked past me. "Don't you think you should be worrying about saving your own life?"

"My life means nothing without the people I love," I began, "Now, take me to him!" I hollered.

"Mortal, do not push me. I will end you!"

"Fine –," I began, shifting my gaze to his ghastly features, "but can you first take me to my friend?"

He chuckled at my persistence. "You'll be putting yourself between Abaddon and me. I'm not sure which of the two wants to kill you more."

"I don't care what you do with me. I need to see Tyler!"

Bernael walked in circles around me visibly frustrated. "Why is the choice so easy for you?" he asked, stopping only a foot away.

"What choice would that be?"

"Sacrificing everything you are for the people who've obviously hurt you deeply."

"They did what they thought was best for me. No blaming them for not knowing any better."

He reached to touch my face, but just as fast dropped his hand to the side. "You astound me young mortal, and all this time I thought you were on a course for self-destruction. Instead you seek sainthood."

"I seek no such thing," I protested. "This is who I am. This is how I feel. You and your brother would rather have me, instead of Tyler; that much I'm sure of."

"Do you hear what you are saying? You would be willing to exchange places with your friend, forsaking your own life? You would follow us into damnation for the sheer satisfaction of seeing your friend safe?"

I simply nodded.

"Take it from me infant, no one person deserves such a heavy sacrifice. People tend to forget such virtuous actions. You'd best concentrate on your own mortality and leave the Ascended to my brother."

Without any warning Bernael snapped his head to the side and looked around, inhaling rather deeply. "Ah, Ramiel old friend," he sneered in disdain, "Don't you have better things to do?"

"Brother, you need to spend more time with our young Caitlin," said the young Immortal as he materialized only a couple yards away "She seems to be doing you a world of good."

"Is she now?" he laughed dryly.

"Too bad you changed back to the animal you've become. Your former self suited you," added Ramiel, taking a step closer.

"Your dear master made me who I am," Bernael slithered, morphing into the dark mist, but before he faded away, he turned to me with contempt. "There will be a day when no one will come for you, Caitlin."

Remaining transfixed to the spot where the monster once stood, I quickly realized that it was the first time Bernael ever spoke my name, and I wasn't sure how I felt about it.

"Come Caitlin," summoned Ramiel smiling. "You should be heading home. This is no time for you to be anywhere alone. Bernael will not be so well-mannered next time."

"He's radiant," I exclaimed. "Why does he do this to

himself? Why in the world did he choose to become this monster? He is simply magnificent."

"Ah, yes, he was once that, and what you saw was only skin deep. If only you knew him back then. His soul was even more magnificent; a real treasure."

"How can someone so wonderful become engulfed in pure darkness?"

"It's what Alexander and Justin told you. The negative feelings submerged him into his own hell." Ramiel took my hand. "You seem to have made quite an impact on him. Threats aside, the poor soul likes you. He hates feeling the way he does, but thankfully there's no fighting such deep rooted emotions, especially for him. He feels things much stronger than any of us. You are like a beam of light into his decrepit soul; spreading your radiance like wildfire."

"He still wants to kill me."

"I wouldn't be so sure of that. I saw something in him today that I haven't seen in thousands of years."

"What's that," I asked impatiently.

He smiled and patted me on the back. "Admiration! He's seeing what we all see."

I kicked the dirt and walked to the stream. "I wish I saw what you all see in me. I'm a mess, and now I've put Tyler in harm's way. They took Tyler to get to me."

"Caitlin, don't blame yourself. We are on the brink of war. There is absolutely nothing that you did to cause any of this."

"They want me," I cried, "It's all because of me."

Ramiel stood next to me in silence, and placed his small hand into mine. "We are all victims of our destiny. We all have a specific role to play in this life. The sooner we come to grips with what that role is, the faster we can accept who we are." He turned to look at me. "Give yourself time to grow and learn."

Wiping my tears away with my sleeve, I turned to Ramiel. "At the graduation –," I started to say, but Ramiel quickly cut me off. "You were great, Caitlin. You didn't even flinch at the sight of the Shadow Guard."

"I was way too angry to realize the danger I was in. My gift simply took the reins."

"You speak of your gift as though it's a separate entity. Why is that?"

I sat Indian style on the ground. "It seems to have a mind of its own; that's why," I finally answered. "I don't even recognize my own voice. It's like I'm in a trance."

"You and your gift are one, and the sooner you accept that, the sooner you will be able to control it entirely. You allow your anger to trigger it into a spiraling mess of unleashed energy. There must be a balance inside here," he advised, pointing to my head, "and here," he then went on to point to my heart. "Only when these two find their equilibrium will you be able to focus and harness all that energy."

"It's hopeless, I assure you." I hugged my knees. "There's no way I can do what you think I can. You all have this mistaken idea of what it is I do."

"Do we?" he asked, and sat next to me.

"Why does everything have to be so cryptic?"

"You're just worried about your friend right now. It's natural to feel lost."

I nodded. "I just want to see Tyler to make sure he's okay."

Ramiel stood there contemplating something; something against his better judgment. "What is it?" I asked excitedly.

TWENTY-ONE

SURREAL

R AMIEL STOOD AND STRETCHED out his hand for me
to take. "Come," he started, helping me up. "I truly
hope you're ready for this, otherwise Justin will
have my head."

"I'm ready for anything," I yelled, unintentionally.

He smiled weakly and squeezed my hand. "You must do as
I say; otherwise I'm not taking you anywhere," he warned.

"I promise to behave," I pouted. "Can we go?"

"I'm going to regret this, aren't I?" he sighed, and shook his
head.

"What can possibly go wrong with you around?" I assured
him. He rolled his tender little eyes and reluctantly said, "Okay,
well you best close your eyes."

In an instant, I felt as light as a feather being carried in the
wind. "You can open your eyes, now," I heard Ramiel say in
my head. "Remember, you must be silent. Don't make the
slightest sound."

As I opened my eyes, I gasped in utter shock. What I witnessed was not the stuff of an ordinary world. My surroundings were as irrational and surreal as a dream. "What is this place?" I asked, holding Ramiel's hand even tighter.

The world seemed upside down; like one of those nondescript dreams made up of characterless collages; the type of that confuses and disorients. The only other way to describe what I saw would be to cite a painting by Salvador Dali; one of those you can't stop staring at, but yet never figure out what it all means. Everything around me was obscured, but yet so clear; dark but yet light; in color but yet black and white.

"It's where Tyler and the others are. Don't let the location distract you. We are deep in the Inner Realm, and all this is projections of Tyler's mind meant to confuse him. Abaddon has reached deep into your friend's subconscious and extrapolated this scene for one reason or another."

"Beats the hellish surroundings he had created for me," I offered, following Ramiel across what looked like a suspended bridge. At closer analysis we were traversing the backbone of a fish.

"Weird," I whispered.

"We need to be quiet. They can't sense you so you should be safe." Ramiel stopped in mid-stride. "There," he pointed.

From where we stood, we had a panoramic view of the foreign area which did not contain or derive from the essential nature of something. Beneath us was a bottomless ravine that ran the length of a waterfall canyon. Several hundred yards away, standing on what looked like a large turtle shell, was Abaddon with his arm around Tyler. Marcellus stood across from them looking rather distraught.

"What's happening?" I whispered, turning to Ramiel momentarily, utterly discombobulated by the perplexed state of Tyler's inner world.

"The boy's father is trying to talk some sense into the Immortal. Hopefully the balance of reasons will be against Abaddon's carrying out his intention; otherwise there is no way of avoiding a conflict."

"Where are the other Immortals; the Nobe should be here?"

"We can't interfere just yet. If we do, it will surely get messy."

"Tyler is in mortal danger and you all refuse to take action; stupid, irrational rules!" I muttered, getting ready to help my best friend.

Just then I felt a hand pulling me to a full stop. "This isn't the time for heroics." I heard Justin's angst voice say. "You have no business being here."

I pulled my hand free. "Spare me the lecture," I railed, irritated by how everyone was ignoring the problem at hand. My friend needed help and they all refused to intervene. I looked away from Justin's fixed gaze and turned my attention to where Tyler was standing.

"Is anyone going to get him out of this crazy place or shall I?"

Ramiel turned to Justin and quickly back to me. "You need to talk some sense into your friend if you're going to save him. He has to see that what Abaddon is promising him is not as it seems."

Justin snapped his head towards the young immortal and looked at him angrily. "She's doing no such thing. She's staying put," he uttered in a sharp, abrupt tone. "Do you hear me?"

"She's the only one who can help the Healer. He will listen to her."

"And Abaddon? What is she supposed to do about him? She's not ready yet. I won't risk her to save Tyler."

I looked at Justin annoyed. "I won't stand by and watch that devil hurt Tyler; I won't; I can't."

Justin took my hand and kissed it. "Caitlin if anything happens to you, I –,"

Kissing him lightly on the lips was an instrumentality for accomplishing some end. It was the only means I had in stopping his impending threat. I gazed into his worry filled eyes and smiled. "You'll be right here if I need you, won't you?"

He looked down at our intertwined hands. "I can't get involved, so as to alter or hinder Abaddon's actions, or force him to retreat. If any of us intervene it will trigger a war we're all trying to avoid with any means necessary." He kept his eyes lowered, clearly hating not being able to do this for me. "None of us can help Tyler. He has to want to be released from Abaddon's hold. The only thing left for us to do is wait until Abaddon breaches the laws; until then, Tyler is on his own."

My suspicions of a deep rooted change in Justin suddenly resurfaced. "Why are you including yourself in with the Nobe's inability to do something? I mean, you are only an Ascended, right?"

"Caitlin, focus," Ramiel pleaded. "This is neither the time nor the place for insignificant suspicions."

Even though I set the whole thing aside, I knew there was something going on with him. It was in the way he spoke and in the way everybody around him reacted.

I turned my gaze back to Ramiel, and then to where Tyler stood. There was no time to get into a heated argument over another secret they were all keeping from me. "Justin, I have to do this. Please understand."

Without another word he reluctantly let go of my hand, and walked away without another word; fading away into the background; disappearing like a ghost right before my eyes.

"He hates me!"

"Caitlin, focus," Ramiel repeated. "You must stay alert and don't let Abaddon lay a hand on you. The last thing we need right now is for Justin to get involved."

I looked at him puzzled. "I thought Justin can't interfere?"

"He's not supposed to, but who's to stop him if anything happens to you? I certainly can't."

My eyes widened in shock. "A Nobe unable to stop Justin? What in the world is going on, Ramiel?"

"Caitlin please; this isn't the time nor the place."

I nodded and tried to concentrate. "Ramiel, whatever happens down there you have to promise me that you'll keep Justin far from here. Whatever happens to me," I pronounced looking intently at Ramiel. "I don't care what you're all hiding from me, or how powerful Justin's become. I need you to keep him away!"

"Don't fret over things you have no control over," he said, stretching out his hand in a motion to touch my arm. "Just do as I say this time, and don't let Abaddon come close enough to touch you. Now, if you're ready, close your eyes."

The moment Ramiel touched my arm I felt light as air again, as if everything and everyone around me had disappeared.

"Caitlin –," I heard the majestic whisper say.

It was one of the voices I kept hearing when I slipped into my solace. Slowly opening my eyes I looked around only to find myself in the confines of my own little sanctuary. "How is this even possible?" I asked, looking around. "How did I slip into my solace without intending to?"

"Be heedful of Ramiel's warning," said the melodious sound. "Keep your wits about you. Abaddon is not to be taken lightly." It was a whisper within a whisper; male, female; both sounds were interlaced. I couldn't tell when one finished and the other began. The sounds were ethereal; harmoniously uniform. "You need to pull Tyler out of this place, but he needs to go willingly."

"I don't know how," I confessed, talking to the air.

I sat there in the depths of my own mind wishing that at least this once I would be given proper instructions.

"Take hold of the Ellri's hand, and then coax Tyler to take yours. It won't be easy. Tyler is confused at this point. He doesn't know right from wrong. He must be willing to break from Abaddon. You can't force him."

"Okay, so I hold his hand; then what?"

"The Ellri will do the rest." The angelic whispers started tapering off at the end. "Make sure Abaddon doesn't touch you. Now go!"

I had no sooner blinked back the urgency of the beings tone than I found myself standing inches from Marcellus.

Surprised to see me, the Ellri attempted to smile, but quickly circled his head back, and glared at the immortal that held Tyler by the shoulder.

Abaddon grinned hugely at the sight of me. "Ah, you have chosen to join your friend." His pleased look abruptly evaporated, leaving behind a kind of repulsiveness the second he realized my hands were throbbing with pure energy.

I stood there in silence, trying to figure out how to attract Tyler's attention. He did turn to look at me but his face was sullen and cold.

Marcellus' gaze didn't leave Abaddon; not for a second. Color rose to his face and he began to move forward then stopped again, clenching his fists. I took his arm and gently pulled him back next to me. "Don't," I muttered, easing my grip off.

"You're all pathetic," yelled Abaddon, seeing how fast Marcellus responded to me. "You allow this child to guide you."

I ignored the demon and continued looking at Tyler. I stretched out my hand and offered it to my friend. "Come Tyler, let's go home."

He looked at me questionably. "I am home," he replied, looking around. "This is where I belong."

I took a step forward and stood to Tyler's right side. "This is not your home Tyler. This is all in your head." I reached up and stroked his cheek. "Take my hand and come home with me."

Abaddon circled around, and moved in closer. "Tyler, this girl is only toying with you," he whispered in my friend's ear. "It's not you that she loves."

Tyler's expression instantly froze; his face was etched in discordant hatred. "Don't touch me," he snarled, and shrugged me away. "Go away and leave me the hell alone!"

"Don't listen to Abaddon, Tyler. He doesn't care about you. He's only manipulating you into believing everything he says. He's not your friend, Tyler," I continued to press. "He doesn't know what a wonderful person you are. Can't you see that he's only using you? Abaddon is evil."

Abaddon chuckled wholeheartedly. "And what are you?" he asked, edging dangerously close. I slowly took a step back trying to look comfortable. "You have caused more pain to this young man than I ever could. You've been the one manipulating him; not me mortal."

Tyler instantly took a step away from me.

"Please Tyler, don't listen to him. He's lying."

"Am I?" said Abaddon turning to Tyler. "I offer him eternal happiness; a lifetime of euphoria. What do you have to offer him except for more heart ache?"

"Tyler, Abaddon is trying to confuse you. Don't listen to him. He's clouding your mind with all this nonsense. He's using you to satisfy his own personal need. You are but a puppet to him."

Knowing Tyler for so many years I was able to read his every expression. He was truly and most definitely confused.

"Tyler, whatever power Abaddon has over you is blurring your judgment. Please snap out of it!" I heard his father say.

Abaddon circled to my left lessening the space between us.

I stepped back yet again.

The demon was toying with me, dancing around me effortlessly, visibly aware of my discomfort.

Marcellus strategically placed himself between me and the demon, giving me ample space to feel safe. "You'll do best to keep your distance," the Ellri barked. "If you want to get to her, you'll have to go through me."

"Don't tempt me," slithered the damned.

Sensing that I had little time left, I turned back to my friend.

"Tyler, can't you see what he's doing," I implored. "Abaddon doesn't want you. His only agenda is to get to me. He wants to kill me, Tyler! This is what all this is about."

The second I finished my sentence the bright blue sky went balefully dark. My words were finally getting through to him. The vivid surroundings turned to ash, leaving a bleak grayish outline of what once was.

"Abaddon is out to get me, and is using you to do it," I continued to say ignoring the ring of fire that suddenly encircled us.

Tyler's state of violent mental agitation was fabricating rather disturbing surroundings; responding primarily to how he truly felt.

"Please Tyler," I begged. "Just take my hand and help me out of here," I continued. "I need you to get me out of here."

Tyler circled his head around looking quite confused at his maddening surroundings. "Where the hell am I?" he finally asked, snapping out of his delirium.

"Tyler!" I called petulantly. "I'll explain later, now please take my hand."

Disoriented and still quite confused, Tyler continued to look around at the insane landscape.

"Tyler, why would you ever believe her? Don't listen to her," Abaddon hissed contemptuously. "I offer you the world. What does she have to give you?"

Marcellus was quite aware of how thin Abaddon's patience was running and in one swift maneuver; the Ellri quickly took my hand and held it tight. "Now, Caitlin," he enunciated rather sternly causing me to turn to Tyler who seemed to be preoccupied by our surreal surroundings.

"Give me your hand!" I yelled, drawing his eyes to me. "Please Tyler, take me out of here."

Tyler momentarily looked past me towards Abaddon, and then to his father.

"Please, son," Marcellus pleaded in a soft but shaky voice. "Please, do as Caitlin says. I won't leave here without you. No matter what you choose to do, I will always be right here for you. Now please, take Caitlin's hand, and everything will be all right; I promise."

"Don't listen to them," Abaddon roared, awakening the sounds of sinister wails. "What I offer will gratify your every whim. Look at how pathetic and weak they are in front of us. They offer nothing but sorrow and pain. With them you will gain nothing but hollow promises, but with me, you will gain an eternity of unadulterated satisfaction."

"Tyler, please," I begged, offering my hand. "Look at me. Just concentrate on me and ignore all that he promises. He is a predator, seeks to destroy lives; takes what is not his to take. Look at me!" I yelled louder, "Look and decide who you can trust. It's your choice and your choice alone."

Tyler's features exhibited his conflicting mind. It was heart-wrenching to see him so lost inside his own thoughts, but there, in the midst of it all was a shift in our surroundings, a silence so complete that it fell like a veil over our heads. This was all Tyler's doing. His mind went silent, his thoughts just stopped, and then I heard him say, "Caitlin?"

Tyler's features softened as he pronounced my name. He was visibly fighting against something deep down, fighting the demon within us all. He once again looked over to the angel of death before he turned his gaze back to me. "You shouldn't be here," he voiced, looking concerned. "This is no place for you. It's dangerous here. You really need to go."

"Then please take my hand and get me out of here," I begged, hoping he would make the right choice.

With slight reluctance, he finally reached for my hand and took hold, and instantly everything went black.

P acing was counterproductive, and in no way did it make the hands on the clock move any faster. On the contrary, each minute seemed longer, drawn out to excruciating lengths.

"Oh come on already," I muttered, looking at the clock in anticipation for the hand to strike twelve. Justin's birthday was officially in five minutes and some ridiculously long seconds.

Impatiently, I traversed the length of my room and picked up the porcelain doll Tyler had given me on my eighth birthday. I hugged it tight hoping my friend would be okay after the ordeal with Abaddon.

Tyler was, from what little I saw of him, doing much better. I wasn't allowed to see him as often as I had liked, but the Ellri felt I deserved some freedom to come and go. He was in bed for the remainder of the week fighting some sort of inner battle. Possessed is what he seemed to be; ranting on and on about things that made absolutely no sense. Everything he articulated was poorly enunciated; unintelligible by any means. It was hard to see him weak and confused, but knowing he was out of Abaddon's clutches kept me calm.

Marcellus had said something about all the Ascended having to make a life choice, and until that choice was clear; Tyler would not pass to the next level of his Ascension. It was some sort of choice between Light and Shadow. For most, the path to enlightenment was quite clear, but for Healers it required great physical and mental effort to accomplish and comprehend; above all, endure. Both dominions had the same pull. Shadow seemed to be more tempting for them; offering ample stimulus for their gift, drawing them all the more closer to the Fallen.

In my heart I hoped and prayed he would make the right choice in the end. This time there was nothing I could do to help. He had to do this on his own as I would have to when my time came. The ageless choice between good and evil was what Tyler was called on to choose between. Easy as that might be for some; for him it was an inner struggle of his incapability of conscious choice and intention.

I looked at the clock once again.

Two minutes to go, I thought, and pushed myself up against the headboard. I closed my eyes and instantly found my ghostly figure cutting through the night and into Justin's bedroom. Transcending was becoming effortless. I could've easily reached his room without leaving my earthly body, but I didn't want Justin to see me since it was meant to be a surprise, however, to my great disappointment he was nowhere to be found. Failing in my quest for the perfect birthday surprise, I slowly glided outside onto his balcony and let my gaze roam over the moonlit surroundings. A warm breeze swept past me causing the sheer curtains to flail in its wake.

"Where are you?" I whispered with my eyes closed, basking in the soft midnight air, and just then, I felt a kiss as light as a butterfly on the nape of my neck. Stunned, I turned around. "How's that possible?" I asked. "You're not supposed to be able to see me."

"Is that really important?" he asked, smiling brilliantly. "What are you doing here anyway?" He took my translucent hand and lifted it to his brilliant lips.

"I wanted to surprise you," I pouted, "Not the other way round."

"You did surprise me," he whispered against my ear. "It's not every day I see an angel standing on my balcony; a gorgeous one at that."

I smiled involuntarily. "You think I'm an angel?"

He raised my hand and twirled me around. "How else would you describe how you look?"

"I simply wanted to be the first to wish you a happy birthday," I said pouting.

A wide grin spread slowly across his face; he seemed extremely pleased. "I completely forgot about my birthday," he confessed shaking his head forgetfully. His eyebrow suddenly lifted cunningly. "Are you offering yourself as a gift?"

"No!" I exclaimed girlishly shy. "I just came to wish you a happy birthday."

He chuckled at my instant discomfort. "You're so sweet," he said, pulling me into his embrace. "But you know better than to use your gift frivolously."

"Frivolously?" I exclaimed, taking a small step back. "It's your birthday. I simply wanted to surprise you; that's all. There's nothing frivolous about that, is there?"

Justin let out a heavy sigh, and walked back inside. I stood there for a couple of minutes before I followed him in.

"You're right," he began turning to look at me. "You always have good intentions, but still, you need to be more careful. The Fallen are keeping very close tabs on you. Leaving your body is not exactly the best thing to do at this time. When you are in this form you leave your physical self in the real world while you transcend in the inner realm. You're more vulnerable than ever," he explained and turned his back to me. In one seamless motion, Justin slipped out of his shirt. "You need to be more careful, Caitlin," he repeated as he turned to face me with his shirt in hand.

Watching him, made my pulse speed just a little as his bare chest exposed his muscled strength in inches. Seeing him undress only whetted my appetite for him. Justin casually threw the worn shirt on the arm of the side chair and picked another from the dresser. But by doing so, he let me see the long line of his back and shoulders. The muscled smoothness of his back triggered an erratic awakening in my heart. His every move drove me nearly mad and had me biting my bottom lip to keep me from making small eager noises. The view was lovely as always.

"Caitlin –,"

The sound of my name on his lips snapped me out of the hypnotic hold Justin's presence had on me. I looked up at that impossibly lovely face.

"Caitlin, you need to return to your body," he urged. "Your gift is not a toy."

Tears burned at the back of my eyes and tightened my throat so that I could choke on the regret; on the realization that he was right once again. I breathed in, holding back the tears.

"Fine, I'll leave," I said curtly, "By the way, happy birthday." Within milliseconds I was back in my room sitting on the edge of my bed exactly where Justin wanted me to be; back in my earthly body. It wasn't exactly how I thought that night was going to pan out. Not a minute later, the swift knock on my door startled me. "Come in," I offered as I stood straightening out my clothes.

Uncle Abbot poked his head in the door smiling sheepishly. "Normally, I wouldn't allow this, but seeing that you kids today don't seem to be taking the house rules seriously –,"

"What are you talking about?" I asked, pulling my hair in a loose ponytail.

"Justin is downstairs."

"He's here?" I asked eagerly.

"Now just wait one second Caitlin. It's past midnight."

"So?" I exclaimed looking pleadingly at him.

"So –," he smiled, pausing for a few seconds, pondering his next words, "So, you shouldn't keep him waiting."

Unable to contain my excitement, I leaped into my uncle's embrace and squeezed him as tight as humanly possible. "I love you," I squealed, and kissed him on the cheek.

"Sure, you say that now that you got your way."

I took a step back. "You know that's not true. I love you very, very much; always have, and always will."

He smiled and caressed my cheek. "Good to know, sweetie. Now get going before the poor boy collapses from anticipation. He thinks you don't want to see him."

"Why would he think that?

"He said that you're mad at him; are you? Did he do something that I should know about?" my uncle asked sternly.

"No! This is Justin you're talking about. He should be mad at me for always doing stupid things."

His features softened. "I do things without thinking; just really stupid juvenile things," I confessed.

"Yes, I know," my uncle agreed, displaying a wide smile. "You did leave his room rather sudden, wouldn't you say?"

It wasn't exactly what I meant, but nonetheless, I looked at him through lowered eyes. "You know about that, do you?"

Uncle Abbot brought my chin up to face him. "Don't worry Caitlin, I'm not mad. It's just that Justin was right. You should be more careful."

"I'm tired of people telling me how careful I should be. Once; just once, I'd like to be able to act impulsively and not be reprimanded for it; just once!" I huffed.

"Much as I'd like to say how much of a point you have. We, Caitlin, cannot afford such a luxury. We are all with one foot in the grave." He stroked my cheek again trying to comfort my anguish ridden expression. "Sweetheart, if this cat and mouse act continuous with the Fallen for much longer, I fear that there could only be one outcome. We must all be careful of our every move. You of all people should be most careful. Abaddon and Bernael are but followers of a power much stronger than you and I could ever imagine. Being marked –," He lifted my branded wrist to eye level, "Exposes you to many dangers. This is not the time to delve into your gift unguided. This is the time to practice. You need to train and you haven't been."

"I know; I know!" I exclaimed. "I simply wanted to surprise Justin for his birthday. Where's the harm in that?"

"Let's just drop the subject. I know that you are aware of the dangers and besides, Justin is in my head right now driving me mad. So if you could darling, spare your uncle the pain, and go to your young man before I'm forced to put a stop to his insufferable probing."

I smiled contently, and just as I was about to turn and leave, my uncle grabbed my arm and said, "Keep an open mind." He let go just as quickly, and before I could even get a word in, my uncle simply turned and walked away, leaving me unsettled and uncertain of what he meant. Heading down the hall, I contemplated what to say to Justin once I saw him.

Standing in the foyer was the reason I woke up each and every day. The sight of him alone was so intoxicating that I had to find something else for my eyes to meet. I tried to shift my gaze away, but in the end his eyes drew me in. Thankfully, I couldn't read a hint of anger on his brilliant features; just a faint crooked smile filled with the contentment one feels when one has fulfilled a need.

"I didn't want you to leave," he began, and took a few steps to lessen the distance between us.

I remained silent.

"I worry, that's all," he continued to say, now only a breath away. "If anything ever happens to you –," His voice tattered off as he lifted his hand to caress my face.

"I should be more careful," I admitted, leaning into his hand. "Tyler was right, you know."

Justin instrumentally moved his free hand to my back and pulled me up against him. "Right about what," he asked, giving me a quick kiss on the lips.

"He said I should come with a warning label."

Justin let out a good laugh.

"I guess you agree with him, then?"

He kissed me again. "With a warning label; no, but with a manual would have been nice."

"So, you're funny now, is that it?"

Justin smiled and pulled me into a tight embrace.

We stood there for a few minutes, neither of us uttering a sound until Justin said, "There's something I need you to know before my birthday party."

I pulled back, wondering if this is what my uncle tried to prepare me for. My expression must've said it all because at that moment Justin racked his fingers nervously through his hair and took an abrupt step back. "I've been meaning to tell you this for a while now, but –,"

"What is it?" I asked. "Why so serious all of a sudden?"

"It's just something I've been meaning to tell you, but it never seems to be the right time."

"Okay, so what is it?" I urged.

Justin let out another sigh. "I can't do this here, Caitlin," he muttered.

"Why? If it's so important, just tell me already. The suspense is killing me."

"Would you mind if we go for a walk?"

"A walk? Really? You want to take a walk at this hour."

"You had no problem meeting Tyler at this hour."

I rolled my eyes at him. "Not this again. You know that whatever I feel for Tyler is pure friendship. Why are you so hell bent on making it out to be something that it's not? I never once liked him in that way and you know it"

"I'm sorry. I didn't mean it to come out like that."

I smiled at his awkwardness. "Apology accepted."

"Good, now about that walk; I really need to talk to you."

Fighting the urge to pressure him into telling me what that was all about, I reluctantly agreed and allowed him to lead me to the back yard.

TWENTY-TWO

CONFESSION

T HE LIGHT OF EARLY DAWN was filtering through the tree tops, shimmering faintly on the crumbling stone wall that separated the two properties. The sun was in my eyes, as doubt dug into my heart, sending streams of uncertainty to my mind.

Justin had slumped against the wall next to the decrepit metal gate, and rubbed his temples clearly not wanting to tell me what I had gone out there to hear. I began pacing with my arms folded against my chest, fighting back the tears that threatened to reveal my true feelings on the matter.

I did not speak. I couldn't.

He looked at me, and there was something unsettling in that look. "I've changed," he finally voiced, causing me to turn to face him.

"What do you mean, you've changed? How have you changed?"

"Nobody thought it would happen so quickly, but it has."

"Justin, you're not making any sense. Stop talking in riddles and tell me what's going on?"

"You said it yourself, Caitlin; you were the first person to notice a change in me. Even the Nobe were unaware of the change, but you picked up on it without realizing it."

"You're not making any sense," I repeated, sitting next to him on the wall. "Tell me, what's going on."

"I've Ascended," he finally blurted out.

I looked at him wide eyed. "Ascended? Again?" I asked, and then quickly realized how I sounded and said, "That's great."

"Yeah, I guess it is, considering."

"When did this all happen?" I asked. "Where was I?"

"The first time was when you were in Tirion."

I stood up in utter shock. "The first time? You mean to tell me you've Ascended twice?"

"It would seem so," he muttered, keeping his gaze lowered.

"So what does all this mean, and why in the world did you keep something so great a secret?"

"So great –," he huffed.

I sat back down and took his hand in mine. "There's something you're not telling me, isn't there?"

He squeezed my hand momentarily and then stood up. "This change is rather permanent," he started to explain. "I'm not like you guys anymore."

My heart leaped to my mouth. "What does that mean?"

He pushed his fingers through his hair again and then blurted out, "I'm not mortal anymore."

There are moments when nature holds its breath. When the very air seems to pause, as if time itself has taken that last deep breath before reality crashes down and smothers the very essence of life. This was that time, the rare moment when my mortality seemed too real, and suddenly his immortality too large. "You're a Nobe?" I mustered up the courage to ask.

"Don't look at me like that," he implored, reaching for my hand. "You look spooked."

"Shouldn't I be?"

"No, no; of course not," he answered unconvincingly. "I'm not a Nobe or will I ever be."

I looked at him confused. "But you said you're an immortal, doesn't that translate into Nobe?"

"It would for any other member of the five families, but –," He paused, and continued to look at me as though I was supposed to figure it all out on my own.

"But what?" I asked impatiently.

"I wanted to tell you all this the moment I Ascended; the moment I came to Tirion, but The Nobe instructed me not to. You have to believe that nobody knew; not even my parents."

"I believe you, it's just –,"

"Caitlin, I know I'm not making much sense, but you need to give me a few minutes. I don't know how to word all this. It's been murder keeping all this from you. I tried to tell you on the night of your prom, but the Ellri intervened. There was always something going on."

My mind drew a blank.

His face was solemn, but I sensed desperation behind his words. "Caitlin!" he called petulantly, "are you listening?"

My eyes ached. It was all too much to think about.

"Ehm, no," I shook my head, "I mean yes; yes I'm listening. I'm just trying to make sense out of all this. If you're not a Nobe than what are you?" He sat back down on the wall. "Do you remember what Alexander said about the prophecy?"

"Yeah, but what does that have to do with you?"

"Well, it would seem to my great and unexpected surprise that I'm the Chosen One," he revealed abruptly, waiting to see my reaction.

Stunned, I simply gawked at him.

"Did you hear me?" he asked impatiently. "I'm the freaking person who's supposedly going to unite Light and Darkness."

"The Chosen One," I mumbled, unable to believe my ears. "From the legend; that Chosen One?"

Justin nodded.

"What does that mean?"

"I'm not sure," he answered taking my hand.

"If you don't know, then who does?"

Justin shrugged his shoulders. "Gabriel was a test to see if I was the One. They needed to make sure. The Sentinels had foreseen it years ago, but the Nobe needed proof."

"Well, that certainly explains the way you looked that day of the confrontation with Gabriel, but it still doesn't explain how Gabriel was a test?"

"The Nobe needed to see if I was going to be corrupted by my unlimited power. All the newly Ascended go through a phase much like Tyler is going through now. The third Ascension is even harder. When an Ellri ascends into Nobe the appeal of the Fallen is sensational, and quite hard to resist, but for some unexplained reason I ascended effortlessly. I mean our Ellri don't fall into darkness either, but they have a harder time adjusting."

"Why is that?" My voice was, unintentionally sharper.

Justin eyed me doubtfully as he answered. "Our Ellri train

with unflagging resolve in the art of balance between light and darkness; it's the reason they refrain from using their gift. It helps them fight the temptation once they ascend, and keeps them clear minded and centered." He looked to see if I was keeping up. "Each time I ascended I felt absolutely no pull to the dark side. It was so natural that nobody even noticed."

"I still don't understand what the confrontation with Gabriel proved."

Justin smiled warmly. "Don't you see? I didn't kill him. I could've easily, but I didn't. I toyed with him a bit, but I wasn't in any way tempted to step over that line into darkness as most newly ascended would have. That was the last test; the last piece of evidence the Nobe needed. It was the reason why the Book of Truths responded to me in that way. It was why it wrapped its pages around me." Justin looked at me. He gave me every ounce of those beautiful blue eyes. "Only the Chosen One would've been able to decode the writing. It was the last test Alexander needed to be sure."

"But how can that be?" I said shortly, "I was the one who found and unlocked the book. It responded to me. It was only when you pushed my hands away that it wrapped around yours."

"Yes, I know," he began. "Actually, both of us were needed."

He said no more, but instead raised a brow, awaiting a much deeper understanding on my part. His long face gave away little. But I saw the tiny widening of his eyes, heard the faint catch of his breath. I blinked. Angry, happy, baffled, I wasn't sure what to feel – what to think. A chill ran down my spine. Then, in that split second the realization of what it all meant sunk in everything fell into place. "If you're the Chosen One –," I swallowed back the burn of reality, "If you're the Chosen One that would make me the Guardian, wouldn't it?"

The second Justin nodded in acknowledgement; I stood up fearing the worst.

"That would mean that I'm supposed to open the path for you; to protect you from the Fallen, and keep everybody safe." My heart was beating a mile a minute. "There must be some mistake. This can't be right. I'm not that person. I can't do this."

"This is what we were born to do, Caitlin."

My back was to the wall, metaphorically and literally. I slumped down and put my head on my knees. "I'm going to get everyone killed," I cried. "There must be some kind of a mistake. I am not cut-out for this, Justin. I can't go up against immortals and win."

"Let's hope none of us will need to go up against anyone. Everyone is doing what needs to be done to keep the war at bay."

"I'm not who you say I am; I can't be."

Justin kneeled down in front of me. "You are the Guardian of us all, Caitlin. You feel it in your bones. You have this unyielding need to protect anyone at any personal cost. You yield to no one, no matter how powerful they are. Your gift escalates to such heights to meet your needs in battle. It is who you are. It has always been who you are. Caitlin, you were born a fighter. Er'el knew that the moment he saw you."

"That night at the celebrations in Tirion, when I was supposed to lift all the Ellri off the ground Er'el told me that next time I should choose the Nobe Sentinels not 'them'. By them, he meant the Shadow Guard, didn't he?"

"It sounds right."

"So Er'el knew then that I would be leading them, and yet he threatened me with a spear through the heart or head."

"Yeah, well, you're not their leader yet," Justin said attempting a joke.

"Is that why the Shadow Guard bowed down to me at the graduation? Do they know?"

"That was only a test," Justin said unconvincingly.

I placed my head back on my knees and said, "I don't know what the hell I'm doing half the time. How am I supposed to lead anyone anywhere, when I myself don't know where the hell I'm going?"

Justin stretched out his hand to help me up. "It's time you saw who you really are," he said, pulling me to my feet. "Stand tall, and prepare to be amazed."

Without any warning, ethereal beings appeared bright as the sun and stood in a circle around us. A hand clamped onto my wrist so hard it hurt. But the pain brought me back from the wilderness of confusion I'd wandered into. It was Justin squeezing my wrist tight as he pulled me to his side. "It's only the Nobe," he said whispering in my ear.

I wasn't as surprised to see them as I should've been. My mind was too busy trying to wrap itself around the information I had, only moments to absorb.

There in the middle of this angel laden circle Justin and I stood holding hands. From the corner of my eye I saw one of the bright beings approaching. The closer it got the lesser the brightness, until it was in complete human form. The woman stood about a foot away. Her long silver hair cascaded loosely on either side framing her creamy white complexion. Her face was veiled in soft light making it nearly impossible to make out her features. I watched as the godly creature laid her hand on Justin's shoulder and chanted softly, her head bowed. In answer came a hum like a whisper of wind, but I knew to look to the Nobe for the source of the majestic sound. Instantly, as I stood there in awe, the supernatural being looked to the sky and there, right before my eyes, a lustrous dome like structure started configuring, encompassing the makeshift circle, bottling us in.

No one spoke, and as the silence grew, I became more and more aware of the power imbued in the lucent structure around us. Fear tried to claim me, but I refused to give into it. Instead, I circled my gaze back to Justin and my breath quickly caught in my chest at the sight of him looking like them – angelic in every way – radiant from head to toe.

I impulsively pulled my hand free and stepped back wanting to distance myself. Fearing that I was losing him to them, my eyes stung with tears and my heart was heavy with sadness in the knowledge that things would never be the same between us. I fell short of Guardian status, I was sure. According to the legend, the Guardian was to clear the path for the Chosen One but standing there, I couldn't see how or even why Justin would need any protecting especially by me.

Neither Justin nor the others spoke. The vast stillness echoed in them. But I had a question – many really, but my courage failed me. I was too stunned by Justin's appearance to think clearly.

"Why so afraid, my child?" said the women in a soft melody. Her hand remained on Justin's shoulder. "We are here to help you understand." The sound of her voice didn't simply enter my ears, but penetrated deep into my soul.

"I'm not afraid," I confessed, keeping my gaze on Justin.

Without hesitation and as if responding to my own thoughts, the being raised her hand off Justin's shoulder and took a step back. In that instant, the translucent light, that permeated his every fiber, slowly faded returning Justin back to normal.

"Are you okay?" I asked not sure of what else to say.

He chuckled. "Of course I'm okay. You're the one who looks like she's going to faint."

I smiled at the awkwardness of the situation I seemed to have found myself in. "No, I'm fine," I lied, distracting his probing gaze by looking up at the dome that surrounded us. "What's all this for? Why all the drama?" I asked feigning comfort.

"It's a shield to keep the Fallen out. They are Nobe as well and can go anywhere they please. This –," he pointed to the force field that encapsulated us, "is to keep what we say from being heard. It will keep them guessing for a while longer."

"Oh, I see." I scratched my head confused. "Keep them guessing about what?" I finally asked.

Instead of answering immediately, Justin took a few steps towards me and took my hand in his – his eyes molten. "It's me Caitlin –," he began, laying my palm on his chest, "Nothing's changed between us. I need you to see that." He leaned in and kissed me so abruptly hard and full of unspoken demand, that I just stood there and let him kiss me. "Don't give up on me," he continued in a low voice, as his thumb brushed a line along my jaw. "It's me Caitlin."

I smiled weakly. "I know. It's just taking me longer than

usual to come to terms with all this." He smiled and kissed me lightly on the lips. I eased back and looked him in the eyes. "Keep the Fallen guessing about what?" I asked again.

Before I could even blink, the breathtaking Nobe was right next to me. "They believe that you are the Chosen One. They are not aware of Justin's role in all this. The Fallen know that he has ascended, but that is as far as it goes. They remain in the dark about the details and we hope it continues to stay that way. It will keep him safe."

"How can they not know yet? Justin and I were just talking about all this on the wall. They could've easily listened in, right?"

The bright being shook her head in disagreement. "They do not know the truth yet. The symbols on your wrists have led them to believe that you are the One."

"Wait!" I exclaimed. "You mean to tell me that once they find out the truth, the Fallen will want Justin dead?" I asked, refusing to look at him in fear of meeting his gaze, but my gift didn't take long to ignite as rapids of energy coursed through my veins.

The being nodded her head. "Justin is the link that binds all the families. When he takes his rightful place many of their followers will kneel to the light. This is what the Fallen fear most. They fear that they will lose their army to the Chosen One."

I turned back to Justin. "The Shadow Guard? Is that who she means? Who are they anyway?"

Justin caressed my cheek in an attempt to calm me. "For many, many millennia almost since the beginning of the first war, there have been a few gifted who have slipped into shadow following the way of the Fallen as Gabriel did. Many have died under the hands of the Sentinels for transgressions against the Gifted or even mankind as a whole. But enough survived to summon up an army against the Illumine and Varjatus."

I suddenly felt sick, and Justin fell silent. A little voice in the back of my mind whimpered about the part I was to play against these powerful immortals. I chewed my lower lip, swallowing back the bile that crept up my throat. A moment later I realized that my hand remained on Justin's chest; clenching at his shirt, gripping it in a tight fist. He didn't seem to mind that my hand was fully charged and quite lethal.

Justin tilted his head and smiled. "You really need to relax." He placed his hand on top of mine. "You'll be safe."

"It's not me that I'm worried about," I admitted, ironing out the creases I created on his shirt with my hand.

A look of bafflement replaced the masklike expression on the Nobe's glorious face. "Your need to protect us all is commendable, but you have more important things to do at this time and that's to grow. If and when the Fallen realize that you are the Guardian, they will not be so civil. You are the only obstacle that will stand in their way when the time comes because you will command all armies at will, and this they fear above all else."

Afraid to ask about when that time would be, I shook my head in utter disbelief. "I don't see how I can help any of you," I admitted. "You are all supreme beings and I'm a common house fly in comparison."

Justin chuckled. "I've told you a million times before Caitlin. There's nothing common about you. You will grow and evolve into the role you are meant to take. The role you know and feel is your rightful calling. Give it time."

"And until then? What do I do in the meantime? How am I supposed to keep you safe?"

His face beamed with pleasure. "How about you let me keep you safe for the time being?" Justin wrapped his hand around my waist and brought me up against his body. "Nothing will happen to me, I promise you." He leaned down and kissed me, and this time I kissed him back. This time I melted into his arms, his body, because I could do nothing more. "I love you," he whispered and held me close.

"You both need to be extra careful," said the seraphic presence drawing our attention. Justin released his hold and we both turned to face The Nobe. "The Fallen might not be able to read your thoughts Caitlin, but Bernael is able to sense what you feel. Who Justin is must be kept a secret. Since you have not ascended yet, they don't see you as a threat. They will, however, try to coax you to join their little world. Hopefully, they will keep to our laws and cause you no harm."

I struggled to block out the feeling of danger that surged within me. I gritted my teeth and turned to Justin, unwilling to give into the sensation, I held his hand in an attempt to focus on what the Nobe was saying and not what my mind was generating. "Abaddon wants me dead, I'm absolutely sure of that," I finally said, fighting to control my breathing, denying the need to scream as the black thoughts swirled in my mind.

"Abaddon wants us all dead," said the Nobe.

My gaze dropped at those last words, and tears welled up, as I desperately tried to brush off the clinging sense of a nightmare.

Out of nowhere, a disquieting feeling of something threatening heading our way was steadily escalating as the sense of foreboding crashed over me, almost making me gasp with the intensity of it. My hair on the back of my neck stood on end. Instantly, I looked around our enclosure to everyone's face, trying to decide if it was someone within our enclosure that was having this ominous effect on me, but they all seemed too engrossed in each other's thoughts.

"Is everything okay?" asked Justin. "You look as if you've seen a ghost."

I didn't answer.

I couldn't begin to describe what I felt. I had a momentary image in my mind of a shadow stalking through the woods, the scent of death and decay so pungent it almost burned my nose.

"Caitlin –," Justin enounced caringly, "what's going on in that head of yours?"

His voice distracted me for a moment. "Can't you feel that?" I asked, shifting my gaze past the outer perimeter of the translucent dome.

Justin's eyebrow lifted. "Feel what?" The words came out hard and short, causing the radiant Nobe to turn and stare.

Slowly, as if pulled by an invisible rope, I inched closer to the transparent wall that separated us and the outside world, looking past the iridescent force field that kept our thoughts and voices hidden from any intruder wanting to listen in.

"Caitlin, what's going on?" Justin's voice was tight with worry.

I blinked the sensation aside and rubbed the back of my neck as I tried to focus my attention on what Justin was saying. Then, as I stood there in complete silence I felt the gathering of evil approaching. It was a feeling like no other. This time accompanied with an acute piercing at the depths of my mind. Instantly, I closed my eyes and attempted to swallow back the pain when in that split second I was thrown to my knees by the intensity of the vision swirling in the darkness of my mind.

Justin shot me a curious look, part concern, part aggravation. I rubbed my forehead and wondered why my mind had chosen that particular moment to snap. He eased his arm around my waist supporting most of my weight.

"My head is killing me," I complained, leaning into the shoulder that supported me unable to explain what was going on.

The entire area started spinning into a gray swirl of confusion as the image of a dark silhouette made its way to my conscious mind. It moved in a blur of speed that left a wake of streamers of color.

It was almost as if the shadow didn't so much touch the ground or the surrounding trees, but was moving so quickly that the air wasn't solid enough to stop it. My head was about to explode as I fell limp in Justin's arms.

"Caitlin –," Justin implored.

He carefully set me on the ground, holding onto my waist while I waited to see if the world would stop spinning.

"What's happening to her?" he yelled, looking around to The Nobe.

They all stood there in sheer silence looking up to the sky.

"Damn it!" Justin screamed annoyed. "What the hell is happening? I can't read her! Will somebody please tell me what the hell is going on?"

TWENTY-THREE

SACRIFICE

Y MIND WAS screaming out for clarity. I tried to pull myself together, tried to rationalize what was going on, but once again the stabbing pain was potent and malicious. I seemed to be a pawn to a force I didn't understand.

Another surge of pain; again, the image was a swirl of darkness and decay. The wind brushed against the ghostly figure as he swooshed through the woods, driven by the need to reach me. The taste of rot was back in my mouth.

"Bernael," I whispered, and looked up at Justin's worried face. "It must be him. The taste in my throat is all too familiar," I continued to say. "He's coming. He's on his way," I warned trying to get back on my feet.

"You can sense the Fallen?" he asked as he helped me to my feet.

"I don't sense him. I see him," I answered in a weak voice, closing my eyes as tight as possible. "He's not that far." I pushed the worry of my potential insanity aside, and tried to ease Justin's despairing gaze. "I can see him approaching in a cloud of darkness and he's moving fast."

"How? How is that possible? You haven't even ascended yet. How is it that you sense the immortal? Bernael of all people? Only the Watcher can sense these things."

I smiled contently.

"What is it?" Justin asked.

"I'm just happy that I'm not the only one with so many questions."

Justin smiled as well and caressed my cheek. "But really, how is it that you feel the Fallen? I must know why you feel what you feel."

"For the love of God Justin," I whimpered in sheer agony and annoyance at his inability to focus on the bigger picture, "Who cares why it's happening; how do I stop it from hurting so much?"

His hold instantly tightened around my waist, quieting the beast that howled within my head. "Make it stop, please!" I implored, pressing both hands against the throbbing veins of my temples, and shut my eyes momentarily. "I sense great change. Something big is going to happen," I warned, returning my gaze to him. "I'm not sure what it is, but it's big."

If Justin wasn't holding on so tight, I was sure to collapse from the sheer force of the image. The closer Bernael approached, the more vivid the vision became.

The Angel of darkness caused the wind to rise to an unbearable volume, shrieking and screaming out sounds of tormented souls in anguish and pain, but just when I thought I was going to scream myself, just when my mind was about to lapse into the dark obese of my own solace; all was suddenly deathly quiet. I pried my eyes open, hoping that the images wouldn't return. Slowly, I lifted my head from Justin's shoulder. At that particular moment I knew the reason for the sudden stop and stillness. Bernael had come. I only needed to turn around to see that he was right there on the other side of the dome that separated us.

Fear seized me as I saw Justin's menacing expression. My breath was a solid lump in my chest as I scrambled to think of a way to keep myself from turning to the demon my mind had foreseen, but instantly the overwhelming need to protect Justin resurfaced, banishing any fear that lurked in the depths of my mind.

"He won't hurt me," I stated, gazing into the dark pools of Justin's eyes. "He'd never hurt me."

Justin momentarily shifted his menacing gaze from Bernael back to me. "That's what he wants you to think, Caitlin. He knows that if we act; if I act to protect you then we will have a war on our hands. That's what he wants; that's what he lives for."

I breathed in deep trying to summon up the courage to deal with the demon on my own. "He's here for me Justin," I said, clutching onto his arm in a feeble attempt to make him see that I wasn't at all scared. "None of you need to get involved."

My gaze quickly swept the area and noticed that the Nobe were nowhere to be seen, but the majestic dome remained; protecting us within its power. I casually turned to look in the other direction only to see a dark mist surrounding the entire perimeter, circling at unfathomable speeds, covering the entire exterior wall of the protective shield.

"He's trying to find a way in," muttered Justin in response to my questionable expression. "He insists on talking to you."

The pain that had been sprouting in the back of my head eased, fading with the uneasiness and nausea. I slowly slipped out of Justin's tight grip and let my gaze fall on the dark silhouette standing only a few yards away.

"Caitlin –," Justin begged, pulling me back into his strong embrace, "you don't need to do this. I can get us both out of here."

He wasn't actually pressuring me to choose, rather waiting to see how I'd react. He didn't sound as persistent as I'd thought he'd be. There was something in his smooth voice that guided me in the right direction. It wasn't going with him that I needed to do, but stay there and see what Bernael wanted. Justin looked at me with more intent. "What will it be?" he asked stroking a finger down the outline of my jaw.

Darkness descended once again as it entered the depths of my soul, filling my mind with unceasing despair, ripping my sanity until there was nothing left. I backed away from Justin not wanting him to be anywhere near the hell I was envisioning. I stared at him, shaking my head as he watched me. "You must leave," I ordered, trying to sound as confident as possible.

"I will do no such thing!"

I threw a quick glance at Bernael trying to understand everything he was pouring into my mind. "You must," I whispered, returning my gaze to Justin.

Visions of death and destruction corroded through the barriers of my mind making me shiver at the intensity and vileness of what I saw.

"Caitlin," I heard Bernael's slithering voice call. "Come to me, sweet child."

Justin took a threatening step forward, on the edge of reason. "You're coming with me, and that's final!" he ordered, changing his previous calm tone, pulling me towards him with force. "Hell with what they all think. I'm not letting you go anywhere near that bastard!"

"No," I stumped, like a petulant child unable to take my eyes off of him. I backed away a couple of steps, pulling free from his vice. "Please Justin, just go," I implored, "Bernael is here for me. No one needs to get involved."

Justin took a step toward me, his hand held out with the palm up. "I'm not going anywhere without you."

Refusing to take his extended arm I withdrew a couple more steps. "Don't do this," I pleaded. "I need to see what he wants."

Dropping his hand to his side, Justin momentarily dropped his gaze. "Go, I'll be standing right here in case he tries anything."

I shook my head. "It's you I'm trying to protect," I explained, trying to get him to leave.

"Nonsense!" he spat out. "Now go see what the demon wants before I change my mind. I don't like this Caitlin! I don't like it one bit." I kept my gaze on Justin for what seemed an eternity before turning on my heel and slowly walked towards Bernael. The demon stood rather close to the dividing wall, scratching his razor sharp nails against the force field in an attempt to break through. "Come Caitlin," he said, putting both hands up against the translucent barrier.

Bernael's face grew serious and something like fear filled his eyes. Feigning a smile, he kept his gaze on me as I approached, and I returned the smile knowing all too well that I needed to have my wits about me. I needed him to believe that I was comfortable and that I didn't fear him. There was no room for error as far as Bernael was concerned. Ramiel did warn me that the angel of darkness was not going to be so civil the next time he saw me, and here we were, a mere mortal facing down one of the deadliest hunters on the planet.

I was only a foot away looking into his piercing eyes. Then his face sobered, and there was something far too serious in his monstrous expression. Bernael dropped both hands to the side and simply stared. He then fluttered his hands anxiously and his dark eyes filled with fear once again.

He grunted in an effort to speak. "Caitlin, I did not mean to cause you any pain," he said tilting his head to the side as if reading my every emotion. "I hurt you. It was unintentional, I assure you." He lied, smoothly, effortlessly; lied as if it were the truth.

Allowing my instinct to guide me, I walked up to the perimeter and placed my hand up against the opalescent dome.

"I saw you," I started to say, "I felt you approaching. It was a vision far too real for my own liking," I admitted, hoping my honesty would lift his angelic side to the surface. "I felt your anxiety; your need to reach me."

Unexpectedly, Bernael lifted his arm and placed his hand directly in front of mine. He didn't speak; instead he just stood there staring at our hands.

"What's on your mind?" I asked remaining still. "Why here? Why now?" He froze momentarily, peering upward, and frowned broadly. "They have you on a very tight leash," he said, turning his dark features to me.

I looked around to see who he was talking about, but saw no one other than Justin at the farthest part of the enclosure. "No one has me on a leash," I exclaimed dropping my hand to my side.

His smile suddenly warm, in a trifle wry. "Ah, but they do. You might not see them, but they are all around us watching and waiting."

"Damn it!" I mumbled under my breath. "They don't seem to trust me." My frustration wasn't meant to be verbalized, and I quickly bit my bottom lip the second I spoke the words.

In that instant, Bernael let out a husky laugh.

"What are you laughing at?" I scolded him, raising my voice louder than I had intended.

"You are face to face with the angle of darkness, and you think it's you they don't trust." He laughed again. "Amazing is what you are mortal; simply amazing!" His voice was tight with controlled rage.

I attempted a weak smile and rolled my eyes.

He took a step back. "Well, are you going to do something about this divider or are we going to stand on either side pretending to be something that we're not. You and I both know Caitlin that we have a connection. What it is I'm not sure, but your presence has been haunting my existence."

"As yours, mine," I admitted.

His gaze dropped.

I took the opportunity and exchanged a quick glance with Justin. He didn't seem as anxious as I'd thought he'd be.

"Wield the dome to disappear," Bernael instructed.

"I'm not sure I can."

"Of course you can. Just walk through it."

I looked at him wondering what trick he had up his sleeve. I didn't fear him. There was no logical reason I shouldn't, but I didn't. Bernael had many opportunities to do me harm, but he chose not to.

"And then what?" I asked keeping my gaze on him.

"I will not hurt you," he promised. His once raspy voice slipped around me to whisper velvety-soft against the depths of my soul. "I will never hurt you, of that I swear."

B ernael had a calming effect on me. His voice lingered in my mind like a quiet song intended to lull a child to sleep. Seconds later, I did as he said and took a step closer to the transparent wall pushing my hand forward to see if I could actually pass through. The once solid wall seemed to be made of molten light which bent to the touch. I held my breath and in one great big stride walked right through. As soon as I was on the other side, the massive force field collapsed inward and vanished into thin air. Justin remained glued to the spot visibly unscathed by the whole incident.

"Much better, wouldn't you say?" asked Bernael.

"Only time will tell."

"Don't be like that young mortal. I prefer your confidence and sharp tongue."

"What's all this really about, Bernael? What's going on?"

He closed his eyes and sniffed the air around him. "I don't have much time," he stated ominously, allowing me a slight glimpse into the endless torment that held him in its grip and in no time at all, sorrow gusted through my mind like a storm. My heart felt like it had stopped. There was something going on, something millennia in the making.

"What is it?" I finally spoke, taking a step closer. "Bernael, what's wrong? What's going on?"

He closed his eyes again and took a deep breath. As he did, the grey mist that enveloped him retracted leaving him stand there in complete human form; black-robed from head to toe.

"The Korbs is where you should be. You're not safe here," he warned in a low whisper.

"What are you saying? And why are you warning me?"

I felt the blood drain from my face. Bernael looked uncertain, and almost reached out for me. Involuntarily, I took a quick step back.

"This hour I'm here for a different reason." He licked his lips and I prayed that he was being honest. "Don't ask me why I'm doing this," he finally added, pushing back his long flowing robe displaying the red satin lining underneath the rich woven material. "I'm not sure myself. You seem to have seeped in somehow," he admitted uncomfortably, pausing for a few minutes. "I feel your every emotion as my own. For some reason I sense you more than I do others and I'm frightened for you."

His gaze bore into mine until something distracted him; something bigger than him. "The armies of darkness are ready to rise and crumble everything and anyone that is dear to you. You must go to Velius. The Korbs are much more than you think. They can help keep all of you safe at least until you ascend." He took a step back and closed his eyes again. "I'm going against everything I believe in by telling you this."

The angel of Darkness took a step closer and slowly lifted his hand to my face. I remained still. I could feel Justin's instant discomfort, it stung in my veins the second he felt it. Softly,

Bernael caressed my cheek and smiled warmly as he turned his gaze towards Justin. "You must get her out of here, and fast," he ordered, looking over my shoulder. "She's not safe out here. He's not coming for her, but for me. It's best her presence not rouse him."

I circled my head and saw Justin standing inches away. "What's going on?" I asked worriedly. "Bernael, why are you helping me?"

"For everything that's holly Caitlin, you must go. He's on his way. I shouldn't have come."

"Bernael, you're not making any sense," I urged with tear-filled eyes, taking a hold of his arm, causing him to turn. "Who's coming for you?"

He looked down at my hand, and then slowly placed his other hand on top of mine. "I finally see what Alexander sees in you," he confessed softly. "Please, do what I say. It is imperative that you see this to the end. Don't become a victim of your own thoughts and feelings. Stand strong against them all."

"Bernael, what the hell is going on?" I yelled.

"The Primoris is approaching," Justin quickly warned as he grabbed my arm, "Bernael is right, I need to get you out of here."

I pulled my hand free. "I'm not going anywhere. I'm not leaving Bernael alone. I'll leave only if he comes too!"

Justin nodded. "Yes, of course you're right," he agreed. "Bernael, you must join us."

"Take the child away," Bernael ordered. "She speaks nonsense."

Justin shook his head. "She's right. I hate to admit it, but

Caitlin has a point. You have betrayed your kind by coming here, by warning her. I cannot stand by and allow the Fallen to destroy you."

Bernael smiled. "So, it is you then," he muttered, glowing with satisfaction. "I knew it couldn't be Caitlin, she's too headstrong to lead us, but you – you are most definitely perfect for the role. You are led by pure light and truth. Justin the Just – how appropriate. The Chosen One and the Guardian bound in life – how poetic."

I gasped in fear. If Bernael could figure out that Justin was the Chosen One that would mean that the rest of the Fallen would know as well.

"If either of you fails in fulfilling your destiny the other dies; you both die." Bernael started muttering to himself as though solving a complex puzzle. "It makes sense that the connection must exist." He lifted his bewildered gaze to look at us. "One more reason why this must be done," he finally said.

I took hold of Bernael's sleeve. "Please, please Bernael nobody must know."

"Don't worry child, your secret is safe with me."

"Why? Why after all you've said and done? Why should I trust you?"

"That's unimportant," stated Bernael half smiling. "What is important is getting the two of you to a safe distance."

Everything was happening way too fast for my mind to process. Bernael, the person who swore to kill me was helping me and Justin escape the hands of the oldest and most powerful immortal.

"Please, you don't need to do this," I pleaded standing face-to-face with him. "He'd rather have me. Please just go and let me deal with this. I can't allow you to sacrifice yourself for me. I'm no one."

Just then I realized that his true nature was too glorious to hide under the darkness and evil. It simply needed thousands of years to seep back to the surface.

His eyes fixed on me. "You must go child," he said wiping away my free-flowing tears. "Don't make me out to be a saint. I do this for my own conscious and for my own peace of mind. I have touched eternity. My whole life has been cloaked in darkness, never to know the feel of the light. Caitlin, I have lived in silent torment wishing I had the strength to do what you so easily offer. I am cursed, an abomination to every living thing. Do not take pity on me."

"No!" I yelled turning to Justin. "We must do something."

Justin continued to stare at Bernael, but now something else was working behind his eyes; tightness came to his features. Bernael shook his head and looked once to me and Justin and the expression on his face had changed again.

"Go!" he wailed and suddenly turned, shielding us from whatever shrieked in the distance.

There was no sound but a continuous shrill in my ears. I applied pressure with a hand over each ear trying to stifle the deafening sound. The wind fluttered our clothing – the wind or insubstantial sounds. The sound turned to whispers that slowly rose into a drone of many agitated soft, but piercing cries.

Justin instantly pulled me back. "We need to go," he ordered tightening his hold, "It's here."

I didn't know how long I had been staring into the dark woods. For a moment I thought it was all but a dream – a nightmare to be exact, but surely this strange feeling was something all too real – real and deadly. The images before me seemed to shift and blur along their edges as though the world had suddenly twisted ever so slightly out of its natural shape.

"I'm not leaving Bernael," I pronounced, trying to break free of Justin's unyielding grip.

He pulled me harder against his taut body and forced me to look at him. "This is not your fight, Caitlin. You must learn when to back away and let things take their course. Bernael is one of them. There is absolutely nothing you or your gift can do to help. You will only implicate the Nobe if you get involved. Is it a war you want?"

I shook my head unwilling to yield to his wishes.

"Damn it, Caitlin. Just do what I say. This is not the time or the place. Bernael has made his choice."

I looked over my shoulder and saw that Bernael stood there alone, staring in the direction of the murmurs. There was no one, or, if someone was indeed near, they stood silently, waiting to make their move. Suddenly, I felt a curious, abrupt unsteadiness, as the ground tilted beneath my feet. The nondescript shapes in the distance shifted into hundreds of shadows silhouetted against the break of dawn.

"Close your eyes," ordered Justin as he coaxed my head to face him. "I need to get you out of here."

"No! Please, I can't just leave him."

For a moment I thought Justin had carried me far away, but then I realized that we were still standing on the same spot – imbedded in a sphere of pure light, much like the dome that engulfed us earlier.

"What's going on?" I asked stunned.

"We'll be safe for the time being," explained Justin.

"Nobody can see us or sense us for the time being. Hopefully, the Primoris will be too preoccupied with Bernael to notice our presence."

The wind instantly grew shriller.

"Is that the Shadow Guard?" I asked, shuddering by the sheer force of the evil the dark shadows imbued.

"Yes," Justin said pulling me back against his chest. "The Guard protects the Fallen as the Nobe Sentinels protect us all. The Primoris never travels anywhere without them. They are all immortals and never ever have taken human form."

Realizing that at my graduation I was up against these powerful beings made me gasp in shock. "They're all powerful immortals?" I turned in his arms to look at him. "Justin you must leave. If all those beings are the Fallen then you shouldn't be here. What if they figure out who you are?"

He slowly leaned in and kissed me on the lips. It wasn't the most appropriate time to be basking in the effect he was having on me, but there was little I could do when it came to his perfect mouth. "I'll be fine," he said smiling. "They're all here for Bernael, not me."

I impulsively grabbed Justin's arm with all my might as the deafening sound pierced through my skull. The sound didn't seem to faze Justin. "Make it stop!" I begged looking to him for help.

"I'm afraid there's not much I can do. You'll get used to it soon enough," Justin tried to explain. "The reason you hear it is because you have some strange connection to them."

"What do you mean?"

"The sound that you hear is the immortals communicating; actually they're arguing. They speak on a whole different wavelength than mere mortals. Once you ascend you will be able to understand them."

"Enough!" Bernael spat. The madness in his eyes was all too clear. "I have but one father!"

I looked at Justin. "What's happening? Who's he talking to?"

"The Primoris is pretty mad. He's ordering Bernael to kneel for his retribution."

"There must be something we can do. He's put his life on the line for me. I can't just stand here and watch him be destroyed. This is all my doing. I need to stop this."

"The swiftness of divine retribution is what Bernael seeks," Justin explained. "He's tired. He's had enough of this world and all the pain that goes with it. He feels everything on this planet. Can you imagine how it feels to sense every last emotion? He simply wants to sleep."

"What are you saying? He wants to be killed?"

"Immortals cannot take their own life. It's not like they can commit suicide. Only another immortal is able to put an end to his misery. That's what this is all about. Bernael seems to have finally looked into the mirror and clearly hated the creature that stared back at him."

"This is all my fault."

"How can you say that? How is this your fault?"

I circled my head and looked in Bernael's direction. "It was my idea for Alexander to remove his scar, for Alexander to forgive him. If I didn't intervene, if I kept my mouth shut, none of this would be happening."

"What Bernael chooses to do is not your doing. He's been fighting an inner battle for eons. You simply reminded him of how warm standing in the light is. You can't blame yourself for this; you shouldn't. Bernael appreciates what you've done. In a way you've helped him snap out of his self-destructive path."

A long moment passed and nothing was happening. Bernael turned for a second and we exchanged a quick glance. There was so much more to it than what Justin said, so much more that had been revealed in the fallen angel's pale, emotionless eyes.

"Please don't," I mouthed falling to my knees. "Please, Bernael, you don't need to do this."

He smiled and sprawled his arms to the side surrendering himself to darkness. In seconds, the shadowy figures meshed into one great swirl of dark cloud and spiraled towards Bernael.

Without my meaning to, my gift instantly ignited to unfathomable levels and the throbbing in both my wrists pulsated to the rhythm of my heart, if not faster. It was like nothing I had ever felt before. In that speck of time, the submerging need to protect Bernael was beyond my common understanding as my body and mind worked without my conscious guidance and what I did from that point on I did instinctively; defying my own inner will.

The protective shield around us disintegrated, but Justin didn't react; instead he turned to me and said, "Do what you must."

Then, without a second thought I extended my hand in front of me and yelled at the top of my lungs for the oncoming swirl of destruction to stop, but the sound that resonated from my lungs was anything but human. I was being heard, for Bernael instantly turned to face me and his strained expression was awash with shock. I felt a pulse greater than anything I could imagine. The energy emanating from my body was like a shock wave being carried by every air particle in its wake. I felt the sheer power released through the sharp transient wave causing the great black swirl to stop dead.

The dark cloud dispersed into what seemed like hundreds of rain drops, each dropping to the ground and materializing into the Shadow Guard they once were. They stood yards away frozen like statues and then a loud roar came from the depths of the far forest; a menacing rumble that ripped right through my soul.

"Daughter," I heard the foul voice say. The mere sound of the word in my head hurt. It felt like someone was digging a knife right into my skull and I fell to my knees in pain.

"Don't answer," I heard Justin whisper in my mind. "Don't let the Primoris in."

Fear was slowly creeping up. It was then that I noticed that Bernael stood as a barrier between me and the Shadow Guard.

"Step to the side brother," I heard the slithering voice of Abaddon say. "The child is mine."

"Over my dead body," rasped Bernael determined to block Abaddon from advancing.

"Caitlin, stand up," ordered Justin. I circled my head to glance at him, but he remained in the distance with his eyes closed, however his angst voice was in my mind guiding me. I quickly stood and held onto Bernael's long black robe, like a child holding onto its mother's skirt. He instantly distributed his weight so that I was completely blocked from the angel of death.

Abaddon craned his neck to the side and smirked. "Why brother; why do this now?"

"Leave the child alone," answered Bernael calmly.

"No matter how powerful you are, brother. I will end the child."

Bernael stood even higher.

"So brother," Abaddon began, "you would give up your immortality for this insignificant mortal. The child is obviously the Chosen One. Her powers are like no other. Help me finish her and we can all return to our duties. Let's get this over with, shall we? Our master is waiting."

Bernael simply shook his head. "He is my master no more," he pronounced pushing his robe to the side. "Why did you summon the Shadow Guard Abaddon? Can't find it in your heart to kill me yourself, brother?"

"You forget your place," Abaddon hissed in contempt. "We are bound by darkness. It is who we are."

"It is who we have become," corrected Bernael in a much softer voice. "I will not be following you in the depths of hell anymore."

I heard a loud thunder clap rip through the clear, early morning sky. The Shadow Guard instantly took a step forward in unison, causing the ground to tremor.

"Is that going to be your last word?" asked Abaddon wryly.

I took hold of Bernael's robe even tighter, fearing for his life. He half circled his head in response to my tug and then returned to look forward.

Silence fell.

"Close your eyes Caitlin," ordered Justin, but I refused to listen to anything anyone had to say, and in that moment I saw Bernael look up to the heavens and whisper softly, "Forgive me father for I have done you wrong," and with the quickness of the wind he held out his hands to the side blocking my view completely. A mere second later, Bernael let out a maddened shriek of pain and collapsed to the ground, sprawled unconscious at my feet. I instantly fell to my knees next to him trying to shake him awake, but the roar of murmurs drew my gaze up to where Abaddon was holding something in his hands and waving it around for the Shadow Guard to see. As the angel of death turned to face me, I noticed that what he was holding was Bernael's beating heart.

"No!" I screamed from the pits of despair. "No, this can't be. Where's the blood? I see no blood," I kept saying, refusing to accept the reality of the situation. A flood of grief brought fresh tears to my eyes as I cried silently, caught up in Bernael's demise. Abaddon turned his attention back to the Shadow Guard who was aggressively excited at the site of blood.

"Caitlin, back away," said Justin sounding angst. "I can't intervene, not yet."

I didn't move. I sat on the ground pulling Bernael's lifeless body into my lap and wrapped the rich material around his motionless body. "I'm so sorry," I cried.

"Caitlin, please back away. Don't force my hand," Justin pleaded. "It's a war they want."

I slowly placed Bernael on the ground and attempted to retreat when out of nowhere Abaddon appeared in front of me, blocking my path.

My grief weighed heavily on me, smothering my own powers into an insignificant pulse, leaving me stand across a powerful immortal as a common human.

Another clap of thunder shook the ground as I tried to pull back from Abaddon, but it was the howling sounds of the rowdy Shadow Guard that drew my attention.

An insanely alluring awareness awakened within me, triggered by their war sounds as though they were calling to me to join them, but it was when my gaze fell to where Bernael lay that I quickly snapped out of the delirium of thoughts brought about by the Shadow Guard, but soon enough the sounds from the army of darkness again enticed me, inciting a quickening in my heart, an excitement matching their own. I felt a thirst for power, a thirst to conquer and destroy. It was, however, Abaddon's incessant prowling that kept me on my toes.

"What is it that you want?" I yelled, surprisingly annoyed at the way he severed my wayward bond with the Guard.

"They call to you," Abaddon stated in a surprised manner. "The Guard calls to no one let alone an insignificant child." He took an inquisitive step closer to me and I stood there like a rabbit staring down a massive lion when out of nowhere the sound of thunder tore through the sky causing me to jump.

The angel of death displayed a wide grin.

"You're a monster!" I yelled.

"That's an understatement," he taunted, and stood directly in front of me. "Now let's pull out that poisonous tongue of yours."

I took a fearful step back, causing him to smile and look to where Justin was standing. "Too bad he can't save you. Poor, insignificant mortal; no one can come to your rescue without inciting a war."

"I will not be the cause of this war," I pronounced. "No matter what you do to me, a war will not come of it."

TWENTY-FOUR

PROCESSION

MY EYES BRIMMED with tears. "I failed you," I wept softly as I kneeled over Bernael's lifeless body knowing full well that Abaddon was preparing to end me once and for all.

"Don't waste your tears on him, mortal child for it's your life that you should lament," Abaddon sneered, approaching dangerously close.

I stood up to run, but there was nowhere to go that the angel of death couldn't reach faster. My predator stealthily prowled about me preparing to pounce on me like a lion to his next meal. Each and every time I had attempted to move, he would, with a mere flick of his hand, cast me effortlessly to the ground like a ragdoll, landing me with a thud onto the hard soil.

Long torturous moments later, I laid sprawled numb on the ground, too stunned to do anything but wait for my brain to register all of what was happening around me. The pain hit and it hit hard, leaving me gasping for air as I tried to drag my limp body to a kneeling position, but it was then that I sensed Justin tensing up in every fiber of my being, felt him preparing to attack. Wanting to avoid any bigger conflict I lifted my head off the dirt and turned my attention to Justin feigning a smile, and motioned that I was fine.

"Stay down," he ordered. His voice was ruthless and unyielding in my mind. "Stay down and don't provoke him."

I willed my legs to stand, to run, but they had all the strength of jelly, and back down I went once again. The immortal approached in a stride as slow and deliberate as a stalking lion.

Justin was not going to stand there much longer; that I was sure of. Sprawled on the ground in the middle of the darkest part of my existence I had no more to give. It was at that moment that my mind simply gave up and called out for help.

"Alexander, please don't just watch this time," I cried, with my cheek against the dirt. I asked for Alexander over and over again, hoping that he would put an end to the whole ordeal before Justin had a chance to jump in; sparking a war. I needed to shout, to jump up and run to Justin and keep him safe, but my body did not obey.

Just as I had finally collected enough strength to stand, the sky darkened instantaneously as the air became charged with unremitting fear and the droning sounds of the Shadow Guard ceased their piercing cries. The monstrous Guard looked spooked and in one uniform motion, they quickly pulled back. An agitated roar broke the silence as another clap of thunder shook the very ground we stood on.

Then nothing – a complete stillness veiled the entire area.

There was only one immortal that I knew powerful enough

to place everyone in suspended animation. *Alexander*, I thought.

"I'm here," he said softly as he appeared kneeling next to Bernael's lifeless body.

"This is my fault," I began, placing my hand on top of his. "Bernael wouldn't have done this if it weren't for me."

"Nonsense," he spoke softly. The great Immortal didn't seem to want to believe the state Bernael was in. "My son," he finally whispered with a heavy heart, "What has become of you?"

At that moment, Alexander placed his hand on Bernael's face and caressed his cheek tenderly; fatherly like. Miraculously, the dark lifeless corpse that lay on the hard earth had morphed into the glorious creature Bernael once was. Tears flowed freely down my face as the sixteen-year-olds body lay limp and motionless.

With Abaddon being in suspended animation as he was, I took the opportunity and dragged my weary body to Alexander's side. I knew the pathetic whimper was mine, but I didn't care. I crawled toward Alexander as he stood above a still Bernael. Alexander slowly dropped his gaze to me, but he didn't utter a sound, just stared for what seemed forever.

Reaching down to stroke my cheek, he wiped away my tears and quickly stood upright. With his back turned to me he stretched out his hands to the side and stood there motionless for a few minutes. "Why?" He suddenly screamed, "Why now?" he asked much softer this time with pain lining each syllable.

He cocked his head to the side and looked down at Bernael one last time. I wanted to reach for him, but I knew that there was nothing I could say or do to bring back the lost angel.

Alexander's eyes were a stormy green, immersed in thought and contemplation. He seemed to be fighting a battle of will and fighting one against himself. Slowly, he lifted his gaze to me and the moment our eyes locked I knew that something dark was brewing deep inside. His calm exterior masked the anger smoldering within.

"Alex –," I started to say, hoping to calm him. My voice instantly trailed off seeing that he was in no mood for comforting.

"Abaddon," he suddenly bellowed menacingly, returning everything to its natural rhythm, but the sky darkened even more, changing with Alexander's mood. "Will you never learn?" he continued to say, glaring threateningly at the demon standing a couple yards away. The power and deadly menace surrounding Alexander made the warm air turn icy-cold and the day turn to night. He reigned over nature as though it yielded to his needs and thoughts.

Abaddon dropped his head instantly, refusing to look up.

There was an instant drop in temperature and I could see my own breath as I pushed and pulled my body behind where Bernael lay, and out of nowhere there came a murderous shrill carried through the wind making my hair stand on end. Its place of origin was much further from where the Guard stood.

As though summoned by the shrill, the Shadow Guard took a thunderous step forward in a preparedness state to attack the powerful Ancient. Alexander, however, seemed rather annoyed, and roared angrily, "You dare defy me!"

They froze instantly.

"Don't be coy with me immortal," said Alexander talking in the direction of the high-pitched tone. "Show yourself! Why hide behind your pawns? After all these years, you still hide behind your soldiers. This is between the two of us. Don't make it about anything else." Yet again, a conspicuously and offensively loud outcry as loud and pungent as a locomotive bellowed from the depths of the woods. The Primoris was not enjoying this reunion.

The Guard took another defiant step forward.

"You will sacrifice your whole army? For what purpose?" asked Alexander, "Come out and face me; here, now. Let's put an end to this. Don't use the child to get to me."

The Shadow Guard took one last stride forward.

"Enough!" roared Alexander visibly annoyed, and took a step forward without wavering. "Disperse, you foul creatures," he commanded. His voice rang raucously, and in a manner one would use to blow out their birthday candles, Alexander exhaled deeply and blew in the direction of the Guard. In seconds, as soon as his breath reached the sinister shadows a terrible, high-pitched noise resembling a human cry echoed in the distance; rippling through the air in a long, endless cry of death and despair. The Guard instantly scattered like smoke on a windy day, and Abaddon was quick to back away when Alexander responded instantly to the Immortals attempt to weasel out of his predicament.

"You shall remain in my presence until you are told otherwise," roared Alexander, motioning for Abaddon to stop. The angel of death bowed his head immediately, but was clearly contemplating a swift exit. "You will stand over your brother's body and lament his lose," ordered Alexander. "Pray that I don't snatch out your heart in the same cowardly manner. Now beg him to forgive you, for I am on the edge of reason."

Abaddon shook his head; his momentary paralysis of terror finally broke. "No," he yelled again and again.

Alexander stared rigidly at him, forcing Abaddon to his knees. "Then you shall join your brother in death," Alexander howled emphatically. "Where is your master now, Fallen? Where is the one that has promised you eternal glory?"

Abaddon stiffened. "You have no right to intervene," the monster finally said, raising his eyes to meet Alexander's.

"You dare lecture me on rights? What right did you have to take your brother's life?"

Just then, I noticed that Alexander was doing everything to avoid looking at Bernael's lifeless body. He seemed calm and in control, but I feared that losing Bernael had cost him dearly.

"Bernael betrayed his kind," yelled Abaddon. "He betrayed his brothers. He had to be punished."

"And what then should your punishment be for attempting to kill the child?" He pointed to me. "Isn't it an abomination for our kind to want to kill a mortal? Especially, when the child hasn't even ascended yet?"

"These are your rules, not ours. We live by a different code."

"As long as you enter this realm, you play by my rules," growled Alexander, visibly annoyed at Abaddon's persistence.

"Will you kill me then?" slithered Abaddon, playing with Alexander's better judgment trying to force his hand.

"Your life is insignificant for me to take. You will soon kneel and beg for the light. You will beg for salvation."

"Never!" howled Abaddon, clearly angst at the mere mention of the prophecy.

Alexander smiled. "The wheel is in motion immortal; eons in the making. Nothing you do or say will stop the loom of life from weaving. Tell that perfidious master of yours that the child is to be left alone. She needs to first ascend. No one will do her ill. Tell your master that the child is not to be harmed or used to get to me. Do you understand?"

Abaddon turned a benign smile upon him, bowing once again. "I will relay the message to my master, but I tell you this; the child is ours for the taking. She will choose rightly. We are her kind."

Alexander was visibly angered by Abaddon's response. "The child will remain in this realm. Tell that unyielding, stubborn master of yours that hiding is not the answer to all this. If anyone goes against my wishes and forces my hand, I will hunt them down myself and rejoice in tearing out their heart."

Alexander's resolve was monstrous as he meant every word.

Abaddon's eyes grew in fear.

"Now go before I lose my temper, for I will not be as merciful with you as I was with your Shadow Guard," roared the Ancient as he waved him away. Before I could even blink back the menacing sound in Alexander's voice Abaddon had disappeared.

"Are you hurt?" asked Justin surprising me as he kneeled next to me. "Everything will be okay."

I hugged him tight needing to feel the security of his embrace.

"He's dead Justin. He's really dead," I kept repeating, crying into his shoulder. His hold instantly tightened. "It's my fault," I cried, lifting my head. "I'm the source of all this. Bernael came to warn me, and now because of me he's dead!"

"None of this is your fault. None of it! Get that through you head. Bernael knew exactly what he was doing."

Alexander came and stood over Bernael's corpse.

"I'm so sorry Alex," I cried, "This wasn't supposed to happen; none of this was. I'm supposed to protect all of you! I'm so sorry." I buried my face in my hands and cried against Bernael's chest. "I did this, I did this." My tears streamed down my face with every gasp of air.

Justin pulled me back against his chest and held me tight. "None of this is your fault. You need to understand that."

"All of this is my fault; all of it," I snapped angrily and broke free from Justin's embrace. I breathed in a numbing breath and stood up. "I can't be the person you think I am," I dictated, turning my gaze to Alexander. He just stared at me. "There's no way I can protect any of you. This –," I pronounced, pointing to Bernael, "this is my doing. This is all I'm good at."

Alexander caressed my cheek and said in a soothing voice, "It is your calling, child. You are their rightful leader. The Shadow Guard felt it, the Sentinels know it, but it's up to you to accept it."

The second he finished he looked away and the whole area was infused with light. The members of the Nobe Council as well as all the Ellri formed two circles around us. The Nobe stood in the inner circle holding hands while the hooded Ellri remained motionless in the outer circle dressed from head to toe in white.

Justin took hold of my hand and pulled me away from Bernael's body. "Let them do what they came here to do," he instructed and squeezed my hand.

"What's happening?"

"Just look," he said and smiled reassuringly.

In no time at all, the body of the exquisite angel of darkness lifted off the ground and was suspended in mid-air at waist height. Bernael's long chestnut hair flailed in the light breeze as Alexander approached the levitating corpse and lovingly folded Bernael's limp arms across his lifeless chest.

"Your Long Journey has come to its end, son." He said falteringly. "It's time you joined our creator." With that Alexander kissed Bernael on the forehead and whispered something in his ear. He stayed in that position for a few minutes – pressing his cheek against Bernael's. "My son," he whispered in deep lament and just as I was about to reach for Alex's hand he vanished into thin air.

Justin pulled me further from the body.

Tears streaked freely down my cheeks in short, choppy cries of sorrow and grief.

Two by two the Nobe broke formation and streamed into a double line at the foot of Bernael's suspended body. Three Nobe stood on either side of Bernael, facing forward. Simultaneously, they all looked up to the sky and started walking forward; gliding along the surface with the levitating body alongside them and faded into nothingness as they continued to proceed forward. One by one, the Nobe gradually disappeared as they got further and further away until they were no more.

I turned and burrowed my head in Justin's chest deeply moved by Bernael's angelic funeral procession. "Everything will be okay," he said kissing me on the top of my head, "you'll see."

I tightened my hold on Justin wanting to make the morbid scenes go away. The knowledge that I had to move away from

Oaks once again was slowly creeping into my conscious mind.

"I have to leave again, don't I?" I asked, looking up at Justin. "It is after all the reason Bernael risked his own life. He needed to warn me – lead me to the Korbs."

Before Justin had a chance to answer, I felt a hand on my shoulder which caused me to turn around. Aunt Leslie stood there smiling a weak smile. "Sweetie, everything will be okay. I promise."

I went from Justin's embrace into my aunt's. She wrapped her arms around me squeezing me tight as she did when I was a little girl. "Sweetie, today you should how courageous you are. You held your ground against Abaddon, and kept us all from a war."

With my head against her shoulder, I released the tears that threatened to choke me. "Poor Alexander," I cried, my lips trembling as more tears spilled down my cheeks. I lifted my head to look at my aunt. "This whole ordeal will cost him dearly."

With her flowing sleeve, she wiped my tears away and cupped my chin. "The Ancient will be fine, but you will not be if you don't get some sleep, sweetie." She lifted her gaze and looked over to Justin. "Please take her to her room. She has had enough," she began loosening her hold, "she needs her rest."

J ustin and I walked back to the house in complete silence. The overwhelming impact of what had transpired hung over us like a dark veil disabling us from holding any sort of conversation. Just as he was about to open the back door, I turned and looked at him, but he stared back expressionless.

"This wasn't exactly what I had planned for your birthday

surprise," I told him, trying to lighten the mood. "I simply wanted to make this day special, and be the first to wish you a happy birthday, and then all this happened."

He leaned in and kissed me softly on the lips. "Every day with you is special," he answered and wrapped his arms around me. "I must admit –," he began, sweeping my annoyingly stray hair behind my ear, "it worries me at how easily you brush aside your true emotions. I know that at some point you let Bernael in. You truly liked him, and I sensed he felt the same about you." He kissed me on the forehead. "I can't understand how you do it. Why you do it? Why you feel you have to hide how you really feel. What happened today was –"

I shook my head not wanting to hear anymore. "I don't care. I really don't want to think about what happened. I failed him and that's that. No matter what anyone says, he lost his life because of me. He would be alive right now if he didn't come to warn me."

"You don't get it, do you?" Justin insisted, leading me indoors. "Bernael changed because of you. He chose for once in his life to do something good. If it weren't for you, he'd continue being the dark monster that he always was."

"Even so, he'd still be alive."

"What kind of life would that be? He would've continued to be soulless, lacking any sort of sensitivity or even the capacity for deep feeling. Feelings, is what Bernael's gift was all about. For so many years he's repressed his natural need to help, to soothe. By acting as he was he was going against his natural urges, tormenting himself on purpose for the sake of getting back at Alexander. He was, in his own twisted way, begging for the Ancient's attention. Unlike Abaddon, who was born in darkness, Bernael was created of purity and beauty. What he did today returned him to that stage. There's so much more to life than what we experience here, now. So much more for those who chose to live in the light. Your compassion taught him to feel. It showed him who he was born to be. Bernael did what he thought was right and what he needed to do to repent for all his sins. You shouldn't blame yourself for any of this because nothing but good has come out of this whole ordeal. He might be gone from this world, but where he's heading we all strive to reach."

I stopped in the middle of the hall and hugged Justin. "I love you," I whispered against his cheek.

Justin lifted me off the floor. "I love you more," he declared.

"Humanly impossible," I answered as the mere touch of his lips to mine suddenly set my heart palpitating.

"You need your rest young lady," he ordered between breaths, trying to sound calm.

"But it's your birthday," I replied smiling. Slowly and determined to seduce the love of my life, I intentionally trailed kisses down the smoothness of his neck. There was nothing as sweet as the taste of Justin's skin against my lips. His little utterances of pleasure were enough to drive me crazy.

"You're not playing fair," he groaned, tugging me toward him until I was flush against him.

"Who says I want to play fair?"

"Don't try covering how you really feel deep down Caitlin. I know you. I know how much his death has affected you, and don't think that I don't know that you're feigning being over all this for my sake."

I pulled a face. "But, it's your birthday!"

"Yes, I know, but you are what I'm concerned about so, stop pretending that you're okay with everything." I bobbed my head in acknowledgement. Justin came closer, his lips almost touching mine. "Besides, we'll have time to celebrate later. You need your rest," he said and gave me a warm kiss. "I want you to rest up so you can enjoy yourself at the barbeque Kyle is throwing for me."

"You're right. You're absolutely right." I reached up and gave him a quick kiss. "Will you at least stay with me until I fall asleep?"

"I would love to, but I can't. There's something I need to see Abbot about. He's already waiting for me in the den."

"Oh! What do you and uncle Abbot have to discuss?"

He kissed me softly on the lips. "I need him to give me something, something important."

"Like what?"

Justin smiled contently. "I can't tell you just yet. You'll have to wait for the party. Now go to your room and get some rest. I'll see you later."

He quickly pecked me on the lips and walked away. "Why can't you tell me?" I called after him. "Does it have anything to do with me?"

He stopped in mid-stride and turned momentarily and beamed an amazingly bright smile. "It has nothing to do with you," he said turning to walk away again. "It has to do with us," he yelled as he descended the stairs.

"Us?" I was flabbergasted.

TO BE CONTINUED.....

MORE FROM ANNA LAZARIDIS
THE AUTHOR OF

LINES THAT BIND

BOOK ONE
CIRCLE OF TRUST

BOOK TWO
WITHIN THE WHISPERS

BOOK THREE
LIGHT TO DARKNESS

BOOK FOUR
AMONG THE SHADOWS

BOOK FIVE
COMING 2018

www.linesthatbind.com

www.ingramcontent.com/pod-product-compliance
Lightning Source LLC
Chambersburg PA
CBHW070615260626
47161CB00007B/2440